...an is the author of the ....
Aubrey-Maturin tales and the biographer of Joseph
Banks and Picasso. His first novel, *Testimonies*, and
his *Collected Short Stories* have recently been
reprinted by HarperCollins. He translated many
works from French into English, among them the
novels and memoirs of Simone de Beauvoir and the
first volume of Jean Lacouture's biography of Charles
de Gaulle. In 1995 he was the first recipient of the
Heywood Hill Prize for a lifetime's contribution to
literature. In the same year he was awarded the CBE.
In 1997 he was awarded an honorary doctorate of
letters by Trinity College, Dublin. He died in January
2000 at the age of 85.

The Works of Patrick O'Brian

The Aubrey/Maturin Novels
in order of publication

MASTER AND COMMANDER
POST CAPTAIN
HMS SURPRISE
THE MAURITIUS COMMAND
DESOLATION ISLAND
THE FORTUNE OF WAR
THE SURGEON'S MATE
THE IONIAN MISSION
TREASON'S HARBOUR
THE FAR SIDE OF THE WORLD
THE REVERSE OF THE MEDAL
THE LETTER OF MARQUE
THE THIRTEEN-GUN SALUTE
THE NUTMEG OF CONSOLATION
CLARISSA OAKES
THE WINE-DARK SEA
THE COMMODORE
THE YELLOW ADMIRAL
THE HUNDRED DAYS
BLUE AT THE MIZZEN

Novels

TESTIMONIES
THE CATALANS
THE GOLDEN OCEAN
THE UNKNOWN SHORE
RICHARD TEMPLE
CAESAR
HUSSEIN

Tales

THE LAST POOL
THE WALKER
LYING IN THE SUN
THE CHIAN WINE
COLLECTED SHORT STORIES

Biography

PICASSO
JOSEPH BANKS

Anthology

A BOOK OF VOYAGES

PATRICK O'BRIAN

Master and Commander

HarperCollinsPublishers

HarperCollins*Publishers*
1 London Bridge Street
London SE1 9GF

www.harpercollins.co.uk

This paperback edition 2002

30

Previously published in B-format paperback
by HarperCollins 1996
Reprinted four times

Previously published in Great Britain by
HarperCollins*Publishers* 1993
Reprinted three times

Also published in paperback by Fontana 1971
Reprinted thirteen times

First published in Great Britain by
William Collins Sons & Co. Ltd 1970

Patrick O'Brian asserts the moral right
to be identified as the author of this work

ISBN 978 0 00 649915 2

Set in Imprint by
Rowland Phototypesetting Ltd,
Bury St Edmunds, Suffolk

Printed and bound by
CPI Group (UK) Ltd, Croydon, CR0 4YY

CONTENTS

MARIAE LEMBI NOSTRI
DUCI ET MAGISTRAE
DO DEDICO

The sails of a square-rigged ship, hung out to dry in a calm.

1 Flying jib
2 Jib
3 Fore topmast staysail
4 Fore staysail
5 Foresail, or course
6 Fore topsail
7 Fore topgallant
8 Mainstaysail
9 Main topmast staysail
10 Middle staysail
11 Main topgallant staysail

12 Mainsail, or course
13 Maintopsail
14 Main topgallant
15 Mizzen staysail
16 Mizzen topmast staysail
17 Mizzen topgallant staysail
18 Mizzen sail
19 Spanker
20 Mizzen topsail
21 Mizzen topgallant

AUTHOR'S NOTE

When one is writing about the Royal Navy of the eighteenth and early nineteenth centuries it is difficult to avoid understatement; it is difficult to do full justice to one's subject; for so very often the improbable reality outruns fiction. Even an uncommonly warm and industrious imagination could scarcely produce the frail shape of Commodore Nelson leaping from his battered seventy-four-gun *Captain* through the quarter-gallery window of the eighty-gun *San Nicolas*, taking her, and hurrying on across her deck to board the towering *San Josef* of a hundred and twelve guns, so that 'on the deck of a Spanish first-rate, extravagant as the story may seem, did I receive the swords of the vanquished Spaniards; which, as I received, I gave to William Fearney, one of my bargemen, who put them, with the greatest *sang-froid*, under his arm'.

The pages of Beatson, James and the *Naval Chronicle*, the Admiralty papers in the Public Record Office, the biographies in Marshall and O'Byrne are filled with actions that may be a little less spectacular (there was only one Nelson), but that are certainly no less spirited – actions that few men could invent and perhaps none present with total conviction. That is why I have gone straight to the source for the fighting in this book. From the great wealth of brilliantly-fought, baldly-described actions I have picked some I particularly admire; and so when I describe a fight I have log-books, official letters, contemporary accounts or the participants' own memoirs to vouch for every exchange. Yet, on the other hand, I have not felt slavishly bound to precise chronological sequence; and the naval historian will notice, for example, that Sir James Saumarez' action in the Gut of Gibraltar has been postponed until after the grape-harvest, just as he will see that at least one of my *Sophie*'s battles was fought by quite another sloop, though one of exactly the same strength. Indeed, I have taken great liberties; I have seized upon documents, poems, letters; in short, *j'ai pris mon bien là où je l'ai trouvé*, and within a context of general historical accuracy I have changed names, places and minor events to suit my tale.

My point is that the admirable men of those times, the Cochranes, Byrons, Falconers, Seymours, Boscawens and the many less famous sailors from whom I have in some degree compounded my characters, are best celebrated in their own splendid actions rather than in imaginary contests; that authenticity is a jewel; and that the echo of their words has an abiding value.

At this point I should like to acknowledge the advice and assistance I have had from the patient, erudite officials of the Public Record Office and of the National Maritime Museum at Greenwich, as well as the Commanding Officer of HMS *Victory*: no one could have been kinder or more helpful.

P.O'B.

Chapter One

The music-room in the Governor's House at Port Mahon, a tall, handsome, pillared octagon, was filled with the triumphant first movement of Locatelli's C major quartet. The players, Italians pinned against the far wall by rows and rows of little round gilt chairs, were playing with passionate conviction as they mounted towards the penultimate crescendo, towards the tremendous pause and the deep, liberating final chord. And on the little gilt chairs at least some of the audience were following the rise with an equal intensity: there were two in the third row, on the left-hand side; and they happened to be sitting next to one another. The listener farther to the left was a man of between twenty and thirty whose big form overflowed his seat, leaving only a streak of gilt wood to be seen here and there. He was wearing his best uniform – the white-lapelled blue coat, white waistcoat, breeches and stockings of a lieutenant in the Royal Navy, with the silver medal of the Nile in his buttonhole – and the deep white cuff of his gold-buttoned sleeve beat the time, while his bright blue eyes, staring from what would have been a pink-and-white face if it had not been so deeply tanned, gazed fixedly at the bow of the first violin. The high note came, the pause, the resolution; and with the resolution the sailor's fist swept firmly down upon his knee. He leant back in his chair, extinguishing it entirely, sighed happily and turned towards his neighbour with a smile. The words 'Very finely played, sir, I believe' were formed in his gullet if not quite in his mouth when he caught the cold and indeed inimical look and heard the whisper, 'If you really must beat

I

the measure, sir, let me entreat you to do so in time, and not half a beat ahead.'

Jack Aubrey's face instantly changed from friendly ingenuous communicative pleasure to an expression of somewhat baffled hostility: he could not but acknowledge that he *had* been beating the time; and although he had certainly done so with perfect accuracy, in itself the thing was wrong. His colour mounted; he fixed his neighbour's pale eye for a moment, said, 'I trust . . .', and the opening notes of the slow movement cut him short.

The ruminative 'cello uttered two phrases of its own and then began a dialogue with the viola. Only part of Jack's mind paid attention, for the rest of it was anchored to the man at his side. A covert glance showed that he was a small, dark, white-faced creature in a rusty black coat – a civilian. It was difficult to tell his age, for not only had he that kind of face that does not give anything away, but he was wearing a wig, a grizzled wig, apparently made of wire, and quite devoid of powder: he might have been anything between twenty and sixty. 'About my own age, in fact, however,' thought Jack. 'The ill-looking son of a bitch, to give himself such airs.' With this almost the whole of his attention went back into the music; he found his place in the pattern and followed it through its convolutions and quite charming arabesques to its satisfying, logical conclusion. He did not think of his neighbour again until the end of the movement, and then he avoided looking in his direction.

The minuet set Jack's head wagging with its insistent beat, but he was wholly unconscious of it; and when he felt his hand stirring on his breeches and threatening to take to the air he thrust it under the crook of his knee. It was a witty, agreeable minuet, no more; but it was succeeded by a curiously difficult, almost harsh last movement, a piece that seemed to be on the edge of saying something of the very greatest importance. The volume of sound died away to the single whispering of a fiddle, and the steady hum of low conversation that had never stopped at the back of the room threatened to drown it: a soldier exploded in a stifled guffaw and Jack looked angrily round. Then the rest of the quartet joined the fiddle and all of them worked back to the point from which the statement might arise: it was essential to get straight back into the current, so as the 'cello came in with its predictable and necessary contribution of *pom, pom-pom-pom, poom,* Jack's chin sank upon his breast and in unison with the 'cello he went *pom, pom-pom-pom, poom.* An elbow drove into his ribs and the sound *shshsh* hissed in his ear. He found that his hand was high in the air, beating time; he lowered it, clenched his mouth shut and looked down at his feet until the music was over. He heard the noble conclusion and recognized that it was far beyond the straightforward winding-up that he had foreseen, but he could take no pleasure in it. In the applause and general din his neighbour looked at him, not so much with defiance as with total, heart-felt disapprobation: they did not speak, but sat in rigid awareness of one another while Mrs Harte, the commandant's wife, went through a long and technically difficult piece on her harp. Jack Aubrey looked out of the long, elegant windows into the night: Saturn was rising in the south-south-east, a glowing ball in the Minorcan sky. A nudge, a thrust of that kind, so vicious and deliberate, was very like a blow. Neither his personal temper nor his professional code could patiently suffer an affront: and what affront was graver than a blow?

As it could not for the moment find any outward expression, his anger took on the form of melancholy: he thought of his shipless state, of half and whole promises made to him and broken, and of the many schemes he had built up on visionary foundations. He owed his prize-agent, his man of business, a hundred and twenty pounds; and its interest of fifteen per cent was about to fall due; and his pay was five pounds twelve shillings a month. He thought of men he knew, junior to him but with better luck or better interest, who were now lieutenants in command of brigs or cutters, or who had even been promoted master and commander: and all of them snapping up trabacaloes in the Adriatic, tartans in the Gulf of Lions, xebecs and settees along the whole of the Spanish coast. Glory, professional advancement, prize-money.

The storm of applause told him that the performance was over, and he beat his palms industriously, stretching his mouth into an expression of rapturous delight. Molly Harte curtseyed and smiled, caught his eye and smiled again; he clapped louder; but she saw that he was either not pleased or that he had not been attending, and her pleasure was sensibly diminished. However, she continued to acknowledge the compliments of her audience with a radiant smile, looking very well in pale blue satin and a great double rope of pearls – pearls from the *Santa Brigida*.

Jack Aubrey and his neighbour in the rusty black coat stood up at the same time, and they looked at one another: Jack let his face return to its expression of cold dislike – the dying remnants of his artificial rapture were peculiarly disagreeable, as they faded – and in a low voice he said, 'My name is Aubrey, sir: I am staying at the Crown.'

'Mine, sir, is Maturin. I am to be found any morning at Joselito's coffee-house. May I beg you to stand aside?'

For a moment Jack felt the strongest inclination to snatch up his little gilt chair and beat the white-faced man down with it; but he gave way with a tolerable show of civility – he had no choice, unless he was to be run into – and shortly afterwards he worked through the crowd of tight-packed blue or red coats with the occasional civilian black as far as the circle round Mrs Harte, called out 'Charming – capital – beautifully played' over heads three deep, waved his hand and left the room. As he went through the hall he exchanged greetings with two other sea-officers, one of them a former messmate in the gun-room of the *Agamemnon*, who said, 'You are looking very hipped, Jack,' and with a tall midshipman, stiff with the sense of occasion and the rigour of his starched, frilled shirt, who had been a youngster in his watch in the *Thunderer*; and lastly he bowed to the commandant's secretary, who returned his bow with a smile, raised eyebrows and a very significant look.

'I wonder what that infamous brute has been up to now,' thought Jack, walking down towards the harbour. As he walked memories of the secretary's duplicity and of his own ignoble truckling to that influential personage came into his mind. A beautiful, newly-coppered, newly-captured little French privateer had been virtually promised to him: the secretary's brother had appeared from Gibraltar – adieu, kiss my hand to that command. 'Kiss my arse,' said Jack aloud, remembering the politic tameness with which he had received the news, together with the secretary's renewed professions of good will and of unspecified good offices to be performed in the future. Then he remembered his own conduct that evening, particularly his withdrawing to let the small man walk by, and his inability to find any remark, any piece of repartee that would have been both crushing and well clear of boorishness. He was profoundly dissatisfied with himself, and with the man in the black coat, and with the service. And with the velvet softness of the April night, and the choir of nightingales in the orange-trees, and the host of stars hanging so low as almost to touch the palms.

The Crown, where Jack was staying, had a certain resemblance to its famous namesake in Portsmouth: it had the same immense gilt and scarlet sign hanging up outside, a relic of former British occupations, and the house had been built about 1750 in the purest English taste, with no concessions whatever to the Mediterranean except for the tiles; but there the likeness stopped. The landlord was from Gibraltar and the staff was Spanish, or rather Minorcan; the place smelt of olive oil, sardines and wine; and there was not the least possibility of a Bakewell tart, an Eccles cake or even a decent suet pudding. Yet, on the other hand, no English inn could produce a chambermaid so very like a dusky peach as Mercedes. She bounced out on to the dim landing, filling it with vitality and a kind of glow, and she called up the stairs, 'A letter, Teniente: I bring him . . .' A

5

moment later she was at his side, smiling with innocent delight: but he was only too clearly aware of what any letter addressed to him might have in it, and he did not respond with anything more than a mechanical jocosity and a vague dart at her bosom.

'And Captain Allen come for you,' she added.

'Allen? Allen? What the devil can he want with me?' Captain Allen was a quiet, elderly man; all that Jack knew of him was that he was an American Loyalist and that he was considered very set in his ways – invariably tacked by suddenly putting his helm hard a-lee, and wore a long-skirted waistcoat. 'Oh, the funeral, no doubt,' he said. 'A subscription.'

'Sad, Teniente, sad?' said Mercedes, going away along the corridor. 'Poor Teniente.'

Jack took his candle from the table and went straight to his room. He did not trouble with the letter until he had thrown off his coat and untied his stock; then he looked suspiciously at the outside. He noticed that it was addressed, in a hand he did not know, to *Captain* Aubrey, R. N.: he frowned, said 'Damned fool', and turned the letter over. The black seal had been blurred in the impression, and although he held it close to the candle, directing the light in a slanting manner over its surface, he could not make it out.

'I cannot make it out,' he said. 'But at least it ain't old Hunks. He always seals with a wafer.' Hunks was his agent, his vulture, his creditor.

At length he went so far as to open the letter, which read:

By the Right Honourable Lord Keith, Knight of the Bath, Admiral of the Blue and Commander in Chief of His Majesty's Ships and Vessels employed and to be employed in the Mediterranean, etc., etc., etc.

Whereas Captain Samuel Allen of His Majesty's Sloop *Sophie* is removed to the *Pallas*, Captain James Bradby deceased –

6

You are hereby required and directed to proceed on board the *Sophie* and take upon you the Charge and Command of Commander of her; willing and requiring all the Officers and Company belonging to the said Sloop to behave themselves in their several Employments with all due Respect and Obedience to you their Commander; and you likewise to observe as well the General Printed Instructions as what Orders and Directions you may from time to time receive from any of your superior Officers for His Majesty's Service. Hereof nor you nor any of you may fail as you will answer the contrary at your Peril.

And for so doing this shall be your Order.

Given on board the *Foudroyant*
at sea, 1st April, 1800.

To John Aubrey, Esqr,
hereby appointed Commmander of
His Majesty's Sloop *Sophie*
By command of the Admiral Thos Walker

His eyes took in the whole of this in a single instant, yet his mind refused either to read or to believe it: his face went red, and with a curiously harsh, severe expression he obliged himself to spell through it line by line. The second reading ran faster and faster: and an immense delighted joy came welling up about his heart. His face grew redder still, and his mouth widened of itself. He laughed aloud and tapped the letter, folded it, unfolded it and read it with the closest attention, having entirely forgotten the beautiful phrasing of the middle paragraph. For an icy second the bottom of the new world that had sprung into immensely detailed life seemed to be about to drop out as his eyes focused upon the unlucky date. He held the letter up to the light, and there, as firm, comforting and immovable as the rock of Gibraltar, he saw the Admiralty's watermark, the eminently respectable anchor of hope.

He was unable to keep still. Pacing briskly up and down the room he put on his coat, threw it off again and uttered a series of disconnected remarks, chuckling as he did so. 'There I was, worrying . . . ha, ha . . . such a neat little brig – know her well . . . ha, ha . . . should have thought myself the happiest of men with the command of the sheer-hulk, or the *Vulture* slop-ship . . . any ship at all . . . admirable copperplate hand – singular fine paper . . . almost the only quarterdeck brig in the service: charming cabin, no doubt . . . capital weather – so warm . . . ha, ha . . . if only I can get men: that's the great point . . .' He was exceedingly hungry and thirsty: he darted to the bell and pulled it violently, but before the rope had stopped quivering his head was out in the corridor and he was hailing the chambermaid. 'Mercy! Mercy! Oh, there you are, my dear. What can you bring me to eat, manger, mangiare? Pollo? Cold roast pollo? And a bottle of wine, *vino* – two bottles of *vino*. And Mercy, will you come and do something for me? I want you, désirer, to do something for me, eh? Sew on, cosare, a button.'

'Yes, Teniente,' said Mercedes, her eyes rolling in the candlelight and her teeth flashing white.

'Not teniente,' cried Jack, crushing the breath out of her plump, supple body. 'Capitan! Capitano, ha, ha, ha!'

He woke in the morning straight out of a deep, deep sleep: he was fully awake, and even before he opened his eyes he was brimming with the knowledge of his promotion.

'She is not quite a first-rate, of course,' he observed, 'but who on earth wants a blundering great first-rate, with not the slightest chance of an independent cruise? Where is she lying? Beyond the ordnance quay, in the next berth to the *Rattler*. I shall go down directly and have a look at her – waste not a minute. No, no. That would never do – must give them fair warning. No: the first thing I must do is to go and render thanks in the proper quarters and make an appointment with Allen – dear old Allen – I must wish him joy.'

The first thing he did in point of fact was to cross the road to the naval outfitter's and pledge his now elastic credit to the extent of a noble, heavy, massive epaulette, the mark of his present rank – a symbol which the shopman fixed upon his left shoulder at once and upon which they both gazed with great complacency in the long glass, the shopman looking from behind Jack's shoulder with unfeigned pleasure on his face.

As the door closed behind him Jack saw the man in the black coat on the other side of the road, near the coffee-house. The evening flooded back into his mind and he hurried across, calling out, 'Mr – Mr Maturin. Why, there you are, sir. I owe you a thousand apologies, I am afraid. I must have been a sad bore to you last night, and I hope you will forgive me. We sailors hear so little music – are so little used to genteel company – that we grow carried away. I beg your pardon.'

'My dear sir,' cried the man in the black coat, with an odd flush rising in his dead-white face, 'you had every reason to be carried away. I have never heard a better quartetto in my life – such unity, such fire. May I propose a cup of chocolate, or coffee? It would give me great pleasure.'

'You are very good, sir. I should like it of all things. To tell the truth, I was in such a hurry of spirits I forgot my breakfast. I have just been promoted,' he added, with an off-hand laugh.

'Have you indeed? I wish you joy of it with all my heart, sure. Pray walk in.'

At the sight of Mr Maturin the waiter waved his forefinger in that discouraging Mediterranean gesture of negation – an inverted pendulum. Maturin shrugged, said to Jack, 'The posts are wonderfully slow these days,' and to the waiter, speaking in the Catalan of the island, 'Bring us a pot of chocolate, Jep, furiously whipped, and some cream.'

'You speak the Spanish, sir?' said Jack, sitting down and flinging out the skirts of his coat to clear his sword in a wide gesture that filled the low room with blue. 'That must be a splendid thing, to speak the Spanish. I have often tried, and with French and Italian too; but it don't answer. They generally understand me, but when *they* say anything, they speak so quick I am thrown out. The fault is here, I dare say,' he observed, rapping his forehead. 'It was the same with Latin when I was a boy: and how old Pagan used to flog me.' He laughed so heartily at the recollection that the waiter with the chocolate laughed too, and said, 'Fine day, Captain, sir, fine day!'

'Prodigious fine day,' said Jack, gazing upon his rat-like visage with great benevolence. 'Bello soleil, indeed. But,' he added, bending down and peering out of the upper part of the window, 'it would not surprise me if the tramontana were to set in.' Turning to Mr Maturin he said, 'As soon as I was out of bed this morning I noticed that greenish look in the nor-nor-east, and I said to myself, "When the sea-breeze dies away, I should not be surprised if the tramontana were to set in."'

'It is curious that you should find foreign languages difficult, sir,' said Mr Maturin, who had no views to offer on the weather, 'for it seems reasonable to suppose that a good ear for music would accompany a facility for acquiring – that the two would necessarily run together.'

'I am sure you are right, from a philosophical point of view,' said Jack. 'But there it is. Yet it may well be that my musical ear is not so very famous, neither; though indeed I love music dearly. Heaven knows I find it hard enough to pitch upon the true note, right in the middle.'

'You play, sir?'

'I scrape a little, sir. I torment a fiddle from time to time.'

'So do I! So do I! Whenever I have leisure, I make my attempts upon the 'cello.'

'A noble instrument,' said Jack, and they talked about Boccherini, bows and rosin, copyists, the care of strings, with great satisfaction in one another's company until a brutally ugly clock with a lyre-shaped pendulum struck the hour: Jack Aubrey emptied his cup and pushed back his chair.

'You will forgive me, I am sure. I have a whole round of official calls and an interview with my predecessor. But I hope I may count upon the honour, and may I say the pleasure – the great pleasure – of your company for dinner?'

'Most happy,' said Maturin, with a bow.

They were at the door. 'Then may we appoint three o'clock at the Crown?' said Jack. 'We do not keep fashionable hours in the service, and I grow so devilish hungry and peevish by then that you will forgive me, I am sure. We will wet the swab, and when it is handsomely awash, why then perhaps we might try a little music, if that would not be disagreeable to you.'

'Did you see that hoopoe?' cried the man in the black coat.

'What is a hoopoe?' cried Jack, staring about.

'A bird. That cinnamon-coloured bird with barred wings. Upupa epops. There! There, over the roof. There! There!'

'Where? Where? How does it bear?'

'It has gone now. I had been hoping to see a hoopoe ever since I arrived. In the middle of the town! Happy Mahon, to have such denizens. But I beg your pardon. You were speaking of wetting a swab.'

'Oh, yes. It is a cant expression we have in the Navy. The swab is this' – patting his epaulette – 'and when first we ship it, we wet it: that is to say, we drink a bottle or two of wine.'

'Indeed?' said Maturin with a civil inclination of his head. 'A decoration, a badge of rank, I make no doubt? A most elegant ornament, so it is, upon my soul. But, my dear sir, have you not forgot the other one?'

'Well,' said Jack, laughing, 'I dare say I shall put them both on, by and by. Now I will wish you a good day and thank you for the excellent chocolate. I am so happy that you saw your epop.'

The first call Jack had to pay was to the senior captain, the naval commandant of Port Mahon. Captain Harte lived in a big rambling house belonging to one Martinez, a

Spanish merchant, and he had an official set of rooms on the far side of the patio. As Jack crossed the open spaces he heard the sound of a harp, deadened to a tinkle by the shutters – they were drawn already against the mounting sun, and already geckoes were hurrying about on the sunlit walls.

Captain Harte was a little man, with a certain resemblance to Lord St Vincent, a resemblance that he did his best to increase by stooping, by being savagely rude to his subordinates and by the practice of Whiggery: whether he disliked Jack because Jack was tall and he was short, or whether he suspected him of carrying on an intrigue with his wife, it was all one – there was a strong antipathy between them, and it was of long standing. His first words were, 'Well, Mr Aubrey, and where the devil have you been? I expected you yesterday afternoon – Allen expected you yesterday afternoon. I was astonished to learn that he had never seen you at all. I wish you joy, of course,' he said without a smile, 'but upon my word you have an odd notion of taking over a command. Allen must be twenty leagues away by now, and every real sailorman in the *Sophie* with him, no doubt, to say nothing of his officers. And as for all the books, vouchers, dockets, and so on, we have had to botch it up as best we could. Precious irregular. Uncommon irregular.'

'*Pallas* has sailed, sir?' cried Jack, aghast.

'Sailed at midnight, sir,' said Captain Harte, with a look of satisfaction. 'The exigencies of the service do not wait upon our pleasure, Mr Aubrey. And I have been obliged to make a draft of what he left for harbour duty.'

'I only heard last night – in fact this morning, between one and two.'

'Indeed? You astonish me. I am amazed. The letter certainly went off in good time. It is the people at your inn who are at fault, no doubt. There is no relying on your foreigner. I give you joy of your command, I am sure, but how you will ever take her to sea with no people to work her out of the harbour I must confess I do not know. Allen took his lieutenant, and his surgeon, and all the promising

12

midshipmen; and I certainly cannot give you a single man fit to set one foot in front of another.'

'Well, sir,' said Jack, 'I suppose I must make the best of what I have.' It was understandable, of course: any officer who could would get out of a small, slow, old brig into a lucky frigate like the *Pallas*. And by immemorial custom a captain changing ships might take his coxswain and boat's crew as well as certain followers; and if he were not very closely watched he might commit enormities in stretching the definition of either class.

'I can let you have a chaplain,' said the commandant, turning the knife in the wound.

'Can he hand, reef and steer?' asked Jack, determined to show nothing. 'If not, I had rather be excused.'

'Good day to you, then, Mr Aubrey. I will send you your orders this afternoon.'

'Good day, sir. I hope Mrs Harte is at home. I must pay my respects and congratulate her – must thank her for the pleasure she gave us last night.'

'Was you at the Governor's then?' asked Captain Harte, who knew it perfectly well – whose dirty little trick had been based upon knowing it perfectly well. 'If you had not gone a-caterwauling you might have been aboard your own sloop, in an officerlike manner. God strike me down, but it is a pretty state of affairs when a young fellow prefers the company of Italian fiddlers and eunuchs to taking possession of his own first command.'

The sun seemed a little less brilliant as Jack walked diagonally across the patio to pay his call on Mrs Harte; but it still struck precious warm through his coat, and he ran up the stairs with the charming unaccustomed weight jogging there on his left shoulder. A lieutenant he did not know and the stuffed midshipman of yesterday evening were there before him, for at Port Mahon it was very much the thing to pay a morning call on Mrs Harte; she was sitting by her harp, looking decorative and talking to the lieutenant, but when he came in she jumped up, gave him both hands and cried, 'Captain Aubrey, how happy I am to see you! Many, many congratulations. Come, we must wet the swab. Mr Parker, pray touch the bell.'

'I wish you joy, sir,' said the lieutenant, pleased at the mere sight of what he longed for so. The midshipman hovered, wondering whether he might speak in such august company and then, just as Mrs Harte was beginning the introductions, he roared out, 'Wish you joy, sir,' in a wavering bellow, and blushed.

'Mr Stapleton, third of the *Guerrier*,' said Mrs Harte, with a wave of her hand. 'And Mr Burnet, of the *Isis*. Carmen, bring some Madeira.' She was a fine dashing woman, and without being either pretty or beautiful she gave the impression of being both, mostly from the splendid way she carried her head. She despised her scrub of a husband, who truckled to her; and she had taken to music as a relief from him. But it did not seem that music was enough, for now she poured out a bumper and drank it off with a very practised air.

A little later Mr Stapleton took his leave, and then after five minutes of the weather – delightful, not too hot even at midday – heat tempered by the breeze – north wind a little trying – healthy, however – summer already – preferable to the cold and rain of an English April – warmth in general more agreeable than cold – she said, 'Mr Burnet, I wonder whether I might beg you to be very kind? I left my reticule at the Governor's.'

'How charmingly you played, Molly,' said Jack, when the door had closed.

'Jack, I am so happy you have a ship at last.'

'So am I. I don't think I have ever been so happy in my life. Yesterday I was so peevish and low in my spirits I could have hanged myself, and then I went back to the Crown and there was this letter. Ain't it charming?' They read it together in respectful silence.

'*Answer the contrary at your peril*,' repeated Mrs Harte.

'Jack, I do beg and pray you will not attempt to make prize of neutrals. That Ragusan bark poor Willoughby sent in has not been condemned, and the owners are to sue him.'

'Never fret, dear Molly,' said Jack. 'I shall not be taking any prizes for a great while, I do assure you. This letter was delayed – damned curious delay – and Allen has gone off with all my prime hands; ordered to sea in a tearing hurry before I could see him. And the commandant has made hay of what was left for harbour duty: not a man to spare. We can't work out of harbour, it seems; so I dare say we shall ground upon our own beef-bones before ever we see so much as the smell of a prize.'

'Oh, indeed?' cried Mrs Harte, her colour rising: and at that moment in walked Lady Warren and her brother, a captain in the Marines. 'Dearest Anne,' cried Molly Harte, 'come here at once and help me remedy a very shocking injustice. Here is Captain Aubrey – you know one another?'

'Servant, ma'am,' said Jack, making a particularly deferential leg, for this was an admiral's wife, no less.

'– a most gallant, deserving officer, a thorough-paced Tory, General Aubrey's son, and he is being most abominably used . . .'

The heat had increased while he was in the house, and when he came out into the street the air was hot on his face, almost like another element; yet it was not at all choking, not at all sultry, and there was a brilliance in it that took away all oppression. After a couple of turns he reached the tree-lined street that carried the Ciudadela road down to the high-perched square, or rather terrace, that overlooked the quays. He crossed to the shady side, where English houses with sash windows, fanlights and cobbled forecourts stood on unexpectedly good terms with their neighbours, the baroque Jesuit church and the withdrawn Spanish mansions with great stone coats of arms over their doorways.

A party of seamen went by on the other side, some wearing

broad striped trousers, some plain sailcloth; some had fine red waistcoats and some ordinary blue jackets; some wore tarpaulin hats, in spite of the heat, some broad straws, and some spotted handkerchiefs tied over their heads; but they all of them had long swinging pigtails and they all had the indefinable air of man-of-war's men. They were Bellerophons, and he looked at them hungrily as they padded by, laughing and roaring out mildly to their friends, English and Spanish. He was approaching the square, and through the fresh green of the very young leaves he could see the *Généreux*'s royals and topgallants twinkling in the sun far over on the other side of the harbour, hanging out to dry. The busy street, the green, and the blue sky over it was enough to make any man's heart rise like a lark, and three-quarters of Jack's soared high. But the remaining part was earthbound, thinking anxiously about his crew. He had been familiar with this nightmare of manning since his earliest days in the Navy, and his first serious wound had been inflicted by a woman in Deal with a flat-iron who thought her man should not be pressed; but he had not expected to meet it quite so early in his command, nor in this form, nor in the Mediterranean.

Now he was in the square, with its noble trees and its great twin staircases winding down to the quay – stairs known to British sailors for a hundred years as Pigtail Steps, the cause of many a broken limb and battered head. He crossed it to the low wall that ran between the stair-heads and looked out over the immense expanse of enclosed water before him, stretching away left-handed to the distant top of the harbour and right-handed past the hospital island miles away to its narrow, castle-guarded mouth. To his left lay the merchantmen: scores and, indeed, hundreds of feluccas, tartans, xebecs, pinks, polacres, polacre-settees, houarios and barca-longas – all the Mediterranean rigs and plenty from the northern seas as well – bean-cods, cats, herring-busses. Opposite him and to his right lay the men-of-war: two ships of the line, both seventy-fours; a pretty twenty-eight gun frigate, the *Niobe*, whose people were painting a vermilion band under the chequered line of her gunports and up over her delicate transom, in imitation of a Spanish ship her captain had admired; and a number of transports and other vessels; while between them all and the steps up to the quay, innumerable boats plied to and fro – long-boats, barges from the ships of the line, launches, cutters, yawls and gigs, right down to the creeping jolly-boat belonging to the *Tartarus* bomb-ketch, with her enormous purser weighing it down to a bare three inches off the water. Still farther to the right the splendid quay curved away towards the dockyard, the ordnance and victualling wharfs and the quarantine island, hiding many of the other ships: Jack stared and craned with one foot on the parapet in the hope of catching a glimpse of his joy; but she was not to be seen. He turned reluctantly away to the left, for that was where Mr Williams' office lay. Mr Williams was the Mahon correspondent of Jack's prize-agent in Gibraltar, the eminently respectable house of Johnstone and Graham, and his office was the next and most necessary port of call; for besides feeling that it was ridiculous to have gold on his shoulder but none to jingle in his pocket, Jack would presently need ready money for a whole series of grave and unavoidable expenses – customary gifts, douceurs and the like, which could not possibly be done on credit.

He walked in with the utmost confidence, as if he had just won the battle of the Nile in person, and he was very well received: when their business was over the agent said, 'I suppose you have seen Mr Baldick?'

'The *Sophie*'s lieutenant?'

'Just so.'

'But he has gone with Captain Allen – he is aboard the *Pallas*.'

'There, sir, you are mistaken, if I may say so, in a manner of speaking. He is in the hospital.'

'You astonish me.'

The agent smiled, raising his shoulders and spreading his

hands in a deprecating gesture: he possessed the true word and Jack had to be astonished; but the agent begged pardon for his superiority. 'He came ashore late yesterday afternoon and was taken to the hospital with a low fever – the little hospital up past the Capuchins, not the one on the island. To tell you the truth' – the agent held the flat of his hand in front of his mouth as a token of secrecy and spoke in a lower tone – 'he and the *Sophie*'s surgeon did not see eye to eye, and the prospect of a cruise under his hands was more than Mr Baldick could abide. He will rejoin at Gib, no doubt, as soon as he is better. And now, Captain,' said the agent, with an unnatural smile and a shifty look, 'I am going to make so bold as to ask you a favour, if I may. Mrs Williams has a young cousin who is with child to go to sea – wants to be a purser later on. He is a quick boy and he writes a good clear hand; he has worked in the office here since Christmas and I know he is clever at figures. So, Captain Aubrey, sir, if you have no one else in mind for your clerk, you would infinitely oblige . . .' The agent's smile came and went, came and went: he was not used to be on the asking side in a favour, not with sea officers, and he found the possibility of a refusal wonderfully unpleasant.

'Why,' said Jack, considering, 'I have no one in mind, to be sure. You answer for him, of course? Well then, I tell you what, Mr Williams, you find me an able seaman to come along with him and I'll take your boy.'

'Are you in earnest, sir?'

'Yes . . . yes, I suppose I am. Yes: certainly.'

'Done, then,' said the agent, holding out his hand. 'You won't regret it, sir, I give you my word.'

'I'm sure of it, Mr Williams. Perhaps I had better have a look at him.'

David Richards was a plain, colourless youth – literally colourless except for some mauve pimples – but there was something touching in his intense, repressed excitement and his desperate eagerness to please. Jack looked at him kindly and said, 'Mr Williams tells me you write a fine clear hand, sir. Should you like to take down a note for me? It is addressed to the master of the *Sophie*. What's the master's name, Mr Williams?'

'Marshall, sir, William Marshall. A prime navigator, I hear.'

'So much the better,' said Jack, remembering his own struggles with the Requisite Tables and the bizarre conclusions he had sometimes reached. 'To Mr William Marshall, then, Master of His Majesty's sloop the *Sophie*. Captain Aubrey presents his compliments to Mr Marshall and will come aboard at about one o'clock in the afternoon. There, that should give them decent warning. Very prettily written, too. You will see that it reaches him?'

'I shall take it myself this minute, sir,' cried the youth, an unhealthy red with pleasure.

'Lord,' said Jack to himself as he walked up to the hospital, gazing about him at the vast spread of severe, open, barren country on either side of the busy sea, 'Lord, what a fine thing it is to play the great man, once in a while.'

'Mr Baldick?' he said. 'My name is Aubrey. Since we were so nearly shipmates I have called in to ask how you do. I hope I see you on the way to recovery, sir?'

'Very kind in you, sir,' cried the lieutenant, a man of fifty whose crimson face was covered with a silvery glinting stubble, although his hair was black, 'more than kind. Thankee, thankee, Captain. I am far better, I am glad to say, now I am out of the clutches of that bloody-minded sawbones. Would you credit it, sir? Thirty-seven years in the service, twenty-nine of them as a commissioned officer, and I am to be treated to the water-cure and a low diet. Ward's pill and Ward's drop are no good – quite exploded, we hear: but they saw me through the West Indies in the last war, when we lost two-thirds of the larboard watch in ten days from the yellow jack. They preserved me from that, sir, to say nothing of scurvy, and sciatica, and rheumatism, and the bloody flux; but they are of no use, we are told. Well, they may say what they please, these jumped-up young fellows from the Surgeons' Hall with the ink scarcely dry on their warrants, but I put my faith on Ward's drop.'

'And in Brother Bung,' remarked Jack privately, for the place smelt like the spirit-room of a first-rate. 'So the *Sophie* has lost her surgeon,' he said aloud, 'as well as the more valuable members of her crew?'

'No great loss, I do assure you, sir: though, indeed, the ship's company did make great case of him – swore by him and his silly nostrums, the damned set of gabies; and were much distressed at his going off. And how ever you will replace him in the Med I do not know, by the by, such rare birds they are. But he's no great loss, whatever they may say: and a chest of Ward's drop will answer just as well; nay, better. And the carpenter for amputations. May I offer you a glass, sir?' Jack shook his head. 'As for the rest,' the lieutenant went on, 'we really were very moderate. The *Pallas* has close on her full complement. Captain A only took his nephew and a friend's son and the other Americans, apart from his cox'n and his steward. And his clerk.'

'Many Americans?'

'Oh no, not above half a dozen. All people from his own part – the country up behind Halifax.'

'Well, that's a relief, upon my word. I had been told the brig was stripped.'

'Who told you that, sir?'

'Captain Harte.'

Mr Baldick narrowed his lips and sniffed. He hesitated and took another pull at his mug; but he only said, 'I've known him off and on these thirty years. He is very fond of practising upon people: by way of having a joke, no doubt.' While they contemplated Captain Harte's devious sense of fun, Mr Baldick slowly emptied his mug. 'No,' he said, setting it down, 'we've left you what might be called a very fair crew. A score or two of prime seamen, and a good half of the people real man-of-war's men, which is more than you can say for most line of battle ships nowadays. There are some untoward sods among the other half, but so there are in every ship's company – by the by, Captain A left you a note about one of 'em – Isaac Wilson, ordinary – and at least you have no damned sea-lawyers aboard. Then there are your standing officers: right taut old-fashioned sailormen, for the most part. Watt, the bosun, knows his business as well as any man in the fleet. And Lamb, the carpenter, is a good, steady fellow, though maybe a trifle slow and timid. George Day, the gunner – he's a good man, too, when he's well, but he has a silly way of dosing himself. And the purser, Ricketts, is well enough, for a purser. The master's mates, Pullings and young Mowett, can be trusted with a watch: Pullings passed for a lieutenant years ago, but he has never been made. And as for the youngsters, we've only left you two, Ricketts' boy and Babbington. Blockheads, both of them; but not blackguards.'

'What about the master? I hear he is a great navigator.'

'Marshall? Well, so he is.' Again Mr Baldick narrowed his lips and sniffed. But by now he had drunk a further pint of grog, and this time he said, 'I don't know what *you* think about this buggery lark, sir; but *I* think it's unnatural.'

'Why, there is something in what you say, Mr Baldick,' said Jack. Then, feeling the weight of interrogation still upon him, he added, 'I don't like it – not my line at all. But I must confess I don't like to see a man hanged for it. The ship's boys, I suppose?'

Mr Baldick slowly shook his head for some time. 'No,' he said at last. 'No. I don't say he *does* anything. Not now. But come, I do not like to speak ill of a man behind his back.'

'The good of the service . . .' said Jack, with a general wave of his hand; and shortly afterwards he took his leave, for the lieutenant had come out in a pale sweat; was poorly, lugubrious and intoxicated.

The tramontana had freshened and now it was blowing a two-reef topsail breeze, rattling the fronds of the palms; the sky was clear from rim to rim; a short, choppy sea was getting up outside the harbour, and now there was an edge to the hot air like salt or wine. He tapped his hat firmly on his head, filled his lungs and said aloud, 'Dear God, how good it is to be alive.'

He had timed it well. He would pass by the Crown, make sure that dinner would be suitably splendid, brush his coat and maybe drink a glass of wine: he would not have to pick up his commission, for it had never left him – there it was against his bosom, crackling gently as he breathed.

Walking down at a quarter to one, walking down to the waterside with the Crown behind him, he felt a curious shortness of his breath; and as he sat in the waterman's boat he said nothing but the word '*Sophie*', for his heart was beating high, and he had a curious difficulty in swallowing. 'Am I afraid?' he wondered. He sat looking gravely at the pommel of his sword, scarcely aware of the boat's smooth passage down the harbour, among the crowded ships and vessels, until the *Sophie's* side rose in front of him and the waterman rattled his boathook.

A quick automatic searching look showed him yards exactly squared, the side dressed, ship's boys in white gloves running down with baize-covered side-ropes, the bosun's call poised, winking silver in the sun. Then the boat's motion stopped, there was the faint crunch as it touched the sloop, and he went up the side to the weird screaming of the call. As his foot touched the gangway there was the hoarse order, the clump and crash of the marines presenting arms, and every officer's hat flew off; and as he stepped upon the quarterdeck he raised his own.

The warrant-officers and midshipmen were drawn up in their best uniforms, blue and white on the shining deck, a less rigid group than the scarlet rectangle of the marines. Their eyes were fixed very attentively on their new commander. He looked grave and, indeed, rather stern: after a second's pause in which the boatman's voice could be heard over the side, muttering to himself, he said, 'Mr Marshall, name the officers to me, if you please.'

Each came forward, the purser, the master's mates, the

midshipmen, the gunner, the carpenter and the bosun, and each made his bow, intently watched by the crew. Jack said, 'Gentlemen, I am happy to make your acquaintance. Mr Marshall, all hands aft, if you please. As there is no lieutenant I shall read my commission to the ship's company myself.'

There was no need to turn anybody up from below: every man was there, washed and shining, staring hard. Nevertheless, the calls of the bosun and his mates piped *All hands aft* for a good half-minute down the hatchways. The shrilling died away. Jack stepped forward to the break of the quarter-deck and took out his commission. As soon as it appeared there came the order 'Off hats', and he began in a firm but somewhat forced and mechanical voice.

'By the right Honourable Lord Keith . . .'

As he ran through the familiar lines, now so infinitely more full of meaning, his happiness returned, welling up through the gravity of the occasion, and he rolled out the 'Hereof nor you nor any of you may fail as you will answer the contrary at your peril' with a fine relish. Then he folded the paper, nodded to the men and returned it to his pocket. 'Very good,' he said. 'Dismiss the hands and we will take a look at the brig.'

In the hushed ceremonial procession that followed Jack saw exactly what he had expected to see – a vessel ready for inspection, holding her breath in case any of her beautifully trim rigging with its geometrically perfect fakes and perpendicular falls should be disturbed. She bore as much resemblance to her ordinary self as the rigid bosun, sweating in a uniform coat that must have been shaped with an adze, did to the same man in his shirt-sleeves, puddening the topsail yard in a heavy swell; yet there was an essential relationship, and the snowy sweep of the deck, the painful brilliance of the two brass quarter-deck four-pounders, the precision of the cylinders in the cable-tier and the parade-ground neatness of the galley's pots and tubs all had a meaning. Jack had whited too many sepulchres to be easily deceived; and he was pleased with what he saw. He saw and appreciated all he was meant to see. He was blind to the things he was not meant to see – the piece of ham that an officious fo'c'sle cat dragged from behind a bucket, the girls the master's mates had hidden in the sail-room and who would keep peeping out from behind mounds of canvas. He took no notice of the goat abaft the manger, that fixed him with an insulting devilish split-pupilled eye and defecated with intent; nor of the dubious object, not unlike a pudding, that someone in a last-minute panic had wedged beneath the gammoning of the bowsprit.

Yet his was an eminently professional eye – it had been nominally at sea since he was nine and, in fact, since he was twelve – and it picked up a great many other impressions. The master was not at all what he had expected, but a big, good-looking, capable middle-aged man – the sodden Mr Baldick had probably got the whole thing wrong. The bosun was: his character was written in his rigging – cautious, solid, conscientious, traditional. The purser and the gunner neither here nor there, though indeed the gunner was obviously too ill to do himself justice, and half-way through he quietly vanished. The midshipmen were more presentable than he had expected: brig's and cutter's midshipmen were often a pretty squalid lot. But that child, that youngster Babbington, could not be allowed ashore in those garments: his mother must have counted upon a growth that had not taken place, and he was so extinguished by his hat alone that it would bring discredit to the sloop.

His chief impression was of old-fashionedness: the *Sophie* had something archaic about her, as though she would rather have her bottom hobnailed than coppered, and would rather pay her sides than paint them. Her crew, without being at all elderly – indeed, most of the hands were in their twenties – had an old-fashioned look; some were wearing petticoat-breeches and shoes, a rig that had already grown uncommon when he was a midshipman no bigger than little Babbington. They moved about in an easy, unconstrained manner, he noticed: they seemed decently curious, but not in the least bloody-minded, resentful or cowed.

Yes: old-fashioned. He loved her dearly – had loved her from the moment his eye first swept along her sweetly curving deck – but calm intelligence told him that she was a slow brig, an old brig and a brig that was very unlikely to make his fortune. She had fought a couple of creditable actions under his predecessor, one against a French twenty-gun ship-rigged privateer from Toulon, and the other in the Gut of Gibraltar, protecting her convoy from a swarm of Algeciras gunboats rowing out in a calm; but as far as he could remember she had never taken a prize of any real value.

They were back at the break of the odd little quarter-deck – it was really more like a poop – and bending his head he stepped into the cabin. Crouching low, he made his way to the lockers beneath the stern-windows that stretched from one side to the other of the after end – an elegant, curving frame for an extraordinarily brilliant, Canaletto view of Port Mahon, all lit with the silent noon-day sun and (seen from this comparative dimness) belonging to a different world. Sitting down with a cautious sideways movement he found he could hold his head up with no difficulty at all – a good eighteen inches to spare – and he said, 'There we are, Mr Marshall. I must congratulate you upon the *Sophie's* appearance. Very trim: very shipshape.' He thought he might go as far as that, so long as he kept his voice quite official, but he was certainly not going to say any more; nor was he going to address the men or announce any indulgence to mark the occasion. He loathed the idea of a 'popular' captain. 'Thank you, sir,' said the master.

'Now I am going ashore. But I shall sleep aboard, of course; so pray be good enough to send a boat for my chest and dunnage. I am at the Crown.'

He sat on for a while, savouring the glory of his day-cabin. It had no guns in it, for the peculiar build of the *Sophie* would have brought their muzzles to within six inches of the surface if there had been, and the two four-pounders that would ordinarily have taken up so much space were immediately over his head; but even so there was not much room, and one table running athwart was all that the cabin would hold, apart from the lockers. Yet it was far more than he had ever owned before, at sea, and he surveyed it with glowing complacency, looking with particular delight at the handsomely mounted inward-sloping windows, all as bright as glass could very well be, seven sets of panes in a noble sweep quite furnishing the room.

It was more than he had ever had, and more than he had ever really hoped for so early in his career; so why was there something as yet undefined beneath his exultation, the *aliquid amari* of his schooldays?

As he rowed back to the shore, pulled by his own boat's crew in white duck and straw hats with *Sophie* embroidered on the ribbon, a solemn midshipman silent beside him in the stern-sheets, he realized the nature of this feeling. He was no longer one of 'us': he was 'they'. Indeed, he was the immediately-present incarnation of 'them'. In his tour of the brig he had been surrounded with deference – a respect different in kind from that accorded to a lieutenant, different in kind from that accorded to a fellow human-being: it had surrounded him like a glass bell, quite shutting him off from the ship's company; and on his leaving the *Sophie* had let out a quiet sigh of relief, the sigh he knew so well: 'Jehovah is no longer with us.'

'It is the price that has to be paid,' he reflected. 'Thank you, Mr Babbington,' he said to the child, and he stood on the steps while the boat backed out and pulled away down the harbour, Mr Babbington piping, 'Give way now, can't you? Don't go to sleep, Simmons, you grog-faced villain.'

'It is the price that has to be paid,' he reflected. 'And by God it's worth it.' As the words formed in his mind so the look of profound happiness, of contained delight, formed once more upon his shining face. Yet as he walked off to his meeting at the Crown – to his meeting with an equal – there was a little greater eagerness in his step than the mere Lieutenant Aubrey would have shown.

Chapter Two

They sat at a round table in a bow window that protruded from the back of the inn high above the water, yet so close to it that they had tossed the oyster-shells back into their native element with no more than a flick of the wrist: and from the unloading tartan a hundred and fifty feet below them there arose the mingled scents of Stockholm tar, cordage, sail-cloth and Chian turpentine.

'Allow me to press you to a trifle of this ragoo'd mutton, sir,' said Jack.

'Well, if you insist,' said Stephen Maturin. 'It is so very good.'

'It is one of the things the Crown does well,' said Jack. 'Though it is hardly decent in me to say so. Yet I had ordered duck pie, alamode beef and soused hog's face as well, apart from the kickshaws. No doubt the fellow misunderstood. Heaven knows what is in that dish by you, but it is certainly not hog's face. I said, *visage de porco*, many times over; and he nodded like a China mandarin. It is provoking, you know, when one desires them to prepare five dishes, *cinco platos*, explaining carefully in Spanish, only to find there are but three, and two of those the wrong ones. I am ashamed of having nothing better to offer you, but it was not from want of good will, I do assure you.'

'I have not eaten so well for many a day, nor' – with a bow – 'in such pleasant company, upon my word,' said Stephen Maturin. 'Might it not be that the difficulty arose from your own particular care – from your explaining in Spanish, in Castilian Spanish?'

'Why,' said Jack, filling their glasses and smiling through

his wine at the sun, 'it seemed to me that in speaking to Spaniards, it was reasonable to use what Spanish I could muster.'

'You were forgetting, of course, that Catalan is the language they speak in these islands.'

'What is Catalan?'

'Why, the language of Catalonia – of the islands, of the whole of the Mediterranean coast down to Alicante and beyond. Of Barcelona. Of Lerida. All the richest part of the peninsula.'

'You astonish me. I had no notion of it. Another language, sir? But I dare say it is much the same thing – a *putain*, as they say in France?'

'Oh no, nothing of the kind – not like at all. A far finer language. More learned, more literary. Much nearer the Latin. And by the by, I believe the word is *patois*, sir, if you will allow me.'

'*Patois* – just so. Yet I swear the other is a word: I learnt it somewhere,' said Jack. 'But I must not play the scholar with you, sir, I find. Pray, is it very different to the ear, the unlearned ear?'

'As different as Italian and Portuguese. Mutually incomprehensible – they sound entirely unlike. The intonation of each is in an utterly different key. As unlike as Gluck and Mozart. This excellent dish by me, for instance (and I see that they did their best to follow your orders), is *jabalí* in Spanish, whereas in Catalan it is *senglar*.'

'Is it swine's flesh?'

'Wild boar. Allow me . . .'

'You are very good. May I trouble you for the salt? It is capital eating, to be sure; but I should never have guessed it was swine's flesh. What are these well-tasting soft dark things?'

'There you pose me. They are *bolets* in Catalan: but what they are called in English I cannot tell. They probably have no name – no country name, I mean, though the naturalist will always recognize them in the boletus edulis of Linnaeus.'

'How . . . ?' began Jack, looking at Stephen Maturin with candid affection. He had eaten two or three pounds of mutton, and the boar on top of the sheep brought out all his benevolence. 'How . . . ?' But finding that he was on the edge of questioning a guest he filled up the space with a cough and rang the bell for the waiter, gathering the empty decanters over to his side of the table.

The question was in the air, however, and only a most repulsive or indeed a morose reserve would have ignored it. 'I was brought up in these parts,' observed Stephen Maturin. 'I spent a great part of my young days with my uncle in Barcelona or with my grandmother in the country behind Lerida – indeed, I must have spent more time in Catalonia than I did in Ireland; and when first I went home to attend the university I carried out my mathematical exercises in Catalan, for the figures came more naturally to my mind.'

'So you speak it like a native, sir, I am sure,' said Jack. 'What a capital thing. That is what I call making a good use of one's childhood. I wish I could say as much.'

'No, no,' said Stephen, shaking his head. 'I made a very poor use of my time indeed: I did come to a tolerable acquaintance with the birds – a very rich country in raptores, sir – and the reptiles; but the insects, apart from the lepidoptera, and the plants – what deserts of gross sterile brutish ignorance! It was not until I had been some years in Ireland and had written my little work on the phanerogams of Upper Ossory that I came to understand how monstrously I had wasted my time. A vast tract of country to all intents and purposes untouched since Willughby and Ray passed through towards the end of the last age. The King of Spain invited Linnaeus to come, with liberty of conscience, as no doubt you remember; but he declined: I had had all these unexplored riches at my command, and I had ignored them. Think what Pallas, think what the learned Solander, or the Gmelins, old and young, would have accomplished! That was why I fastened upon the first opportunity that offered and agreed to accompany old Mr Browne: it is true that

Minorca is not the mainland, but then, on the other hand, so great an area of calcareous rock has its particular flora, and all that flows from that interesting state.'

'Mr Brown of the dockyard? The naval officer? I know him well,' cried Jack. 'An excellent companion – loves to sing a round – writes a charming little tune.'

'No. My patient died at sea and we buried him up there by St Philip's: poor fellow, he was in the last stages of phthisis. I had hoped to get him here – a change of air and regimen can work wonders in these cases – but when Mr Florey and I opened his body we found so great a . . . In short, we found that his advisers (and they were the best in Dublin) had been altogether too sanguine.'

'You cut him up?' cried Jack, leaning back from his plate.

'Yes: we thought it proper, to satisfy his friends. Though upon my word they seem wonderfully little concerned. It is weeks since I wrote to the only relative I know of, a gentleman in the county Fermanagh, and never a word has come back at all.'

There was a pause. Jack filled their glasses (how the tide went in and out) and observed, 'Had I known you was a surgeon, sir, I do not think I could have resisted the temptation of pressing you.'

'Surgeons are excellent fellows,' said Stephen Maturin with a touch of acerbity. 'And where should we be without them, God forbid: and, indeed, the skill and dispatch and dexterity with which Mr Florey at the hospital here everted Mr Browne's eparterial bronchus would have amazed and delighted you. But I have not the honour of counting myself among them, sir. I am a physician.'

'I beg your pardon: oh dear me, what a sad blunder. But even so, Doctor, even so, I think I should have had you run aboard and kept under hatches till we were at sea. My poor *Sophie* has no surgeon and there is no likelihood of finding her one. Come, sir, cannot I prevail upon you to go to sea? A man-of-war is the very thing for a philosopher, above all in the Mediterranean: there are the birds, the fishes – I could promise you some monstrous strange fishes – the natural phenomena, the meteors, the chance of prize-money. For even Aristotle would have been moved by prize-money. Doubloons, sir: they lie in soft leather sacks, you know, about so big, and they are wonderfully heavy in your hand. Two is all a man can carry.'

He had spoken in a bantering tone, never dreaming of a serious reply, and he was astonished to hear Stephen say, 'But I am in no way qualified to be a naval surgeon. To be sure, I have done a great deal of anatomical dissection, and I am not unacquainted with most of the usual chirurgical operations; but I know nothing of naval hygiene, nothing of the particular maladies of seamen . . .'

'Bless you,' cried Jack, 'never strain at gnats of that kind. Think of what we are usually sent – surgeon's mates, wretched half-grown stunted apprentices that have knocked about an apothecary's shop just long enough for the Navy Office to give them a warrant. They know nothing of surgery, let alone physic; they learn on the poor seamen as they go along, and they hope for an experienced loblolly boy or a beast-leech or a cunning-man or maybe a butcher among the hands – the press brings in all sorts. And when they have picked up a smattering of their trade, off they go into frigates and ships of the line. No, no. We should be delighted to have you – more than delighted. Do, pray, consider of it, if only for a while. I need not say,' he added, with a particularly earnest look, 'how much pleasure it would give me, was we to be shipmates.'

The waiter opened the door, saying, 'Marine,' and immediately behind him appeared the red-coat, bearing a packet. 'Captain Aubrey, sir?' he cried in an outdoor voice. 'Captain Harte's compliment.' He disappeared with a rumble of boots, and Jack observed, 'Those must be my orders.'

'Do not mind me, I beg,' said Stephen. 'You must read them directly.' He took up Jack's fiddle and walked away to the end of the room, where he played a low, whispering scale, over and over again.

The orders were very much what he had expected: they required him to complete his stores and provisions with the utmost possible dispatch and to convoy twelve sail of merchantmen and transports (named in the margin) to Cagliari. He was to travel at a very great pace, but he was by no means to endanger his masts, yards or sails: he was to shrink from no danger, but on the other hand he was on no account to incur any risk whatsoever. Then, labelled *secret*, the instructions for the private signal – the difference between friend and foe, between good and bad: 'The ship first making the signal is to hoist a red flag at the foretopmast head and a white flag with a pendant over the flag at the main. To be answered with a white flag with a pendant over the flag at the maintopmast head and a blue flag at the foretopmast head. The ship that first made the signal is to fire one gun to windward, which the other is to answer by firing three guns to leeward in slow time.' Lastly, there was a note to say that Lieutenant Dillon had been appointed to the *Sophie*, vice Mr Baldick, and that he would shortly arrive in the *Burford*.

'Here's good news,' said Jack. 'I am to have a capital fellow as my lieutenant: we are only allowed one in the *Sophie*, you know, so it is very important . . . I do not know him personally, but he is an excellent fellow, that I am sure of. He distinguished himself very much in the *Dart*, a hired cutter – set about three French privateers in the Sicily Channel, sank one and took another. Everyone in the fleet talked about it at the time; but his letter was never printed in the Gazette, and he was not promoted. It was infernal bad luck. I wonder at it, for it was not as though he had no interest: Fitzgerald, who knows all about these things, told me he was a nephew, or cousin was it? to a peer whose name I forget. And in any case it was a very creditable thing – dozens of men have got their step for much less. I did, for one.'

'May I ask what you did? I know so little about naval matters.'

'Oh, I simply got knocked on the head, once at the Nile and then again when the *Généreux* took the old *Leander*: rewards were obliged to be handed out, so I being the only surviving lieutenant, one came my way at last. It took its time, upon my word, but it was very welcome when it came, however slow and undeserved. What do you say to taking tea? And perhaps a piece of muffin? Or should you rather stay with the port?'

'Tea would make me very happy,' said Stephen. 'But tell me,' he said, walking back to the fiddle and tucking it under his chin, 'do not your naval appointments entail great expense, going to London, uniforms, oaths, levees . . . ?'

'Oaths? Oh, you refer to the swearing-in. No. That applies only to lieutenants – you go to the Admiralty and they read you a piece about allegiance and supremacy and utterly renouncing the Pope; you feel very solemn and say "to this I swear" and the chap at the high desk says "and that will be half a guinea", which does rather take away from the effect, you know. But it is only commissioned officers – medical men are appointed by a warrant. *You* would not object to taking an oath, however,' he said, smiling; and then feeling that this remark was a little indelicate, a little personal, he went on, 'I was shipmates with a poor fellow once that objected to taking an oath, any oath, on principle. I never could like him – he was for ever touching his face. He was nervous, I believe, and it gave him countenance; but whenever you looked at him there he was with a finger at his mouth, or pressing his cheek, or pulling his chin awry. It is nothing, of course; but when you are penned up with it in the same wardroom it grows tedious, day after day all through a long commission. In the gun-room or the cockpit you can call out "Leave your face alone, for God's sake," but in the wardroom you must bear with it. However, he took to reading in his Bible, and he conceived this notion that he must not take an oath; and when there was that foolish court-martial on poor Bentham he was called as a witness and refused, flatly refused, to be sworn. He told Old

Jarvie it was contrary to something in the Gospels. Now that might have washed with Gambier or Saumarez or someone given to tracts, but not with Old Jarvie, by God. He was broke, I am sorry to say: I never could like him – to tell you the truth, he smelt too – but he was a tolerably good seaman and there was no vice in him. That is what I mean when I say you would not object to an oath – *you* are not an enthusiast.'

'No, certainly,' said Stephen. 'I am not an enthusiast. I was brought up by a philosopher, or perhaps I should say a *philosophe*; and some of his philosophy has stuck to me. He would have called an oath a childish thing – otiose if voluntary and rightly to be evaded or ignored if imposed. For few people today, even among your tarpaulins, are weak enough to believe in Earl Godwin's piece of bread.'

There was a long pause while the tea was brought in. 'You take milk in your tea, Doctor?' asked Jack.

'If you please,' said Stephen. He was obviously deep in thought: his eyes were fixed upon vacancy and his mouth was pursed in a silent whistle.

'I wish . . .' said Jack.

'It is always said to be weak, and impolitic, to show oneself at a disadvantage,' said Stephen, bearing him down. 'But you speak to me with such candour that I cannot prevent myself from doing the same. Your offer, your suggestion, tempts me exceedingly; for apart from those considerations that you so obligingly mention, and which I reciprocate most heartily, I am very much at a stand, here in Minorca. The patient I was to attend until the autumn has died. I had understood him to be a man of substance – he had a house in Merrion Square – but when Mr Florey and I looked through his effects before sealing them we found nothing whatever, neither money nor letters of credit. His servant decamped, which may explain it: but his friends do not answer my letters; the war has cut me off from my little patrimony in Spain; and when I told you, some time ago, that I had not eaten so well for a great while, I did not speak figuratively.'

'Oh, what a very shocking thing!' cried Jack. 'I am heartily sorry for your embarrassment, and if the – the *res angusta* is pressing, I hope you will allow me . . .' His hand was in his breeches pocket, but Stephen Maturin said 'No, no, no,' a dozen times smiling and nodding. 'But you are very good.'

'I am heartily sorry for your embarrassment, Doctor,' repeated Jack, 'and I am almost ashamed to profit by it. But my *Sophie* must have a medical man – apart from anything else, you have no notion of what a hypochondriac your seaman is: they love to be physicked, and a ship's company without someone to look after them, even the rawest half-grown surgeon's mate, is not a happy ship's company – and then again it is the direct answer to your immediate difficulties. The pay is contemptible for a learned man – five pounds a month – and I am ashamed to mention it; but there is the chance of prize-money, and I believe there are certain perquisites, such as Queen Anne's Gift, and something for every man with the pox. It is stopped out of their pay.'

'Oh, as for money, I am not greatly concerned with that. If the immortal Linnaeus could traverse five thousand miles of Lapland, living upon twenty-five pounds, surely I can . . . But is the thing in itself really feasible? Surely there must be an official appointment? Uniform? Instruments? Drugs, medical necessities?'

'Now that you come to ask me these fine points, it is surprising how little I know,' said Jack, smiling. 'But Lord love you, Doctor, we must not let trifles stand in the way. A warrant from the Navy Office you must have, that I am sure of; but I know the admiral will give you an acting order the minute I ask him – delighted to do so. As for uniform, there is nothing particular for surgeons, though a blue coat is usual. Instruments and so on – there you have me. I believe Apothecaries' Hall sends a chest aboard: Florey will know, or any of the surgeons. But at all events come aboard directly. Come as soon as you like – come tomorrow, say, and we will dine together. Even the acting order will take some little time, so make this voyage as my guest. It will not be comfortable – no elbow-room in a brig, you know – but it will introduce you to naval life; and if you have a saucy landlord, it will dish him instantly. Let me fill your cup. And I am sure you will like it, for it is amazingly philosophical.'

'Certainly,' said Stephen. 'For a philosopher, a student of human nature, what could be better? The subjects of his inquiry shut up together, unable to escape his gaze, their passions heightened by the dangers of war, the hazards of their calling, their isolation from women and their curious, but uniform, diet. And by the glow of patriotic fervour, no doubt.' – with a bow to Jack – 'It is true that for some time past I have taken more interest in the cryptogams than in my fellow-men; but even so, a ship must be a most instructive theatre for an inquiring mind.'

'Prodigiously instructive, I do assure you, Doctor,' said Jack. 'How happy you make me: to have Dillon as the *Sophie*'s lieutenant and a Dublin physician as her surgeon – by the way, you are countrymen, of course. Perhaps you know Mr Dillon?'

'There are so many Dillons,' said Stephen, with a chill settling about his heart. 'What is his Christian name?'

'James,' said Jack, looking at the note.

'No,' said Stephen deliberately. 'I do not remember to have met any James Dillon.'

'Mr Marshall,' said Jack, 'pass the word for the carpenter, if you please. I have a guest coming aboard: we must do our best to make him comfortable. He is a physician, a great man in the philosophical line.'

'An astronomer, sir?' asked the master eagerly.

'Rather more of a botanist, I take it,' said Jack. 'But I have great hopes that if we make him comfortable he may stay with us as the *Sophie*'s surgeon. Think what a famous thing that would be for the ship's company!'

'Indeed it would, sir. They were right upset when Mr Jackson went off to the *Pallas*, and to replace him with a physician would be a great stroke. There's one aboard the flagship and one at Gibraltar, but not another in the whole fleet, not that I know of. They charge a guinea a visit, by land; or so I have heard tell.'

'Even more, Mr Marshall, even more. Is that water aboard?'

'All aboard and stowed, sir, except for the last two casks.'

'There you are, Mr Lamb. I want you to have a look at the bulkhead of my sleeping-cabin and see what you can do to make it a little more roomy for a friend: you may be able to shift it for'ard a good six inches. Yes, Mr Babbington, what is it?'

'If you please, sir, the *Burford* is signalling over the headland.'

'Very good. Now let the purser, the gunner and the bosun know I want to see them.'

From that moment on the captain of the *Sophie* was plunged deep into her accounts – her muster-book, slop-book, tickets, sick-book, complete-book, gunner's, bosun's and carpenter's expenses, supplies and returns, general account of provisions received and returned, and quarterly account of same, together with certificates of the quantity of spirits, wine, cocoa and tea issued, to say nothing of the log, letter and order books – and what with having dined extremely well and not being good with figures at any time, he very soon lost his footing. Most of his dealings were with Ricketts, the purser; and as Jack grew irritable in his confusion it seemed to him that he detected a certain smoothness in the way the purser presented his interminable sums and balances. There were papers here, quittances, acknowledgements and receipts that he was being asked to sign; and he knew very well that he did not understand them all.

'Mr Ricketts,' he said, at the end of a long, easy explanation that conveyed nothing to him at all, 'here in the muster-book, at number 178, is Charles Stephen Ricketts.'

'Yes, sir. My son, sir.'

'Just so. I see that he appeared on November 30th, 1797. From *Tonnant*, late *Princess Royal*. There is no age by his name.'

'Ah, let me see: Charlie must have been rising twelve by then, sir.'

'He was rated Able Seaman.'

'Yes, sir. Ha, ha!'

It was a perfectly ordinary little everyday fraud; but it was illegal. Jack did not smile. He went on, 'AB to September 20th, 1798, then rated Clerk. And then on November 10th, 1799, he was rated Midshipman.'

'Yes, sir,' said the purser: not only was there that little awkwardness of the eleven-year-old able seaman, but Mr Ricketts' quick ear caught the slight emphasis on the word *rated* and its slightly unusual repetition. The message it conveyed was this: 'I may seem a poor man of business; but if you try any purser's tricks with me, I am athwart your hawse and I can rake you from stem to stern. What is more, one captain's rating can be disrated by another, and if you trouble my sleep, by God, I shall turn your boy before the mast and flog the tender pink skin off his back every day for the rest of the commission.' Jack's head was aching; his eyes were slightly rimmed with red from the port, and there was so clear a hint of latent ferocity in them that the purser took the message very seriously. 'Yes, sir,' he said again. 'Yes. Now here is the list of dockyard tallies: would you like me to explain the different headings in detail, sir?'

'If you please, Mr Ricketts.'

This was Jack's first direct, fully responsible acquaintance with book-keeping, and he did not much relish it. Even a small vessel (and the *Sophie* barely exceeded a hundred and fifty tons) needs a wonderful amount of stores: casks of beef, pork and butter all numbered and signed for, puncheons, butts and half-pieces of rum, hard-tack by the ton from Old Weevil, dried soup with the broad arrow upon it, quite apart from the gunner's powder (mealed, corned and best patent), sponges, worms, matches, priming-irons, wads and shot – bar, chain, case, langrage, grape or plain round – and the countless objects needed (and so *very* often embezzled) by the bosun – the blocks, the long-tackle, single, double, parrel, quarter-coak, double-coak, flat-side, double thin-coak, single thin-coak, single strap-bound and sister blocks alone made up a whole Lent litany. Here Jack was far more at home, for the difference between a single double-scored and a single-shoulder block was as clear to him as that between night and day, or right and wrong – far clearer, on occasion. But by now his mind, used to grappling with concrete physical problems, was thoroughly tired: he looked wistfully over the dog-eared, tatty books piled up on the curving rim of the lockers out through the cabin windows at the brilliant air and the dancing sea. He passed his hand over his forehead and said, 'We will deal with the rest another time, Mr Ricketts. What a God-damned great heap of paper it is, to be sure: I see that a clerk is a very necessary member of the ship's company. That reminds me, I have appointed a young man – he will be coming aboard today. I am sure you will ease him into his duties, Mr Ricketts. He seems willing and competent, and he is nephew to Mr Williams, the prize-agent. I think it is to the *Sophie*'s advantage that we should be well with the prize-agent, Mr Ricketts?'

'Indeed it is, sir,' said the purser, with deep conviction.

'Now I must go across to the dockyard with the bosun before the evening gun,' said Jack, escaping into the open air. As he set foot upon deck so young Richards came up the larboard side, accompanied by a Negro, well over six feet tall. 'Here is the young man I was telling you about, Mr Ricketts. And this is the seaman you have brought me, Mr Richards? A fine stout fellow he looks, too. What is his name?'

'Alfred King, if you please, sir.'

'Can you hand, reef and steer, King?'

The Negro nodded his round head; there was a fine flash of white across his face and he grunted aloud. Jack frowned, for this was no way to address a captain on his own quarter-deck. 'Come, sir,' he said sharply, 'haven't you got a civil tongue in your head?'

Looking suddenly grey and apprehensive the Negro shook his head. 'If you please, sir,' said the clerk, 'he has no tongue. The Moors cut it out.'

'Oh,' said Jack, taken aback, 'oh. Well, stow him for'ard. I will read him in by and by. Mr Babbington, take Mr Richards below and show him the midshipmen's berth. Come, Mr Watt, we must get to the dockyard before the idle dogs stop work altogether.'

'There is a man to gladden your heart, Mr Watt,' said Jack, as the cutter sped across the harbour. 'I wish I could find another score or so like him. You don't seem very taken with the idea, Mr Watt?'

'Well, sir, I should never say no to a prime seaman, to be sure. And to be sure we could swap some of our landmen (not that we have many left, being as we've been in commission so long, and them as was going to run having run and most of the rest rated ordinary, if not able . . .' The bosun could not find his way out of his parenthesis, and after a staring pause he wound up by saying, 'But as for mere numbers, why no, sir.'

'Not even with the draft for harbour-duties?'

'Why, bless you, sir, they never amounted to half a dozen, and we took good care they was all the hard bargains and right awkward buggers. Beg pardon, sir: the idle men. So as for mere numbers, why no, sir. In a three-watch brig like the *Sophie* it's a puzzle to stow 'em all between-decks as it is: she's a trim, comfortable, home-like little vessel, right enough, but she ain't what you might call roomy.'

Jack made no reply to this; but it confirmed a good many of his impressions, and he reflected upon them until the boat reached the yard.

'Captain Aubrey!' cried Mr Brown, the officer in charge of the yard. 'Let me shake you by the hand, sir, and wish you joy. I am very happy to see you.'

'Thank you, sir; thank you very much indeed.' They shook hands. 'This is the first time I have seen you in your kingdom, sir.'

'Commodious, ain't it?' said the naval officer. 'Rope-walk over there. Sail-loft behind your old *Généreux*. I only wish there were a higher wall around the timber-yard: you would never believe how many flaming thieves there are in this island, that creep over the wall by night and take away my spars: or try to. It is my belief they are sometimes set on it by the captains; but captains or not, I shall crucify the next son of a bitch I find so much as looking at a dog-pawl.'

'It is my belief, Mr Brown, that you will never be really happy until there is not a King's ship left in the Mediterranean and you can walk round your yard mustering a full complement of paint-pots every day of the week, never issuing out so much as a treenail from one year's end to the next.'

'You just listen to me, young man,' said Mr Brown, laying his hand on Jack's sleeve. 'Just you listen to age and experience. Your *good* captain never wants anything from a dockyard. He makes do with what he has. He takes great care of the King's stores: nothing is ever wasted: he pays his bottom with his own slush: he worms his cables deep with twice-laid stuff and serves and parcels them so there is never any fretting in the hawse *anywhere*: he cares for his sails far more than for his own skin, and he never sets his royals – nasty, unnecessary, flash, gimcrack things. And the result is promotion, Mr Aubrey; for we make our report to the Admiralty, as you know, and it carries the greatest possible weight. What made Trotter a post-captain? The fact that he was the most economical master and commander on the station. Some men carried away topmasts two and three times in a year: never Trotter. Take your own good Captain Allen. Never did he come to me with one of those horrible lists as long as his own pennant. And look at him now, in command of as pretty a frigate as you could wish. But why do I tell you all this, Captain Aubrey? I know very well you are not one of these spendthrift, fling-it-down-the-kennel young commanders, not after the care you took bringing in the *Généreux*. Besides, the *Sophie* is perfectly well found in every possible respect. Except conceivably in the article of paint. I might, at great inconvenience to other captains, find you some yellow paint, a very little yellow paint.'

'Why, sir, I should be grateful for a pot or two,' said Jack, his eye ranging carelessly over the spars. 'But what I really came for was to beg the favour of the loan of your duettoes. I am taking a friend on this cruise and he particularly desires to hear your B minor duetto.'

'You shall have them, Captain Aubrey,' said Mr Brown. 'You shall most certainly have them. Mrs Harte is transcribing one for the harp at the present moment, but I shall step round there directly. When do you sail?'

'As soon as I have completed my water and my convoy is assembled.'

'That will be tomorrow evening, if the *Fanny* comes in: and the watering will not take you long. The *Sophie* only carries ten ton. You shall have the book by noon tomorrow, I promise you.'

'I am most obliged, Mr Brown, infinitely obliged. Good night to you, then, and my best respects wait on Mrs Brown and Miss Fanny.'

'Christ,' said Jack, as the shattering din of the carpenter's hammer prised him from his hold on sleep. He clung to the soft darkness as hard as he could, burying his face in his pillow, for his mind had been racing so that he had not dropped off until six – indeed, it was his appearance on deck at first light, peering at the yards and rigging, that had given rise to the rumour that he was up and about. And this was the reason for the carpenter's untimely zeal, just as it was for the nervous presence of the gun-room steward (the former captain's steward had gone over to the *Pallas*) hovering with what had been Captain Allen's invariable breakfast – a mug of small beer, hominy grits and cold beef.

But there was no sleeping; the echoing crash of the hammer right next to his ear, ludicrously followed by the sound of whispering between the carpenter and his mates, made certain of that. They were in his sleeping-cabin, of course. Jets of pain shot through Jack's head as he lay there. "Vast that bloody hammering,' he called, and almost against his shoulder came the shocked reply, 'Aye aye, sir,' and the tip-toe pittering away.

His voice was hoarse. 'What made me so damned garrulous yesterday?' he said, still lying there in his cot. 'I am as hoarse as a crow, with talking. And what made me launch out in wild invitations? A guest I know nothing about, in a very small brig I have scarcely seen.' He pondered gloomily upon the extreme care that should be taken with shipmates – cheek by jowl – very like marriage – the inconvenience of pragmatic, touchy, assuming companions – incompatible tempers mewed up together in a box. In a box: his manual of seamanship – and how he had conned it as a boy, poring over the impossible equations.

Let the angle YCB, to which the yard is braced up, be called the trim of the sails, and expressed by the symbol b. This is the complement of the angle DCI. Now $CI:ID = rad.:tan. DCI = I:tan. DCI = \,|\, : cotan. b$. Therefore we have finally $\,|\, : cotan. b = A^1:B^1:tan.^2x$, and $A^1 cotan. b = B\, 'angent^2$, and $tan. \,^1x = \frac{A}{B} cot$. This equation evidently ascertains the mutual relation between the trim of the sails and the leeway . . .

'It *is* quite evident, is it not, Jacky darling?' said a hopeful voice, and a rather large young woman bent kindly over him (for at this stage in his memory he was only twelve, a stocky little boy, and tall, nubile Queeney sailed high above).

'Why, no, Queeney,' said the infant Jack. 'To tell you the truth, it ain't.'

'Well,' said she, with untiring patience. 'Try to remember

what a cotangent is, and let us begin again. Let us consider the ship as an oblong box . . .'

For a while he considered the *Sophie* as an oblong box. He had not seen a great deal of her, but there were two or three fundamentals that he knew with absolute certainty: one was that she was under-rigged – she might be well enough close to the wind, but she would be a slug before it; another was that his predecessor had been a man of a temper entirely unlike his own; and another was that the *Sophie*'s people had come to resemble their captain, a good sound quiet careful unaggressive commander who never set his royals, as brave as could be when set upon, but the very opposite of a Sallee rover. 'Was discipline to be combined with the spirit of a Sallee rover,' said Jack, 'it would sweep the ocean clean.' And his mind descending fast to the commonplace dwelt on the prize-money that would result from sweeping the ocean even moderately clean.

'That despicable main-yard,' he said. 'And surely to God I can get a couple of twelve-pounders as chasers. Would her timbers stand it, though? But whether they can or not, the box can be made a little more like a fighting vessel – more like a real man-of-war.'

As his thoughts ranged on so the low cabin brightened steadily. A fishing-boat passed under the *Sophie*'s stern, laden with tunny and uttering the harsh roar of a conch; at almost the same time the sun popped up from behind St Philip's fort – it did, in fact, *pop* up, flattened like a sideways lemon in the morning haze and drawing its bottom free of the land with a distinct jerk. In little more than a minute the greyness of the cabin had utterly vanished: the deck-head was alive with light glancing from the rippling sea; and a single ray, reflected from some unmoving surface on the distant quay, darted through the cabin windows to light up Jack's coat and its blazing epaulette. The sun rose within his mind, obliging his dogged look to broaden into a smile, and he swung out of his cot.

*   *   *

The sun had reached Dr Maturin ten minutes earlier, for he was a good deal higher up: he, too, stirred and turned away, for he too had slept uneasily. But the brilliance prevailed. He opened his eyes and stared about very stupidly: a moment before he had been so solidly, so warmly and happily in Ireland, with a girl's hand under his arm, that his waking mind could not take in the world he saw. Her touch was still firm upon his arm and even her scent was there: vaguely he picked at the crushed leaves under him – dianthus perfragrans. The scent was reclassified – a flower, and nothing more – and the ghostly contact, the firm print of fingers, vanished. His face reflected the most piercing unhappiness, and his eyes misted over. He had been exceedingly attached; and she was so bound up with that time . . .

He had been quite unprepared for this particular blow, striking under every conceivable kind of armour, and for some minutes he could hardly bear the pain, but sat there blinking in the sun.

'Christ,' he said at last. 'Another day.' With this his face grew more composed. He stood up, beat the white dust from his breeches and took off his coat to shake it. With intense mortification he saw that the piece of meat he had hidden at yesterday's dinner had oozed grease through his handkerchief and his pocket. 'How wonderfully strange,' he thought, 'to be upset by this trifle; yet I am upset.' He sat down and ate the piece of meat (the eye of a mutton chop); and for a moment his mind dwelt on the theory of counter-irritants, Paracelsus, Cardan, Rhazes. He was sitting in the ruined apse of St Damian's chapel high above Port Mahon on the north side, looking down upon the great winding inlet of the harbour and far out beyond it over a vast expanse of sea, a variegated blue with wandering lanes; the flawless sun, a hand's breadth high, rising from the side of Africa. He had taken refuge there some days before, as soon as his landlord began to grow a shade uncivil; he had not waited for a scene, for he was too emotionally worn to put up with any such thing.

Presently, he took notice of the ants that were taking away his crumbs. Tapinoma erraticum. They were walking in a steady two-way stream across the hollow, or dell, of his inverted wig, as it lay there looking very like an abandoned bird's nest, though once it had been as neat a physical bob as had ever been seen in Stephen's Green. They hurried along with their abdomens high, jostling, running into one another: his gaze followed the wearisome little creatures and while he was watching them a toad was watching him: their eyes met, and he smiled. A splendid toad: a two-pound toad with brilliant tawny eyes. How did he manage to make a living in the sparse thin grass of that stony, sun-beaten landscape, so severe and parched, with no more cover than a few tumbles of pale stone, a few low creeping hook-thorned caper-bushes and a cistus whose name Stephen did not know? Most remarkably severe and parched, for the winter of 1799–1800 had been uncommonly dry, the March rains had failed and now the heat had come very early in the year. Very gently he stretched out his finger and stroked the toad's throat: the toad swelled a little and moved its crossed hands; then sat easy, gazing back.

The sun rose and rose. The night had not been cold at any time, but still the warmth was grateful. Black wheatears that must have a brood not far: one of the smaller eagles in the sky. There was a sloughed snake's skin in the bush where he pissed, and its eye-covers were perfect, startlingly crystalline.

'What am I to think of Captain Aubrey's invitation?' he said aloud, in that great emptiness of light and air – all the more vast for the inhabited patch down there and its movement, and the checkered fields behind, fading into pale dun formless hills. 'Was it merely Jack ashore? Yet he was such a pleasant, ingenuous companion.' He smiled at the recollection. 'Still and all, what weight can be attached to . . . ? We had dined extremely well: four bottles, or possibly five. I must not expose myself to an affront.' He turned it over and over, arguing against his hopes, but coming at last to the conclusion that if he could make his coat passably respectable – and the dust does seem to be getting it off, or at least disguising it, he said – he would call on Mr Florey at the hospital and talk to him, in a general way, about the naval surgeon's calling. He brushed the ants from his wig and settled it on his head: then as he walked down towards the edge of the road – the magenta spikes of gladioli in the taller grass – the recollection of that unlucky name stopped him in his stride. How had he come to forget it so entirely in his sleep? How was it possible that the name James Dillon had not presented itself at once to his waking mind?

'Yet it is true there are hundreds of Dillons,' he reflected. 'And a great many of them are called James, of course.'

'*Christe*,' hummed James Dillon under his breath, shaving the red-gold bristles off his face in what light could make its way through the scuttle of the *Burford's* number twelve gunport. '*Christe eleison. Kyrie...*' This was less piety in James Dillon than a way of hoping he should not cut himself; for like so many Papists he was somewhat given to blasphemy. The difficulty of the planes under his nose silenced him, however, and when his upper lip was clean he could not hit the note again. In any case, his mind was too busy to be seeking after an elusive neume, for he was about to report to a new captain, a man upon whom his comfort and ease of mind was to depend, to say nothing of his reputation, career and prospects of advancement.

Stroking his shining smoothness, he hurried out into the ward-room and shouted for a marine. 'Just brush the back of my coat, will you, Curtis? My chest is quite ready, and the bread-sack of books is to go with it,' he said. 'Is the captain on deck?'

'Oh no, sir, no,' said the marine. 'Breakfast only just carrying in this moment. Two hard-boiled eggs and one soft.'

The soft-boiled egg was for Miss Smith, to recruit her from her labours of the night, as both the marine and Mr Dillon knew very well; but the marine's knowing look met with a total lack of response. James Dillon's mouth tightened, and for a fleeting moment as he ran up the ladder to the sudden brilliance of the quarter-deck it wore a positively angry expression. Here he greeted the officer of the watch and the *Burford*'s first lieutenant. 'Good morning. Good morning to you. My word, you're very fine,' they said. 'There she lies: just beyond the *Généreux*.'

His eyes ranged over the busy harbour: the light was so nearly horizontal that all the masts and yards assumed a strange importance, and the little skipping waves sent back a blinding sparkle.

'No, no,' they said. 'Over by the sheer-hulk. The felucca has just masked her. There – now do you see her?'

He did indeed. He had been looking far too high and his gaze had swept right over the *Sophie* as she lay there, not much above a cable's length away, very low in the water. He leant both hands on the rail and looked at her with unwinking concentration. After a while he borrowed the telescope from the officer of the watch and did the same again, with a most searching minute scrutiny. He could see the gleam of an epaulette, whose wearer could only be her captain: and her people were as active as bees just about to swarm. He had been prepared for a little brig, but not for quite such a dwarfish vessel as this. Most fourteen-gun sloops were between two hundred and two hundred and fifty tons in burthen: the *Sophie* could scarcely be more than a hundred and fifty.

'I like her little quarter-deck,' said the officer of the watch. 'She was the Spanish *Vencejo*, was she not? And as for being rather low, why, anything you look at close to from a seventy-four looks rather low.'

There were three things that everybody knew about the *Sophie*: one was that unlike almost all other brigs she had a quarter-deck; another was that she had been Spanish; and a third was that she possessed an elm-tree pump on her fo'c'sle, that is to say, a bored-out trunk that communicated directly with the sea and that was used for washing her deck

– an insignificant piece of equipment, really, but one so far above her station that no mariner who saw it or heard of this pump ever forgot it.

'Maybe your quarters will be a little cramped,' said the first lieutenant, 'but you will have a quiet, restful time of it, I am sure, convoying the trade up and down the Mediterranean.'

'Well . . .' said James Dillon, unable to find a brisk retort to this possibly well-intentioned kindness. 'Well . . .' he said with a philosophical shrug. 'You'll let me have a boat, sir? I should like to report as early as I can.'

'A boat? God rot my soul,' cried the first lieutenant, 'I shall be asked for the barge, next thing I know. Passengers in the *Burford* wait for a bumboat from shore, Mr Dillon; or else they swim.' He stared at James with cold severity until the quartermaster's chuckle betrayed him; for Mr Coffin was a great wag, a wag even before breakfast.

'Dillon, sir, reporting for duty, if you please,' said James taking off his hat in the brilliant sun and displaying a blaze of dark red hair.

'Welcome aboard, Mr Dillon,' said Jack, touching his own, holding out his hand and looking at him with so intense a desire to know what kind of man he was, that his face had an almost forbidding acuity. 'You would be welcome in any case, but even more so this morning: we have a busy day ahead of us. Masthead, there! Any sign of life on the wharf?'

'Nothing yet, sir.'

'The wind is exactly where I want it,' said Jack, looking for the hundredth time at the rare white clouds sailing evenly across the perfect sky. 'But with this rising glass there is no trusting to it.'

'Your coffee's up, sir,' said the steward.

'Thank you, Killick. What is it, Mr Lamb?'

'I haven't no ring-bolts anywheres near big enough, sir,' said the carpenter. 'But there's a heap on 'em at the yard, I know. May I send over?'

'No, Mr Lamb. Don't you go near that yard, to save your life. Double the clench-bolts you have; set up the forge and fashion a serviceable ring. It won't take you half an hour. Now, Mr Dillon, when you have settled in comfortably below, perhaps you will come and drink a cup of coffee with me and I will tell you what I have in mind.'

James hurried below to the three-cornered booth that he was to live in, whipped out of his reporting uniform into trousers and an old blue coat, reappearing while Jack was still blowing thoughtfully upon his cup. 'Sit down, Mr Dillon, sit down,' he cried. 'Push those papers aside. It's a sad brew, I'm afraid, but at least it is wet, that I can promise you. Sugar?'

'If you please, sir,' said young Ricketts, 'the *Généreux*'s cutter is alongside with the men who were drafted off for harbour-duty.'

'All of 'em?'

'All except two, sir, that have been changed.'

Still holding his coffee-cup, Jack writhed from behind the table and with a twist of his body out through the door. Hooked on to the larboard main-chains there was the *Généreux*'s boat, filled with seamen, looking up, laughing and exchanging witticisms or mere hoots and whistles with their former shipmates. The *Généreux*'s midshipman saluted and said, 'Captain Harte's compliments, sir, and he finds the draft can be spared.'

'God bless your heart, dear Molly,' said Jack: and aloud, 'My compliments and best thanks to Captain Harte. Be so good as to send them aboard.'

They were not much to look at, he reflected, as the whip from the yardarm hoisted up their meagre belongings: three or four were decidedly simple, and two others had that inde-finable air of men of some parts whose cleverness sets them apart from their fellows, but not nearly so far as they imagine. Two of the boobies were quite horribly dirty, and one had managed to exchange his slops for a red garment with remains of tinsel upon it. Still, they all possessed two hands; they could all clap on to a rope; and it would be strange if the bosun and his mates could not induce them to heave.

'Deck,' hailed the midshipman aloft. 'Deck. There is someone moving about on the wharf.'

'Very good, Mr Babbington. You may come down and have your breakfast now. Six hands I thought lost for good,' he said to James Dillon with intense satisfaction, turning back to the cabin. 'They may not be much to look at – indeed, I think we must rig a tub if we are not to have an itchy ship – but they will help us weigh. And I hope to weigh by half-past nine at the latest.' Jack rapped the brass-bound wood of the locker and went on, 'We will ship two long twelves as chase-pieces, if I can get them from Ordnance. But whether or no I am going to take the sloop out while this breeze lasts, to try her paces. We convoy a dozen merchantmen to Cagliari, sailing this evening if they are all here, and we must know how she handles. Yes, Mr . . . Mr . . . ?'

'Pullings, sir: master's mate. *Burford*'s long-boat alongside with a draft.'

'A draft for us? How many?'

'Eighteen, sir.' *And rum-looking cullies some of 'em are*, he would have added, if he had dared.

'Do you know anything about them, Mr Dillon?' asked Jack.

'I knew the *Burford* had a good many of the *Charlotte*'s people and some from the receiving ships as drafts for Mahon, sir; but I never heard of any being meant for the *Sophie*.'

Jack was on the point of saying, 'And there I was, worrying about being stripped bare,' but he contented himself with chuckling and wondering why this cornucopia should have poured itself out on him. 'Lady Warren,' came the reply, in a flash of revelation. He laughed again, and said, 'Now I am going across to the wharf, Mr Dillon. Mr Head is a businesslike man and he will tell me whether the guns are to be had or not within half an hour. If they are, I will break out my handkerchief and you can start carrying out the warps directly. What now, Mr Richards?'

'Sir,' said the pale clerk, 'Mr Purser says I should bring you the receipts and letters to sign this time every day, and the fair-copied book to read.'

'Quite right,' said Jack mildly. 'Every ordinary day. Presently you will learn which is ordinary and which is not.' He glanced at his watch. 'Here are the receipts for the men. Show me the rest another time.'

The scene on deck was not unlike Cheapside with road-work going on: two parties under the carpenter and his crew were making ready the places for the hypothetical bow- and stern-chasers, and parcels of assorted landmen and boobies stood about with their baggage, some watching the work with an interested air, offering comments, others gaping vacantly about, gazing into the sky as though they had never seen it before. One or two had even edged on to the holy quarter-deck.

'What in God's name is this infernal confusion?' cried Jack. 'Mr Watt, this is a King's ship, not the Margate hoy. You, sir, get away for'ard.'

For a moment, until his unaffected blaze of indignation galvanized them into activity, the *Sophie's* warrant officers gazed at him sadly: he caught the words 'all these people . . .'

'I am going ashore,' he went on. 'By the time I come back this deck will present a very different appearance.'

He was still red in the face as he went down into the boat after the midshipman. 'Do they really imagine I shall leave an able-bodied man on shore if I can cram him aboard?' he said to himself. 'Of course, their precious three watches will have to go. And even so, fourteen inches will be hard to find.'

The three-watch system was a humane arrangement that allowed the men to sleep a whole night through from time to time, whereas with two watches four hours was the most they could ever hope for; but on the other hand it did mean that half the men had the whole of the available space to sling their hammocks, since the other half was on deck. 'Eighteen and six is twenty-four,' said Jack, 'and fifty or thereabout, say seventy-five. And of those how many shall I watch?' He worked out this figure in order to multiply it by fourteen, for fourteen inches was the space the regulations allowed for each hammock: and it seemed to him very doubtful whether the *Sophie* possessed anything like that amount of room, whatever her official complement might be. He was still working at it when the midshipman called, 'Unrow. Boat your oars,' and they kissed gently against the wharf.

'Go back to the ship now, Mr Ricketts,' said Jack on an impulse. 'I do not suppose I shall be long, and it may save a few minutes.'

But with the *Burford*'s draft he had missed his chance: other captains were there before him now and he had to wait his turn. He walked up and down in the brilliant morning sun with one whose epaulette matched his own – Middleton, whose greater pull had enabled him to snap up the command of the *Vertueuse*, the charming French privateer that would have been Jack's had there been any justice in the world. When they had exchanged the naval gossip of the Mediterranean, Jack remarked that he had come for a couple of twelve-pounders.

'Do you think she'll bear them?' asked Middleton.

'I hope so. Your four-pounder is a pitiful thing: though I must confess I feel anxious for her knees.'

'Well, I hope so, too,' said Middleton, shaking his head. 'At all events you have come on the right day: it seems that Head is to be placed under Brown, and he has taken such a spite at it that he is selling off his stock like a fishwife at the end of the fair.'

Jack had already heard something of this development in the long, long squabble between the Ordnance Board and the Navy Board, and he longed to hear more; but at this moment Captain Halliwell came out, smiling all over his face, and Middleton, who had some faint remains of conscience, said, 'You take my turn. I shall be an age, with all my carronades to explain.'

'Good morning, sir,' said Jack. 'I am Aubrey, of the *Sophie*, and I should like to try a couple of long twelves, if you please.'

With no change in his melancholy expression, Mr Head said, 'You know what they weigh?'

'Something in the nature of thirty-three hundredweight, I believe.'

'Thirty-three hundredweight, three pounds, three ounces, three pennyweight. Have a dozen, Captain, if you feel she will bear them.'

'Thank you: two will be plenty,' said Jack, looking sharply to see whether he were being made game of.

'They are yours, then, and upon your own head be it,' said Mr Head with a sigh, making secret marks upon a worn, curling parchment slip. 'Give it to the master-parker and he will troll you out as pretty a pair as ever the heart of man could desire. I have some neat mortars, if you have room.'

'I am extremely obliged to you, Mr Head,' said Jack, laughing with pleasure. 'I wish the rest of the service were run so.'

'So do I, Captain, so do I,' cried Mr Head, his face growing suddenly dark with passion. 'There are some slack-arsed, bloody-minded men – flute-playing, fiddle-scraping, present-seeking, tale-bearing, double-poxed hounds that would keep you waiting about for a month; but I am not one of them. Captain Middleton, sir: carronades for you, I presume?'

In the sunlight once more Jack threw out his signal and, peering among the masts and criss-crossed yards, he saw a figure at the *Sophie*'s masthead bend as though to hail the deck, before disappearing down a backstay, like a bead sliding upon a thread.

Expedition was Mr Head's watchword, but the master-parker of the ordnance wharf did not seem to have heard of it. He showed Jack the two twelve-pounders with great good will. 'As pretty a pair as the heart of man could desire,' he said, stroking their cascabels as Jack signed for them; but after that his mood seemed to change – there were several other captains in front of Jack – fair was fair – turn and turn about – them thirty-sixes were all in the way and would have to be moved first – he was precious short of hands.

The *Sophie* had warped in long ago and she was lying neatly against the dock right under the derricks. There was more noise aboard her than there had been, more noise than was right, even with the relaxed harbour discipline, and he was sure some of the men had managed to get drunk already. Expectant faces – a good deal less expectant now – looked over her side at her captain as he paced up and down, up and down, glancing now at his watch and now at the sky.

'By God,' he cried, clapping his hand to his forehead. 'What a damned fool. I clean forgot the oil.' Turning short in his stride he hurried over to the shed, where a violent squealing showed that the master-parker and his mates were trundling the slides of Middleton's carronades towards the neat line of their barrels. 'Master-parker,' called Jack, 'come and look at my twelve-pounders. I have been in such a hurry all morning that I do believe I forgot to anoint them.' With these words he privately laid down a gold piece upon each touch-hole, and a slow look of approval appeared on the parker's face. 'If my gunner had not been sick, he would have reminded me,' added Jack.

'Well, thankee, sir. It always has been the custom, and I don't like to see the old ways die, I do confess,' said the parker, with some still-unevaporated surliness: but then brightening progressively he said, 'A hurry, you mentioned, Captain? I'll see what we can do.'

Five minutes later the bow-chaser, neatly slung by its train-loops, side-loops, pommelion and muzzle, floated gently over the *Sophie*'s fo'c'sle within half an inch of its ideal resting-place: Jack and the carpenter were on all fours side by side, rather as though they were playing bears, and they were listening for the sound her beams and timbers would make as the strain came off the derrick. Jack beckoned with his hand, calling 'Handsomely, handsomely now.' The *Sophie* was perfectly silent, all her people watching intently, even the tub-party with their buckets poised, even the human chain who were tossing the twelve-pound round shot from the shore to the side and so down to the gunner's mate in the shot-locker. The gun touched, sat firm: there was a deep, not unhealthy creaking, and the *Sophie* settled a little by the head. 'Capital,' said Jack, surveying the gun as it stood there, well within its chalked-out space. 'Plenty of room all round – great oceans of room, upon my word,' he said, backing a step. In his haste to avoid being trodden down, the gunner's mate behind him collided with his neighbour, who ran into his, setting off a chain-reaction in that crowded, roughly tri-angular space between the foremast and the stem that resulted in the maiming of one ship's boy and very nearly in the watery death of another. 'Where's the bosun? Now, Mr Watt, let me see the tackles rigged: you want a hard-eye becket on that block. Where's the breeching?'

'Almost ready, sir,' said the sweating, harassed bosun. 'I'm working the cunt-splice myself.'

'Well,' said Jack, hurrying off to where the stern-chaser hung poised above the *Sophie*'s quarter-deck, ready to plunge through her bottom if gravity could but have its way, 'a simple thing like a cunt-splice will not take a man-of-war's bosun long, I believe. Set those men to work, Mr Lamb, if you please: this is not fiddler's green.' He looked at his watch again. 'Mr Mowett,' he said, looking at a cheerful young master's mate. Mr Mowett's cheerful look changed to one of extreme gravity. 'Mr Mowett, do you know Joselito's coffee-house?'

'Yes, sir.'

'Then be so good as to go there and ask for Dr Maturin. My compliments and I am very much concerned to say we shall not be back in port by dinner-time; but I will send a boat this evening at any time he chooses to appoint.'

*　　*　　*

They were not back in port by dinner-time: it would indeed have been a logical impossibility, since they had not yet left it, but were sweeping majestically through the close-packed craft towards the fairway. One advantage of having a small vessel with a great many hands aboard is that you can execute manoeuvres denied to any ship of the line, and Jack preferred this arduous creeping to being towed or to threading along under sail with a thoroughly uneasy crew, disturbed in all their settled habits and jostling full of strangers.

In the open channel he had himself rowed round the *Sophie*: he considered her from every angle, and at the same time he weighed the advantages and disadvantages of sending all the women ashore. It would be easy to find most of them while the men were at their dinner: not merely the local girls who were there for fun and pocket-money, but also the semi-permanent judies. If he made one sweep now, then another just before their true departure might clear the sloop entirely. He wanted no women aboard. They only caused trouble, and with this fresh influx they would cause even more. On the other hand, there was a certain lack of zeal aboard, a lack of real spring, and he did not mean to turn it into sullenness, particularly that afternoon. Sailors were as conservative as cats, as he knew very well: they would put up with incredible labour and hardship, to say nothing of danger, but it had to be what they were used to or they would grow brutish. She was very low in the water, to be sure: a little by the head and listing a trifle to port. All that extra weight would have been far better below the water-line. But he would have to see how she handled.

'Shall I send the hands to dinner, sir?' asked James Dillon when Jack was aboard again.

'No, Mr Dillon. We must profit by this wind. Once we are past the cape they may go below. Those guns are breeched and frapped?'

'Yes, sir.'

'Then we will make sail. In sweeps. All hands to make sail.'

The bosun sprang his call and hurried away to the fo'c'sle amidst a great rushing of feet and a good deal of bellowing.

'Newcomers below. Silence there.' Another rush of feet. The *Sophie*'s regular crew stood poised in their usual places, in dead silence. A voice on board the *Généreux* a cable's length away could be heard, quite clear and plain, '*Sophie*'s making sail.'

She lay there, rocking gently, out in Mahon harbour, with the shipping on her starboard beam and quarter and the brilliant town beyond it. The breeze a little abaft her larboard beam, a northerly wind, was pushing her stern round a trifle. Jack paused, and as it came just so he cried, 'Away aloft.' The calls repeated the order and instantly the shrouds were dark with passing men, racing up as though on their stairs at home.

'Trice up. Lay out.' The calls again, and the topmen hurried out on the yards. They cast off the gaskets, the lines that held the sails tight furled to the yards; they gathered the canvas under their arms and waited.

'Let fall,' came the order, and with it the howling peep-peep, peep-peep from the bosun and his mates.

'Sheet home. Sheet home. Hoist away. Cheerly there, in the foretop, look alive. T'garns'l sheets. Hands to the braces. Belay.'

A gentle push from above heeled the *Sophie* over, then another and another, each more delightfully urgent until it was one steady thrust; she was under way, and all along her side there sang a run of living water. Jack and his lieutenant exchanged a glance: it had not been bad – the foretopgallantsail had taken its time, because of a misunderstanding as to how *newcomer* should be defined and whether the six restored Sophies were to be considered in that injurious light, which had led to a furious, silent squabble on the yard; and the sheeting-home had been rather spasmodic; but it had not been disgraceful, and they would not have to support the derision of the other men-of-war in the harbour. There had been moments in the confusion of the morning when each had dreaded just that thing.

The *Sophie* had spread her wings a little more like an unhurried dove than an eager hawk, but not so much so that the expert eyes on shore would dwell upon her with disapprobation; and as for the mere landsmen, their eyes were so satiated with the coming and going of every kind of vessel that they passed over her departure with glassy indifference.

'Forgive me, sir,' said Stephen Maturin, touching his hat to a nautical gentleman on the quay, 'but might I ask whether you know which is the ship called *Sophia*?'

'A King's ship, sir?' asked the officer, returning his salute. 'A man-of-war? There is no ship of that name – but perhaps you refer to the sloop, sir? The sloop *Sophie*?'

'That may well be the case, sir. No man could easily surpass me in ignorance of naval terms. The vessel I have in mind is commanded by Captain Aubrey.'

'Just so: the sloop, the fourteen-gun sloop. She lies almost directly in front of you, sir, in a line with the little white house on the point.'

'The ship with triangular sails?'

'No. That is a polacre-settee. Somewhat to the left, and farther off.'

'The little small squat merchantman with two masts?'

'Well' – with a laugh – 'she *is* a trifle low in the water; but she is a man-of-war, I assure you. And I believe she is about to make sail. Yes. There go her topsails: sheeted home. They hoist the yard. To'garns'ls. What's amiss? Ah, there we are. Not very smartly done, but all's well that ends well, and the *Sophie* never was one of your very brisk performers. See, she gathers way. She will fetch the mouth of the harbour on this wind without touching a brace.'

'She is sailing away?'

'Indeed she is. She must be running three knots already – maybe four.'

'I am very much obliged to you, sir,' said Stephen, lifting his hat.

'Servant, sir,' said the officer, lifting his. He looked after Stephen for a while. 'Should I ask him whether he is well? I have left it too late. However, he seems steady enough now.'

Stephen had walked down to the quay to find out whether the *Sophie* could be reached on foot or whether he should have to take a boat to keep his dinner engagement; for his conversation with Mr Florey had persuaded him that not only was the engagement intended to be kept, but that the more general invitation was equally serious – an eminently practicable suggestion, most certainly to be acted upon. How civil, how more than civil, Florey had been: had explained the medical service of the Royal Navy, and taken him to see Mr Edwardes of the *Centaur* perform quite an interesting amputation, had dismissed his scruples as to lack of purely surgical experience, had lent him Blane on diseases incident to seamen, Hulme's *Libellus de Natura Scorbuti*, Lind's *Effectual Means* and Northcote's *Marine Practice*, and had promised to find him at least the bare essentials in instruments until he should have his allowance and the official chest – 'There are trocars, tenaculums and ball-scoops lying about by the dozen at the hospital, to say nothing of saws and bone-rasps.'

Stephen had allowed his mind to convince itself entirely, and the strength of his emotion at the sight of the *Sophie*, her white sails and her low hull dwindling fast over the shining sea, showed him how much he had come to look forward to the prospect of a new place and new skies, a living, and a closer acquaintance with this friend who was now running fast towards the quarantine island, behind which he would presently vanish.

He walked up through the town with his mind in a curious state; he had suffered so many disappointments recently that it did not seem possible he could bear another. What was more, he had allowed all his defences to disperse – unarm. It was while he was reassembling them and calling out his reserves that his feet carried him past Joselito's coffee-house and voices said, 'There he is – call out – run after him – you will catch him if you run.'

He had not been into the coffee-house that morning because it was a question either of paying for a cup of coffee or of paying for a boat to row him out to the *Sophie*, and he had therefore been unavailable for the midshipman, who now came running along behind him.

'Dr Maturin?' asked young Mowett, and stopped short, quite shocked by the pale glare of reptilian dislike. However, he delivered his message; and he was relieved to find that it was greeted with a far more human look.

'Most kind,' said Stephen. 'What do you imagine would be a convenient time, sir?'

'Oh, I suppose about six o'clock, sir,' said Mowett.

'Then at six o'clock I shall be at the Crown steps,' said Stephen. 'I am very much obliged to you, sir, for your diligence in finding me out.' They parted with a bow apiece, and Stephen said privately, 'I shall go across to the hospital and offer Mr Florey my assistance: he has a compound fracture above the elbow that will call for primary resection of the joint. It is a great while since I felt the grind of bone under my saw,' he added, smiling with anticipation.

Cape Mola lay on their larboard quarter: the troubled blasts and calms caused by the heights and valleys along the great harbour's winding northern shore no longer buffeted them, and with an almost steady tramontana at north by east the *Sophie* was running fast towards Italy under her courses, single-reefed topsails and topgallants.

'Bring her up as close as she will lie,' said Jack. 'How near will she point, Mr Marshall? Six?'

'I doubt she'll do as well as six, sir,' said the master,

shaking his head. 'She's a little sullen today, with the extra weight for'ard.'

Jack took the wheel, and as he did so a last gust from the island staggered the sloop, sending white water along her lee rail, plucking Jack's hat from his head and streaming his bright yellow hair away to the south-south-west. The master leapt after the hat, snatched it from the seaman who had rescued it in the hammock-netting and solicitously wiping the cockade with his handkerchief he stood by Jack's side, holding it with both hands.

'Old Sodom and Gomorrah is sweet on Goldilocks,' murmured John Lane, foretopman, to his friend Thomas Gross: Thomas winked his eye and jerked his head, but without any appearance of censure – they were concerned with the phenomenon, not with any moral judgment. 'Well, I hope he don't take it out of us too much, that's all, mate,' he replied.

Jack let her pay off until the flurry was over, and then, as he began to bring her back, his hands strong on the spokes, so he came into direct contact with the living essence of the sloop: the vibration beneath his palm, something between a sound and a flow, came straight up from her rudder, and it joined with the innumerable rhythms, the creak and humming of her hull and rigging. The keen clear wind swept in on his left cheek, and as he bore on the helm so the *Sophie* answered, quicker and more nervous than he had expected. Closer and closer to the wind. They were all staring up and forward: at last, in spite of the fiddle-tight bowline, the foretopgallantsail shivered, and Jack eased off. 'East by north, a half north,' he observed with satisfaction. 'Keep her so,' he said to the timoneer, and gave the order, the long-expected and very welcome order, to pipe to dinner.

Dinner, while the *Sophie*, as close-hauled on the larboard tack as she could be, made her offing into the lonely water where twelve-pound cannon-balls could do no harm and where disaster could pass unnoticed: the miles streamed out behind her, her white path stretching straight and true a little south of west. Jack looked at it from his stern-window with approval: remarkably little leeway; and a good steady hand must be steering, to keep that furrow so perfect in the sea. He was dining in solitary state – a Spartan meal of sodden kid and cabbage, mixed – and it was only when he realized that there was no one to whom he could impart the innumerable observations that came bubbling into his mind that he remembered: this was his first formal meal as a captain. He almost made a jocose remark about it to his steward (for he was in very high spirits, too), but he checked himself. It would not do. 'I shall grow used to it, in time,' he said, and looked again with loving relish at the sea.

The guns were not a success. Even with only half a cartridge the bow-chaser recoiled so strongly that at the third discharge the carpenter came running up on deck, so pale and perturbed that all discipline went by the board. 'Don't ee do it, sir!' he cried, covering the touch-hole with his hand. 'If you could but see her poor knees – and the spirketting started in five separate places, oh dear, oh dear.' The poor man hurried to the ring-bolts of the breeching. 'There. I knew it. My clench is half drawn in this poor thin old stuff. Why didn't you tell me, Tom?' he cried, gazing reproachfully at his mate.

'I dursen't,' said Tom, hanging his head.

'It won't do, sir,' said the carpenter. 'Not with these here timbers, it won't. Not with this here deck.'

Jack felt his choler rising – it was a ludicrous situation on the overcrowded fo'c'sle, with the carpenter crawling about at his feet in apparent supplication, peering at the seams; and this was no sort of a way to address a captain. But there was no resisting Mr Lamb's total sincerity, particularly as Jack secretly agreed with him. The force of the recoil, all that weight of metal darting back and being brought up with a twang by the breeching was too much, far too much for the *Sophie*. Furthermore, there really was not room to work the ship with the two twelve-pounders and their tackle filling so much of what little space there was. But he was bitterly disappointed: a twelve-pound ball could pierce at five hundred yards: it could send up a shower of lethal splinters, carry away a yard, do great execution. He tossed one up and down in his hand, considering. Whereas at any range a four-pounder . . .

'And was you to fire off t'other one,' said Mr Lamb with desperate courage, still on his hands and knees, 'your wisitor wouldn't have a dry stitch on him: for the seams have opened something cruel.'

William Jevons, carpenter's crew, came up and whispered, 'Foot of water in the well,' in a rumble that could have been heard at the masthead.

The carpenter stood up, put on his hat, touched it and reported, 'There's a foot of water in the well, sir.'

'Very well, Mr Lamb,' said Jack, placidly, 'we'll pump it out again. Mr Day,' he said, turning to the gunner, who had crawled up on deck for the firing of the twelve-pounders (would have crept out of his grave, had he been in it), 'Mr Day, draw and house the guns, if you please. And bosun, man the chain-pump.'

He patted the warm barrel of the twelve-pounder regretfully and walked aft. He was not particularly worried about the water: the *Sophie* had been capering about in a lively way with this short sea coming across, and she would have made a good deal by her natural working. But he was vexed about the chasers, profoundly vexed, and he looked with even greater malignance at the main-yard.

'We shall have to get the topgallants off her presently, Mr Dillon,' he observed, picking up the traverse-board. He consulted it more as a matter of form than anything else, for he knew very well where they were: with some sense that develops in true seamen he was aware of the loom of the land, a dark presence beyond the horizon behind him – behind his right shoulder-blade. They had been beating steadily up into the wind, and the pegs showed almost equal boards – east-north-east followed by west-north-west: they had tacked five times (*Sophie* was not as quick in stays as he could have wished) and worn once; and they had been running at seven knots. These calculations ran their course in his mind, and as soon as he looked for it the answer was ready: 'Keep on this course for half an hour and then put her almost before the wind – two points off. That will bring you home.

'It would be as well to shorten sail now,' he observed. 'We will hold our course for half an hour.' With this he went below, meaning to do something in the way of dealing with the great mass of papers that called for attention: apart from such things as the statements of stores and the pay books there was the *Sophie*'s log, which would tell him something of the past history of the vessel, and her muster-book, which would do the same for her company. He leafed through the pages: *Sunday, September 22, 1799, winds NW, W, S. course N40W, distance 49 miles, latitude 37°59'N longitude 9°38'W, Cape St Vincent S27E 64 miles. PM Fresh breezes and squally with rain, made and shortened sail occasionally. AM hard gales, and 4 handed the square mainsail, at 6 saw a strange sail to the southward, at 8 more moderate, reefed the square mainsail and set it, at 9 spoke her. She was a Swedish brig bound to Barcelona in ballast. At noon weather calm, head round the compass.*' Dozens of entries of that kind of duty; and of convoy work. The plain, unspectacular, everyday sort of employment that made up ninety per cent of a service life: or more. '*People variously employed, read the Articles of War . . . convoy in company, in topgallantsails and second reef topsails. At 6 made private signal to two line of battle ships which answered. All sails set, the people employed working up junk . . . tacked occasionally, in third reef maintopsail . . . light airs inclinable to calm . . . scrubbed hammocks. Mustered by divisions, read Articles of War and punished Joseph Wood, Jno. Lakey, Matt. Johnson and Wm. Musgrave with twelve lashes for drunkenness . . . PM calm and hazy weather, at 5 out sweeps and boats to pull off shore at $^1/_2$ past 6 came to with the stream anchor Cape Mola S6W distance 5 leagues. At $^1/_2$*

past 8 coming on to blow suddenly was obliged to cut the hawser and make sail ... read the Articles of War and performed Divine Service ... punished Geo. Sennet with 24 lashes for contempt ... Fra. Bechell, Robt. Wilkinson and Joseph Wood for drunkenness ...'

A good many entries of that kind: a fair amount of flogging, but nothing heavy – none of your hundred-lash sentences. It contradicted his first impression of laxity: he would have to look into it more thoroughly. Then the muster. *Geo. Williams, ordinary seaman, born Bengal, volunteered at Lisbon 24 August 1797, ran 27 March 1798, Lisbon. Fortunato Carneglia, midshipman, 21, born Genoa, discharged 1 June 1797 per order Rear-Admiral Nelson per ticket. Saml. Willsea, able seaman, born Long Island, volunteered Porto 10 October 1797, ran 8 February 1799 at Lisbon from the boat. Patrick Wade, landman, 21, born County Fermanagh, prest 20 November 1796 at Porto Ferraio, discharged 11 November 1799 to Bulldog, per order Captain Darley. Richard Sutton, lieutenant, joined 31 December 1796 per order Commodore Nelson, discharged dead 2 February 1798, killed in action with a French privateer. Richard William Baldick, lieutenant, joined 28 February 1798 per commission from Earl St Vincent, discharged 18 April 1800 to join Pallas per order Lord Keith.* In the column Dead Mens Cloaths there was the sum of £8.10s. 6d. against his name: clearly poor Sutton's kit auctioned at the mainmast.

But Jack could not keep his mind to the stiff-ruled column. The brilliant sea, darker blue than the sky, and the white wake across it kept drawing his eyes to the stern-window. In the end he closed the book and indulged himself in the luxury of staring out: if he chose he could go to sleep, he reflected; and he looked around, relishing this splendid privacy, the rarest of commodities at sea. As a lieutenant in the *Leander* and other fair-sized ships he had been able to look out of the ward-room windows, of course; but never alone, never unaccompanied by human presence and activity. It was wonderful: but it so happened that just now he longed for human presence and activity – his mind was too eager and restless to savour the full charm of solitude, although he knew it was there, and as soon as the ting-ting, ting-ting of four bells sounded he was up on deck.

Dillon and the master were standing by the starboard brass four-pounder, and they were obviously discussing some part of her rigging visible from that point. As soon as he appeared they moved over to the larboard side in the traditional way, leaving him his privileged area of the quarter-deck. This was the first time it had happened to him: he had not expected it – had not thought of it – and it gave him a ridiculous thrill of pleasure. But it also deprived him of a companion, unless he were to call James Dillon over. He took two or three turns, looking up at the yards: they were braced as sharp as the main and foremast shrouds would allow, but they were not as sharp as they might have been in an ideal world, and he made a mental note to tell the bosun to set up cross catharpings – they might gain three or four degrees.

'Mr Dillon,' he said, 'be so good as to bear up and set the square mainsail. South by west a half south.'

'Aye aye, sir. Double-reefed, sir?'

'No, Mr Dillon, no reef,' said Jack with a smile, and he resumed his pacing. There were orders all round him, the trample of feet, the bosun's calls: his eyes took in the whole of the operation with a curious detachment – curious, because his heart was beating high.

The *Sophie* paid off smoothly. 'Thus, thus,' cried the master at the con, and the helmsman steadied her: as she was coming round before the wind the fore-and-aft mainsail vanished in billowing clouds that quickly subsided into the members of a long sailcloth parcel, greyish, inanimate; and immediately afterwards the square mainsail appeared, ballooning and fluttering for a few seconds and then mastered, disciplined and squared, with its sheets hauled aft. The *Sophie* shot forward, and by the time Dillon called 'Belay' she had increased her speed by at least two knots, plunging her head and raising her stern as though she were surprised at her rider, as well she might have been. Dillon sent another man to the wheel, in case a fault in the wind should broach her to. The square mainsail was as taut as a drum.

'Pass the word for the sailmaker,' said Jack. 'Mr Henry, could you get me another cloth on to that sail, was you to take a deep goring leach?'

'No, sir,' said the sailmaker positively. 'Not if it was ever so. Not with that yard, sir. Look at all the horrible bunt there is now – more like what you might call a hog's bladder, properly speaking.'

Jack went to the rail and looked sharply at the sea running by, the long curve as it rose after the hollow under the lee-bow: he grunted and returned to his staring at the mainyard, a piece of wood rather more than thirty feet long and tapering from some seven inches in the slings, the middle part, to three at the yard-arms, the extremities.

'More like a cro'jack than a mainyard,' he thought, for the twentieth time since he first set eyes upon it. He watched the yard intently as the force of the wind worked upon it: the *Sophie* was running no faster now, and so there was no longer any easing of the load; the yard plied, and it seemed to Jack that he heard it groan. The *Sophie*'s braces led forward, of course, she being a brig, and the plying was greatest at the yard-arms, which irked him; but there was some degree of bowing all along. He stood there with his hands behind his back, his eyes set upon it; and the other officers on the quarter-deck, Dillon, Marshall, Pullings and young Ricketts stood attentively, not speaking, looking sometimes at their new captain and sometimes at the sail. They were not the only men to wonder, for most of the more experienced hands on the fo'c'sle had joined in this double scrutiny – a gaze up, then a sidelong stare at Jack. It was a strange atmosphere. Now that they were before the wind, or very nearly – that is to say, now that they were going in the same direction as the wind – nearly all the song had gone out of the rigging; the *Sophie*'s long slow pitching (no cross-sea to move her quickly) made little noise; and added to this there was the strained quietness of men murmuring together, not to be heard. But in spite of their care a voice drifted back to the quarter-deck: 'He'll carry all away, if he cracks on so.'

Jack did not hear it: he was quite unconscious of the tension around him, far away in his calculations of the opposing forces – not mathematical calculations by any means, but rather sympathetic; the calculations of a rider with a new horse between his knees and a dark hedge coming.

Presently he went below, and after he had stared out of the stern-window for some time he looked at the chart. Cape Mola would be on their starboard now – they should raise it very soon – and it would add a little greater thrust to the wind by deflecting it along the coast. Very quietly he whistled *Deh vieni*, reflecting, 'If I make a success of this, and if I make a mint of money, several hundred guineas, say, the first thing I shall do after paying-off is to go to Vienna, to the opera.'

James Dillon knocked on the door. 'The wind is increasing, sir,' he said. 'May I hand the mainsail, or reef at least?'

'No, no, Mr Dillon . . . no,' said Jack, smiling. Then reflecting that it was scarcely fair to leave this on his lieutenant's shoulders he added, 'I shall come on deck in two minutes.'

In fact, he was there in less than one, just in time to hear the ominous rending crack. 'Up sheets!' he cried. 'Hands to the jears. Tops'l clewlines. Clap on to the lifts. Lower away cheerly. Look alive, there.'

They looked alive: the yard was small; soon it was on deck, the sail unbent, the yard stripped and everything coiled down.

'Hopelessly sprung in the slings, sir,' said the carpenter sadly. He was having a wretched day of it. 'I could try to fish it, but it would never be answerable, like.'

Jack nodded, without any particular expression. He walked across to the rail, put a foot on to it and hoisted himself up into the first ratlines; the *Sophie* rose on the swell, and there indeed lay Cape Mola, a dark bar three points on the starboard beam. 'I think we must touch up the look-out,' he observed. 'Lay her for the harbour, Mr Dillon, if you please. Boom mainsail and everything she can carry. There is not a minute to lose.'

Forty-five minutes later the *Sophie* picked up her moorings, and before the way was off her the cutter splashed into the water; the sprung yard was already afloat, and the boat set off urgently in the direction of the wharf, towing the yard behind like a streaming tail.

'Well, there's the fleet's own brazen smiling serpent,' remarked bow oar, as Jack ran up the steps. 'Brings the poor old *Sophie* in, first time he ever set foot on her, with barely a yard standing at all, her timbers all crazy and half the ship's company pumping for dear life and every man on deck the livelong day, dear knows, with never a pause for the smell of a pipe. And he runs up them old steps smiling like King George was at the top there to knight him.'

'And short time for dinner, as will never be made up,' said a low voice in the middle of the boat.

'Silence,' cried Mr Babbington, with as much outrage as he could manage.

'Mr Brown,' said Jack, with an earnest look, 'you can do me a very essential service, if you will. I have sprung my mainyard hopelessly, I am concerned to tell you, and yet I must sail this evening – the *Fanny* is in. So I beg you to condemn it and issue me out another in its place. Nay, never look so shocked, my dear sir,' he said, taking Mr Brown's arm and leading him towards the cutter. 'I am bringing you back the twelve-pounders – ordnance being now within your purview, as I understand – because I feared the sloop might be over-burthened.'

'With all my heart,' said Mr Brown, looking at the awful chasm in the yard, held up mutely for his inspection by the cutter's crew. 'But there is not another spar in the yard small enough for you.'

'Come, sir, you are forgetting the *Généreux*. She had three spare foretopgalantyards, as well as a vast mound of other spars; and you would be the first to admit that I have a moral right to one.'

'Well, you may *try* it, if you wish; you may sway it up to let us see what it looks like. But I make no promise.'

'Let my men take it out, sir. I remember just where they are stowed. Mr Babbington, four men. Come along now. Look alive.'

''Tis only on trial, remember, Captain Aubrey,' called Mr Brown. 'I will watch you sway it up.'

'Now that is what I call a real spar,' said Mr Lamb, peering lovingly over the side at the yard. 'Never a knot, never a curl: a French spar I dare say: forty-three foot as clean as a whistle. You'll spread a mainsail as a mainsail on that, sir.'

'Yes, yes,' said Jack impatiently. 'Is that hawser brought to the capstan yet?'

'Hawser to, sir,' came the reply, after a moment's pause.

'Then heave away.'

The hawser had been made fast to the middle of the yard and then laid along it almost to its starboard extremity, being tied in half a dozen places from the slings to the yardarm with stoppers – bands of spun yarn; the hawser ran from the yardarm up to the top-block at the masthead and so down through another block on deck and thence to the capstan; so as the capstan turned the yard rose from the water, sloping more and more nearly to the vertical until it came aboard quite upright, steered carefully end-on through the rigging.

'Cut the outer stopper,' said Jack. The spun yarn dropped and the yard canted a little, held by the next: as it rose so the other stoppers were cut, and when the last went the yard swung square, neatly under the top.

'It will never do, Captain Aubrey,' called Mr Brown, hailing over the quiet evening air through his trumpet. 'It is far too large and will certainly carry away. You must saw off the yardarms and half the third quarter.'

Lying stark and bare like the arms of an immense pair of

scales, the yard certainly did look somewhat over-large.

'Hitch on the runners,' said Jack. 'No, farther out. Half way to the second quarter. Surge the hawser and lower away.' The yard came down on deck and the carpenter hurried off for his tools. 'Mr Watt,' said Jack to the bosun. 'Just rig me the brace-pendants, will you?' The bosun opened his mouth, shut it again and bent slowly to his work: anywhere outside Bedlam brace-pendants were rigged after the horses, after the stirrups, after the yard-tackle pendants (or a thimble for the tackle-hook, if preferred): and none of them, ever, until the stop-cleat, the narrow part for them all to rest upon, had been worked on the sawn-off end and provided with a collar to prevent them from drawing in towards the middle. The carpenter reappeared with a saw and a rule. 'Have you a plane there, Mr Lamb?' asked Jack. 'Your mate will fetch you a plane. Unship the stuns'l-boom iron and touch up the ends of the stop-cleats, Mr Lamb, if you please.' Lamb, amazed until he grasped what Jack was about, slowly planed the tips of the yard, shaving off wafers until they showed new and white, a round the size of a halfpenny bun. 'That will do,' said Jack. 'Sway her up again, bracing her round easy all the time square with the quay. Mr Dillon, I must go ashore: return the guns to the ordnance-wharf and stand off and on for me in the channel. We must sail before the evening gun. Oh, and Mr Dillon, all the women ashore.'

'All the women without exception, sir?'

'All without their lines. All the trollops. Trollops are capital things in port, but they will not do at sea.' He paused, ran down to his cabin and came back two minutes later, stuffing an envelope into his pocket. 'Yard again,' he cried, dropping into the boat.

'You will be glad you took my advice,' said Mr Brown, receiving him at the steps. 'It would certainly have carried away with the first puff of wind.'

'May I take the duettoes now, sir?' asked Jack, with a certain pang. 'I am just about to fetch the friend I was

73

speaking of — a great musician, sir. You must meet him, when next we are in Mahon: you must allow me to present him to Mrs Brown.'

'Should be honoured — most happy,' said Mr Brown.

'Crown steps now, and give way like heroes,' said Jack, returning at a shambling run with the book: like so many sailors he was rather fat, and he sweated easily on shore. 'Six minutes in hand,' he said, peering at his watch in the twilight as they came in to the landing. 'Why, there you are, Doctor. I do hope you will forgive me for ratting on you this afternoon. Shannahan, Bussell: you two come with me. The others stay in the boat. Mr Ricketts, you had better lie twenty yards off or so, and deliver them from temptation. Will you bear with me, sir, if I make a few purchases? I have had no time to send for anything, not so much as a sheep or a ham or a bottle of wine; so I am afraid it will be junk, salt horse and Old Weevil's wedding cake for most of the voyage, with four-water grog to wet it. However, we can refresh at Cagliari. Should you like the seamen to carry your dunnage down to the boat? By the way,' he added, as they walked along, with the sailors following some way behind, 'before I forget it, it is usual in the service to draw an advance upon one's pay upon appointment; so conceiving you would not choose to appear singular, I put up a few guineas in this envelope.'

'What a humane regulation,' said Stephen, looking pleased. 'Is it often taken advantage of?'

'Invariably,' said Jack. 'It is a universal custom, in the service.'

'In that case,' said Stephen, taking the envelope, 'I shall undoubtedly comply with it: I certainly should not wish to look singular: I am most obliged to you. May I indeed have one of your men? A violoncello is a bulky object: as for the rest there is only a small chest and some books.'

'Then let us meet again at a quarter past the hour at the steps,' said Jack. 'Lose not a moment, I beg, Doctor; for we are extremely pressed. Shannahan, you look after the Doctor and trundle his dunnage along smartly. Bussell, you come along with me.'

As the clock struck the quarter and the note hung up there unresolved, waiting for the half, Jack said, 'Stow the chest in the fore-sheets. Mr Ricketts, you stow yourself upon the chest. Doctor, you sit down there and nurse the 'cello. Capital. Shove off. Give way together, and row dry, now.'

They reached the *Sophie*, propelled Stephen and his belongings up the side – the larboard side, to avoid ceremony and to make sure they got him aboard: they had too low an opinion of landmen to allow him to venture upon even the *Sophie*'s unaspiring height alone – and Jack led him to the cabin. 'Mind your head,' he said. 'That little den in there is yours: do what you can to make yourself comfortable, pray, and forgive my lack of ceremony. I must go on deck.

'Mr Dillon,' he said, 'is all well?'

'All's well, sir. The twelve merchantmen have made their signal.'

'Very good. Fire a gun for them and make sail, if you please. I believe we shall just get down the harbour with topgallants, if this fag-end of a breeze still holds; and then, out of the lee of the cape, we may make a respectable offing. So make sail; and by then it will be time to set the watch. A long day, Mr Dillon?'

'A very long day, sir.'

'At one time I thought it would never come to an end.'

Chapter Three

Two bells in the morning watch found the *Sophie* sailing steadily eastward along the thirty-ninth parallel with the wind just abaft her beam; she was heeling no more than two strakes under her topgallantsails, and she could have set her royals, if the amorphous heap of merchantmen under her lee had not determined to travel very slowly until full day-light, no doubt for fear of tripping over the lines of longitude.

The sky was still grey and it was impossible to say whether it was clear or covered with very high cloud; but the sea itself already had a nacreous light that belonged more to the day than the darkness, and this light was reflected in the great convexities of the topsails, giving them the lustre of grey pearls.

'Good morning,' said Jack to the marine sentry at the door.

'Good morning, sir,' said the sentry, springing to attention.

'Good morning, Mr Dillon.'

'Good morning, sir,' touching his hat.

Jack took in the state of the weather, the trim of the sails and the likelihood of a fair forenoon; he drew deep gusts of the clean air, after the dense fog of his cabin. He turned to the rail, unencumbered by hammocks at this time of day, and looked at the merchantmen: they were all there, strag-gling over not too vast an area of sea; and what he had taken for a far stern lantern or an uncommonly big top-light was old Saturn, low on the horizon and tangled in their rigging. To windward now, and he saw a sleepy line of gulls, squab-bling languidly over a ripple on the sea – sardines or anchovies or maybe those little spiny mackerel. The sound of the creaking blocks, the gently straining cordage and sail-cloth, the angle of the living deck and the curved line of guns in front of him sent such a jet of happiness through his heart that he almost skipped where he stood.

'Mr Dillon,' he said, overcoming a desire to shake his lieutenant by the hand, 'we shall have to muster the ship's company after breakfast and make up our minds how we are to watch and quarter them.'

'Yes, sir: at the moment things are at sixes and sevens, with the new draft unsettled.'

'At least we have plenty of hands – we could fight both sides easily, which is more than any line of battle ship can say. Though I rather fancy we had the tail end of the draft from the *Burford*; it seemed to me there was an unnatural proportion of Lord Mayor's men among them. No old Charlottes, I suppose?'

'Yes, sir, we have one – the fellow with no hair and a red handkerchief round his neck. He was a foretopman, but he seems quite dazed and stupid still.'

'A sad business,' said Jack shaking his head.

'Yes,' said James Dillon, looking into vacancy and seeing a leaping spring of fire in the still air, a first-rate ablaze from truck to waterline, with eight hundred men aboard. 'You could hear the flames a mile away and more. And sometimes a sheet of fire would lift off and go up into the air by itself, cracking and waving like a huge flag. It was just such a morning as this: a little later in the day, perhaps.'

'You were there, I collect? Have you any notion of the cause? People talk about an infernal machine taken aboard by an Italian in Boney's pay.'

'From all I heard it was some fool who allowed hay to be stowed on the half-deck, close to the tub with the slow-match for the signal-guns. It went up in a blaze and caught the mainsail at once. It was so sudden they could not come to the clew-garnets.'

'Could you save any of her people?'

'Yes, a few. We picked up two marines and a quarter-gunner, but he was most miserably burnt. There were very few saved, not much above a hundred, I believe. It was not a creditable business, not at all. Many more should have been brought away, but the boats hung back.'

'They were thinking of the *Boyne*, no doubt.'

'Yes. The *Charlotte*'s guns were firing as the heat reached them, and everybody knew the magazine might go up at any minute; but even so . . . All the officers I spoke to said the same thing – there was no getting the boats close in. It was the same with my people. I was in a hired cutter, the *Dart* –'

'Yes, yes, I know you were,' said Jack, smiling significantly.

'– three or four miles down-wind, and we had to sweep to get up. But there was no way of inducing them to pull heartily, rope's end or no. There was not a man or boy who was what you would call shy of gunfire – indeed, they were as well-conducted a set of men as you could wish, for boarding or for carrying a shore-battery, or for anything you please. And the *Charlotte*'s guns were not aimed at us, of course – just going off at random. But no, the whole feeling in the cutter was different; quite unlike action or an ugly night on a lee-shore. And there is little to be done with a thoroughly unwilling crew.'

'No,' said Jack. 'There is no forcing a willing mind.' He was reminded of his conversation with Stephen Maturin, and he added, 'It is a contradiction in terms.' He might have gone on to say that a crew thoroughly upset in its ways, cut short in the article of sleep, and deprived of its trollops, was not the best of weapons either; but he knew that any remark passed on the deck of a vessel seventy-eight feet three inches long was in the nature of a public statement. Apart from anything else, the quartermaster at the con and the helmsman at the wheel were within arm's reach. The quartermaster turned the watch-glass, and as the first grains of sand began their tedious journey back into the half they had just so busily emptied he called 'George,' in a low, night-watch voice, and the marine sentry clumped forward to strike three bells.

By now there was no doubt about the sky: it was pure blue from north to south, with no more than a little violet duskiness lingering in the west.

Jack stepped over to the weather-rail, swung himself into the shrouds and ran up the ratlines. 'This may not look quite dignified, in a captain,' he reflected, pausing under the loom of the top to see just how much more clearance well-bowsed cross-catharpings might give the yard. 'Perhaps I had better go up through the lubber's hole.' Ever since the invention of those platforms some way up the mast called tops, sailors have made it a point of honour to get into them by an odd, devious route – by clinging to the futtock-shrouds, which run from the catharpings near the top of the mast to the futtock-plates at the outer edge of the top: they cling to them and creep like flies, hanging backward about twenty-five degrees from the vertical, until they reach the rim of the top and so climb upon it, quite ignoring the convenient square hole next to the mast itself, to which the shrouds lead directly as their natural culmination – a straight, safe path with easy steps from the deck to the top. This hole, this lubber's hole, is as who should say never used, except by those who have never been to sea or persons of great dignity, and when Jack came up through it he gave Jan Jackruski, ordinary seaman, so disagreeable a fright that he uttered a thin scream. 'I thought you were the house-demon,' he said, in Polish.

'What is your name?' said Jack.

'Jackruski, sir. Please: thank you,' said the Pole.

'Watch out carefully, Jackruski,' said Jack, moving easily up the topmast shrouds. He stopped at the masthead, hooked an arm through the topgallant shrouds and settled comfortably in the crosstrees: many an hour had he spent there by way of punishment in his youth – indeed, when first he used to go up he had been so small that he could easily sit on the middle crosstree with his legs dangling, lean forward on his arms folded over the after tree and go to sleep, firmly wedged in spite of the wild gyrations of his seat. How he had slept in those days! He was always sleepy or hungry, or both. And how perilously high it had seemed. It had been higher, of course, far higher, in the old *Theseus* – somewhere about a hundred and fifty feet up: and how it had swung about the sky! He had been sick once, mastheaded in the old *Theseus*, and his dinner had gone straight up into the air, never to be seen again. But even so, this was a comfortable height. Eighty-seven feet less the depth of the kelson – say seventy-five. That gave him a horizon of ten or eleven miles. He looked over those miles of sea to windward – perfectly clear. Not a sail, not the slightest break on the tight line of the horizon. The topgallantsail above him was suddenly golden: then two points on the larboard bow, in the mounting blaze of light, the sun thrust up its blinding rim. For a prolonged moment Jack alone was sunlit, picked out: then the light reached the topsail, travelled down it, took in the peak of the boom mainsail and so reached the deck, flooding it from stem to stern. Tears welled up in his eyes, blurred his vision, overspilt, rolled down his cheeks: they did not use themselves up in lines upon his face but dropped, two, four, six, eight, round drops slanting away through the warm golden air to leeward.

Bending low to look under the topgallantsail he gazed at his charges, the merchantmen: two pinks, two snows, a Baltic cat and the rest barca-longas; all there, and the rearmost was beginning to make sail. Already there was a living warmth in the sun, and a delicious idleness spread through his limbs.

'This will never do,' he said: there were innumerable things to be seen to below. He blew his nose, and with his eyes still fixed on the spar-laden cat he reached out for the weather backstay. His hand curled round it mechanically, with as little thought as if it had been the handle of his own front door, and he slid gently down to the deck, thinking, 'One new landman to each gun-crew might answer very well.'

Four bells. Mowett heaved the log, waited for the red tag

to go astern and called 'Turn.' 'Stop!' cried the quarter-master twenty-eight seconds later, with the little sand-glass close to his eye. Mowett nipped the line almost exactly at the third knot, jerked out the peg and walked across to chalk 'three knots' on the logboard. The quartermaster hurried to the big watch-glass, turned it and called out 'George' in a firm and rounded voice. The marine went for'ard and struck the four bells heartily. A moment later pandemonium broke loose: pandemonium, that is, to the waking Stephen Maturin, who now for the first time in his life heard the unnatural wailing, the strange arbitrary intervals of the bosun and his mates piping 'Up all hammocks'. He heard a rushing of feet and a great terrible voice calling 'All hands, all hands ahoy! Out or down! Out or down! Rouse and bitt! Rise and shine! Show a leg there! Out or down! Here I come, with a sharp knife and a clear conscience!' He heard three muffled dumps as three sleep-sodden landmen were, in fact, cut down: he heard oaths, laughter, the impact of a rope's end as a bosun's mate started a torpid, bewildered hand, and then a far greater trampling as fifty or sixty men rushed up the hatchways with their hammocks, to stow them in the nettings.

On deck the foretopmen had set the elm-tree pump a-wheezing, while the fo'c'slemen washed the fo'c'sle with the fresh sea-water they pumped, the maintopmen washed the starboard side of the quarter-deck and the quarter-deck men all the rest, grinding away with holystones until the water ran like thin milk from the admixture of minute raspings of wood and caulking, and the boys and the idlers – the people who merely worked all day – heaved at the chain-pumps to clear the night's water out of the bilges, and the gunner's crew cosseted the fourteen four-pounders; but none of this had had the electrifying effect of the racing feet.

'Is it some emergency?' wondered Stephen, working his way with rapid caution out of his hanging cot. 'A battle? Fire? A desperate leak? And are they too much occupied to warn me – have forgotten I am here?' He drew on his breeches as fast as he could and, straightening briskly, he brought his head up against a beam with such force that he staggered and sank on to a locker, cherishing it with both hands.

A voice was speaking to him. 'What did you say?' he asked, peering through a mist of pain.

'I said, "Did you bump your head, sir?"'

'Yes,' said Stephen, looking at his hand: astonishingly it was not covered with blood – there was not even so much as a smear.

'It's these old beams, sir' – in the unusually distinct, didactic voice used at sea for landmen and on land for half-wits – 'You want to take care of them; for – they – are very – low.' Stephen's look of pure malevolence recalled the steward to a sense of his message and he said, 'Could you fancy a chop or two for breakfast, sir? A neat beefsteak? We killed a bullock at Mahon, and there's some prime steaks.'

'There you are, Doctor,' cried Jack. 'Good morning to you. I trust you slept?'

'Very well indeed, I thank you. These hanging cots are a most capital invention, upon my word.'

'What would you like for breakfast? I smelt the gunroom's bacon on deck and I thought it the finest smell I had ever smelt in my life – Araby left at the post. What do you say to bacon and eggs, and then perhaps a beefsteak to follow? And coffee?'

'You are of my way of thinking entirely,' cried Stephen, who had great leeway to make up in the matter of victuals. 'And conceivably there might be onions, as an antiscorbutic.' The word onions brought the smell of them frying into his nostrils and their peculiarly firm yet unctuous texture to his palate: he swallowed painfully. 'What's afoot?' he exclaimed, for the howling, and the wild rushing, as of mad beasts, had broken out again.

'The hands are being piped down to breakfast,' said Jack carelessly. 'Light along that bacon, Killick. And the coffee. I'm clemmed.'

'How I slept,' said Stephen. 'Deep, deep, restorative, roborative sleep – none of your hypnogogues, none of your tinctures of laudanum can equal it. But I am ashamed of my appearance. I slept so late that here I am, barbarously unshaved and nasty, whereas you are as smug as a bridegroom. Forgive me for a moment.

'It was a naval surgeon, a man at Haslar,' he said, coming back, smooth, 'who invented these modern short arterial ligatures: I thought of him just now, as my razor passed within a few lines of my external carotid. When it is rough, surely you must get many shocking incised wounds?'

'Why, no: I can't say we do,' said Jack. 'A matter of use, I suppose. Coffee? What we do get is a most plentiful crop of bursten bellies – what's the learned word? – and pox.'

'Hernia. You surprise me.'

'Hernia: exactly so. Very common. I dare say half the idlers are more or less ruptured: that is why we give them the lighter duties.'

'Well, it is not so very surprising, now that I reflect upon the nature of a mariner's labour. And the nature of his amusements accounts for his pox, of course. I remember to have seen parties of seamen in Mahon, wonderfully elated, dancing and singing with sad drabble-tail pakes. Men from the *Audacious*, I recall, and the *Phaëton*: I do not remember any from the *Sophie*.'

'No. The Sophies were a quiet lot ashore. But in any case they had nothing to be elated about, or with. No prizes and so, of course, no prize-money. It's prize-money alone lets a seaman kick up a dust ashore, for precious little does he see of his pay. What do you say to a beefsteak now, and another pot of coffee?'

'With all my heart.'

'I hope I may have the pleasure of introducing my lieutenant to you at dinner. He appears to be a seamanlike, gentlemanly fellow. He and I have a busy morning ahead of us: we must sort out the crew and set them to their duties – we must watch and quarter them, as we say. And I must find you a servant, as well as one for myself, and a cox'n too. The gun-room cook will do very well.'

'We will muster the ship's company, Mr Dillon, if you please,' said Jack.

'Mr Watt,' said James Dillon. 'All hands to muster.'

The bosun sprung his call, his mates sped below roaring 'All hands', and presently the *Sophie*'s deck between the mainmast and the fo'c'sle was dark with men, all her people, even the cook, wiping his hands on his apron, which he balled up and thrust into his shirt. They stood rather uncertainly, over to port, in the two watches, with the newcomers huddled vaguely between them, looking shabby, mean and bereft.

'All hands for muster, sir, if you please,' said James Dillon, raising his hat.

'Very well, Mr Dillon,' said Jack. 'Carry on.'

Prompted by the purser, the clerk brought forward the muster-book and the *Sophie*'s lieutenant called out the names. 'Charles Stallard.'

'Here sir,' cried Charles Stallard, able seaman, volunteer from the *St Fiorenzo*, entered the *Sophie* 6 May 1795, then aged twenty. No entry under Straggling, none under Venereals, none under Cloaths in Sick Quarters: had remitted ten pounds from abroad: obviously a valuable man. He stepped over to the starboard side.

'Thomas Murphy.'

'Here, sir,' said Thomas Murphy, putting the knuckle of his index finger to his forehead as he moved over to join Stallard – a gesture used by all the men until James Dillon reached Assei and Assou, with never a Christian-name between them: able seamen, born in Bengal, and brought here by what strange winds? And they, in spite of years and years in the Royal Navy, put their hands to their foreheads and thence to their hearts, bending quickly as they did so.

'John Codlin. William Witsover. Thomas Jones. Francis Lacanfra. Joseph Bussell. Abraham Vilheim. James Courser.

Peter Peterssen. John Smith. Giuseppe Laleso. William Cozens. Lewis Dupont. Andrew Karouski. Richard Henry . . .' and so the list went on, with only the sick gunner and one Isaac Wilson not answering, until it ended with the newcomers and the boys – eighty-nine souls, counting officers, men, boys and marines.

Then began the reading of the Articles of War, a ceremony that often accompanied divine service and that was so closely associated with it in most minds that the faces of the crew assumed a look of devout blankness at the words, 'for the better regulating of his Majesty's navies, ships of war, and forces by sea, whereon under the good providence of God, the wealth, safety and strength of his kingdom chiefly depend; be it enacted by the King's most excellent Majesty, by and with the advice and consent of the lords spiritual and temporal, and commons, in this present parliament assembled, and by the authority of the same, that from and after the twenty-fifth day of December, one thousand seven hundred and forty-nine, the articles and orders hereinafter following, as well in time of peace as in time of war, shall be duly observed and put in execution, in manner hereinafter mentioned', an expression that they retained throughout, unmoved by 'all flag officers, and all persons in or belonging to his Majesty's ships or vessels of war, being guilty of profane oaths, cursings, execrations, drunkenness, uncleanliness, or other scandalous actions, shall incur such punishment as a court-martial shall think fit to impose'. Or by the echoing repetition of 'shall suffer death'. 'Every flag-officer, captain and commander in the fleet who shall not . . . encourage the inferior officers and men to fight courageously, shall suffer death . . . If any person in the fleet shall treacherously or cowardly yield or cry for quarter – being convicted thereof by the sentence of a court-martial, shall suffer death . . . Every person who through cowardice shall in time of action withdraw or keep back . . . shall suffer death . . . Every person who through cowardice, negligence or disaffection shall forbear to pursue any enemy, pirate, or rebel, beaten or flying . . . shall suffer death . . . If any officer, mariner, soldier or other person in the fleet shall strike any of his superior officers, draw, or offer to draw, or lift up any weapon . . . shall suffer death . . . If any person in the fleet shall commit the unnatural and detestable sin of buggery or sodomy with man or beast, he shall be punished with death.' Death rang through and through the Articles; and even where the words were utterly incomprehensible the death had a fine, comminatory, Leviticus ring, and the crew took a grave pleasure in it all; it was what they were used to – it was what they heard the first Sunday in every month and upon all extraordinary occasions such as this. They found it comfortable to their spirits, and when the watch below was dismissed the men looked far more settled.

'Very well,' said Jack, looking round. 'Make signal twenty-three with two guns to leeward. Mr Marshall, we will set the main and fore stays'ls, and as soon as you see that pink coming up with the rest of the convoy, set the royals. Mr Watt, let the sailmaker and his party get to work on the square mainsail directly, and send the new hands aft one by one. Where's my clerk? Mr Dillon, let us knock these watch-bills into some kind of a shape. Dr Maturin, allow me to present my officers . . .' This was the first time Stephen and James had come face to face in the *Sophie*, but Stephen had seen that flaming red queue with its black ribbon and he was largely prepared. Even so, the shock of recognition was so great that his face automatically took on a look of veiled aggression and of the coldest reserve. For James Dillon the shock was far greater; in the hurry and business of the preceding twenty-four hours he had not chanced to hear the new surgeon's name; but apart from a slight change of colour he betrayed no particular emotion. 'I wonder,' said Jack to Stephen when the introductions were over, 'whether it would amuse you to look over the sloop while Mr Dillon and I attend to this business, or whether you would prefer to be in the cabin?'

'Nothing would give me greater pleasure than to look over

the ship, I am sure,' said Stephen. 'A very elegant complexity of . . .' his voice trailed away.

'Mr Mowett, be so good as to show Dr Maturin everything he would like to see. Carry him into the maintop – it affords quite a visto. You do not mind a little height, my dear sir?'

'Oh no,' said Stephen, looking vaguely about him. 'I do not mind it.'

James Mowett was a tubular young man, getting on for twenty; he was dressed in old sailcoth trousers and a striped Guernsey shirt, a knitted garment that gave him very much the look of a caterpillar; and he had a marlinspike dangling round his neck, for he had meant to take a hand in the making of the new square mainsail. He looked attentively at Stephen to make out what kind of a man he was, and with that mixture of easy grace and friendly deference which comes naturally to so many sailors he made his bow and said, 'Well, sir, where do you choose to start? Shall we go into the top directly? You can see the whole run of the deck from there.'

The whole run of the deck amounted to some ten yards aft and sixteen forward, and it was perfectly visible from where they stood; but Stephen said, 'Let us go up then, by all means. Lead the way, and I will imitate your motions as best I can.'

He watched thoughtfully while Mowett sprang into the ratlines and then, his mind far away, slowly hoisted himself up after him. James Dillon and he had belonged to the United Irishmen, a society that at different times in the last nine years had been an open, public association calling for the emancipation of Presbyterians, dissenters and Catholics and for a representative government of Ireland; a proscribed secret society; an armed body in open rebellion; and a defeated, hunted remnant. The rising had been put down amidst the usual horrors, and in spite of the general pardon the lives of the more important members were in danger. Many had been betrayed – Lord Edward Fitzgerald himself at the very outset – and many had withdrawn, distrusting even their own families, for the events had divided the society and the nation most terribly. Stephen Maturin was not afraid of any vulgar betrayal, nor was he afraid for his skin, because he did not value it: but he had so suffered from the incalculable tensions, rancour and hatreds that arise from the failure of a rebellion that he could not bear any further disappointment, any further hostile, recriminatory confrontation, any fresh example of a friend grown cold, or worse. There had always been very great disagreements within the association; and now, in the ruins of it, it was impossible, once daily contact had been lost, to tell where any man stood.

He was not afraid for his skin, not afraid for himself: but presently his climbing body, now half-way up the shrouds, let him know that for its own part it was in a state of rapidly increasing terror. Forty feet is no very great height, but it seems far more lofty, aerial and precarious when there is nothing but an insubstantial yielding ladder of moving ropes underfoot; and when Stephen was three parts of the way up cries of 'Belay' on deck showed that the staysails were set and their sheets hauled aft. They filled, and the *Sophie* heeled over another strake or two; this coincided with her leeward roll, and the rail passed slowly under Stephen's downward gaze, to be followed by the sea – a wide expanse of glittering water, very far below, and directly underneath. His grip on the ratlines tightened with cataleptic strength and his upward progress ceased: he remained there spread-eagled, while the varying forces of gravity, centrifugal motion, irrational panic and reasonable dread acted upon his motionless, tight-cramped person, now pressing him forward so that the checkered pattern of the shrouds and their crossing ratlines were imprinted on his front, and now plucking him backwards so that he bellied out like a shirt hung up to dry.

A form slid down the backstay to the left of him: hands closed gently round his ankles, and Mowett's cheerful young voice said, 'Now, sir, on the roll. Clap on to the shrouds –

the uprights – and look upwards. Here we go.' His right foot was firmly moved up to the next ratline, his left followed it; and after one more hideous swinging backward lunge in which he closed his eyes and stopped breathing, the lubber's hole received its second visitor of the day. Mowett had darted round by the futtock-shrouds and was there in the top to haul him through.

'This is the maintop, sir,' said Mowett, affecting not to notice Stephen's haggard look. 'The other one over there is the foretop, of course.'

'I am very sensible of your kindness in helping me up,' said Stephen. 'Thank you.'

'Oh, sir,' cried Mowett, 'I beg . . . And that's the main-stays'l they just set, below us. And that's the forestays'l for'ard: you'll never see one, but on a man-of-war.'

'Those triangles? Why are they called staysails?' asked Stephen, speaking somewhat at random.

'Why, sir, because they are rigged on the stays, slide along them like curtains by those rings: we call 'em hanks, at sea. We used to have grommets, but we rigged hanks when we were laying off Cadiz last year, and they answer much better. The stays are those thick ropes that run sloping down, straight for'ard.'

'And their function is to extend these sails: I see.'

'Well, sir, they do extend them, to be sure. But what they are really for is to hold up the masts – to stay them for'ard. To prevent them falling backwards when she pitches.'

'The masts need support, then?' asked Stephen, stepping cautiously across the platform and patting the squared top of the lower mast and the rounded foot of the topmast, two stout parallel columns – close on three feet of wood between them, counting the gap. 'I should scarcely have thought it.'

'Lord, sir, they'd roll themselves overboard, else. The shrouds support them sideways, and the backstays – these here, sir – backwards.'

'I see. I see. Tell me,' said Stephen, to keep the young man talking at any cost, 'tell me, what is the purpose of this platform, and why is the mast doubled at this point? And what is this hammer for?'

'The top, sir? Why, apart from the rigging and getting things up, it comes in handy for the small-arms men in a close action: they can fire down on the enemy's deck and toss stink-pots and grenadoes. And then these futtock-plates at the rim here hold the dead-eyes for the topmast shrouds – the top gives a wide base so that the shrouds have a purchase: the top is a little over ten foot wide. It is the same thing up above. There are the cross-trees, and they spread the topgallant shrouds. You see them, sir? Up there, where the look-out is perched, beyond the topsail yard.'

'You could not explain this maze of ropes and wood and canvas without using sea-terms, I suppose. No, it would not be possible.'

'Using no sea-terms? I should be puzzled to do that, sir; but I will try, if you wish it.'

'No; for it is by those names alone that they are known, in nearly every case, I imagine.' The *Sophie*'s tops were furnished with iron stanchions for the hammock-netting that protected their occupants in battle: Stephen sat between two of them, with an arm round each and his legs dangling, he found comfort in this feeling of being firmly anchored to metal, with solid wood under his buttocks. The sun was well up in the sky by now and it threw a brilliant pattern of light and sharp shadow over the white deck below – geometrical lines and curves broken only by the formless mass of the square mainsail that the sailmaker and his men had spread over the fo'c'sle. 'Suppose we were to take that mast,' he said, nodding forward, for Mowett seemed to be afraid of talking too much – afraid of boring and instructing beyond his station, 'and suppose you were to name the principal objects from the bottom to the top.'

'It is the foremast, sir. The bottom we call the lower mast, or just the foremast; it is forty-nine feet long, and it is stepped on the kelson. It is supported by shrouds on either side – three pair of a side – and it is stayed for'ard by the forestay running down to the bowsprit: and the other rope running parallel with the forestay is the preventer-stay, in case it breaks. Then, about a third of the way up the foremast, you see the collar of the mainstay: the mainstay goes from just under here and supports the mainmast below us.'

'So that is a mainstay,' said Stephen, looking at it vaguely. 'I have often heard them mentioned. A stout-looking rope, indeed.'

'Ten-inch, sir,' said Mowett proudly. 'And the preventer-stay is seven. Then comes the forecourse yard, but perhaps I had best finish the masts before I go on to the yards. You see the foretop, the same kind of thing as we are on now? It lies on the trestletrees and crosstrees about five parts of the way up the foremast: and so the remaining length of lower mast runs double with the topmast, just as these two do here. The topmast, do you see, is that second length going upwards, the thinner piece that rises above the top. We sway it up from below and fix it to the lower mast, rather like a marine clapping a bayonet on to his musket: it comes up through the trestletrees, and when it is high enough, so that the hole in the bottom of it is clear, we ram a fid through, banging it home with the top-maul, which is this hammer you were asking about, and we sing out "Launch ho!" and . . .' the explanation ran eagerly on.

'Castlereagh hanging at the one masthead and Fitzgibbon at the other,' thought Stephen, but with only the weariest gleam of spirit.

'. . . and it's stayed for'ard to the bowsprit again: you can just see a corner of the foretopmast stays'l if you crane over this way.'

His voice reached Stephen as a pleasant background against which he tried to arrange his thoughts. Then Stephen was aware of an expectant pause: the words 'foretopmast' and 'crane over' had preceded it.

'Just so,' he said. 'And how long might that topmast be?'

'Thirty-one feet, sir, the same as this one here. Now, just above the foretop you see the collar of the maintopmast stay, which supports this topmast just above us. Then come the topmast trestletrees and crosstrees, where the other lookout is stationed; and then the topgallantmast. It is swayed up and held the same way as the topmast, only naturally its shrouds are slighter; and it is stayed for'ard to the jib-boom – do you see, the spar that runs out beyond the bowsprit? The bowsprit's topmast, as it were. It is twenty-three feet six inches long. The topgallantmast, I mean, not the jib-boom. That is twenty-four.'

'It is a pleasure to hear a man who thoroughly understands his profession. You are very exact, sir.'

'Oh, I hope the captains will say the same, sir,' cried Mowett. 'When next we put into Gibraltar I am to go for my lieutenant's examination again. Three senior captains sit upon you; and last time a very devilish captain asked me how many fathoms I should need for the main crowfoot, and how long the euphroe was. I could tell him now: it is fifty fathoms of three-quarter-inch line, though you would never credit it, and the euphroe is fourteen inches. I believe I could tell him anything that can even be attempted to be measured, except perhaps for the new mainyard, and I shall measure that with my tape before dinner. Should you like to hear some dimensions, sir?'

'I should like it of all things.'

'Well, sir, the *Sophie*'s keel is fifty-nine feet long; her gun-deck seventy-eight foot three inches; and she is ten foot ten inches deep. Her bowsprit is thirty-four foot, and I have told you all the other masts except for the main, which is fifty-six. Her maintopsail yard – the one just above us, sir – is thirty-one foot six inches; the maintopgallant, the one above that, twenty-three foot six; and the royal, up at the top, fifteen foot nine. And the stuns'l booms – but I ought to explain the yards first, sir, ought I not?'

'Perhaps you ought.'

'They are very simple, indeed.'

'I am happy to learn it.'

'On the bowsprit, now, there's a yard across, with the

spritsail furled upon it. That's the sprits'l yard, naturally. Then, coming to the foremast, the bottom one is the foreyard and the big square sail set upon it is the fore course; the foretopsail yard crosses above it; then the foretopgallant and the little royal with its sail furled. It is the same with the mainmast, only the mainyard just below us has no sail bent – if it had it would be called the *square* mainsail, because with this rig you have two mainsails, the square course set on the yard and the boom mainsail there behind us, a fore-and-aft sail set on a gaff above and a boom below. The boom is forty-two feet nine inches long, sir, and ten and a half inches through.'

'Ten and a half inches, indeed?' How absurd it had been to affect not to know James Dillon – and a very childish reaction – the most usual and dangerous of them all.

'Now to finish with the square sails, there are the stuns'ls, sir. We only set them when the wind is well abaft the beam, and they stand outside the leeches – the edges of the square sails – stretched by booms that run out along the yard through boom-irons. You can see them as clear as can be –'

'What is that?'

'The bosun piping hands to make sail. They will be setting the royals. Come over here, sir, if you please, or the topmen will trample you down.'

Stephen was scarcely out of the way before a swarm of young men and boys darted over the edge of the top and raced on grunting up the topmast shrouds.

'Now, sir, when the order comes you will see them let the sail fall, and then the men on deck will haul home the lee sheet first, because the wind blows it over that way and it comes home easy. Then the weather sheet: and as soon as the men are off the yard they will hoist away at the halliards and up she'll go. Here are the sheets, leading through by the block with a patch of white on it: and these are the halliards.'

A few moments later the royals were drawing, the *Sophie* heeled another strake and the hum of the breeze in her rigging rose by half a tone: the men came down less hurriedly than they had mounted; and the *Sophie*'s bell sounded five times.

'Tell me,' said Stephen, preparing to follow them, 'what is a brig?'

'This is a brig, sir; though we *call* her a sloop.'

'Thank you. And what is a – there is that howling again.'

''Tis only the bosun, sir: the square mainsail must be ready, and he desires the men to bend it to the yard.

> *O'er the ship the gallant bosun flies*
> *Like a hoarse mastiff through the storm he cries.*
> *Prompt to direct th'unskilful still appears,*
> *The expert he praises, and the timid cheers.'*

'He seems very free with that cane: I wonder they don't knock him down. So you are a poet, sir?' asked Stephen, smiling: he was beginning to feel that he could cope with the situation.

Mowett laughed cheerfully, and said, 'It would be easier this side, sir, with her heeling so. I will just get round a little below you. They say it is a wonderful plan not to look down, sir. Easy now. Easy does it. Handsomely wins the day. There you are, sir, all a-tanto.'

'By God,' said Stephen, dusting his hands. 'I am glad to be down.' He looked up at the top, and down again. 'I should not have thought myself so timid,' he reflected inwardly; and aloud he said, 'Now shall we look downstairs?'

'Perhaps we may find a cook among this new draft,' said Jack. 'That reminds me – I hope I may have the pleasure of your company to dinner?'

'I should be very happy, sir,' said James Dillon with a bow. They were sitting at the cabin table with the clerk at their side and the *Sophie*'s muster-book, complete-book, description-book and various dockets spread out before them.

'Take care of that pot, Mr Richards,' said Jack, as the

Sophie gave a skittish lee-lurch in the freshening breeze. 'You had better cork it up and hold the ink-horn in your hand. Mr Ricketts, let us see these men.'

They were a lacklustre band, compared with the regular Sophies. But then the Sophies were at home; the Sophies were all dressed in the elder Mr Ricketts' slops, which gave them a tolerably uniform appearance; and they had been tolerably well fed for the last few years – their food had at least been adequate in bulk. The newcomers, with three exceptions, were quota-men from the inland counties, mostly furnished by the beadle; there were seven ardent spirits from Westmeath who had been taken up in Liverpool for causing an affray, and so little did they know of the world (they had come over for the harvest, no more) that when they were offered the choice between the dampest cells of the common gaol and the Navy, they chose the latter, as the dryer place; and there was a bee-master with a huge lamentable face and a great spade beard whose bees had all died; an out-of-work thatcher; some unmarried fathers; two starving tailors; a quiet lunatic. The most ragged had been given clothes by the receiving-ships, but the others were still in their own worn corduroy or ancient second-hand coats – one countryman still had his smock-frock on. The exceptions were three middle-aged seamen, one a Dane called Christian Pram, the second mate of a Levanter, and the two others Greek sponge fishers whose names were thought to be Apollo and Turbid, pressed in circumstances that remained obscure.

'Capital, capital,' said Jack, rubbing his hands. 'I think we can rate Pram quartermaster right away – we are one quartermaster shy – and the brothers Sponge able as soon as they can understand a little English. As for the rest, all landmen. Now, Mr Richards, as soon as you have finished those descriptions, go along to Mr Marshall and tell him I should like to see him.'

'I think we shall watch almost exactly fifty men, sir, said James, looking up from his calculation.

'Eight fo'c'sle men, eight foretop – Mr Marshall, come and sit down and let us have the benefit of your lights. We must work out this watch-bill and quarter the men before dinner: there's not a minute to be lost.'

'And this, sir, is where we live,' said Mowett, advancing his lantern into the midshipmen's berth. 'Pray mind the beam. I must beg your indulgence for the smell: it is probably young Babbington here.'

'Oh, it is not,' cried Babbington, springing up from his book. 'You are *cruel*, Mowett,' he whispered, with seething indignation.

'It is a pretty luxurious berth, sir, as these things go,' said Mowett. 'There is some light from the grating, as you see, and a little air gets down when the hatch-covers are off. I remember in the after-cockpit of the old *Namur* the candles used to go out for want of anything in that line, and we had nothing as odorous as young Babbington.'

'I can well imagine it,' said Stephen, sitting down and peering about him in the shadows. 'How many of you live here?'

'Only three now, sir: we are two midshipmen short. The youngsters sling their hammocks by the breadroom, and they used to mess with the gunner until he took so poorly. Now they come here and eat our food and destroy our books with their great greasy thumbs.'

'You are studying trigonometry, sir?' said Stephen, whose eyes, accustomed to the darkness, could now distinguish an inky triangle.

'Yes, sir, if you please,' said Babbington. 'And I believe I have nearly found out the answer.' (And should have, if that great ox had not come barging in, he added, privately.)

'In canvassed berth, profoundly deep in thought,
His busy mind with sines and tangents fraught,
A Mid reclines! In calculation lost,
His efforts still by some intruder crost,' said Mowett.
'Upon my word and honour, sir, I am rather proud of that.'

'And well you may be,' said Stephen, his eyes dwelling on the little ships drawn all round the triangle. 'And pray, what in sea-language is meant by a ship?'

'She must have three square-rigged masts, sir,' they told him kindly, 'and a bowsprit; and the masts must be in three – lower, top and topgallant – for we never call a polacre a ship.'

'Don't you, though?' said Stephen.

'Oh no, sir,' they cried earnestly, 'nor a cat. Nor a xebec; for although you may *think* xebecs have a bowsprit, it is really only a sorts of wooded boomkin.'

'I shall take particular notice of that,' said Stephen. 'I suppose you grow used to living here,' he observed, rising cautiously to his feet. 'At first it must seem a little confined.'

'Oh, sir,' said Mowett, '*think not meanly of this humble seat,*

Whence spring the guardians of the British fleet!
Revere the sacred spot, however low,
Which formed to martial acts an Hawke! An Howe!'

'Pay no attention to him, sir,' cried Babbington, anxiously. 'He means no disrespect, I do assure you, sir. It is only his disgusting way.'

'Tush, tush,' said Stephen. 'Let us see the rest of the – of the vessel, the conveyance.'

They went for'ard and passed another marine sentry; and groping his way along the dim space between two gratings, Stephen stumbled over something soft that clanked and called out angrily, 'Can't you see where you're a-coming to, you grass-combing bugger?'

'Now then, Wilson, you stow your gob,' cried Mowett. 'That's one of the men in the bilboes – lying in irons,' he explained. 'Never mind him, sir.'

'What is he lying in irons for?'

'For being rude, sir,' said Mowett, with a certain primness.

'Come, now, here's a fair-sized room, although it is so low. For the inferior officers, I take it?'

'No, sir. This is where the hands mess and sleep.'

'And the rest of them downstairs again, I presume.'

'There is no downstairs from here, sir. Below us is the hold, with only a bit of a platform as an orlop.'

'How many men are there?'

'Counting the marines, seventy-seven, sir.'

'Then they cannot all sleep here: it is physically impossible.'

'With respect, sir, they do. Each man has fourteen inches to sling his hammock, and they sling 'em fore and aft: now, the midship beam is twenty-five foot ten, which gives twenty-two places – you can see the numbers written up here.'

'A man cannot lie in fourteen inches.'

'No, sir, not very comfortably. But he can in eight and twenty; for, do you see, in a two-watch ship at any one time about half the men are on deck for their watch, which leaves all their places free.'

'Even in twenty-eight inches, two foot four, a man must be touching his neighbour.'

'Why, sir, it is tolerably close, to be sure; but it gets them all in out of the weather. We have four ranges, as you see: from the bulkhead to this beam; and so to this one; then to the beam with the lantern hanging in front of it; and the last between that and the for'ard bulkhead, by the galley. The carpenter and the bosun have their cabins up there. The first range and part of the next is for the marines; then come the seamen, three and a half ranges of them. So with an average of twenty hammocks to a row, we get them all in, in spite of the mast.'

'But it must be a continuous carpet of bodies, when even half the men are lying there.'

'Why, so it is, sir.'

'Where are the windows?'

'We have nothing like what you would call windows,' said Mowett, shaking his head. 'There are the hatches and gratings overhead, but of course they are mostly covered up when it blows.'

'And the sick-quarters?'

'We have none of them either, sir, rightly speaking. But sick men have cots slung right up against the for'ard bulk-head on the starboard side, by the galley; and they are indulged in the use of the round-house.'

'What is that?'

'Well, it is not really a round-house, more like a little row-port: not like in a frigate or a ship of the line. But it serves.'

'What for?'

'I hardly know how to explain, sir,' said Mowett, blushing. 'A necessary-house.'

'A jakes? A privy?'

'Just so, sir.'

'But what do the other men do? Have they chamber-pots?'

'Oh no, sir, Heavens above! They go up the hatch there and along to the heads – little places on either side of the stem.'

'Out of doors?'

'Yes, sir.'

'But what happens in inclement weather?'

'They still go to the heads, sir.'

'And they sleep forty or fifty together down here, with no windows? Well, if ever a man with the gaol-fever, or the plague, or the cholera morbus, sets foot in this apartment, God help you all.'

'Amen, sir,' said Mowett, quite aghast at Stephen's immovable, convincing certainty.

'That is an engaging young fellow,' said Stephen, walking into the cabin.

'Young Mowett? I am happy to hear you say so,' said Jack, who was looking worn and harried. 'Nothing pleasanter than good shipmates. May I offer you a whet? Our seaman's drink, that we call grog – are you acquainted with it? It goes down gratefully enough, at sea. Simpkin, bring us some grog. Damn that fellow – he is as slow as Beelzebub . . . Simpkin! Light along that grog. God rot the flaming son of a bitch. Ah, there you are. I needed that,' he said, putting down his glass. 'Such a tedious damned morning. Each watch has to have just the same proportions of skilled hands in the various stations, and so on. Endless discussion. And,' said he, hitching himself a little closer to Stephen's ear, 'I blundered into one of those unhappy gaffes . . . I picked up the list and read off Flaherty, Lynch, Sullivan, Michael Kelly, Joseph Kelly, Sheridan and Aloysius Burke – those chaps that took the bounty at Liverpool – and I said "More of these damned Irish Papists; at this rate half the starboard watch will be made up of them, and we shall not be able to get by for beads" – meaning it pleasantly, you know. But then I noticed a damned frigid kind of a chill and I said to myself, "Why, Jack, you damned fool, Dillon is from Ireland, and he takes it as a national reflexion." Whereas I had not meant anything so illiberal as a national reflexion, of course; only that I hated Papists. So I tried to put it right by a few well-turned flings against the Pope; but perhaps they were not as clever as I thought for they did not seem to answer.'

'And do you hate Papists, so?' asked Stephen.

'Oh, yes: and I hate paper-work. But the Papists are a very wicked crew, too, you know, with confession and all that,' said Jack. 'And they tried to blow up Parliament. Lord, how we used to keep up the Fifth of November. One of my very best friends – you would not believe how kind – was so upset when her mother married one that she took to mathematics and Hebrew directly – aleph, beth – though she was the prettiest girl for miles around – taught me navigation – splendid headpiece, bless her. She told me quantities of things about the Papists: I forget it all now, but they are certainly a very wicked crew. There is no trusting them. Look at the rebellion they have just had.'

'But my dear sir, the United Irishmen were primarily

Protestants – their leaders were Protestants. Wolfe Tone and Napper Tandy were Protestants. The Emmets, the O'Connors, Simon Butler, Hamilton Rowan, Lord Edward Fitzgerald were Protestants. And the whole idea of the club was to unite Protestant and Catholic and Presbyterian Irishmen. The Protestants it was who took the initiative.'

'Oh? Well, I don't know much about it, as you see – I thought it was the Papists. I was on the West Indies station at the time. But after a great deal of this damned paper-work I am quite ready to hate Papists and Protestants, too, and Anabaptists and Methodies. And Jews. No – I don't give a damn. But what really vexes me is that I should have got across Dillon's hawse like that; as I was saying, there is nothing pleasanter than good shipmates. He has a sad time of it, doing a first lieutenant's duty *and* keeping a watch – new ship – new ship's company – new captain – and I particularly wished to ease him in. Without there is a good understanding between the officers a ship cannot be happy: and a happy ship is your only good fighting ship – you should hear Nelson on that point: and I do assure you it is profoundly true. He will be dining with us, and I should take it very kindly if you would, as it were . . . ah, Mr Dillon, come and join us in a glass of grog.'

Partly for professional reasons and partly because of an entirely natural absence, Stephen had long ago assumed the privilege of silence at table; and now from the shelter of this silence he watched James Dillon with particular attention. It was the same small head, held high; the same dark-red hair, of course, and green eyes; the same fine skin and bad teeth – more were decaying now; the same very well-bred air; and although he was slim and of no more than the average height, he seemed to take up as much room as the fourteen-stone Jack Aubrey. The main difference was that the look of being just about to laugh, or of having discovered a private joke, had quite vanished – wiped out: no trace of it. A typically grave, humourless Irish countenance now. His

behaviour was reserved, but perfectly attentive and civil –
not the least appearance of sullen resentment.

They ate an acceptable turbot – acceptable when the
flour-and-water paste had been scraped off him – and then
the steward brought in a ham. It was a ham that could only
have come from a hog with a long-borne crippling disease,
the sort of ham that is reserved for officers who buy their
own provisions; and only a man versed in morbid anatomy
could have carved it handsomely. While Jack was struggling
with his duties as a host and adjuring the steward 'to clap
on to its beakhead' and 'to look alive', James turned to
Stephen with a fellow-guest's smile and said, 'Is it not possible that I have already had the pleasure of being in your
company, sir? In Dublin, or perhaps at Naas?'

'I do not believe I have had the honour, sir. I am often
mistaken for my cousin, of the same name. They tell me
there is a striking resemblance, which makes me uneasy, I
confess; for he is an ill-looking fellow, with a sly, Castle-
informer look on his face. And the character of an informer
is more despised in our country than in any other, is it not?
Rightly so, in my opinion. Though, indeed, the creatures
swarm there.' This was in a conversational tone, loud enough
to be heard by his neighbour over Jack's 'Easy, now . . .
wish it may not be infernally tough . . . get a purchase on
its beam, Killick; never mind thumbs . . .'

'I am entirely of your way of thinking,' said James with
complete understanding in his look. 'Will you take a glass
of wine with me, sir?'

'With all my heart.'

They pledged one another in the sloe-juice, vinegar
and sugar of lead that had been sold to Jack as wine and
then turned, the one with professional interest and the
other with professional stoicism, to Jack's dismembered
ham.

The port was respectable, however, and after the cloth
was drawn there was an easier, far more comfortable atmosphere in the cabin.

'Pray tell us about the action in the *Dart*,' said Jack, filling Dillon's glass. 'I have heard so many different accounts . . .'

'Yes, pray do,' said Stephen. 'I should look upon it as a most particular favour.'

'Oh, it was not much of an affair,' said James Dillon. 'Only with a contemptible set of privateers – a squabble among small-craft. I had temporary command of a hired cutter – a one-masted fore-and-aft vessel, sir, of no great size.' Stephen bowed. '– called the *Dart*. She had eight four-pounders, which was very well; but I only had thirteen men and a boy to fight them. However, orders came down to take a King's Messenger and ten thousand pounds in specie to Malta; and Captain Dockray asked me to give his wife and her sister a passage.'

'I remember him as first of the *Thunderer*,' said Jack. 'A dear, good, kind man.'

'So he was,' said James, shaking his head. 'Well, we had a steady tops'l libeccio, made our offing, tacked three or four leagues west of Egadi and stood a little west of south. It came on to blow after sundown, so having the ladies aboard and being short-handed in any case, I thought I should get under the lee of Pantelleria. It moderated in the night and the sea went down, and there I was at half-past four the next morning. I was shaving, as I remember very well, for I nicked my chin.'

'Ha,' said Stephen, with satisfaction.

'– when there was a cry of sail-ho and I hurried up on deck.'

'I'm sure you did,' said Jack, laughing.

'– and there were three French lateen-rigged privateers. It was just light enough to make them out, hull-up already, and presently I recognized the two nearest with my glass. They carried each a brass long six-pounder and four one-pounder swivels in their bows, and we had had a brush with them in the *Euryalus*, when they had the heels of us, of course.'

'How many men in them?'

'Oh, between forty and fifty apiece, sir: and they each had maybe a dozen musketoons or patareroes on their sides. And I made no doubt the third was just such another. They had been haunting the Sicily Channel for some time, lying off Lampione and Lampedusa to refresh. Now they were under my lee, lying thus –' he drew in wine on the table – 'with the wind blowing from the decanter. They could outsail me, close-hauled, and clearly their best plan was to engage me on either side and board.'

'Exactly,' said Jack.

'So taking everything into consideration – my passengers, the King's Messenger, the specie, and the Barbary coast ahead of me if I were to bear up – I thought the right thing to do was to attack them separately while I had the weather-gage and before the two nearest could join forces: the third was still three or four miles away, beating up under all sail. Eight of the cutter's crew were prime seamen, and Captain Dockray had sent his cox'n along with the ladies, a fine strong fellow named William Brown. We soon cleared for action and treble-shotted the guns. And I must say the ladies behaved with great spirit: rather more than I could have wished. I represented to them that their place was below – in the hold. But Mrs Dockray was not going to be told her duty by any young puppy without so much as an epaulette to his name and did I think a post-captain's wife with nine years' seniority was going to ruin her sprigged muslin in the bilges of my cockleshell? She should tell my aunt – my cousin Ellis – the First Lord of the Admiralty – bring me to a court-martial for cowardice, for temerity, for not knowing my business. She understood discipline and subordination as well as the next woman, or better; and "Come, my dear," says she to Miss Jones, "you ladle out the powder and fill the cartridges, and I will carry them up in my apron." By this time the position was so –' he redrew the plan. 'The nearest privateer two cables' lengths away and to the lee of the other: both of them had been firing for ten minutes with their bow-chasers.'

'How long is a cable?' asked Stephen.

'About two hundred yards, sir,' said James. 'So I put my helm down – she was wonderfully quick in stays – and steered to ram the Frenchman amidships. With the wind on her quarter, the *Dart* covered the distance in little more than a minute, which was as well, since they were peppering us hard. I steered myself until we were within pistol-shot and then ran for'ard to lead the boarders, leaving the tiller to the boy. Unhappily, he misunderstood me and let the privateer shoot too far ahead, and we took her abaft her mizen, our bowsprit carrying away her larboard mizen shrouds and a good deal of her poop-rail and stern-works. So instead of boarding we passed under her stern: her mizen went by the board with the shock, and we flew to the guns and poured in a raking broadside. There were just enough of us to fight four guns, with the King's Messenger and me working one and Brown helping us run it out when he had fired his own. I luffed up to range along under her lee and get across her bows, so as to prevent her from manoeuvring; but with that great spread of canvas they have, you know, the *Dart* was becalmed for a while, and we exchanged as hot a fire as quickly as we could keep it up. But at last we forged ahead, found our wind again and tacked as quickly as we could, right athwart the Frenchman's stem – quicker, indeed, for we could only spare two hands to the sheet and our boom came crack against her foreyard, carrying it away – the falling sail dowsed her bow-chaser and the swivels. And as we came round there was our starboard broadside ready, and we fired it so close that the wads set light to her foresail and the wreckage of the mizen lying there all over her deck. Then they called for quarter and struck.'

'Well done, well done!' cried Jack.

'It was high time,' said James, 'for the other privateer had been coming up fast. By something like a miracle our bowsprit and boom were still standing, so I told the captain of the privateer that I should certainly sink him if he attempted to make sail and bore up directly for his consort.

I could not spare a single hand to take possession, nor the time.'

'Of course not.'

'So here we were approaching on opposite tacks, and they were firing as the whim took them – everything they had. When we were fifty yards away I paid off four points to bring the starboard guns to bear, gave her the broadside, then luffed up directly and gave her the other, from perhaps twenty yards. The second was very remarkable, sir. I did not think four-pounders could have done such execution. We fired on the down-roll, a trifle later than I should have thought right, and all four shot struck her on the waterline at the height of her rise – I saw them go home, all on the same strake. A moment later her people left their guns – they were running about and hallooing. Unhappily, Brown had stumbled as our gun recoiled and the carriage had mangled his foot most cruelly. I bade him go below, but he would have none of it – would sit there and use a musket – and then he gave a cheer and said the Frenchman was sinking. And so he was: first they were awash, and then they went down, right down, with their sails set.'

'My God!' cried Jack.

'So I stood straight on for the third, all hands knotting and splicing, for our rigging was cut to pieces. But the mast and boom were so wounded – a six-pound ball clean through the mast, and many deep scores – that I dared not carry a press of sail. So I am afraid she ran clean away from us, and there was nothing for it but to beat back to the first privateer. Luckily, they had been busy with their fire all this time, or they might have slipped off. We took six aboard to work our pumps, tossed their dead overboard, battened the rest down, took her in tow, set course for Malta and arrived two days later, which surprised me, for our sails were a collection of holes held together with threads, and our hull not much better.'

'Did you pick up the men from the one that sank?' asked Stephen.

'No, sir,' said James.

'Not corsairs,' said Jack. 'Not with thirteen men and a boy aboard. What were your losses, though?'

'Apart from Brown's foot and a few scratches we had no one wounded, sir, nor a single man killed. It was an astonishing thing: but then we were pretty thin on the ground.'

'And theirs?'

'Thirteen dead, sir. Twenty-nine prisoners.'

'And the privateer you sank?'

'Fifty-six, sir.'

'And the one that got away?'

'Well, forty-eight, or so they told us, sir. But she hardly counts, since we only had a few random shots from her before she grew shy.'

'Well, sir,' said Jack, 'I congratulate you with all my heart. It was a noble piece of work.'

'So do I,' said Stephen. 'So do I. A glass of wine with you, Mr Dillon,' he said, bowing and raising his glass.

'Come,' cried Jack, with a sudden inspiration. 'Let us drink to the renewed success of Irish arms, and confusion to the Pope.'

'The first part ten times over,' said Stephen, laughing. 'But never a drop will I drink to the second, Voltairian though I may be. The poor gentleman has Boney on his hands, and that is confusion enough, in all conscience. Besides, he is a very learned Benedictine.'

'Then confusion to Boney.'

'Confusion to Boney,' they said, and drank their glasses dry.

'You will forgive me, sir, I hope,' said Dillon. 'I relieve the deck in half an hour, and I should like to check the quarter-bill first. I must thank you for a most enjoyable dinner.'

'Lord, what a pretty action that was,' said Jack, when the door was closed. 'A hundred and forty-six to fourteen; or fifteen if you count Mrs Dockray. It is just the kind of thing Nelson might have done – prompt – straight at 'em.'

'You know Lord Nelson, sir?'

'I had the honour of serving under him at the Nile,' said Jack, 'and of dining in his company twice.' His face broke into a smile at the recollection.

'May I beg you to tell me what kind of a man he is?'

'Oh, you would take to him directly, I am sure. He is very slight – frail – I could pick him up (I mean no disrespect) with one hand. But you know he is a very great man directly. There is something in philosophy called an electrical particle, is there not? A charged atom, if you follow me. He spoke to me on each occasion. The first time it was to say, "May I trouble you for the salt, sir?" – I have always said it as close as I can to his way ever since – you may have noticed it. But the second time I was trying to make my neighbour, a soldier, understand our naval tactics – weather-gage, breaking the line, and so on – and in a pause he leant over with such a smile and said, "Never mind manoeuvres, always go at them." I shall never forget it: never mind manoeuvres – always go at 'em. And at that same dinner he was telling us all how someone had offered him a boat-cloak on a cold night and he had said no, he was quite warm – his zeal for his King and country kept him warm. It sounds absurd, as I tell it, does it not? And was it another man, any other man, you would cry out "oh, what pitiful stuff" and dismiss it as mere enthusiasm; but with him you feel your bosom glow, and – now what in the devil's name is it, Mr Richards? Come in or out, there's a good fellow. Don't stand in the door like a God-damned Lenten cock.'

'Sir,' said the poor clerk, 'you said I might bring you the remaining papers before tea, and your tea is just coming up.'

'Well, well: so I did,' said Jack. 'God, what an infernal heap. Leave them here, Mr Richards. I will see to them before we reach Cagliari.'

'The top ones are those which Captain Allen left to be

written fair – they only need to be signed, sir,' said the clerk, backing out.

Jack glanced at the top of the pile, paused, then cried, 'There! There you are. Just so. There's the service for you from clew to earing – the Royal Navy, stock and fluke. You get into a fine flow of patriotic fervour – you are ready to plunge into the thick of the battle – and you are asked to sign this sort of thing.' He passed Stephen the carefully-written sheet.

His Majesty's Sloop *Sophie*
at sea

My Lord,

    I am to beg you will be pleased to order a Court Martial to be held on Isaac Wilson (seaman) belonging to the Sloop I have the honour to Command for having committed the unnatural Crime of Sodomy on a Goat, in the Goathouse, on the evening of March 16th.

    I have the Honour to remain, my Lord,

    Your Lordship's most obedient very humble servant

The Rt. Hon. Lord Keith, K.B., etc., etc.
Admiral of the Blue.

'It is odd how the law always harps upon the unnaturalness of sodomy,' observed Stephen. 'Though I know at least two judges who are pæderasts; and of course barristers . . . What will happen to him?'

'Oh, he'll be hanged. Run up at the yard-arm, and boats attending from every ship in the fleet.'

'That seems a little extreme.'

'Of course it is. Oh, what an infernal bore – witnesses going over to the flagship by the dozen, days lost . . . The *Sophie* a laughing-stock. Why will they report these things? The goat must be slaughtered – that's but fair – and it shall be served out to the mess that informed on him.'

'Could you not set them both ashore – on separate shores, if you have strong feelings on the moral issue – and sail quietly away?'

'Well,' said Jack, whose anger had died down. 'Perhaps there is something in what you propose. A dish of tea? You take milk, sir?'

'Goat's milk, sir?'

'Why, I suppose it is.'

'Perhaps without milk, then, if you please. You told me, I believe, that the gunner was ailing. Would this be a convenient time for seeing what I can do for him? Pray, which is the gun-room?'

'You would expect to find him there, would you not? But in fact his cabin is elsewhere nowadays. Killick will show you. The gun-room, in a sloop, is where the officers mess.'

In the gun-room itself the master stretched and said to the purser, 'Plenty of elbow-room now, Mr Ricketts.'

'Very true, Mr Marshall,' said the purser. 'We see great changes these days. And how they will work out I do not know.'

'Oh, I think they may answer well enough,' said Mr Marshall, slowly picking the crumbs off his waistcoat.

'All these capers,' went on the purser, in a low, dubious voice. 'The mainyard. The guns. The drafts he pretended to know nothing about. All these new hands there is not room for. The people at watch and watch. Charlie tells me there is a great deal of murmuring.' He jerked his head towards the men's quarters.

'I dare say there is. I dare say there is. All the old ways changed and all the old messes broken up. And I dare say we may be a little flighty, too, so young and fine with our brand-new epaulette. But if the steady old standing officers back him up, why, then I think it may answer well enough. The carpenter likes him. So does Watt, for he's a good seaman, and that's certain. And Mr Dillon seems to know his profession, too.'

'Maybe. Maybe,' said the purser, who knew the master's enthusiasms of old.

'And then again,' went on Mr Marshall, 'things may be a little more lively under the new proprietor. The men will like that, when they grow used to it; and so will the officers, I am sure. All that is wanted is for the standing officers to back him up, and it will be plain sailing.'

'What?' said the purser, cupping his ear, for Mr Dillon was having the guns moved, and amid the general rumbling thunder that accompanied this operation an occasional louder bang obliterated speech. Incidentally, it was this all-pervasive thunder that made their conversation possible, for in general there could be no such thing as private talk in a vessel twenty-six yards long, inhabited by ninety-one men, whose gun-room had even smaller apartments opening off it, screened by very thin wood and, indeed, sometimes by no more than canvas.

'Plain sailing. I say, if the officers back him up, it will all be plain sailing.'

'Maybe. But if they do not,' went on Mr Ricketts, 'if they do *not*, and if he persists in capers of this kind – which I believe it is his nature so to do – why then, I dare say he will exchange out of the old *Sophie* as quick as Mr Harvey did. For a brig is not a frigate, far less a ship of the line: you are right on top of your people, and they can give you hell or cause you to be broke as easy as kiss my hand.'

'You don't have to tell *me* a brig is not a frigate, nor yet a ship of the line, Mr Ricketts,' said the master.

'Maybe I don't have to tell you a brig is not a frigate, nor yet a ship of the line, Mr Marshall,' said the purser warmly. 'But when you have been at sea as long as I have, Mr Marshall, you will know there is a great deal more than mere seamanship required of a captain. Any damned tarpaulin can manage a ship in a storm,' he went on in a slighting voice, 'and any housewife in breeches can keep the decks clean and the falls just so; but it needs a headpiece' – tapping his own – 'and true bottom and steadiness, as well as conduct, to be the captain of a man-o'-war: and these are qualities not to be found in every Johnny-come-lately – nor in every Jack-lie-by-the-wall, neither,' he added, more or less to himself. 'I don't know, I'm sure.'

Chapter Four

The drum rolled and thundered at the *Sophie*'s hatchway. Feet came racing up from below, a desperate rushing sound that made even the tense drum-beat seem more urgent. But apart from the landmen's in the new draft, the men's faces were calm; for this was beating to quarters, an afternoon ritual that many of the crew had performed some two or three thousand times, each running to a particular place by one allotted gun or to a given set of ropes that he knew by heart.

No one could have called this a creditable performance, however. Much had been changed in the *Sophie*'s comfortable old routine; the manning of the guns was different; a score of worried, sheep-like landmen had to be pushed and pulled into something like the right place; and since most of the newcomers could not yet be allowed to do anything more than heave under guidance, the sloop's waist was so crowded that men trampled upon one another's toes.

Ten minutes passed while the *Sophie*'s people seethed about her upper deck and her fighting-tops: Jack stood watching placidly abaft the wheel while Dillon barked orders and the warrant-officers and midshipmen darted furiously about, aware of their captain's gaze and conscious that their anxiety was not improving anything at all. Jack had expected something of a shambles, though not anything quite so unholy as this; but his native good-humour and the delight of feeling even the inept stirring of this machine under his control overcame all other, more righteous, emotions.

'Why do they do this?' asked Stephen, at his elbow. 'Why do they run about so earnestly?'

'The idea is that every man shall know exactly where to go in action – in an emergency,' said Jack. 'It would never do if they had to stand pondering. The gun-teams are there at their stations already, you see; and so are Sergeant Quinn's marines, here. The foc's'le men are all there, as far as I can make out; and I dare say the waisters will be in order presently. A captain to each gun, do you see; and a sponger and boarder next to him – the man with the belt and cutlass; they join the boarding-party; and a sail-trimmer, who leaves the gun if we have to brace the yards round, for example, in action; and a fireman, the one with the bucket – his task is to dash out any fire that may start. Now there is Pullings reporting his division ready to Dillon. We shall not be long now.'

There were plenty of people on the little quarter-deck – the master at the con, the quartermaster at the wheel, the marine sergeant and his small-arms party, the signal midshipman, part of the afterguard, the gun-crews, James Dillon, the clerk, and still others – but Jack and Stephen paced up and down as though they were alone, Jack enveloped in the Olympian majesty of a captain and Stephen caught up within his aura. It was natural enough to Jack, who had known this state of affairs since he was a child, but it was the first time that Stephen had met with it, and it gave him a not altogether disagreeable sensation of waking death: either the absorbed, attentive men on the other side of the glass wall were dead, mere phantasmata, or he was – though in that case it was a strange little death, for although he was used to this sense of isolation, of being a colourless shade in a silent private underworld, he now had a companion, an audible companion.

'. . . your station, for example, would be below, in what we call the cockpit – not that it is a real cockpit, any more than that fo'c'sle is a real fo'c'sle, in the sense of being raised: but we *call* it the cockpit – with the midshipmen's sea-chests as your operating table and your instruments all ready.'

'Is that where I should live?'

'No, no. We shall fix you up with something better than that. Even when you come under the Articles of War,' said Jack with a smile, 'you will find that we still honour learning; at least to the extent of ten square feet of privacy, and as much fresh air on the quarter-deck as you may choose to breathe in.'

Stephen nodded. 'Tell me,' he said, in a low voice, some moments later. 'Were I under naval discipline, could that fellow have me whipped?' He nodded towards Mr Marshall.

'The master?' cried Jack, with inexpressible amazement.

'Yes,' said Stephen, looking attentively at him, with his head slightly inclined to the left.

'But he is the *master* . . .' said Jack. If Stephen had called the *Sophie*'s stem her stern, or her truck her keel, he would have understood the situation directly; but that Stephen should confuse the chain of command, the relative status of a captain and a master, of a commissioned officer and a warrant officer, so subverted the natural order, so undermined the sempiternal universe, that for a moment his mind could hardly encompass it. Yet Jack, though no great scholar, no judge of a hexameter, was tolerably quick, and after gasping no more than twice he said, 'My dear sir, I believe you have been led astray by the words *master* and *master and commander* – illogical terms, I must confess. The first is subordinate to the second. You must allow me to explain our naval ranks some time. But in any case you will never be flogged – no, no; *you* shall not be flogged,' he added, gazing with pure affection, and with something like awe, at so magnificent a prodigy, at an ignorance so very far beyond anything that even his wide-ranging mind had yet conceived.

James Dillon broke through the glass wall. 'Hands at quarters, sir, if you please,' he said, raising his three-corner hat.

'Very well, Mr Dillon,' said Jack. 'We will exercise the great guns.'

A four-pounder may not throw a very great weight of metal, and it not be able to pierce two feet of oak half a mile away, as a thirty-two-pounder can; but it does throw a solid three-inch cast-iron ball at a thousand feet a second, which is an ugly thing to receive; and the gun itself is a formidable machine. Its barrel is six feet long; it weighs twelve hundred-weight; it stands on a ponderous oak carriage; and when it is fired it leaps back as though it were violently alive.

The *Sophie* possessed fourteen of these, seven a side; and the two aftermost guns on the quarter-deck were gleaming brass. Each gun had a crew of four and a man or boy to bring up powder from the magazine. Each group of guns was in charge of a midshipman or a master's mate – Pullings had the six forward guns, Ricketts the four in the waist and Babbington the four farthest aft.

'Mr Babbington, where is this gun's powder horn?' asked Jack coldly.

'I don't know, sir,' stammered Babbington, very red. 'It seems to have gone astray.'

'Quarter-gunner,' said Jack, 'go to Mr Day – no, to his mate, for he is sick – and get another.' His inspection showed no other obvious shortcomings: but when he had had both broadsides run in and out half a dozen times – that is to say when the men had been through all the motions short of actually firing the guns – his face grew long and grave. They were quite extraordinarily slow. They had obviously been trained to fire nothing but whole broadsides at once – very little independent firing. They seemed quite happy with easing their guns gently up to the port at the rate of the slowest of them all: and the whole exercise had an artificial, wooden air. It was true that ordinary convoy-duty in a sloop did not give the men any very passionate conviction of the guns' vital reality, but even so . . . 'How I wish I could afford a few barrels of powder,' he thought, with a clear image of the gunner's accounts in his mind: forty-nine half barrels in all, seven under the *Sophie*'s full allowance; forty-one of the red, large grain, seven of them white, large grain – restored powder of doubtful strength – and one barrel of fine grain for priming. The barrels held forty-five pounds, so the *Sophie* would nearly empty one with each double broadside. 'But even so,' he went on, 'I think we can have a couple of rounds: God knows how long these charges have been lying in the guns. Besides,' he added in a voice within his inner voice – a voice from a far deeper level, 'think of the lovely smell.'

'Very well,' he said aloud. 'Mr Mowett, be so good as to go into my cabin. Sit down by the table-watch and take exact note of the time that elapses between the first and second discharge of each gun. Mr Pullings, we'll start with your division. Number one. Silence, fore and aft.'

Dead silence fell over the *Sophie*. The wind sang evenly in her taut weather-rigging, steady at two points abaft the beam. Number one's crew licked their lips nervously. Their gun was in its ordinary position of rest, bowsed up tight against its port and lashed there – put away, as it were.

'Cast loose your gun.'

They cast loose the tackles that held the gun hard against the side and cut the spun-yarn frapping that clenched the breeching to hold it firmer still. With a gentle squeal of trucks the gun showed that it was free: a man held each side-tackle, or the *Sophie*'s heel (which made the rear-tackle unnecessary) would have brought the gun inboard before the next word of command.

'Level your gun.'

The sponger pushed his handspike under the thick breech of the gun and with a quick heave levered it up, while number one's captain thrust the wooden wedge more than half-way under, bringing the barrel to the horizontal point-blank position.

'Out tompion.'

They let the gun run in fast: the breeching checked its inward course when the muzzle was a foot or so inboard: the sail-trimmer whipped out the carved and painted tompion that plugged it.

'Run out your gun.'

Clapping on to the side-tackles they heaved her up hand over hand, running the carriage hard against the side and coiling the falls, coiling them down in wonderfully neat little fakes.

'Prime.'

The captain took his priming-iron, thrust it down the touch-hole and pierced the flannel cartridge lying within the gun, poured fine powder from his horn into the open vent and on to the pan, bruising it industriously with the nozzle. The sponger put the flat of his hand over the powder to prevent its blowing away, and the fireman slung the horn behind his back.

'Point your gun.' And to this order Jack added, 'As she lies,' since he wished to add no complications of traversing or elevating for range at this stage. Two of the gun's crew were now holding the side tackles: the sponger knelt on one side with his head away from the gun, blowing gently on the smouldering slow-match he had taken from its little tub (for the *Sophie* did not run to flintlocks): the powder-boy stood with the next cartridge in its leather box over on the starboard side directly behind the gun: the captain, holding his vent-bit and sheltering the priming, bent over the gun, staring along its barrel.

'Fire.'

The slow-match whipped across. The captain stubbed it hard down on to the priming. For an infinitesimal spark of time there was a hissing, a flash, and then the gun went off with the round, satisfying bang of a pound and more of hard-rammed powder exploding in a confined space. A stab of crimson flame in the smoke, flying morsels of wad, the gun shooting eight feet backwards under the arched body of its captain and between the members of its crew, the deep twang of the breeching as it brought up the recoil – all these were virtually inseparable in time; and before they were over the next order came.

'Stop your vent,' cried Jack, watching for the flight of the ball as the white smoke raced streaming down to leeward. The captain stabbed his vent-piece into the touch-hole; and the ball sent up a fleeting plume in the choppy sea four hundred yards to windward, then another and another, ducks and drakes for fifty yards before it sank. The crew clapped on to the rear-tackle to hold the gun firmly inboard against the roll.

'Sponge your gun.'

The sponger darted his sheepskin swab into the fireman's bucket, and pushing his face into the narrow space between the muzzle and the side he shot the handle out of the port and thrust the swab down the bore of the gun: he twirled it conscientiously and brought it out, blackened, with a little smoking rag on it.

'Load with cartridge.'

The powder-boy had the tight cloth bag there ready: the sponger entered it and rammed it hard down. The captain, with his priming-iron in the vent to feel for its arrival, cried, 'Home!'

'Shot your gun.'

The ball was there to hand in its garland, and the wad in its cheese; but an unlucky slip sent the ball trundling across the deck towards the fore-hatch, with the anxious captain, sponger and powder-boy following its erratic course. Eventually it joined the cartridge, with the wad rammed down over it, and Jack cried, 'Run out your gun. – Prime. – Point your gun. – Fire. Mr Mowett,' he called, through the cabin skylight, 'what was the interval?'

'Three minutes and three-quarters, sir.'

'Oh dear, oh dear,' said Jack, almost to himself. There were no words in the vocabulary at his command to express his distress. Pullings' division looked apprehensive and ashamed: number three gun-crew had stripped to the waist and had tied their handkerchiefs round their heads against the flash and the thunder: they were spitting on their hands, and Mr Pullings himself was fussing anxiously about with the crows, handspikes and swabs.

'Silence. Cast loose your gun. Level your gun. Out tompion. Run out your gun . . .'

This time it was rather better – just over three minutes.

But then they had not dropped their shot and Mr Pullings had helped run up the gun and haul on the rear-tackle, gazing absently into the sky as he did so, to prove that he was not in fact there at all.

As the firing came aft gun by gun, so Jack's melancholy increased. One and three had not been unlucky bands of bobbies: this was the *Sophie*'s true average rate of fire. Archaic. Antediluvian. And if there had been any question of aiming, of traversing the guns, heaving them round with crows and handspikes, it would have been even slower. Number five would not fire, damp having got at the powder, and the gun had to be wormed and drawn. That could happen in any ship: but it was a pity that it also occurred twice in the starboard broadside.

The *Sophie* had come up into the wind to fire her starboard guns, out of a certain delicacy about shooting at random into her convoy, and she was lying there, pitching easily with almost no way on her, while the last damp charge was being extracted, when Stephen, feeling that in this lull he might without impropriety address the captain, said to Jack, 'Pray tell me why those ships are so very close together. Are they conversing – rendering one another mutual assistance?' He pointed over the neat wall of hammocks in the quarter-netting: Jack followed his finger and gazed for an unbelieving second at the rearmost vessel in his convoy, the *Dorthe Engelbrechtsdatter*, the Norwegian cat.

'Hands to the braces,' he shouted. 'Port your helm. Flat in for'ard – jump to it. Brail up the mainsail.'

Slowly, then faster and faster with all the wind in her sharp-braced headsails, the *Sophie* paid off. Now the wind was on her port beam: a few moments later she was right before it, and in still another moment she steadied on her course, with the wind three points on her starboard quarter. There had been a good deal of trampling to and fro, with Mr Watt and his mates roaring and piping like fury, but the Sophies were better hands with a sail than a gun, and quite soon Jack could cry, 'Square mains'l. Topmast stuns'ls. Mr

Watt, the top-chains and puddening – but I need not tell you what to do, I see.'

'Aye aye, sir,' said the bosun, clanking away aloft, already loaded with the chains that were to prevent the yards falling in action.

'Mowett, run up with a glass and tell me what you see. Mr Dillon, you'll not forget that look-out? We'll have the hide off him tomorrow, if he lives to see it. Mr Lamb, you have your shot-plugs ready?'

'Ready, aye ready, sir,' said the carpenter, smiling, for this was not a serious question.

'Deck!' hailed Mowett, high above the taut, straining canvas. 'Deck! She's an Algerine – a quarter-galley. They've boarded the cat. They have not carried her yet. I think the Norwegians are holding out in their close-quarters.'

'Anything to windward?' called Jack.

In the pause that followed the peevish crackling of pistols could be heard from the Norwegian, struggling faintly up through the streaming of the wind.

'Yes, sir. A sail. A lateen. Hull down in the wind's eye. I can't make her out for sure. Standing east . . . standing due east, I think.'

Jack nodded, looking up and down his two broadsides. He was a big man at any time, but now he seemed to be at least twice his usual size; his eyes were shining in an extraordinary manner, as blue as the sea, and a continuous smile showed a gleam across the lively scarlet of his face. Something of the same change had come over the *Sophie*; with her big new square mainsail and her topsails immensely broadened by the studdingsails at either side of them she, like her master and commander, seemed to have doubled in size as she tore heavily through the sea. 'Well, Mr Dillon,' he cried, 'this is a bit of luck, is it not?'

Stephen, looking at them curiously, saw that the same extraordinary animation had seized upon James Dillon – indeed, the whole crew was filled with a strange ebullience. Close by him the marines were checking the flints of their muskets, and one of them was polishing the buckle of his cross-belt, breathing on it and laughing happily between the carefully-directed breaths.

'Yes, sir,' said James Dillon. 'It could not have fallen more happily.'

'Signal the convoy to haul two points to larboard and to reduce sail. Mr Richards, have you noted the time? You must carefully note the time of everything. But, Dillon, what can the fellow be thinking of? Did he suppose we were engaged? Blind? However, this is not time to ... We will board, of course, if only the Norwegians can hold out long enough. I hate firing into a galley, in any event. I believe you may have all our pistols and cutlasses served out. Now, Mr Marshall,' he said, turning to the master, who was at his action-station by the wheel, and who was now responsible for sailing the *Sophie*, 'I want you to lay us alongside that damned Moor. You may set the lower-stuns'ls if she will bear them.' At this moment the gunner crept up the ladder. 'Well, Mr Day,' said Jack, 'I am happy to see you on deck. Are you a little better?'

'Much better, sir, I thank you,' said Mr Day, 'thanks to the gentleman' – nodding towards Stephen. 'It worked,' he said, directing his voice towards the taffrail. 'I just thought I'd report as I was in my place, sir.'

'Glad of it – I'm very glad of it. This is a bit of luck, master-gunner, I believe?' said Jack.

'Why, so it is, sir – it worked, Doctor: it worked, sir, like a maiden's dream. – So it is,' said the gunner, looking complacently over the mile or so of sea at the *Dorthe Engelbrechtsdatter* and the corsair, at the *Sophie*, with all her guns warm, freshly-loaded, run out, perfectly ready, her crew on tip-toe and her decks cleared for action.

'Here we were exercising,' went on Jack, almost to himself. 'And that impudent dog rowed up-wind on the far side and made a snatch at the cat – what can he be thinking of? – and would be running off with her now if our good doctor had not brought us to our senses.'

'Never was such a doctor, is my belief,' said the gunner. 'Now I fancy I had best get down into my magazine, sir. We've not all that much powder filled; and I dare say you'll be calling for a tidy parcel, ha, ha, ha!'

'My dear sir,' said Jack to Stephen, measuring the *Sophie*'s increasing speed and the distance that separated her from the embattled cat – in this state of triply intensified vitality he could perfectly well calculate, talk to Stephen and revolve a thousand shifting variables all at once – 'my dear sir, do you choose to go below or should you rather stay on deck? Perhaps it would divert you to go to into the maintop with a musket, along with the sharpshooters, and have a bang at the villains?'

'No, no, no,' said Stephen. 'I deprecate violence. My part is to heal rather than to kill; or at least to kill with kindly intent. Pray let me take my place, my station, in the cockpit.'

'I hoped you would say that,' said Jack, shaking him by the hand. 'I had not liked to suggest it to my guest, however. It will comfort the men amazingly – all of us, indeed. Mr Ricketts, show Dr Maturin the cockpit. And give the loblolly boy a hand with the chests.'

A sloop with the depth of a mere ten feet ten inches cannot rival a ship of the line for dank airless obscurity below; but the *Sophie* did astonishingly well, and Stephen was obliged to call for another lantern to check and lay out his instruments and the meagre store of bandages, lint, tourniquets and pledgets. He was sitting there with Northcote's *Marine Practice* held close to the light, carefully reading '. . . having divided the skin, order the same assistant to draw it up as much as possible; then cut through the flesh and bones circularly,' when Jack came down. He had put on Hessian boots and his sword, and he was carrying a pair of pistols.

'May I use the room next door?' asked Stephen, adding in Latin, so that he might not be understood by the loblolly boy, 'it might discourage the patients, were they to see me consulting my printed authorities.'

'Cerainly, certainly,' cried Jack, riding straight over the

Latin. 'Anything you like. I will leave these with you. We shall board, if ever we can come up with them; and then, you know, they may try to board us – there's no telling – these damned Algerines are usually crammed with men. Cut-throat dogs, every one of 'em,' he added, laughing heartily and vanishing into the gloom.

Jack had only been below a very short while, but by the time he returned to the quarter-deck the situation had entirely changed. The Algerines were in command of the cat: she was falling off before the northerly wind; they were setting her crossjack, and it was clear that they hoped to get away with her. The galley lay in its own length away from her, on her starboard quarter: it lay there motionless on its oars, fourteen great sweeps a side, headed directly towards the *Sophie*, with its huge lateen sails brailed up loosely to the yards – a long, low, slim vessel, longer than the *Sophie* but much slighter and narrower: obviously very fast and obviously in enterprising hands. It had a singularly lethal, reptilian air. Its intention was clearly either to engage the *Sophie* or at least to delay her until the prize-crew should have run the cat a mile or so down the wind towards the safety of the coming night.

The distance was now a little over a quarter of a mile, and with a smooth continuous flow the relative positions were perpetually changing: the cat's speed was increasing, and in four or five minutes she was a cable's length to the leeward of the galley, which still lay there on its oars.

A fleeting cloud of smoke appeared in the galley's bows, a ball hummed overhead, at about the level of the topmast crosstrees, followed in half a heart's beat by the deep boom of the gun that had fired it. 'Note down the time, Mr Richards,' said Jack to the pale clerk – the nature of his pallor had changed and his eyes were starting from his head. Jack hurried forward, just in time to see the flash of the galley's second gun. With an enormous smithy-noise the ball struck the fluke of the *Sophie*'s best bower anchor, bent it half over and glanced off into the sea far behind.

'An eighteen-pounder,' observed Jack to the bosun, standing there at his post on the fo'c'sle. 'Maybe even a twenty-four. Oh, for my long twelves,' he added inwardly. The galley had no broadside, naturally, but mounted her guns fore and aft: in his glass Jack could see that the forward battery consisted of two heavy guns, a smaller one and some swivels; and, of course, the *Sophie* would be exposed to their raking fire throughout her approach. The swivels were firing now, a high sharp cracking noise.

Jack returned to the quarter-deck. 'Silence fore and aft,' he cried through the low, excited murmur. 'Silence. Cast loose your guns. Level your guns. Out tompions. Run out your guns. Mr Dillon, they are to be trained as far for'ard as possible. Mr Babbington, tell the gunner the next round will be chain.' An eighteen-pound ball hit the *Sophie*'s side between the larboard number one and three guns, sending in a shower of sharp-edged splintered wood, some pieces two feet long, and heavy: it continued its course along the crowded deck, knocked down a marine and struck against the mainmast, its force almost spent. A dismal 'Oh oh oh' showed that some of the splinters had done their work, and a moment later two seamen hurried by, carrying their mate below, leaving a trail of blood as they went.

'Are those guns trained round?' cried Jack.

'All hard round sir,' came the reply after a gasping pause.

'Starboard broadside first. Fire as they bear. Fire high. Fire for the masts. Right, Mr Marshall, over she goes.'

The *Sophie* yawed forty-five degrees off her course, presenting quarter of her starboard side to the galley, which instantly sent another eighteen-pound ball into it amidships, just above the water-line, its deep resonant impact surprising Stephen Maturin as he put a ligature round William Musgrave's spouting femoral artery, almost making him miss the loop. But now the *Sophie*'s guns were bearing, and the starboard broadside went off on two successive rolls: the sea beyond the galley spat up in white plumes and the *Sophie*'s deck swirled with smoke, acrid, piercing gunpowder smoke.

As the seventh gun fired Jack cried, 'Over again,' and the *Sophie*'s head came round for the larboard broadside. The eddying cloud cleared under her lee: Jack saw the galley fire its whole forward battery and leap into motion under the power of its oars to avoid the *Sophie*'s fire. The galley fired high, on the upward roll, and one of its balls severed the maintopmast stay and struck a great lump of wood from the cap. The lump, rebounding from the top, fell on to the gunner's head just as he put it up through the main hatchway.

'Lively with those starboard guns,' cried Jack. 'Helm amidships.' He meant to bring the sloop back on to the port tack, for if he could manage to get in another starboard broadside he would catch the galley as it was moving across from left to right. A muffled roar from number four gun and a terrible shrieking: in his haste the sponger had not fully cleared the gun and now the fresh charge had gone off in his face as he rammed it down. They dragged him clear, re-sponged, re-loaded the gun and ran it up. But the whole manoeuvre had been too slow: the whole starboard battery had been too slow: the galley was round again – it could spin like a top, with all those oars backing water – and it was speeding away to the south-west with the wind on its starboard quarter and its great lateen sails spread on either side – set in hares' ears, as they say. The cat was now standing south-east; it was half a mile away already, and their courses were diverging fast. The yawing had taken a surprising amount of time – had lost a surprising amount of distance.

'Port half a point,' said Jack, standing on the lee-rail and staring very hard at the galley, which was almost directly ahead of the *Sophie*, a little over a hundred yards away, and gaining. 'Topgallant stuns'ls. Mr Dillon, get a gun into the bows, if you please. We still have the twelve-pounder's ring-bolts.'

As far as he could see they had done the galley no harm: firing low would have meant firing straight into benches packed tight with Christian rowers chained to the oars; firing high . . . His head jerked sideways, his hat darted across the deck: a musket-ball from the corsair had nicked his ear. It was perfectly numb under his investigating hand, and it was pouring with blood. He stepped down from the rail, craning his head out sideways to bleed to windward, while his right hand sheltered his precious epaulette from the flow. 'Killick,' he shouted, bending to keep his eyes on the galley under the taut arch of the square mainsail, 'bring me an old coat and another handkerchief.' Throughout his changing he gazed piercingly at the galley, which had fired twice with its single after gun, both shots going a very little wide. 'Lord, they run that twelve-pounder in and out briskly,' he reflected. The topgallant studdingsails were sheeted home; the *Sophie*'s pace increased; now she was gaining perceptibly. Jack was not the only one to notice this, and a cheer went up from the fo'c'sle, running down the larboard side as the gun-crews heard the news.

'The bow-chaser is ready, sir,' said James Dillon, smiling. 'Are you all right, sir?' he asked, seeing Jack's bloody hand and neck.

'A scratch – nothing at all,' said Jack. 'What do you make of the galley?'

'We're gaining on her, sir,' said Dillon, and although he spoke quietly there was an extraordinarily fierce exultation in his voice. He had been shockingly upset by Stephen's sudden appearance, and although his innummerable present duties had kept him from much consecutive thought, the whole of his mind, apart from its immediate forefront, was filled with unvoiced concern, distress and dark incoherent nightmare shadows: he looked forward to the turmoil on the galley's deck with a wild longing.

'She's spilling her wind,' said Jack. 'Look at that sly villain by the mainsheet. Take my glass.'

'No, sir. Surely not,' said Dillon, angrily clapping the telescope shut.

'Well,' said Jack, 'well . . .' A twelve-pounder ball passed through the *Sophie*'s starboard lower studdingsails – two holes, precisely behind each other, and hummed along four or five feet from them, a visible blur, just skimming the hammocks. 'We could do with one or two of their gunners,' observed Jack. 'Masthead!' he hailed.

'Sir?' came the distant voice.

'What do you make of the sail to windward?'

'Bearing up, sir, bearing up for the head of the convoy.'

Jack nodded. 'Let the captains of the bow guns and the quartergunners serve the chaser. I'll lay her myself.'

'Pring is dead, sir. Another captain?'

'Make it so, Mr Dillon.'

He walked up forward. 'Shall we catch 'un, sir?' asked a grizzled seaman, one of the big boarding-party, with the pleasant friendliness of crisis.

'I hope so, Cundall, I hope so indeed,' said Jack. 'At least we shall have a bang at him.'

'That dog,' he said to himself, staring along the dispart-sight at the Algerine's deck. He felt the first beginning of the upward roll under the *Sophie*'s forefoot, snapped the match down on to the touch-hole, heard the hiss and the shattering crash and the shriek of trucks as the gun recoiled.

'Huzzay, huzzay!' roared the men on the fo'c'sle. It was no more than a hole in the galley's mainsail, about half-way up, but it was the first blow they had managed to get home. Three more shots; and they heard one strike something metallic in the galley's stern.

'Carry on, Mr Dillon,' said Jack, straightening. 'Light along my glass, there.'

The sun was so low now that it was difficult to see as he stood balancing to the sea, shading his object-glass with his far hand and concentrating with all his power on two red-turbanned figures behind the galley's stern-chaser. A musketoon-ball struck the *Sophie*'s starboard knighthead and he heard a seaman rip out a string of furious obscenity. 'John Lakey copped it something cruel,' said a low voice close behind him. 'In the ballocks.' The gun went off at his side, but before its smoke hid the galley from him he had made up his mind. The Algerine was, in fact, spilling his wind – starting his sheets so that his sails, apparently full, were not really drawing with their whole force: that was why the poor old fat heavy dirty-bottomed *Sophie*, labouring furiously and on the very edge of carrying everything away, was gaining slightly on the slim, deadly, fine-cut galley. The Algerine was leading him on – could, in fact, run away at any moment. Why? To draw him far to the leeward of the cat, that was why: together with the real possibility of dis-masting him, raking him at leisure (being independent of the wind) and making a prize of the *Sophie* as well. To draw him to the leeward of the convoy, too, so that the sail to windward might snap up half a dozen of them. He glanced over his left shoulder at the cat. Even if she were to go about they would still fetch her in one board, close-hauled, for she was a very slow creature – no topgallants and, of course, no royals – far slower than the *Sophie*. But in a very little while, on this course and at this pace, he would never be able to reach her except by beating up, tack upon tack, with the darkness coming fast. It would not do. His duty was clear enough: the unwelcome choice, as usual. And this was the time for decision.

''Vast firing,' he said as the gun ran in. 'Starboard broad-side: ready, now. Sergeant Quinn, look to the small-arms men. When we have her dead on the beam, aim for her cabin abaft the rowers' benches, right low. Fire at the word of command.' As he turned and ran back to the quarter-deck he caught a look from James Dillon's powder-blackened face, a look if not of anger or something worse, then at least of bitter contrariety. 'Hands to the braces,' he called, mentally dismissing that as something for another day. 'Mr Marshall, lay her for the cat.' He heard the men's groan – a universal exhalation of disappointment – and said, 'Hard over.'

'We'll catch him unaware and give him something to remember the *Sophie* by,' he added, to himself, standing directly behind the starboard brass four-pounder. At this speed the *Sophie* came round very fast: he crouched, half-bent, not breathing, all his being focused along the central gleam of brass and the turning seascape beyond it. The *Sophie* turned, turned; the galley's oars started into furious motion, churning up the sea, but it was too late. A tenth of a second before he had the galley dead on the beam and just before the *Sophie* reached the middle of her downward roll he cried 'Fire!' and the *Sophie*'s broadside went off as crisply as a ship of the line's, together with every musket aboard. The smoke cleared and a cheer went up, for there was a gaping hole in the galley's side and the Moors were running to and fro in disorder and dismay. In his glass Jack could see the stern-chaser dismounted and several bodies lying on the deck: but the miracle had not happened – he had neither knocked her rudder away nor holed her disastrously below the water-line. However, there was no further trouble to be expected from her, he reflected, turning his attention from the galley to the cat.

'Well, Doctor,' he said, appearing in the cockpit, 'how are you getting along?'

'Tolerably well, I thank you. Has the battle begun again?'

'Oh, no. That was only a shot across the cat's bows. The galley is hull-down in the south-south-west and Dillon has just taken a boat across to set the Norwegians free – the Moors have hung out a white shirt and called for quarter. The damned rogues.'

'I am happy to hear it. It is really impossible to sew one's flaps neatly with the jarring of the guns. May I see your ear?'

'It was only a passing flick. How are your patients?'

'I believe I may answer for four or five of them. The man with the terrible incision in his thigh – they tell me it was a splinter of wood: can this be true?'

'Yes, indeed. A great piece of hard sharp-edged oak flying through the air will cut you up amazingly. It often happens.'

'– has responded remarkably well; and I have patched up the poor fellow with the burn. Do you know that the rammer was actually thrust right through between the head of the biceps, just missing the ulnar nerve? But I cannot deal with the gunner down here – not in this light.'

'The gunner? What's amiss with the gunner? I thought you had cured him?'

'So I had. Of the grossest self-induced costiveness it has ever been my privilege to see, caused by a frantic indulgence in Peruvian bark – self-administered Peruvian bark. But this is a depressed cranial fracture, sir, and I must use the trephine: here he lies – you notice the characteristic stertor? – and I think he is safe until the morning. But as soon as the sun is up I must have off the top of his skull with my little saw. You will see the gunner's brain, my dear sir,' he added with a smile. 'Or at least his dura mater.'

'Oh dear, oh dear,' murmured Jack. Deep depression was settling on him – anticlimax – such a bloody little engagement for so little – two good men killed – the gunner almost certainly dead – no man could survive having his brain opened, that stood to reason – and the others might easily die too – they so often did. If it had not been for that damned convoy he might have had the galley – two could play at that game. 'Now what's to do?' he cried, as a clamour broke out on deck.

'They're carrying on very old-fashioned aboard the cat, sir,' said the master as Jack reached the quarter-deck in the twilight. The master came from some far northern part – Orkney, Shetland – and either that or a natural defect in his speech caused him to pronounce *er* as *ar*: a peculiarity that grew more marked in time of stress. 'It looks as though those infernal buggars were cutting their capars again, sir.'

'Put her alongside, Mr Marshall. Boarders, come along with me.'

The *Sophie* braced round her yards to avoid any more damage, backed her fore-topsail and glided evenly along the cat's side. Jack reached out for the main channels on the

Norwegian's high side and swung himself up through the wrecked boarding netting, followed by a grim and savage-looking band. Blood on the deck: three bodies: five ashy Moors pressed against the roundhouse bulkhead under the protection of James Dillon: the dumb Negro Alfred King with a boarder's axe in his hand.

'Get those prisoners across,' said Jack. 'Stow them in the forehold. What's to do, Mr Dillon?'

'I can't quite make him out, sir, but I think the prisoners must have attacked King between decks.'

'Is that what happened, King?'

The Negro was still glaring about – his mates held his arms – and his answer might have meant anything.

'Is that what happened, Williams?' asked Jack.

'Don't know, sir,' said Williams, touching his hat and looking glassy.

'Is that what happened, Kelly?'

'Don't know, sir,' said Kelly, with a knuckle to his forehead and the same look to a hairsbreadth.

'Where's the cat's master, Mr Dillon?'

'Sir, it seems the Moors tossed them all overboard.'

'Good God,' cried Jack. Yet the thing was not uncommon. An angry noise behind him showed that the news had reached the *Sophie*. 'Mr Marshall,' he called, going to the rail, 'take care of these prisoners, will you? I will not have any foolery.' He looked up and down the deck, up and down the rigging: very little damage. 'You will bring her in to Cagliari, Mr Dillon,' he said in a low voice, quite upset by the savagery of the thing. 'Take what men you need.'

He returned to the *Sophie*, very grave, very grave. Yet he had scarcely reached his own quarter-deck before a minute, discreditable voice within said, 'In that case she's a prize, you know, not just a rescue.' He frowned it down, called for the bosun and began a tour of the brig, deciding the order of the more urgent repairs. She had suffered surprisingly for a short engagement in which not more than fifty shots had been exchanged – she was a floating example of what superior gunnery could do. The carpenter and two of his crew were over the side in cradles, trying to plug a hole very near the water-line.

'I can't rightly come at 'un, sir,' said Mr Lamb, in answer to Jack's inquiry. 'We'm half drowned, but we can't seem to bang 'un home, not on this tack.'

'We'll put her about for you, then, Mr Lamb. But let me know the minute she's plugged.' He glanced over the darkening sea at the cat, now taking her place in the convoy once more: going about would mean travelling right away from the cat, and the cat had grown strangely dear to his heart. 'Loaded with spars, Stettin oak, tow, Stockholm tar, cordage,' continued that inner voice eagerly. 'She might easily fetch two or three thousand – even four . . .' 'Yes, Mr Watt, certainly,' he said aloud. They climbed into the maintop and gazed at the injured cap.

'That was the bit that done poor Mr Day's business for him,' said the bosun.

'So that was it? A devilish great lump indeed. But we must not give up hope. Dr Maturin is going to – going to do something prodigious clever with a saw, as soon as there is light. He needs light for it – something uncommonly skil-ful, I dare say.'

'Oh, yes, I'm sure, sir,' cried the bosun warmly. 'A very clever gentleman he must be, no question. The men are wonderfully pleased. "How kind," they say, "to saw off Ned Evans' leg so trim, and to sew up John Lakey's private parts so neat; as well as all the rest; he being, so to speak, on leave – a visitor, like."'

'It *is* handsome,' said Jack. 'It is very handsome, I agree. We'll need a kind of gammoning here, Mr Watt, until the carpenter can attend to the cap. Hawsers bowsed as tight as can be, and God help us if we have to strike topmasts.'

They saw to half a dozen other points and Jack climbed down, paused to count his convoy – very close and orderly now after its fright – and went below. As he let himself sink on to the long cushioned locker he found that he was in the act of saying 'Carry three,' for his mind was busily working out three eighths of £3,500 – it had now fixed upon this sum as the worth of the *Dorthe Engelbrechtsdatter*. For three-eighths (less one of them for the admiral) was to be his share of the proceeds. Nor was his the only mind to be busy with figures, by any means, for every other man on the *Sophie*'s books was entitled to share – Dillon and the master, an eighth between them; the surgeon (if the *Sophie* had officially borne one on her books), bosun, carpenter and master's mates, another eighth; then the midshipmen, the inferior warrant officers and the marine sergeant another eighth, while the rest of the ship's company shared the remaining quarter. And it was wonderful to see how briskly minds not given to abstract thought rattled these figures, these symbols, up and down, coming out with the acting yeoman of the sheets' share correct to the nearest farthing. He reached for a pencil to do the sum properly, felt ashamed, pushed it aside, hesitated, took it up again and wrote the figures very small, diagonally upon the corner of a leaf, thrusting the paper quickly from him at a knock on the door. It was the still-moist carpenter, coming to report the shot-holes plugged, and no more than eighteen inches of water in the well, 'which is less nor half what I expected, with that nasty rough stroke the galley give us, firing from so low down'. He paused, giving Jack an odd, sideways-looking glance.

'Well, that's capital, Mr Lamb,' said Jack, after a moment.

But the carpenter did not stir; he stood there dripping on the painted sailcloth squares, making a little pool at last. Then he burst out, 'Which, if it is true about the cat, and the poor Norwegians dumped overboard – perhaps wounded, too, which makes you right mad, as being mere cruelty – what harm would they do if battened down? How-soever, the warrant officers of the *Sophie* would wish the gentleman' – jerking his head towards the night-cabin, Stephen Maturin's temporary dwelling-place – 'cut in on their share, fair do's, as a mark of – as an acknowledgement of – his conduct considered very handsome by all hands.'

'If you please, sir,' said Babbington, 'the cat's signalling.'

On the quarter-deck Jack saw that Dillon had run up a motley hoist – obviously all the *Dorthe Engelbrechtsdatter* possessed – stating, among other things, that he had the plague aboard and that he was about to sail.

'Hands to wear ship,' he called. And when the *Sophie* had run down to within a cable's length of the convoy he hailed, 'Cat ahoy!'

'Sir,' came Dillon's voice over the intervening sea, 'you will be pleased to hear the Norwegians are all safe.'

'What?'

'The – Norwegians – are – all – safe.' The two vessels came closer. 'They hid in a secret place in the forepeak – in the forepeak,' went on Dillon.

'Oh, – their forepeak,' muttered the quartermaster at the wheel; for the *Sophie* was all ears – a very religious hush.

'Full and by!' cried Jack angrily, as the topsails shivered under the influence of the quartermaster's emotion. 'Keep her full and by.'

'Full and by it is, sir.'

'And the master says,' continued the distant voice, 'could we send a surgeon aboard, because one of his men hurt his toe hurrying down the ladder.'

'Tell the master, from me,' cried Jack, in a voice that reached almost to Cagliari, his face purple with effort and furious indignation, 'tell the master that he can take his man's toe and – with it.'

He stumped below, £875 the poorer, and looking thoroughly sour and disagreeable.

This, however, was not an expression that his features wore easily, or for long; and when he stepped into the cutter to go aboard the admiral in Genoa roads his face was quite restored to its natural cheerfulness. It was rather grave, of course, for a visit to the formidable Lord Keith, Admiral of the Blue and Commander-in-Chief in the Mediterranean, was no laughing matter. His gravity, as he sat there in the stern-sheets, very carefully washed, shaved and dressed, affected his coxswain and the cutter's crew, and they rowed soberly along, keeping their eyes primly inboard. Yet even so they were going to reach the flagship too early, and Jack, looking at his watch, desired them to pull round the *Audacious* and lie on their oars. From here he could see the whole bay, with five ships of the line and four frigates two or three miles from the land, and inshore of them a swarm of gunboats and mortar-vessels; they were steadily bombarding the noble city that rose steeply in a sweeping curve at the head of the bay – lying there in a cloud of smoke of their own making, lobbing bombs into the close-packed buildings on the far side of the distant mole. The boats were small in the distance; the houses, churches and palaces were smaller still (though quite distinct in that sweet transparent air), like toys; but the continuous rumbling of the fire, and the deeper reply of the French artillery on shore, was strangely close at hand, real and menacing.

The necessary ten minutes passed; the *Sophie*'s cutter approached the flag-ship; and in answer to the hail of Boat ahoy the coxswain answered *Sophie*, meaning that her captain was aboard. Jack went up the side in due form, saluted the quarter-deck, shook hands with Captain Louis and was shown to the admiral's cabin.

He had every reason to be pleased with himself – he had taken his convoy to Cagliari without loss; he had brought up another to Leghorn; and he was here at exactly the appointed time, in spite of calms off Monte Cristo – but for all that he was remarkably nervous, and his mind was so full of Lord Keith that when he saw no admiral in that beautiful great light-filled cabin but only a well-rounded young woman with her back to the window, he gaped like any carp.

'Jacky, dear,' said the young woman, 'how beautiful you are, all dressed up. Let me put your neck-cloth straight, La, Jackie, you look as frightened as if I were a Frenchman.'

'Queeney! Old Queeney!' cried Jack, squeezing her and giving her a most affectionate smacking kiss.

'God damn and blast – a luggit corpis sweenie,' cried a furious Scotch voice, and the admiral walked in from the quarter-gallery. Lord Keith was a tall grey man with a fine leonine head, and his eyes shot blazing sparks of rage.

'This is the young man I told you about, Admiral,' said Queeney, patting poor pale Jack's black stock into place and waving a ring at him. 'I used to give him his bath and take him into my bed when he had bad dreams.'

This might not have been thought the very best possible recommendation to a newly-married admiral of close on sixty, but it seemed to answer. 'Oh,' said the admiral. 'Yes. I was forgetting. Forgive me. I have such a power of captains, and some of them are very mere rakes . . .'

' "And some of them are very mere rakes," says he, piercing me through and through with that damned cold eye of his,' said Jack, filling Stephen's glass and spreading himself comfortably along the locker. 'And I was morally certain that he recognized me from the only three times we were in company – and each time worse than the last. The first was at the Cape, in the old *Reso*, when I was a midshipman: he was Captain Elphinstone then. He came aboard just two minutes after Captain Douglas had turned me before the mast and said, "What's yon wee snotty bairn a-greeting at?" And Captain Douglas said, "That wretched boy is a perfect young whoremonger; I have turned him before the mast, to learn him his duty." '

'Is that a more convenient place to learn it?' said Stephen.

'Well, it is easier for them to teach you deference,' said Jack, smiling, 'for they can seize you to a grating at the gangway and flog the liver and lights out of you with the cat. It means disrating a midshipman – degrading him, so that he is no longer what we call a young gentleman but a common sailor. He becomes a common sailor; he berths and messes with them; and he can be knocked about by anyone with a cane or a starter in his hand, as well as being flogged. I never thought he would really do it, although he had

137

threatened me with it often enough; for he was a friend of my father's and I thought he had a kindness for me – which indeed he did. But, however, he carried it out, and there I was, turned before the mast: and he kept me there six months before rating me midshipman again. I was grateful to him in the end, because I came to understand the lower deck through and through – they were wonderfully kind to me, on the whole. But at the time I bawled like a calf – wept like any girl, ha, ha, ha.'

'What made him take so decided a step?'

'Oh, it was over a girl, a likely black girl called Sally,' said Jack. 'She came off in a bum-boat and I hid her in the cable-tier. But Captain Douglas and I had disagreed about a good many other things – obedience, mostly, and getting out of bed in the morning, and respect for the schoolmaster (we had a schoolmaster aboard, a drunken sot named Pitt) and a dish of tripe. Then the second time Lord Keith saw me was when I was fifth of the *Hannibal* and our first lieutenant was that damned fool Carrol – if there's one thing I hate more than being on shore it's being under the orders of a damned fool that is no seaman. He was so offensive, so designedly offensive, over a trivial little point of discipline that I was obliged to ask him whether he would like to meet me elsewhere. That was exactly what he wanted: he ran to the captain and said I had called him out. Captain Newman said it was nonsense, but I must apologize. But I could not do that, for there was nothing to apologize about – I was in the right, you see. So there I was, hauled up in front of half a dozen post-captains and two admirals: Lord Keith was one of the admirals.'

'What happened?'

'Petulance – I was officially reprimanded for petulance. Then the third time – but I will not go into details,' said Jack. 'It is a very curious thing, you know,' he went on, gazing out of the stern window with a look of mild, ingenuous wonder, 'a prodigious curious thing, but there cannot be many men who are both damned fools and no seamen, who reach post rank in the Royal Navy – men with no interest, I mean, of course – and yet it so happens that I have served under no less than two of them. I really thought I was dished that time – career finished, cut down, alas poor Borwick. I spent eight months on shore, as melancholy as that chap in the play, going up to town whenever I could afford it, which was not often, and hanging about that damned waiting-room in the Admiralty. I really thought I should never get to sea again – a half-pay lieutenant for the rest of my life. If it had not been for my fiddle, and fox-hunting when I could get a horse, I think I should have hanged myself. That Christmas was the last time I saw Queeney, I believe, apart from just once in London.'

'Is she an aunt, a cousin?'

'No, no. No connexion at all. But we were almost brought up together – or rather, *she* almost brought *me* up. I always remember her as a great girl, not a child at all, though to be sure there can't be ten years between us. Such a dear, kind creature. They had Damplow, the next house to ours – they were almost in our park – and after my mother died I dare say I spent as much time there as I did at home. More,' he said reflectively, gazing up at the tell-tale compass overhead. 'You know Dr Johnson – Dictionary Johnson?'

'Certainly,' cried Stephen, looking strange. 'The most respectable, the most amiable of the moderns. I disagree with all he says, except when he speaks of Ireland, yet I honour him; and for his life of Savage I love him. What is more, he occupied the most vivid dream I ever had in my life, not a week ago. How strange that you should mention him today.'

'Yes, ain't it? He was a great friend of theirs, until their mother ran off and married an Italian, a Papist. Queeney was wonderfully upset at having a Papist to her father-in-law, as you may imagine. Not that she ever saw him, however. "Anything but a Papist," says she. "I should rather have had Black Frank a thousand times, I declare." So we burnt thirteen guys in a row that year – it must have been '83 or

'84 – not long after the Battle of the Saints. After that they settled at Damplow more or less for good – the girls, I mean, and their old she-cousin. Dear Queeney. I believe I spoke of her before, did I not? She taught me mathematics.'

'I believe you did: a Hebrew scholar, if I do not mistake?'

'Exactly so. Conic sections and the Pentateuch came as easy as kiss my hand to her. Dear Queeney. I thought she was to be an old maid, though she was so pretty; for how could any man make up to a girl that knows Hebrew? It seemed a sad pity: anyone so sweet-tempered should have a prodigious great family of children. But, however, here she is married to the admiral, so it all ends happy . . . yet, you know, he is amazingly ancient – grey-haired, rising sixty, I dare say. Do you think, as a physician – I mean, is it possible . . . ?'

'*Possibilissima.*'

'Eh?'

'*Possibile è la cosa, e naturale,*' sang Stephen in a harsh, creaking tone, quite unlike his speaking voice, which was not disagreeable. '*E se Susanna vuol, possibilissima,*' discordantly, but near enough to Figaro to be recognized.

'Really? *Really?*' said Jack with intense interest. Then after a pause for reflexion, 'We might try that as a duetto, improvising . . . She joined him at Leghorn. And there I was, thinking it was my own merit, recognized at last, and honourable wounds' – laughing heartily – 'that had won me my promotion. Whereas I make no doubt it was all dear Queeney, do you see? But I have not told you the best – and this I certainly owe to her. We are to have a six weeks' cruise down the French and Spanish coasts, as far as Cape Nao!'

'Aye? Will that be good?'

'Yes, yes! Very good. No more convoy duty, you understand. No more being tied to a lubberly parcel of sneaking rogues, merchants creeping up and down the sea. The French and the Spaniards, their trade, their harbours, their supplies – these are to be our objects. Lord Keith was very

earnest about the great importance of destroying their commerce. He was very particular about it indeed – as important
as your great fleet actions, says he; and so very much more
profitable. The admiral took me aside and dwelt upon it at
length – he is a most acute, far-sighted commander; not
a Nelson, of course, but quite out of the ordinary. I am
glad Queeney has him. And we are under no one's orders,
which is so delightful. No bald-pated pantaloon to
say "Jack Aubrey, you proceed to Leghorn with these
hogs for the fleet", making it quite impossible even to
hope for a prize. Prize-money,' he cried, smiling and slapping his thigh; and the marine sentry outside the door, who
had been listening intently, wagged his head and smiled
too.

'Are you very much attached to money?' asked Stephen.

'I love it passionately,' said Jack, with truth ringing clear
in his voice. 'I have always been poor, and I long to be rich.'

'That's right,' said the marine.

'My dear old father was always poor too,' went on Jack.
'But as open-handed as a summer's day. He gave me fifty
pounds a year allowance when I was a midshipman, which
was uncommon handsome, in those days . . . or would have
been, had he ever managed to persuade Mr Hoare to pay it,
after the first quarter. Lord, how I suffered in the old *Reso*
– mess bills, laundry, growing out of my uniforms . . . of
course I love money. But I think we should be getting under
way – there's two bells striking.'

Jack and Stephen were to be the gun-room's guests, to
taste the sucking-pig bought at Leghorn. James Dillon was
there to bid them welcome, together with the master, the
purser and Mowett, as they plunged into the gloom: the
gun-room had no stern-windows, no sash-ports, and only a
scrap of skylight right forward, for although the peculiarity
of the *Sophie*'s construction made for a very comfortable
captain's cabin (luxurious, indeed, if only the captain's legs
had been sawn off a little above the knee), unencumbered
with the usual guns, it meant that the gun-room lay on a

lower level than the spar-deck and reposed upon a kind of shelf, not unlike an orlop.

Dinner was rather a stiff, formal entertainment to begin with, although it was lit by a splendid Byzantine silver hanging lamp, taken by Dillon out of a Turkish galley, and although it was lubricated by uncommonly good wine, for Dillon was well-to-do, even wealthy, by naval standards. Everyone was unnaturally well behaved: Jack was to give the tone, as he knew very well – it was expected of him, and it was his privilege. But this kind of deference, this attentive listening to every remark of his, required the words he uttered to be worth the attention they excited – a wearing state of affairs for a man accustomed to ordinary human conversation, with its perpetual interruption, contradiction and plain disregard. Here everything he said was right; and presently his spirits began to sink under the burden. Marshall and Purser Ricketts sat mum, saying please and thank you, eating with dreadful precision; young Mowett (a fellow guest) was altogether silent, of course; Dillon worked away at the small talk; but Stephen Maturin was sunk deep in a reverie.

It was the pig that saved this melancholy feast. Impelled by a trip on the part of the steward that coincided with a sudden lurch on the part of the *Sophie*, it left its dish at the door of the gun-room and shot into Mowett's lap. In the subsequent roaring and hullaballoo everyone grew human again, remaining natural long enough for Jack to reach the point he had been looking forward to since the beginning of dinner.

'Well, gentlemen,' he said, after they had drunk the King's health, 'I have news that will please you, I believe; though I must ask Mr Dillon's indulgence for speaking of a service matter at this table. The admiral gives us a cruise on our own down to Cape Nao. And I have prevailed upon Dr Maturin to stay aboard, to sew us up when the violence of the King's enemies happens to tear us apart.'

'Huzzay – well done – hear, hear – topping news – good

– hear him,' they cried, all more or less together, and they looked so pleased – there was so much candid friendliness on their faces that Stephen was intensely moved.

'Lord Keith was delighted when I told him,' Jack went on. 'Said he envied us extremely – had no physician in the flag-ship – was *amazed* when I told him of the gunner's brains – called for his spy-glass to look at Mr Day taking the sun on deck – and wrote out the Doctor's order in his own hand, which is something I have never heard of in the service before.'

Nor had anyone there present – the order had to be wetted – three bottles of port, there Killick – bumpers all round – and while Stephen sat looking modestly down at the table, they all stood up, crouching their heads under the beams, and sang,

'Huzzay, huzzay, huzzay,
Huzzay, huzzay, huzzay,
Hussay, huzzay, huzzay,
Huzzay.'

'There is only one thing I do not care for, however,' he said as the order was passed reverently round the table, 'and that is this foolish insistence upon the word *surgeon*. "Do hereby appoint you *surgeon*. . . take upon you the employment of *surgeon*. . . together with such allowance for wages and victuals for yourself as is usual for the *surgeon* of the said sloop." It is a false description; and a false description is anathema to the philosophic mind.'

'I am sure it is anathema to the philosophic mind,' said James Dillon. 'But the naval mind fairly revels in it, so it does. Take that word sloop, for example.'

'Yes,' said Stephen, narrowing his eyes through the haze of port and trying to remember the definitions he had heard.

'Why, now, a sloop, as you know, is properly a one-masted vessel, with a fore-and-aft rig. But in the Navy a sloop may be ship-rigged – she may have three masts.'

'Or take the *Sophie*,' cried the master, anxious to bring his crumb of comfort. 'She's rightly a brig, you know,

Doctor, with her two masts.' He held up two fingers, in case a landman might not fully comprehend so great a number. 'But the minute Captain Aubrey sets foot in her, why, she too becomes a sloop; for a brig is a lieutenant's command.'

'Or take me,' said Jack. 'I am called captain, but really I am only a master and commander.'

'Or the place where the men sleep, just for'ard,' said the purser, pointing. 'Rightly speaking, and official, 'tis the gun-deck, though there's never a gun on it. *We* call it the spar-deck – though there's no spars, neither – but some say the gun-deck still, and call the right gun-deck the upper-deck. Or take this brig, which is no true brig at all, not with her square mainsail, but rather a sorts of snow, or a her-maphrodite.'

'No, no, my dear sir,' said James Dillon, 'never let a mere word grieve your heart. We have nominal captain's servants who are, in fact, midshipmen; we have nominal able seamen on our books who are scarcely breeched – they are a thousand miles away and still at school; we swear we have not shifted any backstays, when we shift them continually; and we take many other oaths that nobody believes – no, no, you may call yourself what you please, so long as you do your duty. The Navy speaks in symbols, and you may suit what meaning you choose to the words.'

Chapter Five

The fair copy of the *Sophie*'s log was written out in David Richards' unusually beautiful copperplate, but in all other respects it was just like every other log-book in the service. Its tone of semi-literate, official, righteous dullness never varied; it spoke of the opening of beef-cask no. 271 and the death of the loblolly-boy in exactly the same voice, and it never deviated into human prose even for the taking of the sloop's first prize.

> *Thursday, June 28, winds variable, SE by S, course S50W, distance 63 miles. – Latitude 42°32'N, longitude 4°17'E, Cape Creus S76°W 12 leagues. Moderate breezes and cloudy PM. at 7 in first reef topsails. AM d° weather. Exercising the great guns. The people employed occasionally.*
>
> *Friday, June 29, S and Eastward . . . Light airs and clear weather. Exercising the great guns. PM employed worming the cable. AM moderate breezes and clouds, in third reef maintopsail, bent another foretopsail and close reefed it, hard gales at 4 handed the square mainsail at 8 more moderate reefed the square mainsail and set it. At noon calm. Departed this life Henry Gouges, loblolly-boy. Exercising the great guns.*
>
> *Saturday, June 30, light airs inclinable to calm. Exercised the great guns. Punished Jno. Shannahan and Thos. Yates with 12 lashes for drunkenness. Killed a bullock weight 530 lb. Remains of water 3 tons.*
>
> *Sunday, July 1 . . . Mustered the ship's company by divisions read the Articles of War performed Divine*

> *Service and committed the body of Henry Gouges to*
> *the deep. At noon d° weather.*

Ditto weather: but the sun sank towards a livid, purple, tumescent cloud-bank piled deep on the western horizon, and it was clear to every seaman aboard that it was not going to remain ditto much longer. The seamen, sprawling abroad on the fo'c'sle and combing out their long hair or plaiting it up again for one another, kindly explained to the landmen that this long swell from the south and east, this strange sticky heat that came both from the sky and the glassy surface of the heaving sea, and this horribly threatening appearance of the sun, meant that there was to be a coming dissolution of all natural bonds, an apocalyptic upheaval, a right dirty night ahead. The sailormen had plenty of time to depress their hearers, already low in their spirits because of the unnatural death of Henry Gouges (had said, 'Ha, ha, mates, I am fifty years old this day. Oh dear,' and had died sitting there, still holding his untasted grog) – they had plenty of time, for this was Sunday afternoon, when in the course of nature the fo'c'sle was covered with sailors at their ease, their pigtails undone. Some of the more gifted had queues they could tuck into their belts; and now that these ornaments were loosened and combed out, lank when still wet, or bushy when dry and as yet ungreased, they gave their owners a strangely awful and foreboding look, like oracles; which added to the landmen's uneasiness.

The seamen laid it on; but with all their efforts they could scarcely exaggerate the event, for the south-easterly gale increased from its first warning blasts at the end of the last dog-watch to a great roaring current of air by the end of the middle watch, a torrent so laden with warm rain that the men at the wheel had to hold their heads down and cup their mouths sideways to breathe. The seas mounted higher and higher: they were not the height of the great Atlantic rollers, but they were steeper, and in a way more wicked; their heads tore off streaming in front of them so as to race through the *Sophie*'s tops, and they were tall enough to becalm her as she lay there a-try, riding it out under a storm staysail. This was something she could do superbly well: she might not be very fast; she might not look very dangerous or high-bred; but with her topgallantmasts struck down on deck, her guns double-breeched and her hatches battened down, leaving only a little screened way to the after-ladder, and with a hundred miles of sea-room under her lee, she lay to as snug and unconcerned as an eider-duck. She was a remarkably dry vessel too, observed Jack, as she climbed the creaming slope of a wave, slipped its roaring top neatly under her bows and travelled smoothly down into the hollow. He stood with an arm round a back-stay, wearing a tarpaulin jacket and a pair of calico drawers: his streaming yellow hair, which he wore loose and long as a tribute to Lord Nelson, stood straight out behind him at the top of each wave and sank in the troughs between – a natural anemometer – and he watched the regular, dreamlike procession in the diffused light of the racing moon. With the greatest pleasure he saw that his forecast of her qualities as a sea-boat was fulfilled and, indeed, surpassed, 'She is remarkably dry,' he said to Stephen who, preferring to die in the open, had crept up on deck, had been made fast to a stanchion and who now stood, mute, sodden and appalled, behind him.

'Eh?'

'She – is – remarkably – dry.'

Stephen frowned impatiently: this was no time for trifling.

But the rising sun swallowed up the wind, and by half-past seven the next morning all that was left of the storm was the swell and a line of clouds low over the distant Gulf of Lions in the north-west; the sky was of an unbelievable purity and the air was washed so clean that Stephen could see the colour of the petrel's dangling feet as it pattered across the *Sophie*'s wake some twenty yards behind. 'I remember the *fact* of extreme, prostrating terror,' he said, keeping his eye on the tiny bird, 'but the *inward nature* of the emotion now escapes me.'

The man at the wheel and the quartermaster at the con exchanged a shocked glance.

'It is not unlike the case of a woman in childbirth,' went on Stephen, moving to the taffrail to keep the petrel in view and speaking rather more loudly. The man at the wheel and the quartermaster looked hastily away from one another: this was terrible – anybody might hear. The *Sophie*'s surgeon, the opener (in broad daylight and upon the entranced maindeck) of the gunner's brainpan – *Lazarus* Day, as he was called now – was much prized, but there was no telling how far he might go in impropriety. 'I remember an instance . . .'

'Sail ho!' cried the masthead, to the relief of all upon the *Sophie*'s quarter-deck.

'Where away?'

'To leeward. Two points, three points on the beam. A felucca. In distress – her sheets a-flying.'

The *Sophie* turned, and presently those on deck could see the distant felucca as it rose and fell on the long troubled sea. It made no attempt to fly, none to alter course nor yet to heave to, but stood on with its shreds of sail streaming out on the irregular breaths of the dying wind. Nor did it show any answering colours or reply to the *Sophie*'s hail. There was no one at the tiller, and when they came nearer those with glasses could see the bar move from side to side as the felucca yawed.

'That's a body on deck,' said Babbington, full of glee.

'It will be awkward lowering a boat in this,' remarked Jack, more or less to himself. 'Williams, lay her along, will you? Mr Watt, let some men stand by to boom her off. What do you make of her, Mr Marshall?'

Why, sir, I take it she's from Tangiers or maybe Tetuan – the west end of the coast, at all events . . .'

'That man in the square hole died of plague,' said Stephen Maturin, clapping his telescope to.

A hush followed this statement and the wind sighed through the weather-shrouds. The distance between the ves-

sels narrowed fast, and now everyone could see a shape
wedged in the after-hatchway, with perhaps two more
beneath it; an almost naked body among the tangle of gear
near the tiller.

'Keep her full,' said Jack. 'Doctor, are you quite sure of
what you say? Take my glass.'

Stephen looked through it for a moment and handed it
back. 'There is no possible doubt,' he said. 'I will just make
up a bag and then I will go across. There may be some
survivors.'

The felucca was almost touching now, and a tame genet
– a usual creature in Barbary craft, on account of the rats –
stood on the rail, looking eagerly up, ready to spring. An
elderly Swede named Volgardson, the kindliest of men,
threw a swab that knocked it off its balance, and all the
men along the side hooted and shrieked to frighten it
away.

'Mr Dillon,' said Jack, 'we'll get the starboard tacks
aboard.'

At once the *Sophie* sprang to life – bosun's calls shrilling,
hands running to their places, general uproar – and in the
din Stephen cried, 'I insist upon a boat – I protest . . .'

Jack took him by the elbow and propelled him with affectionate violence into the cabin. 'My dear sir,' he said, 'I am
afraid you must not insist, or protest: it is mutiny, you know,
and you would be obliged to be hanged. Was you to set foot
in that felucca, even if you did not bring back the contagion,
we should have to fly the yellow flag at Mahon: and you
know what that means. Forty mortal bloody days on the
quarantine island and shot if you stray outside the pallisado,
that is what. And whether you brought it back or not, half
the hands would die of fright.'

'You mean to sail directly away from that ship, giving it
no assistance?'

'Yes, sir.'

'Upon your own head, then.'

'Certainly.'

The log took little notice of this incident; it scarcely could have found any appropriate official language for saying that the *Sophie*'s surgeon shook his fist at the *Sophie*'s captain, in any case; and it shuffled the whole thing off with the disingenuous *spoke felucca*: *and* ¹/₄ *past* 11 *tacked*, for it was eager to come to the happiest entry it had made for years (Captain Allen had been an unlucky commander: not only had the *Sophie* been almost entirely confined to convoy-duty in his time, but whenever he did have a cruise the sea had emptied before him – never a prize did he take) ... PM *moderate and clear, up topgallantmasts, opened pork cask no.* 113, *partially spoiled. 7 saw strange sail to westward, made sail in chase.*

Westward in this case meant almost directly to the *Sophie*'s lee; and making sail meant spreading virtually everything she possessed – lower, topsail and topgallant studdingsails, royals of course, and even bonnets – for the chase had been made out to be a fair-sized polacre with lateens on her fore and mizen and square sails on her mainmast, and therefore French or Spanish – almost certainly a good prize if only she could be caught. This was the polacre's view, without a doubt, for she had been lying-to, apparently fishing her storm-damaged mainmast, when they first came in sight of one another; but the *Sophie* had scarcely sheeted home her topgallants before the polacre's head was before the wind and she fleeing with all she could spread in that short notice – a very suspicious polacre, unwilling to be surprised.

The *Sophie*, with her abundance of hands trained in setting sail briskly, ran two miles to the polacre's one in the first quarter of an hour; but once the chase had spread all the canvas it could, their speeds became more nearly even. With the wind two points on her quarter and her big square mainsail at its best advantage, the *Sophie* was still the faster, however, and when they had reached their greatest speed she was running well over seven knots to the polacre's six. But they were still four miles apart, and in three hours' time it would be pitch dark – no moon until half-past two. There was the hope, the very reasonable hope, that the chase would carry something away, for she had certainly had a rough night of it; and many a glass was trained upon her from the *Sophie*'s fo'c'sle.

Jack stood there by the starboard knighthead, willing the sloop on with all his might, and feeling that his right arm might not be too great a price for an effective bow-chaser. He stared back at the sails and how they drew, he looked searchingly at the water rising in her bow-wave and sliding fast along her smooth black side; and it appeared to him that with her present trim the after sails were pressing her fore-foot down a trifle much – that the extreme press of canvas might be hindering her progress – and he bade them take in the main royal. Rarely had he given an order more reluctantly obeyed, but the log-line proved that he was right: the *Sophie* ran a little easier, a very little faster, with the wind's thrust more forward.

The sun set over the starboard bow, the wind began to back into the north, blowing in gusts, and darkness swept up the sky from behind them: the polacre was still three-quarters of a mile ahead, holding on to her westward course. As the wind came round on to the beam they set staysails and the fore-and-aft mainsail: looking up at the set of the fore-royal and having it braced round more sharply, Jack could see it perfectly well; but when he looked down it was twilight on deck.

Now, with the studdingsails in, the chase – or the ghost of the chase, a pale blur showing now and then on the lifting swell – could be seen from the quarter-deck, and there he took up his stand with his night-glass, staring through the rapidly gathering darkness, giving a low, conversational order from time to time.

Dimmer, dimmer, and then she was gone: suddenly she was quite gone. The quadrant of horizon that had shown that faint but most interesting bobbing paleness was bare heaving sea, with Regulus setting into it.

'Masthead,' he hailed, 'what do you make of her?'

A long pause. 'Nothing, sir. She ain't there.'

Just so. What was he to do now? He wanted to think: he wanted to think there on deck, in the closest possible touch with the situation – with the shifting wind on his face, the glow of the binnacles just at hand and not the least interruption. And this the conventions and the discipline of the service allowed him to do. The blessed inviolability of a captain (so ludicrous at times, such a temptation to silly pomp) wrapped him about, and his mind could run free. At one time he saw Dillon hurry Stephen away: he recorded the fact, but his mind continued its unbroken pursuit of the answer to his problem. The polacre had either altered its course or would do so presently: the question was, where would this new course bring it to by dawn? The answer depended on a great many factors – whether French or Spanish, whether homeward or outward bound, whether cunning or simple and, above all, upon her sailing qualities. He had a very clear notion of them, having followed her every movement with the utmost attention for the last few hours; so building his reasoning (if such an instinctive process could be called by that name) upon these certainties and a fair estimate of the rest, he came to his conclusion. The polacre had worn; she might possibly be lying there under bare poles to escape detection while the *Sophie* passed her in the darkness to the northward; but whether or no, she would presently be making all sail, close-hauled for Agde or Cette, crossing the *Sophie*'s wake and relying on her lateen's power of lying nearer to run her clear to windward and so to safety before daylight. If this was so the *Sophie* must tack directly and work to windward under an easy sail: that should bring the polacre under her lee at first light; for it was likely that they would rely on their fore and mizen alone – even in the chase they had been favouring their wounded mainmast.

He stepped into the master's cabin, and through narrowed, light-dazzled eyes he checked their position; he checked it again with Dillon's reckoning and went on deck to give his orders.

'Mr Watt,' he said, 'I am going to put her about, and I desire the whole operation shall be carried out in silence. No calls, no starting, no shouts.'

'No calls it is, sir,' said the bosun, and hurried off uttering 'All hands to tack ship,' in a hoarse whisper, wonderfully curious to hear.

The order and its form had a strangely powerful effect: with as much certainty as though it had been a direct revelation, Jack knew that the men were wholly with him; and for a fleeting moment a voice told him that he had better be right, or he would never enjoy this unlimited confidence again.

'Very well, Assou,' he said to the Lascar at the wheel, and smoothly the *Sophie* luffed up.

'Helm's a-lee,' he remarked – the cry usually echoed from one horizon to the other. Then 'Off tacks and sheets'. He heard the bare feet hurrying and the staysail sheets rasping over the stays: he waited, waited, until the wind was one point on her weather bow, and then a little louder, 'Mainsail haul!' She was in stays: and now she was paying off fast. The wind was well round on his other cheek. 'Let go and haul,' he said, and the half-seen waisters hauled on the starboard braces like veteran forecastlemen. The weather bowlines tightened: the *Sophie* gathered way.

Presently she was running east-north-east close-hauled under reefed topsails, and Jack went below. He did not choose to have anything showing from his stern-windows, and it was not worth shipping the dead-lights, so he walked, bending low, into the gun-room. Here, rather to his surprise, he found Dillon (it was Dillon's watch below, certainly; but in his place Jack would never have left the deck) playing chess with Stephen, while the purser read them pieces from the Gentleman's Magazine, with comments.

'Do not stir, gentlemen,' he cried, as they all sprang up. 'I have just come to beg your hospitality for a while.'

They made him very welcome – hurried about with glasses of wine, sweet biscuits, the most recent Navy List – but he was an intruder: he had upset their quiet sociability, dried up the purser's literary criticism and interrupted the chess as effectually as an Olympian thunderbolt. Stephen messed down here now, of course – his cabin was the little boarded cupboard beyond the hanging lantern – and he already looked as though he belonged to this community: Jack felt obscurely hurt, and after he had talked for a while (a dry, constrained interchange, it seemed to him; so very polite) he went up on deck again. As soon as they saw him looming in the dim glow of the hatchway the master and young Ricketts moved silently over to the larboard side, and Jack resumed his solitary pacing from the taffrail to the aftermost deadeye.

At the beginning of the middle watch the sky clouded over, and towards two bells a shower came weeping across, the drops hissing on the binnacles. The moon rose, a faint, lopsided object scarcely to be made out at all: Jack's stomach was pinched and wrung with hunger, but he paced on and on, looking mechanically out over the leeward darkness at every turn.

Three bells. The quiet voice of the ship's corporal reporting all's well. Four bells. There were so many other possibilities, so many things the chase could have done other than bearing up and then hauling her wind for Cette: hundreds of other things . . .

'What, what's this? Walking about in the rain in your shirt? This is madness,' said Stephen's voice just behind him.

'Hush!' cried Mowett, the officer of the watch, who had failed to intercept him.

'Madness. Think of the night air – the falling damps – the fluxion of the humours. If your duty requires you to walk about in the night air, you must wear a woollen garment. A woollen garment, there, for the captain! I will fetch it myself.'

Five bells, and another soft shower of rain. The relieving of the helm, and the whispered repetition of the course, the routine reports. Six bells, and a hint of thinner darkness in the east. The spell of silence seemed as strong as ever; men tiptoed to trim the yards, and a little before seven bells the look-out coughed, hailing almost apologetically, only just loud enough to be heard. 'Upon deck. Deck, sir. I think him vos there, starboard beam. I think . . .'

Jack stuffed his glass into the pocket of the grego Stephen had brought him, ran up to the masthead, twined himself firmly into the rigging and trained the telescope in the direction of the pointing arm. The first grey forerunners of the dawn were straggling through the drifting showers and low torn cloud to leeward; and there, her lateens faintly gleaming, lay a polacre, not half a mile away. Then the rain had hidden her again, but not before Jack had seen that she was indeed his quarry and that she had lost her maintopmast at the cap.

'You're a capital fellow, Anderssen,' he said, clapping him on the shoulder.

To the concentrated mute inquiry from young Mowett and the whole of the watch on deck he replied with a smile that he tried to keep within bounds and the words, 'She is just under our lee. East by south. You may light up the sloop, Mr Mowett, and show her our force: I don't want her to do anything foolish, such as firing a gun – perhaps hurting some of our people. Let me know when you have laid her aboard.' With this he retired, calling for a light and something hot to drink; and from his cabin he heard Mowett's voice, cracked and squeaking with the excitement of this prodigious command (he would happily have died for Jack), as under his orders the *Sophie* bore up and spread her wings.

Jack leant back against the curved run of the stern-window and let Killick's version of coffee down by gulps into his grateful stomach; and at the same time that its warmth spread through him, so there ran a lively tide of settled, pure, unfevered happiness – a happiness that another commander (remembering his own first prize) might have discerned from the log-entry, although it was not specifically mentioned there: *¹/₂ past 10 tacked, 11 in courses, reefed topsail. AM cloudy and rain. ¹/₂ past 4 chase observed E by S, distance ¹/₂ mile. Bore up and took possession of dᵒ, which proved to be* L'Aimable Louise, *French polacre laden with corn and general merchandise for Cette, of about 200 tons, 6 guns and 19 men. Sent her with an officer and eight men to Mahon.*

'Allow me to fill your glass,' said Jack, with the utmost benevolence. 'This is rather better than our ordinary, I believe?'

'Better, dear joy, and very, very much stronger – a healthy, roborative beverage,' said Stephen Maturin. ''Tis a neat Priorato. Priorato, from behind Tarragona.'

'Neat it is – most uncommon neat. But to go back to the prize: the main reason why I am so very happy about it is that it bloods the men, as one might say; and it gives me room to spread my elbows a little. We have a capital prize agent – is obliged to me – and I am persuaded he will advance us a hundred guineas. I can distribute sixty or seventy to the crew, and buy some powder at last. There could be nothing better for these men than kicking up a dust on shore, and for that they must have money.'

'But will they not run away? You have often spoken of desertion – the great evil of desertion.'

'When they have prize-money due to them and a strong notion of more to come they will not desert. Not in Mahon, at all events. And then again, do you see, they will turn to exercising the great guns with a much better heart – do not suppose I do not know how they have been muttering, for indeed I have driven them precious hard. But now they will feel there is some point in it . . . If I can get some powder (I dare not use up much more of the issue) we will shoot larbowlines against starbowlines and watch against watch for a handsome prize; and what with that and what with emulation, I don't despair of making our gunnery at least as dangerous to others as it is to ourselves. And then – God, how sleepy I am – we can set about our cruising in earnest. I have a plan for nightwork, lying close inshore . . . but first I should tell you how I think to divide up our time. A week off Cape Creus, then back to Mahon for stores and water, particularly water. Then the approaches to Barcelona, and coastwise . . . coastwise . . .' He yawned prodigiously: two sleepless nights and a pint of the *Aimable Louise*'s Priorato were bearing him down with an irresistible warm soft delicious weight. 'Where was I? Oh, Barcelona. Then off Tarragona, Valencia . . . Valencia . . . water's the great trouble, of course.' He sat there blinking at the light, musing comfortably; and he heard Stephen's distant voice discoursing upon the coast of Spain – knew it well as far as Denia, could show him many an interesting remnant of Phoenician, Greek, Roman, Visigothic, Arabian occupation; the certainty of both kinds of egret in the marshes by Valencia; the odd dialect and bloody nature of the Valencianos; the very real possibility of flamingoes . . .

The *Aimable Louise*'s ill wind had stirred up the shipping all over the western Mediterranean, driving it far from its intended courses; and not two hours after they had sent their prize away for Mahon, their first fine plump prize, they saw two more vessels, the one a barca-longa heading west and the other a brig to the north, apparently steering due south. The brig was the obvious choice and they set a course to cut her off, keeping closest watch upon her the while: she sailed on placidly enough under courses and topsails, while the *Sophie* set her royals and topgallants and hurried along on the larboard tack with the wind one point free, heeling so that her lee-channels were under the water; and as their courses converged the Sophies were astonished to see that the stranger was extraordinarily like their own vessel, even to the exaggerated steeve of her bowsprit.

'That would be a brig, no doubt,' said Stephen, standing

at the rail next to Pullings, a big shy silent master's mate.

'Yes, sir, so she is; and more exactly like us nor ever you would credit, without you seen it. Do you please to look in my spy-glass, sir?' he asked, wiping it on his handkerchief.

'Thank you. An excellent glass – how clear. But I must venture to disagree. That ship, that brig, is a vile yellow, whereas we are black, with a white stripe.'

'Oh, that's nobbut paintwork, sir. Look at her quarter-deck, with its antic little break right aft, just like ourn – you don't see many of such, even in these waters. Look at the steeve of her bowsprit. And she must gauge the same as us, Thames measurement, within ten ton or less. They must have been off of the same draught, out of the same yard. But there are three rows of reefbands in her fore tops'l, so you can see she's only a merchantman, and not a man-of-war like we.'

'Are we going to take her?'

'I doubt that'd be too good to be true, sir: but maybe we shall.'

'The Spanish colours, Mr Babbington,' said Jack; and looking round Stephen saw the yellow and red break out at the peak.

'We are sailing under false colours,' whispered Stephen. 'Is not that very heinous?'

'Eh?'

'Wicked, morally indefensible?'

'Bless you, sir, we always do that, at sea. But we'll show our own at the last minute, you may be sure, before ever we fire a gun. That's justice. Look at him, now – he's throwing out a Danish waft, and as like as not he's no more a Dane than my grandam.'

But the event proved Thomas Pullings wrong. 'Danish prig *Clomer*, sir,' said her master, an ancient bibulous Dane with pale, red-rimmed eyes, showing Jack his papers in the cabin. 'Captain Ole Bugge. Hides and peeswax from Dripoli to Parcelona.'

'Well, Captain,' said Jack, looking very sharply through

the papers – the quite genuine papers – 'I'm sure you will forgive me for troubling you – we have to do it, as you know. Let me offer you a glass of this Priorato; they tell me it is good of its kind.'

'It is better than good, sir,' said the Dane, as the purple tide ran out, 'it is vonderful vine. Captain, may I ask you the favour of your positions?'

'You have come to the right shop for a position, Captain. We have the best navigator in the Mediterranean. Killick, pass the word for Mr Marshall. Mr Marshall, Captain B . . . – the gentleman would like to know what we make our position.'

On deck the Clomers and the Sophies were gazing at one another's vessels with profound satisfaction, as at their own mirror-images: at first the Sophies had felt that the resemblance was something of a liberty on the part of the Danes, but they came round when their own yeoman of the sheets and their own shipmate Anderssen called out over the water to their fellow-countrymen, talking foreign as easy as kiss my hand, to the silent admiration of all beholders.

Jack saw Captain Bugge to the side with particular affability; a case of Priorato was handed down into the Danish boat; and leaning over the rail Jack called after him, 'I will let you know, next time we meet.'

Her captain had not reached the *Clomer* before the *Sophie*'s yards were creaking round, to carry her as close-hauled as she would lie on her new course, north-east by north. 'Mr Watt,' observed Jack, gazing up, 'as soon as we have a moment to spare we must have cross-catharpings fore and aft; we are not pointing up as sharp as I could wish.'

'What's afoot?' asked the ship's company, when all sail was set and drawing just so, with everything on deck coiled down to Mr Dillon's satisfaction; and it was not long before the news passed along from the gun-room steward to the purser's steward and so to his mate, Jack-in-the-dust, who told the galley and thereby the rest of the brig – the news that the Dane, having a fellow-feeling for the *Sophie* because of her resemblance to his own vessel, and being gratified by Jack's civility, had given word of a Frenchman no great way over the northern horizon, a deep-laden sloop with a patched mainsail that was bearing away for Agde.

Tack followed tack as the *Sophie* beat up into the freshening breeze, and on the fifth leg a scrap of white appeared in the north-north-east, too far and too steady for a distant gull. It was the French sloop, sure enough: from the Dane's description of her rig there was no doubt of that after the first half hour; but her behaviour was so strange that it was impossible to be wholly persuaded of it until she was lying tossing there under the *Sophie*'s guns and the boats were going to and fro over the lane of sea, transferring the glum prisoners. In the first place she had apparently kept no lookout of any kind, and it was not until no more than a mile of water lay between them that she noticed her pursuer at all; and even then she hesitated, wavered, accepted the assurance of the tricolour flag and then rejected it, flying too slowly and too late, only to break out ten minutes later in a flurry of signals of surrender and waving them vehemently at the first warning shot.

The reasons for her behaviour were clear enough to James Dillon once he was aboard her, taking possession: the *Citoyen Durand* was laden with gunpowder – was so crammed with gunpowder that it overflowed her hold and stood in tarpaulined barrels on her deck; and her young master had taken his wife to sea. She was with child – her first – and the rough night, the chase and the dread of an explosion had brought on her labour. James was as stouthearted as the next man, but the continuous groaning just behind the cabin-bulkhead and the awful hoarse, harsh, animal quality of the cries that broke out through the groaning, and their huge volume, terrified him; he gazed at the whitefaced, distracted, tear-stained husband with a face as appalled as his.

Leaving Babbington in sole command he hurried back to the *Sophie* and explained the situation. At the word *powder*

Jack's face lit up; but at the word *baby* he looked very blank.

'I am afraid the poor woman is dying,' said James.

'Well, I don't know, I'm sure,' said Jack hesitantly; and now that he could put a meaning to the remote, dreadful noise he heard it far more clearly. 'Ask the Doctor to come,' he said to a marine.

Now that the excitement of the chase was over, Stephen was at his usual post by the elm-tree pump, peering down its tube into the sunlit upper layers of the Mediterranean; and when they told him there was a woman in the prize, having a baby, he said, 'Aye? I dare say. I thought I recognized the sound,' and showed every sign of returning to his place.

'Surely you can do something about it?' said Jack.

'I am certain the poor woman is dying,' said James.

Stephen looked at them with his odd expressionless gaze and said, 'I will go across.' He went below, and Jack said, 'Well, that's in good hands, thank God. And you tell me all that deck cargo is powder too?'

'Yes, sir. The whole thing is mad.'

'Mr Day – Mr Day, there. Do you know the French marks, Mr Day?'

'Why, yes, sir. They are much the same as ours, only their best cylinder large grain has a white ring round the red: and their halves weigh but thirty-five pound.'

'How much have you room for, Mr Day?'

The gunner considered. 'Squeezing my bottom tier up tight, I might stow thirty-five or six, sir.'

'Make it so, then, Mr Day. There is a lot of damaged stuff aboard that sloop – I can see it from here – that we shall have to take away to prevent further spoiling. So you had better go across and set your hand upon the best. And we can do with her launch, too. Mr Dillon, we cannot entrust this floating magazine to a midshipman; you will have to take her into Mahon as soon as the powder is across. Take what men you think fit, and be so good as to send Dr Maturin back in her launch – we need one badly. God love us, what a terrible cry! I am truly sorry to inflict this upon you, Dillon, but you see how it is.'

'Just so, sir. I am to take the master of the sloop along with me, I presume? It would be inhuman to move him.'

'Oh, by all means, by all means. The poor fellow. What a – what a pretty kettle of fish.'

The little deadly barrels travelled across the intervening sea, rose up and vanished into the *Sophie*'s maw; so did half a dozen melancholy Frenchmen, with their bags or sea-chests; but the usual festive atmosphere was lacking – the Sophies, even the family men, looked guilty, concerned, apprehensive; the dreadful unremitting shrieks went on and on; and when Stephen appeared at the rail to call out that he must stay aboard, Jack bowed to the obscure justice of this deprivation.

The *Citoyen Durand* ran smoothly through the darkness down towards Minorca, a steady breeze behind her; now that the screaming had stopped Dillon posted a reliable man at the helm, visited the little watch below in the galley and came down into the cabin. Stephen was washing, and the husband, shattered and destroyed, held the towel in his drooping hands.

'I hope . . .' said James.

'Oh, yes: yes,' said Stephen deliberately, looking round at him. 'A perfectly straightforward delivery: just a little long, perhaps; but nothing out of the way. Now, my friend' – to the captain – 'these buckets would be best over the side; and then I recommend you to lie down for a while. Monsieur has a son,' he added.

'My best congratulations, sir,' said James. 'And my best wishes for Madame's prompt recovery.'

'Thank you, sir, thank you,' said the captain, his eyes brimming over again. 'I beg you to take a little something – to make yourselves quite at home.'

This they did, sitting each in a comfortable chair and eating away at the hill of cakes laid up against young hasty's christening in Agde next week; they sat there easily enough, and next door the poor young woman slept at last, her husband holding her hand and her crinkled pink baby snorting at her bosom. It was quiet below, wonderfully quiet and peaceful now; and it was quiet on deck with the following wind easing the sloop along at a steady six knots, and with the rigorous barking precision of a man-of-war reduced to an occasional mild 'How does she lie, Joe?' It was quiet; and in that dimly-lighted box they travelled through the night, cradled by the even swell: after a little while of this silence and this uninterrupted slow rhythmic heave they might have been anywhere on earth – alone in the world – in another world altogether. In the cabin their thoughts were far away, and Stephen for one no longer had any sense of movement to or from any particular point – little sense of motion, still less of the immediate present.

'It is only now,' he said in a low voice, 'that we have the opportunity of speaking to one another. I looked forward to this time with great impatience; and now that it is come, I find that in fact there is little to be said.'

'Perhaps nothing at all,' said James. 'I believe we understand each other perfectly.'

This was quite true; it was quite true as far as the heart of the matter was concerned; but nevertheless they talked all through their remaining hours of harboured privacy.

'I believe the last time I saw you was at Dr Emmet's,' said James, after a long, reflective pause.

'No. It was at Rathfarnham, with Edward Fitzgerald. I was going out by the summerhouse as you and Kenmare came in.'

'Rathfarnham? Yes: yes, of course. I remember now. It was just after the meeting of the Committee. I remember . . . You were intimate with Lord Edward, I believe?'

'We knew one another very well in Spain. In Ireland I saw less and less of him as time went on; he had friends I neither liked nor trusted, and I was always too moderate – far too moderate – for him. Though the dear knows I was full enough of zeal for humanity at large, full enough of republicanism in those days. Do you remember the test?'

'Which one?'

'The test that begins *Are you straight?*'

'*I am.*'

'*How straight?*'

'*As straight as a rush.*'

'*Go on then.*'

'*In truth, in trust, in unity and liberty.*'

'*What have you got in your hand?*'

'*A green bough.*'

'*Where did it first grow?*'

'*In America.*'

'*Where did it bud?*'

'*In France.*'

'*Where are you going to plant it?*'

'Nay, I forget what follows. It was not the test I took, you know. Far from it.'

'No, I am sure it was not. I did, however: the word *liberty* seemed to me to glow with meaning, in those days. But even then I was sceptical about *unity* – our society made such very strange bedfellows. Priests, deists, atheists and Presbyterians; visionary republicans, Utopists and men who merely disliked the Beresfords. You and your friends were all primarily for emancipation, as I recall.'

'Emancipation and reform. I for one had no notion of any republic; nor had my friends of the Committee, of course. With Ireland in her present state a republic would quickly become something little better than a democracy. The genius of the country is quite opposed to a republic. A *Catholic* republic! How ludicrous.'

'Is it brandy in that case-bottle?'

'It is.'

'The answer to that last part of the test was *In the crown of Great Britain*, by the way. The glasses are just behind you. I know it was at Rathfarnham,' Stephen went on, 'for

I had spent the whole of that afternoon trying to persuade him not to go on with his shatter-brained plans for the rising: I told him I was opposed to violence – always had been – and that even if I were not I should withdraw, were he to persist with such wild, visionary schemes – that they would be his own ruin, Pamela's ruin, the ruin of his cause and the ruin of God knows how many brave, devoted men. He looked at me with that sweet, troubled look, as though he were sorry for me, and he said he had to meet you and Kenmare. He had not understood me at all.'

'Have you any news of Lady Edward – of Pamela?'

'Only that she is in Hamburg and that the family looks after her.'

'She was the most beautiful woman that ever I saw, and the kindest. None so brave.'

'Aye,' thought Stephen, and stared into his brandy. 'That afternoon,' he said, 'I spent more spirit than ever I spent in my life. Even then I no longer cared for any cause or any theory of government on earth; I would not have lifted a finger for any nation's independence, fancied or real; and yet I had to reason with as much ardour as though I were filled with the same enthusiasm as in the first days of the Revolution, when we were all overflowing with virtue and love.'

'Why? Why did you have to speak so?'

'Because I had to convince him that his plans were disastrously foolish, that they were known to the Castle and that he was surrounded by traitors and informers. I reasoned as closely and cogently as ever I could – better than ever I thought I could – and he did not follow me at all. His attention wandered. "Look," says he, "there's a redbreast in that yew by the path." All he knew was that I was opposed to him, so he closed his mind; if, indeed, he was *capable* of following me, which perhaps he was not. Poor Edward! *Straight as a rush*; and so many of them around him were as crooked as men can well be – Reynolds, Corrigan, Davis ... Oh, it was pitiful.'

'And would you indeed not lift a finger, even for the moderate aims?'

'I would not. With the revolution in France gone to pure loss I was already chilled beyond expression. And now, with what I saw in '98, on both sides, the wicked folly and the wicked brute cruelty, I have had such a sickening of men in masses, and of causes, that I would not cross this room to reform parliament or prevent the union or to bring about the millennium. I speak only for myself, mind – it is my own truth alone – but man as part of a movement or a crowd is indifferent to me. He is inhuman. And I have nothing to do with nations, or nationalism. The only feelings I have – for what they are – are for men as individuals; my loyalties, such as they may be, are to private persons alone.'

'Patriotism will not do?'

'My dear creature, I have done with all debate. But you know as well as I, patriotism is a word; and one that generally comes to mean either *my country*, *right or wrong*, which is infamous, or *my country is always right*, which is imbecile.'

'Yet you stopped Captain Aubrey playing *Croppies lie down* the other day.'

'Oh, I am not consistent, of course; particularly in little things. Who is? He did not know the meaning of the tune, you know. He has never been in Ireland at all, and he was in the West Indies at the time of the rising.'

'And I was at the Cape, thank God. Was it terrible?'

'Terrible? I cannot, by any possible energy of words, express to you the blundering, the delay, the murderous confusion and the stupidity of it all. It accomplished nothing; it delayed independence for a hundred years; it sowed hatred and violence; it spawned out a vile race of informers and things like Major Sirr. And, incidentally, it made us the prey of any chance blackmailing informer.' He paused. 'But as for that song, I acted as I did partly because it is disagreeable to me to listen to it and partly because there were several Irish sailors within hearing, and not one of them an Orangeman; and it would be a pity to have them hate him

166

when nothing in the manner of insult was within his mind's reach.'

'You are very fond of him, I believe?'

'Am I? Yes; perhaps I am. I would not call him a gremial friend – I have not known him long enough – but I am very much attached to him. I am sorry that you are not.'

'I am sorry for it too. I came willing to be pleased. I had heard of him as wild and freakish, but a good seaman, and I was very willing to be pleased. But feelings are not to command.'

'No. But it is curious: at least it is curious to me, the mid-point, with esteem – indeed, more than esteem – for both of you. Are there particular lapses you reproach him with? If we were still eighteen I should say "What's wrong with Jack Aubrey?"'

'And perhaps I should reply "Everything, since he has a command and I have not,"' said James, smiling. 'But come, now, I can hardly criticize your friend to your face.'

'Oh, he has faults, sure. I know he is intensely ambitious where his profession is at issue and impatient of any restraint. My concern was to know just what it was that offended you in him. Or is it merely *non amo te, Sabidi*?'

'Perhaps so: it is hard to say. He can be a very agreeable companion, of course, but there are times when he shows that particular beefy arrogant English insensibility . . . and there is certainly one thing that jars on me – his great eagerness for prizes. The sloop's discipline and training is more like that of a starving privateer than a King's ship. When we were chasing that miserable polacre he could not bring himself to leave the deck all night long – anyone would have thought we were after a man-of-war, with some honour at the end of the chase. And this prize here was scarcely clear of the *Sophie* before he was exercising the great guns again, roaring away with both broadsides.'

'Is a privateer a discreditable thing? I ask in pure ignorance.'

'Well, a privateer is there for a different motive altogether.

A privateer does not fight for honour, but for gain. It is a mercenary. Profit is its *raison d'être*.'

'May not the exercising of the great guns have a more honourable end in view?'

'Oh, certainly. I may very well be unjust – jealous – wanting in generosity. I beg your pardon if I have offended you. And I willingly confess he is an excellent seaman.'

'Lord, James, we have known one another long enough to tell our minds freely, without any offence. Will you reach me the bottle?'

'Well, then,' said James, 'if I may speak as freely as though I were in an empty room, I will tell you this: I think his encouragement of that fellow Marshall is indecent, not to use a grosser word.'

'Do I follow you, now?'

'You know about the man?'

'What about the man?'

'That he is a paederast?'

'Maybe.'

'I have proof positive. I had it in Cagliari, if it had been necessary. And he is enamoured of Captain Aubrey – toils like a galley-slave – would holystone the quarter-deck if allowed – hounds the men with far more zeal than the bosun – anything for a smile from him.'

Stephen nodded. 'Yes,' he said. 'But surely you do not think Jack Aubrey shares his tastes?'

'No. But I do think he is aware of them and that he encourages the man. Oh, this is a very foul, dirty way of speaking ... I go too far. Perhaps I am drunk. We have nearly emptied the bottle.'

Stephen shrugged. 'No. But you are quite mistaken, you know. I can assure you, speaking in all sober earnest, that he has no notion of it. He is not very sharp in some ways; and in his simple view of the world, paederasts are dangerous only to powder-monkeys and choir-boys, or to those epicene creatures that are to be found in Mediterranean brothels. I made a circuitous attempt at enlightening him a little, but he looked very knowing and said, "Don't tell *me* about rears and vices; I have been in the Navy all my life."'

'Then surely he must be wanting a little in penetration?'

'James, I trust there was no *mens rea* in that remark?'

'I must go on deck,' said James, looking at his watch. He came back some time later, having seen the wheel relieved and having checked their course; he brought a gust of cool night air with him and sat in silence until it had dispersed in the gentle lamp-lit warmth. Stephen had opened another bottle.

'There are times when I am not altogether just,' said James, reaching for his glass. 'I am too touchy, I know; but sometimes, when you are surrounded with Proddies and you hear their silly, underbred cant, you fly out. And since you cannot fly out in one direction, you fly out in another. It is a continual tension, as *you* ought to know, if anyone.'

Stephen looked at him very attentively, but said nothing.

'You knew I was a Catholic?' said James.

'No,' said Stephen. 'I was aware that some of your family were, of course; but as for you . . . Do you not find it puts you in a difficult position?' he asked, hesitantly. 'With that oath . . . the penal laws . . . ?'

'Not in the least,' said James. 'My mind is perfectly at ease, as far as that is concerned.'

'That is what you think, my poor friend,' said Stephen to himself, pouring out another glass to hide his expression.

For a moment it seemed that James Dillon might take this further, but he did not: some delicate balance changed, and now the talk ran on and on to friends they had shared and to delightful days they had spent together in what seemed such a very distant past. How many people they had known! How valuable, or amusing, or respectable some of them had been! They talked their second bottle dry, and James went up on deck again.

He came down in half an hour, and as he stepped into the cabin he said, as though he were catching straight on to an interrupted conversation, 'And then, of course, there is that whole question of promotion. I will tell you, just for your secret ear alone and although it sounds odious, that I thought I should be given a command after that affair in the *Dart*; and being passed over does rankle cruelly.' He paused, and then asked, 'Who was it who was said to have earned more by his prick than his practice?'

'Selden. But in this instance I conceive the common gossip is altogether out; as I understand it, this was the ordinary operation of interest. Mark you, I make no claim of outstanding chastity – I merely say that in Jack Aubrey's case the consideration is irrelevant.'

'Well, be that as it may, I look for promotion: like every other sailor I value it very highly, so I tell you in all simplicity; and being under a prize-hunting captain is not the quickest path to it.'

'Well, I know nothing of nautical affairs: but I wonder, I wonder, James, whether it is not too easy for a rich man to despise money – to mistake the real motives . . . To pay too much attention to mere words, and –'

'Surely to God you would never call me rich?'

'I have ridden over your land.'

'It's three-quarters of it mountain, and one quarter bog; and even if they were to pay their rent for the rest it would only be a few hundred a year – barely a thousand.'

'My heart bleeds for you. I have never yet known a man admit that he was either rich or asleep: perhaps the poor man and the wakeful man have some great moral advantage. How does it arise? But to return – surely he is as brave a commander as you could wish, and as likely as any man to lead you to glorious and remarkable actions?'

'Would you guarantee his courage?'

'So here is the true gravamen at last,' thought Stephen, and he said, 'I would not; I do not know him well enough. But I should be astonished, *astonished*, if he were to prove shy. What makes you think he is?'

'I do not say he is. I should be very sorry to say anything against any man's courage without proof. But we should have had that galley. In another twenty minutes we could have boarded and carried her.'

'Oh? I know nothing of these things, and I was downstairs at the time; but I understood that the only prudent thing to do was to turn about, to protect the rest of the convoy.'

'Prudence is a great virtue, of course,' said James.

'Well. And promotion means a great deal to you, so?'

'Of course it does. There never was an officer worth a farthing that did not long to succeed and hoist his flag at last. But I can see in your eye that you think me inconsistent. Understand my position: I want no republic – I stand by settled, established institutions, and by authority so long as it is not tyranny. All I ask is an independent parliament that represents the responsible men of the kingdom and not merely a squalid parcel of placemen and place-seekers. Given that, I am perfectly happy with the English con-nexion, perfectly happy with the two kingdoms: I can drink the loyal toast without choking, I do assure you.'

'Why are you putting out the lamp?'

James smiled. 'It is dawn,' he said, nodding towards the grey, severe light in the cabin window. 'Shall we go on deck? We may have raised the high land of Minorca by now, or we shall very soon; and I think I can promise you some of those birds the sailors call shearwaters if we lay her in towards the cliff of Fornells.'

Yet with one foot on the companion-ladder he turned and looked into Stephen's face. 'I cannot tell what possessed me to speak so rancorously,' he said, passing his hand over his forehead and looking both unhappy and bewildered. 'I do not think I have ever done so before. Have not expressed myself well – clumsy, inaccurate, not what I meant nor what I meant to say. We understood one another better before ever I opened my mouth.'

Chapter Six

Mr Florey the surgeon was a bachelor; he had a large house high up by Santa Maria's, and with the broad, easy conscience of an unmarried man he invited Dr Maturin to stay whenever the *Sophie* should come in for stores or repairs, putting a room at his disposal for his baggage and his collections – a room that already housed the hortus siccus that Mr Cleghorn, surgeon-major to the garrison for close on thirty years, had gathered in countless dusty volumes.

It was an enchanting house for meditation, backing on to the very top of Mahon's cliff and overhanging the merchants' quay at a dizzy height – so high that the noise and business of the harbour was impersonal, no more than an accompaniment to thought. Stephen's room was at the back, on this cool northern side looking over the water; and he sat there just inside the open window with his feet in a basin of water, writing his diary while the swifts (common, pallid and Alpine) raced shrieking through the torrid, quivering air between him and the *Sophie*, a toy-like object far down on the other side of the harbour, tied up to the victualling-wharf.

'So James Dillon is a Catholic,' he wrote in his minute and secret shorthand. 'He used not to be. That is to say, he was not a Catholic in the sense that it would have made any marked difference to his behaviour, or have rendered the taking of an oath intolerably painful. He was not in any way a religious man. Has there been some conversion, some Loyolan change? I hope not. How many crypto-Catholics are there in the service? I should like to ask him; but that would be indiscreet. I remember Colonel Despard's telling me that in England Bishop Challoner gave a dozen dispensations a year for the occasional taking of the sacrament according to the Anglican rite. Colonel T –, of the Gordon riots, was a Catholic. Did Despard's remark refer only to the army? I never thought to ask him at the time. Quaere: is this the cause for James Dillon's agitated state of mind? Yes, I think so. Some strong pressure is certainly at work. What is more, it appears to me that this is a critical time for him, a lesser climacteric – a time that will settle him in that particular course he will never leave again, but will persevere in for the rest of his life. It has often seemed to me that towards this period (in which we all three lie, more or less) men strike out their permanent characters; or have those characters struck into them. Merriment, roaring high spirits before this: then some chance concatenation, or some hidden predilection (or rather inherent bias) working through, and the man is in the road he cannot leave but must go on, making it deeper and deeper (a groove, or channel), until he is lost in his mere character – persona – no longer human, but an accretion of qualities belonging to this character. James Dillon was a delightful being. Now he is closing in. It is odd – will I say heart-breaking? – how cheerfulness goes: gaiety of mind, natural free-springing joy. Authority is its great enemy – the assumption of authority. I know few men over fifty that seem to me entirely human: virtually none who has long exercised authority. The senior post-captains here; Admiral Warne. Shrivelled men (shrivelled in essence: not, alas, in belly). Pomp, an unwholesome diet, a cause of choler, a pleasure paid too late and at too high a price, like lying with a peppered paramour. Yet Ld Nelson, by Jack Aubrey's account, is as direct and unaffected and amiable a man as could be wished. So, indeed, in most ways is JA himself; though a certain careless arrogancy of power appears at times. *His* cheerfulness, at all events, is with him still. How long will it last? What woman, political cause, disappointment, wound, disease, untoward child, defeat, what strange surprising accident will take it all away? But I am concerned for James Dillon: he is as mercurial as ever he was – more so – only now it is all ten octaves lower down and in a darker key; and sometimes I am afraid in a black humour he will do himself a mischief. I would give so much to bring him cordially friends with Jack Aubrey. They are so alike in so many ways, and James is made for friendship: when he sees that he is mistaken about JA's conduct, surely he will come round? But will he ever find this out, or is JA to be the focus of his discontent? If so there is little hope; for the discontent, the inner contest, must at times be very severe in a man so humourless (on occasion) and so very exigent upon the point of honour. He is obliged to reconcile the irreconcilable more often than most men; and he is less qualified to do so. And whatever he may say he knows as well as I do that he is in danger of a horrible confrontation: suppose it had been he who took Wolfe Tone in Lough Swilly? What if Emmet persuades the French to invade again? And what if Bonaparte makes friends with the Pope? It is not impossible. But on the other hand, JD *is* a mercurial creature, and if once, on the upward rise, he comes to love JA as he should, he will not change – never was a more loyal affection. I would give a great deal to bring them friends.'

He sighed and put down his pen. He put it down upon the cover of a jar in which there lay one of the finest asps he had ever seen, thick, venomous, snub-nosed, coiled down in spirits of wine, with its slit-pupilled eye looking at him through the glass. This asp was one of the fruits of the days they spent in Mahon before the *Sophie* came in, a third prize at her tail, a fair-sized Spanish tartan. And next to the asp lay two visible results of the *Sophie*'s activity: a watch and a telescope. The watch pointed at twenty minutes to the hour, so he picked up the telescope and focused it upon the sloop. Jack was still aboard, conspicuous in his best uniform, fussing amidships with Dillon and the bosun over some point of the upper rigging: they were all pointing upwards, and inclining their persons from side to side in ludicrous unison.

Leaning forward against the rail of the little balcony, he trained his glass along the quay towards the head of the harbour. Almost at once he saw the familiar scarlet face of George Pearce, ordinary seaman, thrown back skywards in an ecstasy of mirth: there was a little group of his shipmates with him, along by the huddle of one-storeyed wineshops that stretched out towards the tanneries; and they were passing their time at playing ducks and drakes on the still water. These men belonged to the two prize-crews and they had been allowed to stay ashore, whereas the other Sophies were still aboard. Both had shared in the first distribution of prize-money, however; and looking with closer attention at the silvery gleam of the skipping missiles and at the frenzied diving of the little naked boys out in the noisome shallows, Stephen saw that they were getting rid of their wealth in the most compendious manner known to man.

Now a boat was putting off from the *Sophie*, and in his glass he saw the coxswain nursing Jack's fiddle-case with stiff, conscious dignity. He leant back, took one foot out of the water – tepid now – and gazed at it for a while, musing upon the comparative anatomy of the lower members in the higher mammals – in horses – in apes – in the Pongo of the African travellers, or M. de Buffon's Jocko – sportive and gregarious in youth, sullen, morose and withdrawn in age. Which was the true state of the Pongo? 'Who am I,' he thought, 'to affirm that the gay young ape is not merely the chrysalis, as it were, the pupa of the grim old solitary? That the second state is not the natural inevitable culmination – the Pongo's true condition, alas?'

'I was contemplating on the Pongo,' he said aloud as the door opened and Jack walked in with a look of eager expectation, carrying a roll of music.

'I am sure you were,' cried Jack. 'A damned creditable thing to be contemplating on, too. Now be a good fellow and take your other foot out of that basin – why on earth did you put it in? – and pull on your stockings, I beg. We have not a moment to lose. No, not blue stockings: we are going on to Mrs Harte's party – to her rout.'

'Must I put on silk stockings?'

'Certainly you must put on silk stockings. And do show a leg, my dear chap: we shall be late, without you spread a little more canvas.'

'You are always in such a hurry,' said Stephen peevishly, groping among his possessions. A Montpellier snake glided out with a dry rustling sound and traversed the room in a series of extraordinarily elegant curves, its head held up some eighteen inches above the ground.

'Oh, oh, oh,' cried Jack, leaping on to a chair. 'A snake!'

'Will these do?' asked Stephen. 'They have a hole in them.'

'Is it poisonous?'

'Extremely so. I dare say it will attack you, directly. I have very little doubt of it. Was I to put the silk stockings over my worsted stockings, sure the hole would not show: but then, I should stifle with heat. Do not you find it uncommonly hot?'

'Oh, it must be two fathoms long. Tell me, is it really poisonous? On your oath now?'

'If you thrust your hand down its throat as far as its back teeth you may meet a little venom; but not otherwise. Malpolon monspessulanus is a very innocent serpent. I think of carrying a dozen aboard, for the rats – ah, if only I had more time, and if it were not for this foolish, illiberal persecution of reptiles . . . What a pitiful figure you do cut upon that chair, to be sure. *Barney, Barney, buck or doe, Has kept me out of Channel Row,*' he sang to the serpent; and, deaf as an adder though it was, it looked happily into his face while he carried it away.

Their first visit was to Mr Brown's, of the dockyard, where, after greetings, introductions and congratulations upon Jack's good fortune, they played the Mozart B flat quartet, hunting it along with great industry and good will,

Miss playing a sweet-toned, though weak, viola. They had never played all together before, had never rehearsed this particular work, and the resulting sound was ragged in the extreme; but they took immense pleasure there in the heart of it, and their audience, Mrs Brown and a white cat, sat mildly knitting, perfectly satisfied with the performance.

Jack was in tearing high spirits, but his great respect for music kept him in order throughout the quartet. It was during the collation that followed – a pair of fowls, a glazed tongue, sillabub, flummery and maids of honour – that he began to break out. Being thirsty, he drank off two or three glasses of Sillery without noticing them: and presently his face grew redder and even more cheerful, his voice more decidedly masculine and his laughter more frequent: he gave them a highly-coloured account of Stephen's having sawn the gunner's head off and fixed it on again, better than before; and from time to time his bright blue eye wandered towards Miss's bosom, which the fashion of that year (magnified by the distance from Paris) had covered with no more than a very, very little piece of gauze.

Stephen emerged from his reverie to see Mrs Brown looking grave, Miss looking demurely down at her plate and Mr Brown, who had also drunk a good deal, starting on a story that could not possibly come to good. Mrs Brown made great allowances for officers who had been long at sea, particularly those who had come in from a successful cruise and were disposed to be merry; but she made less for her husband, and she knew this story of old, as well as this somewhat glassy look. 'Come, my dear,' she said to her daughter. 'I think we will leave the gentlemen now.'

Molly Harte's rout was a big, miscellaneous affair, with nearly all the officers, ecclesiastics, civilians, merchants and Minorcan notables – so many of them that she had a great awning spread over Señor Martinez' patio to hold all her guests, while the military band from Fort St Philip played to them from what was ordinarily the commandant's office.

'Allow me to name my friend – my particular friend – and surgeon, Dr Maturin,' said Jack, leading Stephen up to their hostess. 'Mrs Harte.'

'Your servant, ma'am,' said Stephen, making a leg.

'I am very happy to see you here, sir,' said Mrs Harte, instantly prepared to dislike him very much indeed.

'Dr Maturin, Captain Harte,' went on Jack.

'Happy,' said Captain Harte, disliking him already, but for an entirely opposite reason, looking over Stephen's head and holding out two fingers, only a little way in front of his sagging belly. Stephen looked deliberately at them, left them dangling there and silently moved his head in a bow whose civil insolence so exactly matched his welcome that Molly Harte said to herself, 'I shall like that man.' They went on to leave room for others, for the tide was flowing fast – the sea-officers all appeared within seconds of the appointed time.

'Here's Lucky Jack Aubrey,' cried Bennet of the *Aurore*. 'Upon my word, you young fellows do pretty well for yourselves. I could hardly get into Mahon for the number of your captures. I wish you joy of them, in course; but you must leave something for us old codgers to retire upon, Eh? Eh?'

'Why, sir,' said Jack, laughing and going redder still, 'it is only beginner's luck – it will soon be out, I am sure, and then we shall be sucking our thumbs again.'

There were half a dozen sea-officers round him, contemporaries and seniors; they all congratulated him, some sadly, some a little enviously, but all with that direct goodwill Stephen had noticed so often in the Navy; and as they drifted off in a body towards a table with three enormous punch-bowls and a regiment of glasses upon it, Jack told them, in an uninhibited wealth of sea-jargon, exactly how each chase had behaved. They listened silently, with keen attention, nodding their heads at certain points and partially closing their eyes; and Stephen observed to himself that at some levels complete communication between men was possible.

After this both he and his attention wandered; holding a glass of arrack-punch, he took up his stand next to an orange-tree, and he stood looking quite happy, gazing now at the uniforms on the one hand and now through the orange-tree on the other, where there were sofas and low chairs with women sitting in them hoping that men would bring them ices and sorbets; and hoping, as far as the sailors on his left were concerned, in vain. They sighed patiently and hoped that their husbands, brothers, fathers, lovers would not get too drunk; and above all that none of them would grow quarrelsome.

Time passed; an eddy in the party's slow rotatory current brought Jack's group nearer the orange-tree, and Stephen heard him say, 'There a hellish great sea running tonight.'

'It's all very well, Aubrey,' said a post-captain, almost immediately afterward. 'But your Sophies used to be a quiet, decent set of men ashore. And now they have two pennies to rub together they kick up bob's a-dying like – well, I don't know. Like a set of mad baboons. They beat the crew of my cousin Oaks's barge cruelly, upon the absurd pretence of having a physician aboard, and so having the right to tie up ahead of a barge belonging to a ship of the line which carries no more than a surgeon – a very absurd pretence. Their two pennies have sent them out of their wits.'

'I am sorry Captain Oaks's men were beat, sir,' said Jack, with a decent look of concern. 'But the fact is true. We do have a physician aboard – an amazing hand with a saw or a clyster.' Jack gazed about him in a very benevolent fashion. 'He was with me not a pint or so ago. Opened our gunner's skull, roused out his brains, set them to rights, stuffed them back in again – I could not bear to look, I assure you, gentlemen – bade the armourer take a crown piece, hammer it out thin into a little dome, do you see, or basin, and so clapped it on, screwed it down and sewed up his scalp as neatly as a sailmaker. Now that's what I call real physic – none of your damned pills and delay. Why, there he is . . .'

They greeted him kindly, urged him to drink a glass of

punch – another glass of punch – they had all taken a great deal; it was quite wholesome – excellent punch, the very thing for so hot a day. The talk flowed on, with only Stephen and a Captain Nevin remaining a little silent. Stephen noticed a pondering, absorbed look in Captain Nevin's eye – a look very familiar to him – and he was not surprised to be led away behind the orange-tree to be told in a low confidential fluent earnest voice of Captain Nevin's difficulty in digesting even the simplest dishes. Captain Nevin's dyspepsy had puzzled the faculty for years, for *years*, sir; but he was sure it would yield to Stephen's superior powers; he had better give Dr Maturin all the details he could remember, for it was a very singular, interesting case, as Sir John Abel had told him – Stephen knew Sir John? – but to be quite frank (lowering his voice and glancing furtively round) he had to admit there were certain difficulties in – in *evacuation*, too . . . His voice ran on, low and urgent, and Stephen stood with his hands behind his back, his head bowed, his face gravely inclined in a listening attitude. He was not, indeed, inattentive; but his attention was not so wholly taken up that he did not hear Jack cry, 'Oh, yes, yes! The rest of them are certainly coming ashore – they are lining the rail in their shore-going rig, with money in their pockets, their eyes staring out of their heads and their pricks a yard long.' He could scarcely have avoided hearing it, for Jack had a fine carrying voice, and his remark happened to drop into one of those curious silences that occur even in very numerous assemblies.

Stephen regretted the remark; he regretted its effect upon the ladies the other side of the orange-tree, who were standing up and mincing away with many an indignant glance; but how much more did he regret Jack's crimson face, the look of maniac glee in his blazing eyes and his triumphant, 'You needn't hurry, ladies – they won't be allowed off the sloop till the evening gun.'

A determined upsurge of talk drowned any possibility of further observations of this kind, and Captain Nevin was settling down to his colon again when Stephen felt a hand on his arm, and there was Mrs Harte, smiling at Captain Nevin in such a manner that he backed and lost himself behind the punch-bowls.

'Dr Maturin, please take your friend away,' said Molly Harte in a low, urgent tone. 'Tell him his ship is on fire – tell him anything. Only get him away – he will do himself *such* damage.'

Stephen nodded. He lowered his head and walked directly into the group, took Jack by the elbow and said, 'Come, come, come,' in an odd, imperative half-whisper, bowing to those whose conversation he had interrupted. 'There is not a moment to be lost.'

'The sooner we are at sea the better,' muttered Jack Aubrey, looking anxiously into the dim light over against Mahon quay. Was the boat his own launch with the remaining liberty-men, or was it a messenger from the angry, righteous commandant's office, bringing orders that would break off the *Sophie*'s cruise? He was still a little shattered from his night's excess, but the steadier part of his mind assured him from time to time that he had done himself no good, that disciplinary action could be taken against him without any man thinking it unjust or oppressive, and that he was exceedingly averse to any immediate meeting with Captain Harte.

What air was moving came from the westward – an unusual wind, and one that brought all the foul reek of the tanneries drifting wetly across. But it would serve to help the *Sophie* down the long harbour and out to sea. Out to sea, where he could not be betrayed by his own tongue; where Stephen could not get himself into bad odour with authority; and where that infernal child Babbington did not have to be rescued from aged women of the town. And where James Dillon could not fight a duel. He had only heard a rumour of it, but it was one of those deadly little after-supper garrison affairs that might have cost him his lieutenant – as valuable an officer as he had ever sailed with, for all his starchiness and unpredictability.

The boat reappeared under the stern of the *Aurore*. It was the launch and it was filled with liberty-men: there were still one or two merry souls among them, but on the whole the Sophies who could walk were quite unlike those who had gone ashore – they had no money left, for one thing, and they were grey, drooping and mumchance for another. Those who could not walk were laid in a row with the bodies recovered earlier, and Jack said, 'How is the tally, Mr Ricketts?'

'All aboard, sir,' said the midshipman wearily, 'except for Jessup, cook's mate, who broke his leg falling down Pigtail Stairs, and Sennet, Richards and Chambers, of the foretop, who went off to George Town with some soldiers.'

'Sergeant Quinn?'

But there was no answer to be had from Sergeant Quinn: he could, and did, remain upright, bolt upright, but his only reply was 'Yes, sir' and a salute to everything that was proposed to him.

'All but three of the marines are aboard, sir,' said James privately.

'Thank you, Mr Dillon,' said Jack, looking over towards the town again: a few pale lights were moving against the darkness of the cliff. 'Then I think we shall make sail.'

'Without waiting for the rest of the water, sir?'

'What does it amount to? Two tons, I believe. Yes: we will take that up another time, together with our stragglers. Now, Mr Watt, all hands to unmoor; and let it be done silently, if you please.'

He said this partly because of a cruel darting agony in his head that made the prospect of roaring and bellowing wonderfully disagreeable and partly because he wished the *Sophie*'s departure to excite no attention whatsoever. Fortunately she was moored with simple warps fore and aft, so there would be no slow weighing of anchors, no stamp and go at the capstan, no acid shrieking of the fiddle; in any case, the comparatively sober members of the crew were too jaded for anything but a sour, mute, expeditious casting-off – no jolly tars, no hearts of oak, no Britons never, never, in this grey stench of a crapulous dawn. Fortunately, too, he had seen to the repairs, stores and victualling (apart from that cursed last voyage of water) before he or anyone else had set foot on shore; and rarely had he appreciated the reward of virtue more than when the *Sophie*'s jib filled and her head came round, pointing eastward to the sea, a wooded, watered, well-found vessel beginning her journey back to independence.

An hour later they were in the narrows, with the town and its evil smells sunk in the haze behind them and the brilliant open water out in front. The *Sophie*'s bowsprit was pointing almost exactly at the white blaze on the horizon that showed the coming of the sun, and the breeze was turning northerly, freshening as it veered. Some of the night's corpses were in lumpish motion. Presently a hose-pipe would be turned on to them, the deck would return to its rightful condition and the sloop's daily round would begin again.

An air of surly virtue hung over the *Sophie* as she made her tedious, frustrating way south and west towards her cruising-ground through calms, uncertain breezes and head-winds – winds that grew so perverse once they had made their offing that the little Ayre Island beyond the eastern point of Minorca hung obstinately on the northern horizon, sometimes larger, sometimes smaller, but always there.

Thursday, and all hands were piped to witness punishment. The two watches stood on either side of the main-deck, with the cutter and the launch towing behind to make more room; the marines were lined up with their usual precision from number three gun aft; and the little quarter-deck was crowded with the officers.

'Mr Ricketts, where is your dirk?' said James Dillon sharply.

'Forgot it, sir. Beg pardon, sir,' whispered the midshipman.

'Put it on at once, and don't you presume to come on deck improperly dressed.'

Young Ricketts cast a guilty look at his captain as he darted below, and he read nothing but confirmation on Jack's frowning visage. Indeed, Jack's views were identical with Dillon's: these wretched men were going to be flogged and it was their right to have it done with due ceremony – all hands gravely present, the officers with their gold-laced hats and swords, the drummer there to beat a roll.

Henry Andrews, the ship's corporal, brought up his charges one by one: John Harden, Joseph Bussell, Thomas Cross, Timothy Bryant, Isaac Isaacs, Peter Edwards and John Surel, all accused of drunkenness. No one had anything to say for them: not one had anything to say for himself. 'A dozen apiece,' said Jack. 'And if there were any justice on earth you would have two dozen, Cross. A responsible fellow like you – a gunner's mate – for shame.'

It was the *Sophie*'s custom to flog at the capstan, not at a grating: the men came gloomily forward, slowly stripped off their shirts and adapted themselves to the squat cylinder; and the bosun's mates, John Bell and John Morgan, tied their wrists on the far side, more for the form than anything else. Then John Bell stood clear, swinging his cat easily in his right hand, with his eye on Jack. Jack nodded and said, 'Carry on.'

'One,' said the bosun solemnly, as the nine knotted cords sighed through the air and clapped against the seaman's tense bare back. 'Two. Three. Four . . .'

So it went on; and once again Jack's cold, accustomed eye noticed how cleverly the bosun's mate set the knotted ends lashing against the capstan itself, yet without giving any appearance of favouring his shipmate. 'It's very well,' he reflected, 'but either they are getting into the spirit-room or some son of a bitch has brought a store of liquor aboard. If I could find him, I should have a proper grating rigged, and there would be none of this hocus-pocus. This amount of drunkenness was more than was right: seven in one day. It was nothing to do with the men's lurid joys ashore, for that was all over – no more than a memory; and as for the paralytic state of the seamen awash in the scuppers as the sloop stood out, that was forgotten too – put down to the easy ways of port, to relaxed harbour discipline, and never held against them. This was something else. Only yesterday he had hesitated about exercising the guns after dinner, because of the number of men he suspected of having had too much: it was so easy for a tipsy fool to get his foot under a recoiling carriage or his face in front of a muzzle. And in the end he had had them merely run in and out, without firing.

Different ships had different traditions about calling out: the old Sophies kept mum, but Edwards (one of the new men) had been drafted from the *King's Fisher*, where they did not, and he uttered a great howling Oh at the first stroke, which so disturbed the young bosun's mate that the next two or three wavered uncertainly in the air.

'Come now, John Bell,' said the bosun reproachfully, not from any sort of malignance towards Edwards, whom he regarded with the placid impartiality of a butcher weighing up a lamb, but because a job of work had to be done proper; and the rest of the flogging did at least give Edwards some excuse for his shattering crescendo. Shattering, that is to say, to poor John Surel, a meagre little quota-man from Exeter, who had never been beaten before and who now added the crime of incontinence to that of drunkenness; but he was flogged, for all that, in great squalor, weeping and roaring most pitifully, as the flustered Bell laid into him hard and fast, to get it over quickly.

'How utterly barbarous this would seem to a spectator that was not habituated to it,' reflected Stephen. 'And how little it matters to those that are. Though that child does appear concerned.' Babbington was indeed looking a little pale and anxious as the unseemly business came to an end, with the moaning Surel handed over to his shamefaced mess-mates and hurried away.

But how transient was this young gentleman's pallor and anxiety! Not ten minutes after the swabber had removed all traces of the scene, Babbington was flying about the upper rigging in pursuit of Ricketts, with the clerk toiling with laborious, careful delight a great way behind.

'Who is that skylarking?' asked Jack, seeing vague forms through the thin canvas of the main royal. 'The boys?'

'The young gentlemen, your honour,' said the quarter-master.

'That reminds me,' said Jack. 'I want to see them.'

Not long after this the pallor and the anxiety were back again, and with good reason. The midshipmen were sup-posed to take noon observations to work out the vessel's position, which they were to write on a piece of paper. These pieces of paper were called *the young gentlemen's workings* and they were delivered to the captain by the marine sentry, with the words, 'The young gentlemen's workings, sir'; to which Captain Allen (an indolent, easy-going man) had been accustomed to reply, '– the young gentlemen's workings', and toss them out of the window.

Hitherto, Jack had been too busy working up his crew to pay much attention to the education of his midshipmen, but he had looked at yesterday's slips and they, with a very suspicious unanimity, had shown the *Sophie* in 39°21'N., which was fair enough, but also in a longitude that she could only have reached by cleaving the mountain-range behind Valencia to a depth of thirty-seven miles.

'What do you mean by sending me this nonsense?' he asked them. It was not really an answerable question; nor were many of the others that he propounded, and they did not, in fact, attempt to answer them; but they agreed that they were not there to amuse themselves, nor for their manly beauty, but rather to learn their professions; that their jour-nals (which they fetched) were neither accurate, full, nor up to date, and that the ship's cat would have written them

better; that they would for the future pay the greatest attention to Mr Marshall's observation and reckoning; that they
would prick the chart daily with him; and that no man was
fit to pass for a lieutenant, let alone bear any command ('May
God forgive me,' said Jack, in an internal aside) who could
not instantly tell the position of his ship to within a minute
– nay, to within thirty seconds. Furthermore, they would
show up their journals every Sunday, cleanly and legibly
written.

'You *can* write decently, I suppose? Otherwise you must
go to school to the clerk.' They hoped so, sir, they were sure;
they should do their best. But he did not seem convinced and
desired them to sit down on that locker, take those pens and
these sheets of paper, to pass him yonder book, which would
answer admirably for them to be read to out of from.

This was how it came about that Stephen, pausing in the
quietness of his sick-bay to reflect upon the case of the
patient whose pulse beat weak and thin beneath his fingers,
heard Jack's voice, unnaturally slow, grave and terrible,
come wafting down the wind-sail that brought fresh air
below. 'The quarter-deck of a man-of-war may justly be
considered as a national school for the instruction of a
numerous portion of our youth; there it is that they acquire
a habit of discipline and become instructed in all the interesting minutiae of the service. Punctuality, cleanliness, diligence and dispatch are regularly inculcated, and such a habit
of sobriety and even of self-denial acquired, that cannot fail
to prove highly useful. By learning to *obey*, they are also
taught how to *command*.

'Well, well, well,' said Stephen to himself, and then turned
his mind entirely back to the poor, wasted, hare-lipped creature in the hammock beside him, a recent landman belonging
to the starboard watch. 'How old may you be, Cheslin?' he
asked.

'Oh, I can't tell you, sir,' said Cheslin with a ghost of
impatience in his apathy. 'I reckon I might be about thirty,
like.' A long pause. 'I was fifteen when my old father died;

and I could count the harvests back, if I put my mind to it. But I can't put my mind to it, sir.'

'No. Listen, Cheslin: you will grow very ill if you do not eat. I will order you some soup, and you must get it down.'

'Thank you, sir, I'm sure. But there's no relish to my meat; and I doubt they would let me have it, any gate.'

'Why did you tell them your calling?'

Cheslin made no reply for a while, but stared dully. 'I dare say I was drunk. 'Tis mortal strong, that grog of theirn. But I never thought they would be so a-dread. Though to be sure the folk over to Carborough and the country beyond, they don't quite like to name it, either.'

At this moment hands were piped to dinner, and the berth-deck, the long space behind the canvas screen that Stephen had had set up to protect the sick-bay a little, was filled with a tumult of hungry men. An orderly tumult, however: each mess of eight men darted to its particular place, hanging tables appeared, dropping instantly from the beams, wooden kids filled with salt pork (another proof that it was Thursday) and peas came from the galley, and the grog, which Mr Pullings had just mixed at the scuttle-butt by the mainmast, was carried religiously below, everyone skipping out of its way, lest a drop should fall.

A lane instantly formed in front of Stephen, and he passed through with smiling faces and kind looks on either side of him; he noticed some of the men whose backs he had oiled earlier that morning looked remarkably cheerful, particularly Edwards, for he, being black, had a smile that flashed far whiter in the gloom; attentive hands tweaked a bench out of his way, and a ship's boy was slewed violently round on his axis and desired 'not to turn his back on the Doctor – where were his fucking manners?' Kind creatures; such good-natured faces; but they were killing Cheslin.

'I have a curious case in the sick-bay,' he said to James, as they sat digesting figgy-dowdy with the help of a glass of port. 'He is dying of inanition; or will, unless I can stir his torpor.'

'What is his name?'

'Cheslin: he has a hare lip.'

'I know him. A waister – starboard watch – no good to man or beast.'

'Ah? Yet he has been of singular service to men and women, in his time.'

'In what way?'

'He was a sin-eater.'

'Christ.'

'You have spilt your port.'

'Will you tell me about him?' asked James, mopping at the stream of wine.

'Why, it was much the same as with us. When a man died Cheslin would be sent for; there would be a piece of bread on the dead man's breast; he would eat it, taking the sins upon himself. Then they would push a silver piece into his hand and thrust him out of the house, spitting on him and throwing stones as he ran away.'

'I thought it was only a tale, nowadays,' said James.

'No, no. It's common enough, under the silence. But it seems that the seamen look upon it in a more awful light than other people. He let it out and they all turned against him immediately. His mess expelled him; the others will not speak to him, nor allow him to eat or sleep anywhere near them. There is nothing physically wrong with him, yet he will die in about a week unless I can do something.'

'You want to have him seized up at the gangway and given a hundred lashes, Doctor,' called the purser from the cabin where he was casting his accounts. 'When I was in a Guineaman, between the wars, there was a certain sorts of blacks called Whydaws, or Whydoos, that used to die by the dozen in the Middle Passage, out of mere despair at being taken away from their country and their friends. We used to save a good many by touching them up with a horse-whip in the mornings. But it would be no kindness to preserve that chap, Doctor: the people would only smother him or scrag him or shove him overboard in the end. They will abide a great deal, sailors, but not a Jonah. It's like a white crow – the others peck him to death. Or an albatross. You catch an albatross – it's easy, with a line – and paint a red cross on his bosom, and the others will tear him to pieces before the glass is turned. Many's the good laugh we had with them, off the Cape. But the hands will never let that fellow mess with them, not if the commission lasts for fifty years: ain't that so, Mr Dillon?'

'Never,' said James. 'Why in God's name did he ever come into the Navy? He was a volunteer, not a pressed man.'

'I conceive he was tired of being a white crow,' said Stephen. 'But I will not lose a patient because of sailors' prejudices. He must be put to lie out of reach of their malignance, and if he recovers he shall be my loblolly boy, an isolated employment. So much so, indeed, that the present lad –'

'I beg your pardon, sir, but Captain's compliments and would you like to see something amazingly philosophical?' cried Babbington, darting in like a ball.

After the dimness of the gun-room the white blaze on deck made it almost impossible to see, but through his narrowed eyelids Stephen could distinguish Old Sponge, the taller Greek, standing naked in a pool of water by the starboard hances, dripping still and holding out a piece of copper sheathing with great complacency. On his right stood Jack, his hands behind him and a look of happy triumph on his face: on his left most of the watch, craning and staring. The Greek held the corroded copper sheet out a little farther and, watching Stephen's face intently, he turned it slowly over. On the other side there was a small dark fish with a sucker on the back of its head, clinging fast to the metal.

'A remora!' cried Stephen with all the amazement and delight the Greek and Jack had counted upon, and more. 'A bucket, there! Be gentle with the remora, good Sponge, honest Sponge. Oh, what happiness to see the true remora!'

Old Sponge and Young Sponge had been over the side in this flat calm, scraping away the weed that slowed the *Sophie*'s pace: in the clear water they could be seen creeping along ropes weighed down with nets of shot, holding their breath for two minutes at a time, and sometimes diving right under the keel and coming up the other side from lightness of heart. But it was only now that Old Sponge's accustomed eye had detected their sly common enemy hiding under the garboard-strake. The remora was so strong it had certainly torn the sheathing off, they explained to him; but that was nothing – it was so strong it could hold the sloop motionless, or almost motionless, in a brisk gale! But now they had him – there was an end to his capers now, the dog – and now the *Sophie* would run along like a swan. For a moment Stephen felt inclined to argue, to appeal to their common sense, to point to the nine-inch fish, to the exiguity of its fins; but he was too wise, and too happy, to yield to this temptation, and he jealously carried the bucket down to his cabin, to commune with the remora in peace.

And he was too much of a philosopher to feel much vex-ation a little later when a pretty breeze reached them, coming in over the rippling sea just abaft the larboard beam, so that the *Sophie* (released from the wicked remora) heeled over in a smooth, steady run that carried her along at seven knots until sunset, when the mast-head cried, 'Land ho! Land on the starboard bow.'

Chapter Seven

The land in question was Cape Nao, the southern limit of their cruising ground: it stood up there against the western horizon, a dark certainty, hard in the vagueness along the rim of the sky.

'A very fine landfall, Mr Marshall,' said Jack, coming down from the top, where he had been scrutinizing the cape through his glass. 'The Astronomer Royal could not have done better.'

'Thank you, sir, thank you,' said the master, who had indeed taken a most painstaking series of lunars, as well as the usual observations, to fix the sloop's position. 'Very happy to — approbation —' His vocabulary failed him, and he finished by jerking his head and clasping his hands by way of expression. It was curious to see this burly fellow — a hard-faced, formidable man — moved by a feeling that called for a gentle, graceful outlet; and more than one of the hands exchanged a knowing glance with a shipmate. But Jack had no notion of this whatsoever — he had always attributed Mr Marshall's painstaking, scrupulous navigation and his zeal as an executive officer to natural goodness, to his nautical character; and in any case his mind was now quite taken up with the idea of exercising the guns in the darkness. They were far enough from the land to be unheard, with the wind wafting across; and although there had been a great improvement in the *Sophie*'s gunnery he could not rest easy without some daily approach to perfection. 'Mr Dillon,' he said, 'I could wish the starboard watch to fire against the larboard watch in the darkness. Yes, I know,' he went on, dealing with the objection on his lieutenant's lengthening face, 'but if the exercise is carried on *from* light *into* darkness, even the poorest crews will not get under their guns or fling themselves over the side. So we will make ready a couple of casks, if you please, for the daylight exercise, and another couple, with a lantern, or a flambeau, or something of that kind, for the night.'

Since the first time he had watched a repetition of the exercise (what a great while since it seemed), Stephen had tended to avoid the performance; he disliked the report of the guns, the smell of the powder, the likelihood of painful injury to the men and the certainty of a sky emptied of birds, so he spent his time below, reading with half an ear cocked for the sound of an accident – so easy for something to go wrong, with a briskly-moving gun on a rolling, pitching deck. This evening, however, he came up, ignorant of the approaching din, meaning to go forward to the elm-tree pump – the elm-tree pump, whose head the devoted seamen unshipped for him twice a day – to take advantage of the sloping light as it lit up the under-parts of the brig; and Jack said, 'Why, there you are, Doctor. You have come on deck to see what progress we have made, no doubt. It is a charming sight, is it not, to see the great guns fire? And tonight you will see them in the dark, which is even finer. Lord, you should have seen the Nile! And heard it! How happy you would have been!'

The improvement in the *Sophie*'s fire-power was indeed very striking, even to so unmilitary a spectator as Stephen. Jack had devised a system that was both kind to the sloop's timbers (which really could not bear the shock of a united broadside) and good for emulation and regularity: the lee-ward gun of the broadside fired first, and the moment it was at its full recoil its neighbour went off – a rolling fire, with the last gun-layer still able to see through the smoke. Jack explained all this as the cutter pulled out into the fading light with the casks aboard. 'Of course,' he added, 'we make our run at no great range – only enough to get in three rounds. How I long for four!'

The gun-crews were stripped to the waist; their heads were tied up in their black silk handkerchiefs; they looked keenly attentive, at home and competent. There was to be a prize, naturally, for any gun that should hit the mark, but a better one for the watch that should fire the faster, without any wild, disqualifying shots.

The cutter was far away astern and to leeward – it always surprised Stephen to see how smoothly-travelling bodies at sea could appear to be almost together at one moment and then, when one looked round, miles apart without any apparent effort or burst of speed – and the cask was bobbing on the waves. The sloop wore and ran evenly down under her topsails to pass at a cable's length to windward of the cask. 'There is little point in being farther,' observed Jack, with his watch in one hand and a piece of chalk in the other. 'We cannot hit hard enough.'

The moments passed. The cask bore broader on the bow. 'Cast loose your guns,' cried James Dillon. Already the smell of slow-match was swirling along the deck. 'Level your guns . . . out tompions . . . run out your guns . . . prime . . . point your guns . . . fire.'

It was like a great hammer hitting stone at half-second intervals, admirably regular: the smoke streamed racing away in a long roll ahead of the brig. It was the larbowlines who had fired, and the starboard watch, craning their necks a-tiptoe upon any point of vantage, watched jealously for the fall of the shot: they pitched too far, thirty yards too far, but they were well grouped. The larboard watch worked with concentrated fury at their guns, swabbing, ramming, heaving in and heaving out: their backs shone and even ran with sweat.

The cask was not quite abeam when the next broadside utterly shattered it. 'Two minutes five,' said Jack, chuckling. Without even pausing to cheer, the larboard watch raced on; the guns ran up, the great hammer repeated its seven-fold stroke, white water sprang up round the shattered staves. The swabs and rammers flashed, the grunting crews slammed the loaded guns up against their ports, heaving them round with tackles and handspikes as far as ever they would go; but the wreckage was too far behind – they just could not get in their fourth broadside.

'Never mind,' called Jack. 'It was very near. Six minutes and ten seconds.' The larboard watch gave a corporate sigh. They had set their hearts on their fourth broadside, and on beating six minutes, as they knew very well the starboard watch would do.

In fact, the starboard watch achieved five minutes and fifty-seven seconds; but on the other hand they did not hit their cask, and in the anonymous dusk there was a good deal of audible criticism of 'unscrupulous grass-combing buggers that blazed away, blind and reckless – anything to win. And powder at eighteen pence the pound.'

The day had given place to night, and Jack observed with profound satisfaction that it made remarkably little difference on deck. The sloop came up into the wind, filled on the other tack and bore away towards the wavering flare on the third tub. The broadsides rapped out one after another, crimson-scarlet tongues stabbing into the smoke; the powder-boys flitted along the deck, down through the dreadnought screens past the sentry to the magazine and back with cartridge; the gun-crews heaved and grunted; the matches glowed: the rhythm hardly changed. 'Six minutes and forty-two seconds,' he announced after the last, peering closely at his watch by the lantern. 'The larboard watch bears the bell away. A not discreditable exercise, Mr Dillon?'

'Far better than I had expected, sir, I confess.'

'Well now, my dear sir,' said Jack to Stephen, 'what do you say to a little music, if your ears are not quite numbed? Is it any good inviting you, Dillon? Mr Marshall has the deck at present, I believe.'

'Thank you, sir, thank you very much. But you know what a sad waste music is on me – pearls before swine.'

'I am really pleased with tonight's exercise,' said Jack, tuning his fiddle. 'Now I feel I can run inshore with a clearer conscience – without risking the poor sloop too much.'

'I am happy you are pleased; and certainly the mariners seemed to ply their pieces with a wonderful dexterity; but you must allow me to insist that that note is not A.'

'Ain't it?' cried Jack anxiously. 'Is this better?'

Stephen nodded, tapped his foot three times, and they dashed away into Mr Brown's Minorcan divertimento.

'Did you notice my bowing in the pump-pump-*pump* piece?' asked Jack.

'I did indeed. Very sprightly, very agile. I noticed you neither struck the hanging shelf nor yet the lamp. I only grazed the locker once myself.'

'I believe the great thing is not to think of it. Those fellows, rattling their guns in and out, did not think of it. Clapping on to the tackles, sponging, swabbing, ramming – it has grown quite mechanical. I am very pleased with them, particularly three and five of the port broadside. They were the merest parcel of lubbers to begin with, I do assure you.'

'You are wonderfully earnest to make them proficient.'

'Why, yes: there is not a moment to be lost.'

'Well. You do not find this sense of constant hurry oppressive – jading?'

'Lord, no. It is as much part of our life as salt pork – even more so in tide-flow waters. Anything can happen, in five minutes' time, at sea – ha, ha, you should hear Lord Nelson! In this case of gunnery, a single broadside can bring down a mast and so win a fight; and there's no telling, from one hour to the next, when we may have to fire it. There is no telling, at sea.'

How profoundly true. An all-seeing eye, an eye that could pierce the darkness, would have beheld the track of the Spanish frigate *Cacafuego* running down to Carthagena, a track that certainly would have cut the *Sophie*'s if the sloop had not lingered a quarter of an hour to dowse her lighted casks; but as it was the *Cacafuego* passed silently a mile and a half to the westward of the *Sophie*, and neither caught sight of the other. The same eye would have seen a good many other vessels in the neighbourhood of Cape Nao for, as Jack knew very well, everything coming up from Almeria, Alicante or Malaga had to round that headland: it would particularly have noticed a small convoy bound for Valencia under the protection of a letter of marque; and it would have seen that the *Sophie*'s course (if persisted in) would bring her inshore and to the windward of the convoy in the half hour before first light.

'Sir, sir,' piped Babbington into Jack's ear.

'Hush, sweetheart,' murmured his captain, whose dreaming mind was occupied with quite another sex. 'Eh?'

'Mr Dillon says, top lights in the offing, sir.'

'Ha,' said Jack, instantly awake, and ran up on to the grey deck in his nightshirt.

'Good morning, sir,' said James, saluting and offering his night-glass.

'Good morning, Mr Dillon,' said Jack, touching his nightcap in reply and taking the telescope. 'Where away?'

'Right on the beam, sir.'

'By God, you have good eyes,' said Jack, lowering the glass, wiping it and peering again into the shifting sea-haze. 'Two. Three. I think a fourth.'

The *Sophie* was lying there, hove to, with her foretopsail to the mast and her maintopsail almost full, the one counterbalancing the other as she lay right under the dark cliff. The wind — what wind there was — was a puffy, unreliable air from the north-north-west, smelling of the warm hillside; but presently, as the land grew warmer, it would no doubt veer to the north-east or even frankly into the east itself. Jack gripped the shrouds. 'Let us consider the positions from the top,' he said. 'God damn and blast these skirts.'

The light increased; the thinning haze unveiled five vessels in a straggling line, or rather heap; they were all hull-up, and the nearest was no more than a quarter of a mile away. From north to south they ran, first the *Gloire*, a very fast ship-rigged Toulon privateer with twelve eight-pounders,

chartered by a wealthy Barcelona merchant named Jaume
Mateu to protect his two settees, the *Pardal* and the *Xaloc*,
of six guns apiece, the second carrying a valuable (and illegal)
cargo of uncustomed quicksilver into the bargain; the *Pardal*
lay under the privateer's quarter to leeward; then, almost
abreast of the *Pardal* but to windward and only four or five
hundred yards from the *Sophie*, the *Santa Lucia*, a Neopoli-
tan snow, a prize belonging to the *Gloire*, filled with discon-
solate French royalists taken on their passage to Gibraltar;
then came the second settee, the *Xaloc*; and lastly a tartan
that had joined the company off Alicante, glad of the protection from Barbary rovers, Minorcan letters of marque and
British cruisers. They were all smallish vessels; they all
expected danger from the seaward (which was why they kept
inshore – an uncomfortable, perilous way of getting along,
compared with the long course of the open sea, but one that
allowed them to run for the shelter of coastal batteries); and
if any of them noticed the *Sophie* in the stronger light they
said, 'Why, a little brig, creeping along close to the land:
for Denia, no doubt.'

'What do you make of the ship?' asked Jack.

'I cannot count her ports in this light. She seems a little
small for one of their eighteen-gun corvettes. But at all
events she is of some force; and she is the watch-dog.'

'Yes.' That was certain. She lay there to the windward of
the convoy as the wind veered and as they rounded the cape.
Jack's mind was beginning to move fast. The flowing series
of possibilities ran smoothly before his judgment: he was
both the commander of that ship and of this sloop under
his feet.

'May I make a suggestion, sir?'

'Yes,' said Jack in a flat voice. 'So long as we do not hold
a council of war – they never decide anything.' He had asked
Dillon up here as an attention due to him for having detected
the convoy; he really did not want to consult him, or any
other man, and he hoped Dillon would not break in on his
racing ideas with any remarks whatever, however wise. Only

one person could deal with this: the *Sophie*'s master and commander.

'Perhaps I should beat to quarters, sir?' said James stiffly, for the hint had been eminently clear.

'You see that slovenly little snow between us and the ship?' said Jack, breaking across him. 'If we gently square our foreyard we shall be within a hundred yards of her in ten minutes, and she will mask us from the ship. D'ye see what I mean?'

'Yes, sir.'

'With the cutter and the launch full of men you can take her before she's aware. You make a noise, and the ship bears up to protect her: he has no way on him to tack – he must wear; and if you put the snow before the wind, I can pass through the gap and rake him once or twice as he goes round, maybe knocking away a spar aboard the settee at the same time. On deck, there,' he called in a slightly louder voice, 'silence on deck. Send those men below' – for the rumour had spread, and men were running up the forward hatchway. 'The boarders away, then – we should be best advised to send all our black men: they are fine lusty fellows, and the Spaniards dread them – the sloop cleared for action with the least possible show and the men ready to fly to their quarters. But all kept below out of sight: all but a dozen. We must look like a merchantman.' He swung over the edge of the top, his nightshirt billowing round his head. 'The frappings may be cut, but no other preparation that can be seen.'

'The hammocks, sir?'

'Yes, by God,' said Jack, pausing. 'We shall have to get them up precious fast, if we are not to fight without 'em – a damned uncomfortable state. But do not let one come on deck until the boarders are away. Surprise is everything.'

Surprise, surprise. Stephen's surprise at being jerked awake with 'Quarters, sir, quarters,' and at finding himself in the midst of an extraordinarily intense muted activity – people hurrying about in almost pitch darkness – not a glim

– the gentle clash of weapons secretly handed out – the boarders creeping over the landward side and into the boats by twos and threes – the bosun's mates hissing 'Stand by, stand by for quarters, all hands stand by,' in the nearest possible approach to a whispered shout – warrant officers and petty officers checking their teams, quieting the *Sophie*'s fools (she bore a competent share), who urgently wanted to know what? what? and why? Jack's voice calling down into the gloom, 'Mr Ricketts. Mr Babbington.' 'Sir?' 'When I give the word you and the topmen are to go aloft at once: topgallants and courses to be set instantly.' 'Aye aye, sir.'

Surprise. The slow, growing surprise of the sleepy watch aboard the *Santa Lucia*, gazing at this brig as it drifted closer and closer: did it mean to join company? 'She is that Dane who is always plying up and down the coast,' stated Jean Wiseacre. Their sudden total amazement at the sight of two boats coming out from behind the brig and racing across the water. After the first moment's unbelief they did their best: they ran for their muskets, they pulled out their cutlasses and they began to cast loose a gun; but each of the seven men acted for himself, and they had less than a minute to make up their minds; so when the roaring Sophies hooked on at the fore and main chains and came pouring over the side the prize crew met them with no more than one musketshot, a couple of pistols and a half-hearted clash of swords. A moment later the four liveliest had taken to the rigging, one had darted below and two lay upon the deck.

Dillon kicked open the cabin door, glared at the young privateer's mate along a heavy pistol and said, 'You surrender?'

'Oui, monsieur,' quavered the youth.

'On deck,' said Dillon, jerking his head. 'Murphy, Bussell, Thompson, King, clap on to those hatch-covers. Bear a hand, now. Davies, Chambers, Wood, start the sheets. Andrews, flat in the jib.' He ran to the wheel, heaved a body out of the way and put up the helm. The *Santa Lucia* paid off slowly, then faster and faster. Looking over his shoulder he saw the topgallants break out in the *Sophie*, and in almost the same moment the foresail, mainstaysail and boom mainsail: ducking to peer under the snow's forecourse, he saw the ship ahead of him beginning to wear – to turn before the wind and come back on the other tack to rescue the prize. There was great activity aboard her: there was great activity aboard the three other vessels of the convoy – men racing up and down, shouts, whistles, the distant beating of a drum – but in this gentle breeze, and with so little canvas abroad, they all of them moved with a dream-like slowness, quietly following smooth predestinate curves. Sails were breaking out all over, but still the vessels had no way on them, and because of their slowness he had the strangest impression of silence – a silence broken a moment later as the *Sophie* came shaving past the snow's larboard bow with her colours flying, and gave them a thundering cheer. She alone had a fair bow-wave, and with a spurt of pride James saw that every sail was sheeted home, taut and drawing already. The hammocks were piling up at an incredible speed – he saw two go by the board – and on the quarterdeck, stretching up over the nettings, Jack raised his hat high, calling 'Well done indeed, sir,' as they passed. The boarders cheered their shipmates in return; and as they did so the atmosphere of terrible killing ferocity on the deck of the snow changed entirely. They cheered again, and from within the snow, under the hatches, there came a generalized answering howl.

The *Sophie*, all sails abroad, was running at close on four knots. The *Gloire* had little more than steerage-way, and she was already committed to this wheeling movement – was already engaged upon the gradual curve down-wind that would turn her unprotected stern to the *Sophie*'s fire. There was less than a quarter of a mile between them, and the gap was closing fast. But the Frenchman was no fool; Jack saw the ship's mizen topsail laid to the mast and the main and fore yards squared so that the wind should thrust the stern away to leewards and reverse the movement – for the rudder had no bite at all.

'Too late, my friend, I think,' said Jack. The range was narrowing. Three hundred yards. Two hundred and fifty. 'Edwards,' he said to the captain of the aftermost gun, 'Fire across the settee's bows.' The shot, in fact, went through the settee's foresail. She started her halliards, her sails came down with a run and an agitated figure hurried aft to raise his colours and lower them emphatically. There was no time to attend to the settee, however. 'Luff up,' he said. The *Sophie* came closer to the wind: her foresail shivered once and filled again. The *Gloire* was well within the forward traverse of the guns. 'Thus, thus,' he said, and all along the line he heard the grunt and heave as the guns were heaved round a trifle to keep them bearing. The crews were silent, exactly-placed and tense; the spongers knelt with the lighted matches in their hands, gently blowing to keep them in a glow, facing rigidly inboard; the captains crouched glaring along the barrels at that defenceless stern and quarter.

'Fire.' The word was cut off by the roar; a cloud of smoke hid the sea, and the *Sophie* trembled to her keel. Jack was unconsciously stuffing his shirt into his breeches when he saw that there was something amiss – something wrong with the smoke: a sudden fault in the wind, a sudden gust from the north-east, sent it streaming down astern; and at the same moment the sloop was taken aback, her head pushed round to starboard.

'Hands to the braces,' called Marshall, putting up the helm to bring her back. Back she came, though slowly, and the second broadside roared out: but the gust had pushed the *Gloire*'s stern round too, and as the smoke cleared so she replied. In the seconds between Jack had had time to see that her stern and quarter had suffered – cabin windows and little gallery smashed in; that she carried twelve guns; and that her colours were French.

The *Sophie* had lost much of her way, and the *Gloire*, now right back on her original larboard tack, was fast gathering speed; they sailed along on parallel courses, close-hauled to the fitful breeze, the *Sophie* some way behind. They sailed along, hammering one another in an almost continuous din and an unbroken smoke, white, grey-black and lit with darting crimson stabs of fire. On and on: the glass turned, the bell clanged, the smoke lay thick: the convoy vanished astern.

There was nothing to say, nothing to do: the gun-captains had their orders and they were obeying them with splendid fury, firing for the hull, firing as quickly as they could; the midshipmen in charge of the divisions ran up and down the line, bearing a hand, dealing with any beginning of confusion; the powder and shot travelled up from the magazine with perfect regularity; the bosun and his mates roamed gazing up for damage to the rigging; in the tops the sharp-shooters' muskets crackled briskly. He stood there reflecting: a little way to his left, scarcely flinching as the balls came whipping in or hulled the sloop (a great rending thump), stood the clerk and Ricketts, the quarter-deck midshipman. A ball burst through the packed hammock-netting, crossed a few feet in front of him, struck an iron netting-crane and lost its force on the hammocks the other side – an eight-pounder, he noticed, as it rolled towards him.

The Frenchman was firing high, as usual, and pretty wild: in the blue, smokeless, peaceful world to windward he saw splashes as much as fifty yards ahead and astern of them – particularly ahead. Ahead: from the flashes that lit the far side of the cloud and from the change of sound it was clear that the *Gloire* was forging ahead. That would not do. 'Mr Marshall,' he said, picking up his speaking-trumpet, 'we will cross under her stern.' As he raised the trumpet there was a tumult and shouting forward – a gun was over on its side: perhaps two. 'Avast firing there,' he called with great force. 'Stand by, the larboard guns.'

The smoke cleared. The *Sophie* began to turn to starboard, moving to cross the enemy's wake and to bring her port broadside to bear on the *Gloire*'s stern, raking her whole length. But the *Gloire* was having none of it: as though warned by an inner voice, her captain had put up his helm within five seconds of the *Sophie*'s doing so, and now, with the smoke clearing again, Jack, standing by the larboard hammocks, saw him at his taffrail, a small trim grizzled man a hundred and fifty yards away, looking fixedly back. The Frenchman reached behind him for a musket, and resting his elbows on the taffrail he very deliberately aimed it at Jack. The thing was extraordinarily personal: Jack felt an involuntary stiffening of the muscles of his face and chest – a tendency to hold his breath.

'The royals, Mr Marshall,' he said. 'She is drawing away from us.' The gunfire had died away as the guns ceased to bear, and in the lull he heard the musket-shot part almost as if it had been in his ear. In the same second of time Christian Pram, the helmsman, gave a shrill roar and half fell, dragging the wheel over with him, his forearm ploughed open from wrist to elbow. The *Sophie*'s head flew up into the wind, and although Jack and Marshall had the wheel directly, the advantage was gone. The port broadside could only be brought to bear by a further turn that lost still more way; and there was no way to be lost. The *Sophie* was a good two hundred yards behind the *Gloire* now, on her starboard quarter, and the only hope was to gain speed, to range up and renew the battle. He and the master glanced up simultaneously: everything was set that could be set – the wind was too far forward for the studdingsails.

He stared ahead, watching for the stir aboard the chase, the slight change in her wake, that would mean a coming movement to starboard – the *Gloire* in her turn crossing the *Sophie*'s stem, raking her fore and aft and bearing up to protect the scattered convoy. But he stared in vain. The *Gloire* held on to her course. She had drawn ahead of the *Sophie* even without her royals, but now these were setting: and the breeze was kinder to her, too. As he watched, the tears brimming over his eyelids from the concentration of his gaze against the rays of the sun, a slant of wind laid her over and the water ran creaming under her lee, her wake lengthening away and away. The grey-haired captain fired on pertinaciously, a man beside him passing loaded muskets, and one ball severed a ratline two feet from Jack's head; but they were almost beyond musket-range now, and in any case the indefinable frontier between personal animosity and anonymous warfare had been passed – it did not affect him.

'Mr Marshall,' he said, 'pray edge away until we can salute her. Mr Pullings – Mr Pullings, fire as they bear.'

The *Sophie* turned two, three, four points from her course. The bow gun cracked out, followed in even sequence by the rest of the port broadside. Too eager, alas: they were well pitched up, but the splashes showed twenty and even thirty yards astern. The *Gloire*, more attentive to her safety than her honour, and quite forgetful of her duty to Señor Mateu, the unvindictive *Gloire* did not yaw to reply, but hauled her wind. Being a ship, she could point up closer than the *Sophie*, and she did not scruple to do so, profiting to the utmost by the favour of the breeze. She was plainly running away. Of the next broadside two balls seemed to hit her, and one certainly passed through her mizen topsail. But the target was diminishing every minute as their courses diverged, and hope diminished with it.

Eight broadsides later Jack stopped the firing. They had knocked her about shrewdly and they had ruined her looks, but they had not cut up her rigging to make her unmanageable, nor carried away any vital mast or yard. And they had certainly failed to persuade her to come back and fight it out yard-arm to yard-arm. He gazed at the flying *Gloire*, made up his mind and said, 'We will bear away for the cape again, Mr Marshall. South-south-west.'

The *Sophie* was remarkably little wounded. 'Are there any repairs that will not wait half an hour, Mr Watt?' he asked, absently hitching a stray slab-line round a pin.

'No, sir. The sailmaker will be busy for a while; but she sent us no chain nor bar, and she never clawed our rigging, not to say clawed. Poor practice, sir; very poor practice. Not like that wicked little old Turk, and the sharp raps *he* give us.'

'Then we will pipe the hands to breakfast and knot and splice afterwards. Mr Lamb, what damage do you find?'

'Nothing below the water-line, sir. Four right ugly holes amidships and two and four gun-ports well-nigh beat into one: that's the worst. Nothing to what we give her (the sodomite),' he added, under his breath.

Jack went forward to the dismounted gun. A ball from the *Gloire* had shattered the bulwark where the aft ring-bolts were fastened, just as number four was on the recoil. The gun, partly checked on the other side, had slewed round, jamming its run-out neighbour and oversetting. By wonderful good luck the two men who should have been crushed between them were not there – one washing the blood from a graze off his face in the fire-bucket, the other hurrying for more slow-match – and by wonderful good luck the gun had gone over, rather than running murderously about the deck.

'Well, Mr Day,' he said, 'we were in luck one way, if not the other. The gun may go into the bows until Mr Lamb gives us fresh ring-bolts.'

As he walked aft, taking off his coat as he went – the heat was suddenly unbearable – he ran his eye along the south-western horizon. No sign of Cape Nao in the rising haze: not a sail to be seen. He had never noticed the rising of the sun, but there it was, well up into the sky; they must have run a surprising long way. 'By God, I could do with my coffee,' he said, coming abruptly back into a present in which ordinary time flowed steadily once more and appetite mattered. 'But, however,' he reflected, 'I must go below.' This was the ugly side: this was where you saw what happened when a man's face and an iron ball met.

'Captain Aubrey,' said Stephen, clapping his book to the moment he saw Jack in the cockpit. 'I have a grave complaint to make.'

'I am concerned to hear it,' said Jack, peering about in the gloom for what he dreaded to see.

'They have been at my asp. I tell you, sir, they have been at my asp. I stepped into my cabin for a book not three minutes ago, and what did I see? My asp drained – *drained*, I say.'

'Tell me the butcher's bill; then I will attend to your asp.'

'Bah – a few scratches, a man with his forearm moderately scored, a couple of splinters to draw – nothing of consequence – mere bandaging. All you will find in the sick-bay is an obstinate gleet with low fever and a reduced inguinal hernia: and that forearm. Now my asp –'

'No dead? No wounded?' cried Jack, his heart leaping up.

'No, no, no. Now my asp –' He had brought it aboard in its spirits of wine; and at some point in very recent time a criminal hand had taken the jar, drunk up all the alcohol and left the asp dry, stranded, parched.

'I am truly sorry for it,' said Jack. 'But will not the fellow die? Must he not have an emetic?'

'He will not: that is what is so vexing. The bloody man, the more than Hun, the sottish rapparee, he will not die. It was the best double-refined spirits of wine.'

'Pray come and breakfast with me in the cabin; a pint of coffee and a well-broiled chop between you and the asp will take away the sting – will appease . . .' In his gaiety of heart, Jack was very near a witticism; he felt it floating there, almost within reach; but somehow it escaped and he confined himself to laughing as cheerfully as Stephen's vexation would with decency allow and observing, 'The damned villain ran clean away from us; and I am afraid we shall have but a tedious time making our way back. I wonder, I *wonder* whether Dillon managed to pick up the settee, or whether she ran for it, too.'

It was a natural curiosity, a curiosity shared by every man aboard the *Sophie*, apart from Stephen; but it was not to be satisfied that forenoon, nor yet for a great while after the sun had crossed the meridian. Towards noon the wind fell to something very near a calm; the newly-bent sails flapped, hanging in flaccid bulges from their yards, and the men working on the tattered set had to be protected by an awning. It was one of those intensely humid days when the air has no nourishment in it, and it was so hot that even with all his restless eagerness to recover his boarders, secure his prize and move on up the coast, Jack could not find it in his heart to order out the sweeps. The men had fought the ship tolerably well (though the guns were still too slow by far) and they had been very active repairing what damage the *Gloire* had inflicted. 'I will let them be at least until the dog-watch,' he reflected.

The heat pressed down upon the sea; the smoke from the galley funnel hung along the deck, together with the smell of grog and the hundredweight or so of salt beef the Sophies had devoured at dinner-time: the regular tang-tang of the bell came at such long intervals that long before the snow was seen it appeared to Jack that this morning's sharp encounter must belong to another age, another life or, indeed (had it not been for a lingering smell of powder in the cushion under his head), to another kind of experience – to a tale he had read. Stretched out on the locker under his stern window, Jack revolved this in his mind, revolved it again more slowly, and again, and so sank far down and away.

He woke suddenly, refreshed, cool and perfectly aware that the *Sophie* had been running easily for a considerable time, with a breeze that leant her over a couple of strakes, bringing her heels higher than his head.

'I am afraid those damned youngsters woke you, sir,' said Mr Marshall with solicitous vexation. 'I sent 'em aloft, but I fear it was too late. Calling out and hallooing like a pack of baboons. Damn their capars.'

Although he was singularly open and truthful, upon the whole, Jack at once replied, 'Oh, I was not asleep.' On deck he glanced up at the two mastheads, where the midshipmen were peering anxiously down to see whether their offence was reported. Meeting his eye, they at once stared away, with a great demonstration of earnest duty, in the direction of the snow and her accompanying settee, rapidly closing with the *Sophie* on the easterly breeze.

'There she is,' said Jack inwardly, with intense satisfaction. 'And he picked up the settee. Good, active fellow – capital seaman.' His heart warmed to Dillon – it would have been so easy to let that second prize slip away while he was making sure of the crew of the snow. Indeed, it must have called for extraordinary exertions on his part to pin the two of them, for the settee would never have respected her surrender for a moment.

'Well done, Mr Dillon,' he cried, as James came aboard, guiding a figure in a tattered, unknown uniform over the side. 'Did she try to run?'

'She *tried*, sir,' said James. 'Allow me to present Captain La Hire, of the French royal artillery.' They took off their hats, bowed and shook hands. La Hire said, 'Appy,' in a low, pénétré tone: and Jack said, 'Domestique, monsieur.'

'The snow was a Neapolitan prize, sir: Captain La Hire was good enough to take command of the French royalist passengers and the Italian seamen, keeping the prize-crew under control while we pulled across to take possession of the settee. I am sorry to say the tartan and the other settee were too far to windward by the time we had secured her, and they have run down the coast – they are lying under the guns of the battery at Almoraira.'

'Ah? We will look into the bay when we have the prisoners across. Many prisoners, Mr Dillon?'

'Only about twenty, sir, since the snow's people are allies. They were on their way to Gibraltar.'

'When were they taken?'

'Oh, she's a fair prize, sir – a good eight days since.'

'So much the better. Tell me, was there any trouble?'

'No, sir. Or very little. We knocked two of the prize-crew on the head, and there was a foolish scuffle aboard the settee – a man pistolled. I hope all was well with you, sir?'

'Yes, yes – no one killed, no serious wounds. She ran away from us too fast to do much damage: sailed four miles to our three, even without her royals. A most prodigious fine sailer.'

Jack had a notion that some fleeting reserve passed across James Dillon's face, or perhaps showed in his voice; but in the hurry of things to be done, prizes to survey, prisoners to be dealt with, he could not tell why it affected him so unpleasantly until some two or three hours later, when the impression was reinforced and at least half defined.

He was in his cabin: spread out on the table was the chart of Cape Nao, with Cape Almoraira and Cape Ifach jutting out from its massive under-side, and the little village of Almoraira at the bottom of the bay between them: on his right sat James, on his left Stephen, and opposite him Mr Marshall.

'. . . what is more,' he was saying, 'the Doctor tells me the Spaniard says that the other settee has a cargo of quicksilver hidden in sacks of flour, so we must handle *her* with great care.'

'Oh, of course,' said James Dillon. Jack looked at him sharply, then down at the chart and at Stephen's drawing: it showed a little bay with a village and a square tower at the bottom of it: a low mole ran twenty or thirty yards out into the sea, turned left-handed for another fifty and ended in a rocky knob, thus enclosing a harbour sheltered from all but the south-west wind. Steep-to cliffs ran from the village right round to the north-east point of the bay. On the other side there was a sandy beach all the way from the tower to the south-west point, where the cliffs reared up again. 'Could the fellow possibly think I am shy?' he thought. 'That I left off chasing because I did not choose to get hurt and hurried back for a prize?' The tower commanded the entrance to the harbour; it stood some twenty yards to the south of the village and the gravel beach, where the fishing-boats were hauled out. 'Now this knob at the end of the jetty,' he said aloud, 'would you say it was ten foot high?'

'Probably more. It is eight or nine years since I was there,' said Stephen, 'so I will not be absolute; but the chapel on it withstands the tall waves in the winter storms.'

'Then it will certainly protect our hull. Now, with the sloop anchored with a spring on her cable so' – running his finger in a line from the battery to the rock and so to the spot – 'she should be tolerably safe. She opens as heavy a fire as she can, playing on the mole and over the tower. The boats from the snow and the settee land at the Doctor's cove' – pointing to a little indentation just round the south-west point – 'and we run as fast as ever we can along the shore and so take the tower from behind. Twenty yards short of it we fire the rocket and you turn your guns well away from the battery, but blaze away without stopping.'

'Me, sir?' cried James.

'Yes, you, sir; I am going ashore.' There was no answering the decision of this statement, and after a pause he went on to the detailed arrangements. 'Let us say ten minutes to run from the cove to the tower, and . . .'

'Allow twenty, if you please,' said Stephen. 'You portly men of a sanguine complexion often die suddenly, from unconsidered exertion in the heat. Apoplexy – congestion.'

'I wish, I *wish* you would not say things like that, Doctor,' said Jack, in a low tone: they all looked at Stephen with some reproach and Jack added, 'Besides, I am not portly.'

'The captain has an uncommon genteel figgar,' said Mr Marshall.

The conditions were perfect for the attack. The remains of the easterly wind would carry the *Sophie* in, and the breeze that would spring up off the land at about moon-rise would carry her into the offing, together with anything they managed to cut out. In his long survey from the masthead, Jack had made out the settee and a number of other vessels moored to the inner wall of the mole, as well as a row of fishing-boats hauled up along the shore: the settee was at the chapel end of the mole, directly opposite the guns of the tower, a hundred yards on the other side of the harbour.

'I may not be perfect,' he reflected, 'but by God I am not shy; and if we cannot bring her out, then by God I shall burn her where she lies.' But these reflexions did not last long. From the deck of the Neapolitan snow he watched the *Sophie* round Cape Almoraira in the three-quarter darkness and stand into the bay, while the two prizes, with the boats in tow, bore away for the point on the other side. With the settee already in the port there was no possibility of surprise for the *Sophie*, and before she anchored she would have to undergo the fire of the battery. If there was to be a surprise it would lie with the boats: the night was almost certainly too dark now for the prizes to be seen crossing outside the bay to land the boats in Stephen's cove beyond the point – 'one of the few I know where the white-bellied swift builds her nest'. Jack watched her going with a tender and extreme anxiety, torn with longing to be in both places at once: the possibilities of hideous failure flooded into his mind – the shore guns (how big were they? Stephen had been unable to tell) hulling the *Sophie* again and again, the heavy shot passing through both sides – the wind falling, or getting up to blow dead on shore – not enough hands left aboard to sweep her out of range – the boats all astray. It was a fool-hardy attempt, absurdly rash. 'Silence fore and aft,' he cried harshly. 'Do you want to wake the whole coast?'

He had had no idea how deeply he felt about his sloop: he knew exactly how she would be moving in – the particular creak of her mainyard in its parrel, the whisper of her rudder magnified by the sounding-board of her stern; and the passage across the bay seemed to him intolerably long.

'Sir,' said Pullings. 'I think we have the point on our beam now.'

'You are right, Mr Pullings,' said Jack, studying it through his night-glass. 'See the lights of the village going, one after the other. Port your helm, Algren. Mr Pullings, send a good man into the chains: we should have twenty fathom directly.' He walked to the taffrail and called over dark water, 'Mr Marshall, we are standing in.'

The high black bar of the land, sharp against the less solid darkness of the starry sky: it came nearer and nearer, silently eclipsing Arcturus, then the whole of Corona: eclipsing even Vega, high up in the sky. The regular splash of the lead, the steady chant of the man in the weather chains: 'By the deep nine; by the deep nine; by the mark seven; and a quarter five; a quarter less five . . .'

Ahead lay the pallor of the cove beneath the cliff, and a faint white edge of lapping wave. 'Right,' said Jack, and the snow came up into the wind, her foresail backing like a sentient creature. 'Mr Pullings, your party into the launch.' Fourteen men filed fast by him and silently over the side into the creaking boat: each had his white arm-band on. 'Sergeant Quinn.' The marines followed, muskets faintly gleaming, their boots loud on the deck. Someone was grasping at his stomach. It was Captain La Hire, a volunteer attached to the soldiers, looking for his hand. 'Good lucky,' he said, shaking it.

'Merci very much,' said Jack, adding, 'Mon captain,' over the side; and at that moment a flash lit the sky, followed by the deep thump of a heavy gun.

'Is that cutter alongside?' said Jack, his night-eyes half blinded by the flash.

'Here, sir,' said the voice of his coxswain just beneath him. Jack swung over, dropped down. 'Mr Ricketts, where is the dark lantern?'

'Under my jacket, sir.'

'Show it over the stern. Give way.' The gun spoke again, followed almost immediately by two together: they were trying for the range, that was sure: but it was a damned roaring great note for a gun. A thirty-six pounder? Peering round he could see the four boats behind him, a vague line against the loom of the snow and the settee. Mechanically he patted his pistols and his sword: he had rarely felt more nervous, and his whole being was concentrated in his right ear for the sound of the *Sophie*'s broadside.

The cutter was racing through the water, the oars creaking

as the men heaved, and the men themselves grunting deep with the effort – ugh, ugh. 'Rowed-off all,' said the coxswain quietly, and a few seconds later the boat shot hissing up the gravel. The men were out and had hauled it up before the launch grounded, followed by the snow's boat with Mowett, the jolly-boat with the bosun and the settee's launch with Marshall.

The little beach was crowded with men. 'The line, Mr Watt?' said Jack.

'There she goes,' said a voice, and seven guns went off, thin and faint behind the cliff.

'Here we are, sir,' cried the bosun, heaving two coils of one-inch line off his shoulder.

Jack seized the end of one, saying, 'Mr Marshall, clap on to yours, and each man to his knot.' As orderly as though they had been mustering by divisions aboard the *Sophie*, the men fell into place. 'Ready? Ready there? Then tear away.'

He set off for the point, where the beach narrowed to a few feet under the cliff, and behind him, fast to the knotted line, ran his half of the landing-party. There was a bubbling furious excitement rising in his chest – the waiting was over – this was the *now* itself. They came round the point and at once there were blinding fireworks before them and the noise increased tenfold: the tower firing with three, four deep red lances very low over the ground, the *Sophie*, her brailed-up topsails clear in the irregular flashes that lit up the whole sky, hammering away with a fine, busy, rolling fire, playing on the jetty to send stone splinters flying and discourage any attempt at warping the settee ashore. As far as he could judge from this angle, she was in exactly the position they had laid down on the chart, with the dark mass of the chapel rock on her port beam. But the tower was farther than he had expected. Beneath his delight – indeed, his something near a rapture – he could feel his body labouring, his legs heaving him slowly along as his boots sank into the soft sand. He must not, must *not* fall, he thought, after a stumble; and then again at the sound of a man going down on Marshall's rope. He shaded his eyes from the flashes, looked with an unbelievably violent effort away from the battle, ploughed on and on and on, the pounding of his heart almost choking his mind, hardly progressing at all. But now suddenly it was harder ground, and as though he had dropped a ten-stone load he flew along, running, really running. This was packed, noiseless sand, and all along behind him he could hear the hoarse, gasping, catching breath of the landing-party. The battery was hurrying towards them at last, and through the gaps in the parapet he could see busy figures working the Spanish guns. A shot from the *Sophie*, glancing off the chapel rock, howled over their heads; and now an eddy in the breeze brought a choking gust of the tower's powder-smoke.

Was it time for the rocket? The fort was very close – they could hear the voices loud and the rumble of trucks. But the Spaniards were wholly engrossed with answering the *Sophie*'s fire: they could get a little closer, a little closer, closer still. They were all creeping now, by one accord, all clearly visible to one another in the flashes and the general glow. 'The rocket, Bonden,' murmured Jack. 'Mr Watt, the grapnels. Check your arms, all.'

The bosun fixed the three-pronged grapnels to the ropes; the coxswain planted the rockets, struck a spark on to tinder and stood by cherishing it; against the tremendous din of the battery there was a little metallic clicking and the easing of belts; the strong panting lessened.

'Ready?' whispered Jack.

'Ready, sir,' whispered the officers.

He bent. The fuse hissed; and the rocket went away, a red trail and a high blue burst. 'Come on,' he shouted, and his voice was drowned in a great roaring cheer, 'Ooay, ooay!'

Running, running. Dump down into the dry ditch, pistols snapping through the embrasures, men swarming up the ropes on to the parapet, shouting, shouting; a bubbling scream. His coxswain's voice in his ear, 'Give us your fist, mate.' The tearing roughness of stone and there he was, up, whipping his sword out, a pistol in the other hand: but there was no one to fight. The gunners, apart from two on the ground and another kneeling bent over his wound near the great shaded lantern behind the guns, were dropping one by one over the wall and running for the village.

'Johnson! Johnson!' he cried. 'Spike up those guns. Sergeant Quinn, keep up a rapid fire. Light along those spikes.'

Captain La Hire was beating the locks off the heated twenty-four-pounders with a crowbar. 'Better make leap,' he said. 'Make all leap in the air.'

'Vou savez faire leap in the air?'

'Eh, pardi,' said La Hire with a smile of conviction.

'Mr Marshall, you and all the people are to cut along to the jetty. Marines form at the landward end, sergeant, firing all the time, whether they see anyone or not. Get the settee's head round, Mr Marshall, and her sails loosed. Captain La Hire and I are going to blow up the fort.'

'By God,' said Jack, 'I hate an official letter.' His ears were still singing from the enormous bang (a second powder magazine in a vault below the first had falsified Captain La Hire's calculations) and his eyes still swam with yellow shapes from the incandescent leaping half-mile tree of light; his head and neck were horribly painful from all the left-hand half of his long hair having been burnt off – his scalp and face were hideously seared and bruised; on the table in front of him lay four unsatisfactory attempts; and under the *Sophie*'s lee lay the three prizes, urgent to be away for Mahon on the favourable wind, while far behind them the smoke still rose over Almoraira.

'Now just listen to this one, will you,' he said, 'and tell me if it is good grammar and proper language. It begins like the others: Sophie, *at sea; My Lord, I have the honour to acquaint you that pursuant to my orders I proceeded to Cape Nao, where I fell in with a convoy of three sail under the conduct of a French corvetto of twelve guns.* Then I go on to put about the snow – merely touch upon the engagement, with a fling about his *alacrity* – and come to the landing-party. *Upon its appearing that the remainder of the convoy had run under the guns of the Almoraira battery it was determined that they should be attempted to be cut out which was happily accomplished, the battery (a square tower mounting four iron twenty-four-pounders) being blown up at twenty-seven minutes after two, the boats having proceeded to the SSW point of the bay. Three tartans that had been hauled up and chained were obliged to be burnt, but the settee was brought out, when she proved to be the Xaloc, loaded with a valuable cargo of quicksilver concealed in sacks of flour.* Pretty bald, ain't it? However, I go on. *The zeal and activity of Lieutenant Dillon, who took his Majesty's sloop I have the honour to command, in, and kept up an incessant fire on the mole and battery, I am much indebted to. All the officers and men behaved so well that it were insidious to particularize; but I must acknowledge the politeness of Mons. La Hire, of the royal French artillery, who volunteered his services in setting and firing the train to the magazine, and who was somewhat bruised and singed. Enclosed is a list of the killed and wounded: John Hayter, marine, killed; James Nightingale, seaman, and Thomas Thompson, seaman, wounded. I have the honour to be, my Lord* – and so on. What do you think of it?'

'Well, it is somewhat clearer than the last,' said Stephen. 'Though I fancy *invidious* might answer better than *insidious*.'

'Invidious, of course. I knew there was something not quite shipshape there. *Invidious*. A capital word: I dare say you spell it with a V?'

The *Sophie* lay off San Pedro: she had been extraordinarily busy this last week, and she was rapidly perfecting her technique, staying well over the horizon by day, while the military forces of Spain hurried up and down the coast looking for her, and standing in at night to play Old Harry with the little ports and the coast-wise trade in the hours before dawn. It was a dangerous, highly personal way of carrying on; it called for very careful preparation; it made great and continual demands on luck; and it had been remarkably successful. It also made great demands on the *Sophie*'s people, for when they were in the offing Jack exercised them mercilessly at the guns and James at the still brisker setting of sails. James was as taut an officer as any in the service: he liked a clean ship, action or no action, and there was no cutting-out expedition or dawn skirmishing that did not come back to gleaming decks and resplendent brass. He was *particular*, as they said; but his zeal for trim paintwork, perfectly-drawing sails, squared yards, clear tops and flemished ropes was, in fact, surpassed by his delight in taking the whole frail beautiful edifice into immediate contact with the King's enemies, who might wrench it to pieces, shatter, burn or sink it. The *Sophie*'s people bore up under all this with wonderful spirit, however, a worn, lean and eager crew, filled with precise ideas of what they should do the minute they stepped ashore from the liberty-boat – filled, too, with a tolerably precise notion of the change in relations on the quarter-deck: Dillon's marked respect and attention to the captain since Almoraira, their walking up and down together and their frequent consultations had not passed unnoticed; and, of course, the conversation at the gun-room table, in which the lieutenant spoke in the highest terms of the shore-party's action, had at once been repeated throughout the sloop.

'Unless my adding is out,' said Jack, looking up from his paper, 'we have taken, sunk or burnt twenty-seven times our own weight since the beginning of the cruise; and had they all been together they could have fired forty-two guns at us, counting the swivels. That is what the admiral meant by wringing the Spaniard's lugs; and' – laughing heartily – 'if it puts a couple of thousand guineas in our pockets, why, so much the better.'

'May I come in, sir?' asked the purser, appearing in the open door.

'Good morning, Mr Ricketts. Come in, come in and sit down. Are those today's figures?'

'Yes, sir. You will not be pleased, I am afraid. The second butt in the lower tier was started in the head, and it must have lost close on fifty gallon.'

'Then we must pray for rain, Mr Ricketts,' said Jack. But when the purser had gone he turned sadly to Stephen. 'I should have been perfectly happy but for that damned water: everything delightful – people behaving well, charming cruise, no sickness – if only I had completed our water at Mahon. Even at short allowance we use half a ton a day, what with all these prisoners and in this heat; the meat has to be soaked and the grog has to be mixed, even if we do wash in sea-water.' He had wholly set his heart on lying in the sea-lanes off Barcelona, perhaps the busiest convergency in the Mediterranean: that was to have been the culmination of the cruise. Now he would have to bear away for Minorca, and he was by no means sure of what welcome would be waiting for him there, or what orders; not much of his cruising time was left, and capricious winds or a capricious commandant might swallow it entirely – almost certainly would.

'If it is fresh water you are wanting, I can show you a creek not far from here where you may fill all the barrels you choose.'

'Why did you never tell me?' cried Jack, shaking him by the hand and looking delighted – a disagreeable sight, for the left side of his face, head and neck was still seared a baboonish red and blue, it shone under Stephen's medicated grease, and through the grease rose a new frizz of yellow hair; all this, taken with his deep brown, shaved other cheek, gave him a wicked, degenerate, inverted look.

'You never asked.'

'Undefended? No batteries?'

'Never a house, far less a gun. Yet it was inhabited once, for there are the remains of a Roman villa on the top of the promontory, and you can just make out the road beneath the trees and the undergrowth – cistus and lentisk. No doubt they used the spring: it is quite considerable, and it may, I conceive, have real medicinal qualities. The country people use it in cases of impotence.'

'And can you find it, do you think?'

'Yes,' said Stephen. He sat for a moment with his head down. 'Listen,' he said, 'will you do me a kindness?'

'With all my heart.'

'I have a friend who lives some two or three miles inland: I should like you to land me and pick me up, say, twelve hours later.'

'Very well,' said Jack. It was fair enough. 'Very well,' he said again, looking aside to hide the knowing grin that would spread over his face. 'It is the night you would wish to spend ashore, I presume. We will stand in this evening – you are sure we shall not be surprised?'

'Quite sure.'

'– send the cutter in again a little after sunrise. But what if I am forced off the land? What would you do then?'

'I should present myself the next morning, or the morning after that – a whole series of mornings, if need be. I must go,' he said, getting up at the sound of the bell, the still-feeble bell, that his new loblolly boy rang to signify that the sick might now assemble. 'I dare not trust that fellow alone with the drugs.' The sin-eater had discovered a malignance towards his shipmates: he had been found grinding creta alba into their gruel, under the persuasion that it was a far more active substance, far more sinister; and if ill-will had been enough, the sick-bay would have been swept clean days ago.

The cutter, followed by the launch, rowed attentively in through the warm darkness, with Dillon and Sergeant Quinn keeping watch on the sides of the high wooded inlet; and when the boats were two hundred yards from the cliff the exhalation of the stone-pines, mixed with the scent of the gum-cistus, met them – it was like breathing another element.

'If you row a little more to the right,' said Stephen, 'you

may avoid the rocks where the crayfish live.' In spite of the heat he had his black cloak over his shoulders, and sitting huddled there in the stern-sheets he stared into the narrowing cove with a singular intensity, looking deathly pale.

The stream, in times of spate, had formed a little bar, and upon this the cutter grounded: everybody leapt out to float it over, and two seamen carried Stephen ashore. They put him down tenderly, well above the high-water mark, adjured him to take care of all them nasty sticks laying about and hurried back for his cloak. Falling and falling, the water had made a basin in the rock at the top of the beach, and here the sailors filled their barrels, while the marines stood guard at the outward extremities.

'What an agreeable dinner it was,' observed Dillon, sitting with Stephen upon a smooth rock, warm through and through, convenient to their hams.

'I have rarely eaten a better,' said Stephen. 'Never at sea.' Jack had acquired a French cook from the *Santa Lucia*, a royalist volunteer, and he was putting on weight like a prize ox. 'You were in a very copious flow of spirits, too.'

'That was clean against the naval etiquette. At a captain's table you speak when you are spoken to, and you agree; it makes for a tolerably dismal entertainment, but that is the custom. And after all, he does represent the King, I suppose. But I felt I should cast etiquette adrift and make a particular exertion – should try to do the civil thing far more than usual. I have not been altogether fair to himself, you know – far from it,' he added, nodding towards the *Sophie*, 'and it was handsome to invite me.'

'He does love a prize. But prize-taking is not his prime concern.'

'Just so. Though in passing I may say not everyone would know it – he does himself injustice. I do not think the men know it, for example. If they were not kept well in check by the steady officers, the bosun and the gunner, and I must admit that fellow Marshall too, I think there would be trouble with them. There may be still: prize-money is heady stuff. From prize-money to breaking bulk and plunder is no great step – there has been some already. And from plunder and drunkenness to breaking out entirely and even to mutiny itself is not a terrible long way further. Mutinies always happen in ships where the discipline is either too lax or too severe.'

'You are mistaken, sure, when you say they do not know him: unlearned men have a wonderful penetration in these matters – have you ever known a village reputation to be wrong? It is a penetration that seems to dissipate, with a little education, somewhat as the ability to remember poetry will go. I have known peasants who could recite two or three thousand verses. But would you indeed say our discipline is relaxed? It surprises me, but then I know so little of naval things.'

'No. What is commonly called discipline is quite strict with us. What I mean is something else – the intermediate terms, they might be called. A commander is obeyed by his officers because he is himself obeying; the thing is not in its essence personal; and so down. If he does not obey, the chain weakens. How grave I am, for all love. It was that poor unlucky soldier at Mahon I was thinking of brought all this morality into my mind. Do you not find it happens very often, that you are as gay as Garrick at dinner and then by supper-time you wonder why God made the world?'

'I do. Where is the connexion with the soldier?'

'It was prize-money we fought over. He said the whole thing was unfair – he was very angry and very poor. But he would have it we sea-officers were in the Navy for that reason alone. I told him he was mistaken, and he told me I lied. We walked to those long gardens at the top end of the quay – I had Jevons of the *Implacable* with me – and it was over in two passes. Poor, stupid, clumsy fellow: he came straight on to my point. What now, Shannahan?'

'Your honour, the casks are full.'

'Bung 'em up tight, then, and we will get 'em down to the water.'

'Goodbye,' said Stephen, standing up.

'We lose you, then?' said James.

'Yes. I am going up before it grows too dark.'

Yet it would have had to be strangely dark for his feet to have missed this path. It wound up, crossing and recrossing the stream, its steps kept open by the odd fisherman after crayfish, the impotent men going to bathe in the pool and by a few other travellers; and his hand reached out of itself for the branch that would help him over a deep place – a branch polished by many hands.

Up and up: and the warm air sighing through the pines. At one point he stepped out on to a bare rock and there, wonderfully far below already, rowed the boats with their train of almost sunken barrels, not unlike the spaced-out eggs of the common toad; then the path ran back under the trees and he did not emerge again until he was on the thyme and the short turf, the rounded top of the promontory jutting out bare from the sea of pines. Apart from a violet haze on the farther hills and a startling band of yellow in the sky, colour had all gone; but he saw white scuts bobbing away, and as he had expected there were the half-seen forms of shadowy nightjars wheeling and darting, turning like ghosts over his head. He sat down by a great stone that said *Non fui non sum non curo*, and gradually the rabbits came back, nearer and nearer, until on the windward side he could indeed hear their quick nibbling in the thyme. He meant to sit there until dawn, and to establish a continuity in his mind, if that could be done: the friend (though existent) was a mere pretext. Silence, darkness and these countless familiar scents and the warmth of the land had become (in their way) as necessary to him as air.

'I think we may run in now,' said Jack. 'It will do no harm to be before our time, for I should like to stretch my legs a little. In any case, I should like to see him as early as can be; I am uneasy with him ashore. There are times when I feel he should not be allowed out alone; and then again there are times when I feel he could command a fleet, almost.'

The *Sophie* had been standing off and on, and it was now the end of the middle watch, with James Dillon relieving the master; they might just as well take advantage of having all hands on deck to tack the sloop, observed Jack, wiping the dew off the taffrail and leaning upon it to stare down at the cutter towing astern, clearly visible in the phosphorescence of the milk-warm sea.

'That's where we filled, sir,' said Babbington, pointing up the shadowy beach. 'And if it was not so dark you could see the little sorts of path the Doctor went up from here.'

Jack walked over to stare at the path and to view the basin; he walked stumpily, for he could not come by his land legs right away. The ground would not heave and yield like a deck; but as he paced to and fro in the half-light his body grew more used to the earth's rigidity, and in time his legs carried him with an easier, less rough and jerking action. He reflected upon the nature of the ground, upon the slow and uneven coming of the light – a progression by jerks – upon the agreeable change in his lieutenant since the brush at Almoraira and upon the curious alteration in the master, who was quite sullen at times. Dillon had a pack of hounds at home, thirty-five couple – had had some splendid runs – famous country it must be, and prodigious stout foxes to stand up so long – Jack had a great respect for a man who could show good sport with a pack of hounds. Dillon obviously knew a great deal about hunting, and about horses; yet it was strange he should mind so little about the noise his dogs made, for the cry of a tuneful pack . . .

The *Sophie*'s warning gun jerked him from these placid reflexions. He whipped round, and there was the smoke drifting down her side. A hoist of signals was racing up, but without his glass he would not be able to make out the flags in this light: the sloop came round before the wind, and as though she could feel his perplexity of mind she reverted to the oldest of all signals, her topgallants loose and sheets flying, to say *strange sails in sight*; and she emphasized this with a second gun.

Jack glanced at his watch and with longing into the motionless silent pines: said, 'Lend me your knife, Bonden,' and picked up a big flattish stone. *Regrediar* he scratched on it (a notion of secrecy flitting through his mind), with the time and his initials. He struck it into the top of a little heap, took a last hopeless look into the wood and leapt aboard.

The moment the cutter was alongside the *Sophie*'s yards creaked round, she filled and pointed straight out to sea.

'Men-of-war, sir, I am almost certain,' said James. 'I thought you would wish us to get into the offing.'

'Very right, Mr Dillon,' said Jack. 'Will you lend me your glass?'

At the masthead, with his breath coming back and the light of day broad over the sharp, unmisted sea, he could make them out clearly. Two ships to windward, coming up fast from the south with all sails set: men-of-war for a ten-pound note. English? French? Spanish? There was more wind out there and they must be running a good ten knots. He glanced over his left shoulder, at the landing trending away eastwards out to sea. The *Sophie* would have a devil of a job rounding that cape before they were up with her; yet she must do so, or be shut in. Yes, they were men-of-war. They were hull-up now, and although he could not count the ports they were probably heavy frigates, thirty-six gun frigates: frigates for sure.

If the *Sophie* rounded the cape first she might have a chance: and if she ran through the shoal water between the point and the reef beyond it she would gain half a mile, for no deep-drafted frigate could follow her there.

'We will send the people to their breakfast, Mr Dillon,' he said. 'And then clear for action. If there is to be a dust-up, we might just as well have full bellies for it.'

But there were few bellies that filled themselves heartily aboard the *Sophie* that brilliant morning; a kind of impatient rigidity kept the oatmeal and hard-tack from going down regular and smooth; and even Jack's freshly-roasted, freshly-ground coffee wasted its scent on the quarter-deck as the officers stood very carefully gauging the respective courses, speeds and likely points of convergence: two frigates to windward, a hostile coast to leeward and the likelihood of being embayed – it was enough to take the edge off any appetite.

'Deck,' called the look-out from within the pyramid of tightly-drawing canvas, 'she's breaking out her colours, sir. Blue ensign.'

'Aye,' said Jack, 'I dare say. Mr Ricketts, reply with the same.'

Now every glass in the *Sophie* was trained upon the nearer frigate's foretopgallant for the private signal: for although anyone could heave out a blue ensign, only a King's ship could show the secret mark of recognition. There it was: a red flag at the fore, followed a moment later by a white flag and a pendant at the main, and the faint boom of a windward gun.

All the tension slackened at once. 'Very well,' said Jack. 'Reply and then make our number. Mr Day, three guns to leeward in slow time.'

'She's the *San Fiorenzo*, sir,' said James, helping the flustered midshipman with the signal-book, whose prettily-coloured pages would race out of control in the freshening breeze. 'And she is signalling for *Sophie*'s captain.'

'Christ,' said Jack inwardly. The *San Fiorenzo*'s captain was Sir Harry Neale, who had been first lieutenant of the *Resolution* when Jack was her most junior midshipman, and then his captain in the *Success*: a great stickler for promptness, cleanliness, perfection of dress and hierarchy. Jack was unshaved; what hair he had left was in all directions; Stephen's bluish grease covered one half of his face. But there was no help for it. 'Bear up to close her, then,' he said, and darted into his cabin.

*　　*　　*

'Here you are at last,' said Sir Harry, looking at him with marked distaste. 'By God, Captain Aubrey, you take your time.'

The frigate seemed enormous; after the *Sophie* her towering masts might have been those of a first-rate ship of the line; acres of pale deck stretched away on either hand. He had a ludicrous and at the same time a very painful feeling of being crushed down to a far smaller size, as well as that of being reduced all at once from a position of total authority to one of total subservience.

'I beg pardon, sir,' he said, without expression.

'Well. Come into the cabin. Your appearance don't change much, Aubrey,' he remarked, waving towards a chair. 'However, I am quite glad of the meeting. We are overburdened with prisoners and mean to discharge fifty of 'em into you.'

'I am sorry, sir, truly sorry, not to be able to oblige you, but the sloop is crowded with prisoners already.'

'*Oblige*, did you say? You will oblige me, sir, by obeying orders. Are you aware I am the senior captain here, sir? Besides, I know damned well you have been sending prize-crews into Mahon: these prisoners can occupy their room. Anyhow, you can land them in a few days' time; so let us hear no more of it.'

'But what about my cruise, sir?'

'I am less concerned with your cruise, sir, than with the good of the service. Let the transfer be carried out as quickly as possible, because I have further orders for you. We are sweeping for an American ship, the *John B. Christopher*. She is on her passage from Marseilles to the United States, calling at Barcelona, and we expect to find her between Majorca and the main. Among her passengers she may have two rebels, United Irishmen, the one a Romish priest called Mangan and the other a fellow by the name of Roche, Patrick Roche. They are to be taken off, by force if necessary. They will probably be using French names and have French passports: they speak French. Here is their description: *a middle-sized spare man about forty years old, of a brown complexion*

227

and dark brown-coloured hair, but wears a wig; a hooked nose; a sharp chin, grey eyes, and a large mole near his mouth. That's the parson. T'other is *a tall stout man above six foot high, black hair and blue eyes, about thirty-five, has the little finger of his left hand cut off and walks stiff from a wound in his leg.* You had better take these printed sheets.'

'Mr Dillon, prepare to receive twenty-five prisoners from *San Fiorenzo* and twenty-five from *Amelia*,' said Jack. 'And then we are to join in a sweep for some rebels.'

'Rebels?' cried James.

'Yes,' said Jack absently, peering beyond him at the slack foretopsail bowline and breaking off to call out an order. 'Yes. Pray glance at these sheets when you have leisure – leisure, forsooth.'

'Fifty more mouths,' said the purser. 'What do you say to that, Mr Marshall? Three and thirty full allowances. Where in God's name am I supposed to find it all?'

'We shall have to put into Mahon straight away, Mr Ricketts, that's what I say to it, and kiss my hand to the cruise. Fifty is impossible, and that's flat. You never saw two officers look so glum in your life. Fifty!'

'Fifty more of the buggers,' said James Sheehan, 'and all for their own imperial convenience. Jesus, Mary and Joseph.'

'And think of our poor doctor, all alone among them damned trees – why, there might be owls. God damn the service, I say, and the – *San Fiorenzo*, and the bleeding *Amelia*, too.'

'Alone? Don't you think it, mate. But damn the service to hell, just as you say.'

It was in this mood that the *Sophie* stretched away to the north-west, on the outward or right-hand extremity of the sweeping line. The *Amelia* lay half topsails down on her larboard beam and the *San Fiorenzo* the same distance inshore of the *Amelia*, quite out of sight of the *Sophie* and in the best position for picking up any slow prize that offered.

Between them they could oversee sixty miles of the clear-skied Mediterranean; and so they sailed all day long.

It was indeed a long day, full and busy – the fore-hold to clear, the prisoners to stow away and guard (many of them privateer's men, a dangerous crew), three slow-witted heavy merchantmen to scurry after (all neutrals and all unwilling to heave-to; but one did report a ship, thought to be American, fishing her injured foretopmast two days' sail to windward) and the incessant trimming of the sails in the shifting, uncertain, dangerously gusty wind, to keep up with the frigates – the *Sophie*'s very best would only just avoid disgrace. And she was short-handed: Mowett, Pullings and old Alexander, a reliable quartermaster, were away in prizes, together with nearly a third of her best men, so that James Dillon and the master had to keep watch and watch. Tempers ran short, too, and the defaulters' list lengthened as the day wore on.

'I did not think Dillon could be so savage,' thought Jack, as his lieutenant roared up into the foretop, making the weeping Babbington and his reduced band of topmen set the larboard topsail studdingsail afresh for the third time. It was true that the sloop was flying along at a splendid pace (for her); but in a way it was a pity to flog her so, to badger the men – too high a price to pay. However, that was the service, and he certainly must not interfere. His mind returned to its many problems and to worrying about Stephen: it was sheer madness, this rambling about on a hostile shore. And then again he was profoundly dissatisfied with himself for his performance aboard the *San Fiorenzo*. A gross abuse of authority: he should have dealt with it firmly. Yet there he was, bound hand and foot by the Printed Instructions and the Articles of War. And then again there was the problem of midshipmen. The sloop needed at least two more, a youngster and an oldster; he would ask Dillon if there was any boy he chose to nominate – cousin, nephew, godchild; it was a handsome compliment for a captain to pay his lieutenant, not unusual when they liked one another. As for the oldster, he wanted someone with experience, best of all someone who could be rated master's mate almost at once. His thoughts dwelt upon his coxswain, a fine seaman and captain of the maintop; then they moved on to consider the younger men belonging to the lower deck. He would far, far rather have someone who came in through the hawse-hole, a plain sailorman like young Pullings, than most of the youths whose families could afford to send them to sea . . . If the Spaniards caught Stephen Maturin they would shoot him for a spy.

It was almost dark by the time the third merchantman had been dealt with, and Jack was shattered with fatigue – red eyes prickling, ears four times too sharp and a feeling like a tight cord round his temples. He had been on deck all day, an anxious day that began two hours before first light, and he went to sleep almost before his head was down. Yet in that brief interval his darkening mind had time for two darts of intuition, the one stating that all was well with Stephen Maturin, the other that with James Dillon it was *not*. 'I had no notion he minded so about the cruise: though no doubt he has grown attached to Maturin too: a strange fellow,' he said, sinking right down.

Down, down, into the perfect sleep of an exhausted healthy well-fed young fattish man – a rosy sleep; yet not so far that he did not wake sharply after a few hours, frowning and uneasy. Low, urgent, quarrelling voices came whispering in through the stern-window: for a moment he thought of a surprise, a boat-attack, boarding in the night; but then his more woken mind recognized them as Dillon's and Marshall's, and he sank back. 'Yet,' said his mind a great while later, and still in sleep, 'how do they both come to be on the quarter-deck at this time of the night, when they are keeping watch and watch? It is not eight bells.' As if to confirm this statement the *Sophie*'s bell struck three times, and from various points all through the sloop came the low answering cries of *all's well*. But it was not. She was not under the same press of sail. What was amiss? He huddled on his dressing-gown and went on deck. Not only had the *Sophie* reduced sail, but her head was pointing east-north-east by east.

'Sir,' said Dillon, stepping forward, 'this is my responsibility entirely. I overruled the master and ordered the helm to be put up. I believe there is a ship on the starboard bow.'

Jack stared into the silvery haze – moonlight and a half-covered sky: the swell had increased. He saw no ship, no light: but that proved nothing. He picked up the traverse-board and looked at the change of course. 'We shall be in with the coast of Majorca directly,' he said, yawning.

'Yes, sir: so I took the liberty of reducing sail.'

It was an extraordinary breach of discipline. But Dillon knew that as well as he did: there was no good purpose to be served in telling him of it publicly.

'Whose watch is it at present?'

'Mine, sir,' said the master. He spoke quietly, but in a voice almost as harsh and unnatural as Dillon's. There were strange currents here; much stronger than any ordinary disagreement about a ship's light.

'Who is aloft?'

'Assei, sir.'

Assei was an intelligent, reliable Lascar. 'Assei, ahoy!'

'Hollo,' the thin pipe from the darkness above.

'What do you see?'

'See nothing, sir. See star, no more.'

But then there would be nothing obvious about such a fleeting glimpse. Dillon was probably right: he would never have done such an extraordinary thing else. Yet this was a damned odd course. 'Are you quite persuaded about your light, Mr Dillon?'

'Fully persuaded, sir – quite happy.'

Happy was the strangest word to hear said in that grating voice. Jack made no reply for some moments; then he altered the course a point and a half to the north and began pacing up and down his habitual walk. By four bells the light was mounting fast from the east, and there indeed was the dark presence of the land on their starboard bow, dim through the vapours that hung over the sea, though the high bowl of the sky was clear, something between blue and darkness. He went below to put on some clothes, and while the shirt was still over his head there was the cry of a sail.

She came sailing out of a brownish band of mist a bare two miles to leeward, and as soon as he had cleared it Jack's glass picked out the fished foretopmast, with no more than a close-reefed topsail on it. Everything was clear: everything was plain: Dillon had been perfectly right, of course. Here was their quarry, though strangely off its natural course; it must have tacked some time ago off Dragon Island, and now it was slowly making its way into the open channel to the south; in an hour or so their disagreeable task would be done, and he knew very well what he would be at by noon.

'Well done, Mr Dillon,' he cried. 'Well done indeed. We could not have fallen in with her better; I should never have believed it, so far to the east of the channel. Show her our colours and give her a gun.'

The *John B. Christopher* was a little shy of what might prove a hungry man-of-war, eager to impress all her English seamen (or anyone else the boarding-party chose to consider English), but she had not the least chance of escape, above all with a wounded topmast and her topgallantmasts struck down on deck; so after a slight flurry of canvas and a tendency to fall off, she backed her topsails, showed the American flag and waited for the *Sophie*'s boat.

'You shall go,' said Jack to Dillon, who was still hunched over his telescope, as though absorbed in some point of the American's rigging. 'You speak French better than any of us, now the Doctor is away; and after all you discovered her in this extraordinary place – she is your discovery. Should you like the printed papers again, or shall you . . .' Jack broke off. He had seen a very great deal of drunkenness in the Navy; drunken admirals, post-captains, commanders, drunken ship's boys ten years old, and he had been trundled aboard on a wheelbarrow himself before now; but he disliked it on duty – he disliked it very much indeed, above all at such an hour in the morning. 'Perhaps Mr Marshall had better go,' he said coldly. 'Pass the word for Mr Marshall.'

'Oh, no, sir,' cried Dillon, recovering himself. 'I beg your pardon – it was a momentary – I am perfectly well.' And to be sure, the sweating pallor, the boltered staring look had gone, replaced by an unhealthy flush.

'Well,' said Jack, dubiously, and the next moment James Dillon was calling out very actively for the cutter's crew, hurrying up and down, checking their arms, hammering the flints of his own pistols, as clearly master of himself as possible. With the cutter alongside and ready to push off, he said, 'Perhaps I should beg for those sheets, sir. I will refresh my memory as we pull across.'

Gently backing and filling, the *Sophie* kept on the *John B. Christopher*'s larboard bow, prepared to rake her and cross her stem at the first sign of trouble. But there was none. A few more or less derisive cries of 'Paul Jones' and 'How's King George?' floated across from the *John B. Christopher*'s fo'c'sle, and the grinning gun-crews, standing there ready to blow their cousins to a better world without the least hesitation or the least ill-will, would gladly have replied in kind; but their captain would have none of it – this was an odious task, no time for merriment. At the first call of 'Boston beans' he rapped out, 'Silence, fore and aft. Mr Ricketts, take that man's name.'

Time wore on. In its tub the slow-match burned away, coil by coil. All along the deck attention wandered. A gannet passed overhead, brilliant white, and Jack found himself pondering anxiously about Stephen, forgetful of his duty. The sun rose: the sun rose.

Now at last the boarding-party were at the American's gangway, dropping down into the cutter: and there was Dillon, alone. He was replying civilly to the master and to the passengers at the rail. The *John B. Christopher* was filling – the odd colonial twang of her mate urging the men to 'clap on to that tarnation brace' echoed across the sea – and she

233

was under way southwards. The *Sophie*'s cutter was pulling across the intervening space.

On the way out James had not known what he would do. All that day, ever since he had heard of the squadron's mission, he had been overwhelmed by a sense of fatality; and now, although he had had hours to think about it, he still did not know what he would do. He moved as though in a nightmare, going up the American's side without the slightest volition of his own; and he had known, of course, that he would find Father Mangan. Although he had done everything possible, short of downright mutiny or sinking the *Sophie*, to avoid it; although he had altered course and shortened sail, blackmailing the master to accomplish it, he had known that he would find him. But what he had not known, what he had never foreseen, was that the priest should threaten to denounce him if he did not turn a blind eye. He had disliked the man the moment recognition flashed between them, but in that very first moment he had made up his mind – there was not the slightest possibility of his playing the constable and taking them off. And then came this threat. For a second he had known with total certainty that it did not affect him in the least, but he had hardly reached another breath before the squalor of the situation became unbearable. He was obliged to make a slow pretence of examining all the other passports aboard before he could bring himself under control. He had known that there was no way out, that whatever course he took would be dishonourable; but he had never imagined that dishonour could be so painful. He was a proud man; Father Mangan's satisfied leer wounded him beyond anything he had yet experienced, and with the pain of the wound there came a cloud of intolerable doubts.

The boat touched the *Sophie*'s side. 'No such passengers aboard, sir,' he reported.

'So much the better,' said Jack cheerfully, raising his hat to the American captain and waving it. 'West a half south, Mr Marshall; and house those guns, if you please.' The exquisite fragrance of coffee drifted up from the after hatch-way. 'Dillon, come and breakfast with me,' he said, taking him familiarly by the arm. 'You are still looking most ghastly pale.'

'You must excuse me, sir,' whispered James, disengaging himself with a look of utter hatred. 'I am a little out of order.'

Chapter Eight

'I am entirely at a loss, upon my honour; and so I lay the
position before you, confiding wholly in your candour . . .
I am entirely at a loss: I cannot for the life of me conceive
what manner of offence . . . It was not my landing of those
monstrously unjust prisoners on Dragon Island (though he
certainly disapproved of it), for the trouble began before
that, quite early in the morning.' Stephen listened gravely,
attentively, never interrupting; and very slowly, harking
back for details overlooked and forward to straighten his
chronology by anticipation, Jack laid before him the history
of his relations with James Dillon – good, bad; good, bad –
with this last extraordinary descent not only inexplicable
but strangely wounding, because of the real liking that had
grown up, in addition to the esteem. Then there was Marshall's unaccountable conduct, too; but that was of much
less importance.

With the utmost care, Jack reiterated his arguments about
the necessity for having a happy ship if one was to command
an efficient fighting machine; he quoted examples of like
and contrary cases; and his audience listened and approved.
Stephen could not bring his wisdom to the resolution of any
of these difficulties, however, nor (as Jack would somewhat
ignobly have liked) could he propose his good offices; for
he was a merely ideal interlocutor, and his thinking flesh lay
thirty leagues to the south and west, across a waste of sea.
A rough waste, and a cross sea: after frustrating days of
calm, light airs and then a strong south-wester, the wind
had backed easterly in the night, and now it was blowing a
gale across the waves that had built up during the day, so

that the Sophie went thumping along under double-reefed topsails and courses, the cross-sea breaking over the weather-bow and soaking the lookout on the fo'c'sle with a grateful spray, heeling James Dillon as he stood on the quarter-deck communing with the Devil and rocking the cot in which Jack silently harangued the darkness.

His was an exceedingly busy life; and yet since he entered an inviolable solitude the moment he passed the sentry at his cabin door, it let him a great deal of time for reflexion. It was not frittered away in very small exchanges, in listening to three-quarters of a scale on a quavering German flute or in sailors' politics. 'I shall speak to him, when we pick him up. I shall speak in the most general way, of the comfort it is to a man to have a confidential friend aboard; and of this singularity in the sailor's life, that one moment he is so on top of his shipmates, all hugger-mugger in the ward-room, that he can hardly breathe, let alone play anything but a jig on the fiddle, and the next he is pitched into a kind of hermit's solitude, something he has never known before.'

In times of stress Jack Aubrey had two main reactions: he either became aggressive or he became amorous; he longed either for the violent catharsis of action or for that of making love. He loved a battle: he loved a wench.

'I quite understand that some commanders take a girl to sea with them,' he reflected. 'Apart from the pleasure, think of the *refuge* of sinking into a warm, lively, affectionate . . .'

Peace. 'I *wish* there were a girl in this cabin,' he added, after a pause.

This disarray, this open, acknowledged incomprehension, were kept solely for his cabin and his ghostly companion; the outward appearance of the *Sophie*'s captain had nothing hesitant about it, and it would have been a singularly acute observer to tell that the nascent friendship between him and his lieutenant had been cut short. The master was such an observer, however, for although Jack's truly hideous appearance when singed and greased had caused a revulsion for a while, at the same time Jack's obvious liking for James

Dillon had set up a jealousy that worked in the contrary direction. Furthermore, the master had been threatened in terms that left almost no room for doubt, in very nearly direct terms, and so for an entirely different cause he watched the captain and the lieutenant with painful anxiety.

'Mr Marshall,' said Jack in the darkness, and the poor man jumped as though a pistol had been fired behind him, 'when do you reckon we shall raise the land?'

'In about two hours' time, sir, if this wind holds.'

'Yes: I thought as much,' said Jack, gazing up into the rigging. 'I believe you may shake out a reef now, however; and at any further slackening set the topgallants – crack on all you can. And have me called when land is seen, if you please, Mr Marshall.'

Something less than two hours later he reappeared, to view the remote irregular line on the starboard bow: Spain, with the singular mountain the English called Egg-top Hill in line with the best bower anchor, and their watering bay therefore directly ahead.

'By God, you are a prime navigator, Marshall,' he said, lowering his glass. 'You deserve to be master of the fleet.'

It would take them at least an hour to run in, however, and now that the event was so close at hand, no longer at all theoretical, Jack discovered how anxious he was in fact – how very much the outcome mattered to him.

'Send my coxswain aft, will you?' he said, returning to his cabin after he had taken half a dozen uneasy turns.

Barret Bonden, coxswain and captain of the maintop, was unusually young for his post; a fine open-looking creature, tough without brutality, cheerful, perfectly in his place and, of course, a prime seaman – bred to the sea from childhood. 'Sit down, Bonden,' said Jack, a little consciously, for what he was about to offer was the quarter-deck, no less, and the possibility of advancement to the very pinnacle of the sailor's hierarchy. 'I have been thinking . . . should you like to be rated midshipman?'

'Why, no sir, not at all,' answered Bonden at once, his

238

teeth flashing in the gloom. 'But I thank you very kindly for your good opinion, sir.'

'Oh,' said Jack, taken aback. 'Why not?'

'I ain't got the learning, sir. Why' – laughing cheerfully – 'it's all I can do to read the watch-list, spelling it out slow; and I'm too old to wear round now. And then, sir, what should I look like, rigged out like an officer? Jack-in-the-green: and my old messmates laughing up their sleeves and calling out "What ho, the hawse-hole."'

'Plenty of fine officers began on the lower deck,' said Jack. 'I was on the lower deck myself, once,' he added, regretting the sequence as soon as he had uttered it.

'I know you was, sir,' said Bonden, and his grin flashed again.

'How did you know that?'

'We got a cove in the starboard watch, was shipmates with you, sir, in the old *Reso*, off the Cape.'

'Oh dear, oh dear,' cried Jack inwardly, 'and I never noticed him. So there I was, turning all the women ashore as righteous as Pompous Pilate, and they knew all the time . . . well, well.' And aloud, with a certain stiffness, 'Well, Bonden, think of what I have said. It would be a pity to stand in your own way.'

'If I may make so bold, sir,' said Bonden, getting to his feet and standing there, suddenly constrained, lumpish and embarrassed, 'there's my Aunt Sloper's George – George Lucock, foretopman, larboard watch. He's a right scholar, can write so small you can scarcely see it; younger nor I am, and more soople, sir, oh, far more soople.'

'Lucock?' said Jack dubiously. 'He's only a lad. Was not he flogged last week?'

'Yes, sir: but it was only his gun had won again. And he couldn't hold back from his draught, not in duty to the giver.'

'Well,' said Jack, reflecting that perhaps there might be wiser prizes than a bottle (though none so valued), 'I will keep an eye on him.'

* * *

239

Midshipmen were much in his mind during this tedious working in. 'Mr Babbington,' he said, suddenly stopping in his up and down. 'Take your hands out of your pockets. When did you last write home?'

Mr Babbington was at an age when almost any question evokes a guilty response, and this was, in fact, a valid accusation. He reddened, and said, 'I don't know, sir.'

'Think, sir, think,' said Jack, his good-tempered face clouding unexpectedly. 'What port did you send it from? Mahon? Leghorn? Genoa? Gibraltar? Well, never mind.' There was no dark figure to be made out on that distant beach. 'Never mind. Write a handsome letter. Two pages at least. And send it in to me with your daily workings tomorrow. Give your father my compliments and tell him my bankers are Hoares.' For Jack, like most other captains, managed the youngsters' parental allowance for them. 'Hoares,' he repeated absently once or twice, 'my bankers are Hoares,' and a strangled ugly crowing noise made him turn. Young Ricketts was clinging to the fall of the main burton-tackle in an attempt to control himself, but without much success. Jack's cold glare chilled his mirth, however, and he was able to reply to 'And you, Mr Ricketts, have you written to your parents recently?' with an audible 'No, sir' that scarcely quavered at all.

'Then you will do the same: two pages, wrote small, and no demands for new quadrants, laced hats or hangers,' said Jack; and something told the midshipman that this was no time to expostulate, to point out that his loving parent, his only parent, was in daily, even hourly communication with him. Indeed, this awareness of Jack's state of tension was general throughout the brig. 'Goldilocks is in a rare old taking about the Doctor,' they said. 'Watch out for squalls.' And when hammocks were piped up the seamen who had to pass by him to stow theirs in the starboard quarter-deck netting glanced at him nervously; one, trying to keep an eye on the quartermaster, and on the break of the deck, and on his captain, all at the same time, fell flat on his face.

But Goldilocks was not the only one to be anxious, by any manner of means, and when Stephen Maturin was at last seen to walk out of the trees and cross the beach to meet the jolly-boat, a general exclamation of 'There he is!' broke out from waist to fo'c'sle, in defiance of good discipline: 'Huzzay!'

'How *very* glad I am to see you,' cried Jack, as Stephen groped his way aboard, pushed and pulled by well-meaning hands. 'How are you, my dear sir? Come and breakfast directly – I have held it back on purpose. How do you find yourself? Tolerably spry, I hope? Tolerably spry?'

'I am very well, I thank you,' said Stephen, who indeed looked somewhat less cadaverous, flushed as he was with pleasure at the open friendliness of his welcome. 'I will take a look at my sick-bay and then I will share your bacon with the utmost pleasure. Good morning, Mr Day. Take off your hat, if you please. Very neat, very neat: you do us credit, Mr Day. But no exposure to the sun as yet – I recommend the wearing of a close Welsh wig. Cheslin, good morning to you. You have a good account of our patients, I trust?'

'That,' he said, a little greasy from bacon, 'that was a point that exercised my mind a good deal during your absence. Would my loblolly boy pay the men back in their own coin? Would they return to their persecution of him? How quickly could he come by a new identity?'

'Identity?' said Jack, comfortably pouring out more coffee. 'Is not identity something you are born with?'

'The identity I am thinking of is something that hovers between a man and the rest of the world: a mid-point between his view of himself and theirs of him – for each, of course, affects the other continually. A reciprocal fluxion, sir. There is nothing absolute about this identity of mine. Were you, you personally, to spend some days in Spain at present you would find yours change, you know, because of the general opinion there that you are a false harsh brutal murdering villain, an odious man.'

'I dare say they are vexed,' said Jack, smiling. 'And I dare say they call me Beelzebub. But that don't make me Beelzebub.'

'Does it not? Does it not? Ah? Well, however that may be, you have angered, you have stirred up the mercantile interest along the coast to a most prodigious degree. There is a wealthy man by the name of Mateu who is wonderfully incensed against you. The quicksilver belonged to him, and being contraband it was not insured; so did the vessel you cut out at Almoraira; and the cargo of the tartan burnt off Tortosa – half of that was his. He is well with the ministry. He has moved their indolence and they have allowed him and his friends to charter one of their men-of-war . . .'

'Not *charter*, my dear sir: no private person can possibly *charter* a man-of-war, a national vessel, a King's ship, not even in Spain.'

'Oh? Perhaps I use the wrong term: I often use the wrong term in naval matters. However. A ship of force, not only to protect the coasting trade but even more to pursue the *Sophie*, who is perfectly well known now, both by name and by description. This I had from Mateu's own cousin as we danced –'

'You danced?' cried Jack, far more astonished than if Stephen had said 'as we ate our cold roast baby'.

'Certainly I danced. Why would I not dance, pray?'

'Certainly you are to dance – most uncommon graceful, I am sure. I only wondered . . . but did you indeed go about *dancing*?'

'I did. You have not travelled in Catalonia, sir, I believe?'

'Not I.'

'Then I must tell you that on Sunday mornings it is the custom, in that country, for people of all ages and conditions to dance, on coming out of church: so I was dancing with Ramon Mateu i Cadafalch in the square before the cathedral church of Tarragona, where I had gone to hear the Palestrina Missa Brevis. The dance is a particular dance, a round called the sardana; and if you will reach me your fiddle I will play you the air of the one I have in mind. Though you must imagine I am a harsh braying hoboy.' Plays.

'It is a charming melody, to be sure. Somewhat in the Moorish taste, is it not? But upon my word it makes my flesh creep, to think of you rambling about the countryside – in ports – in towns. I had imagined you would have gone to earth, that you would have kept close with your friend, hidden in her room . . . that is to say . . .'

'Yet I had told you, had I not, that I could ride the length and breadth of that country without a question or a moment's uneasiness?'

'So you had. So you had.' Jack reflected for a while. 'And so, of course, if you chose, you could find out what ships and convoys were sailing, when expected, how laden, and so on. Even the galleons themselves, I dare say?'

'Certainly I could,' said Stephen, 'if I chose to play the spy. It is a curious and apparently illogical set of notions, is it not, that makes it right and natural to speak of the *Sophie*'s enemies, yet beyond any question wrong, dishonourable and indecent to speak of her prey?'

'Yes,' said Jack, looking at him wistfully. 'You must give a hare her law, there is no doubt. But what do you tell me about this ship of force? What is her rate? How many guns does she carry? Where does she lie?'

'*Cacafuego* is her name.'

'*Cacafuego*? *Cacafuego*? I have never heard of her. So at least she cannot be a ship of the line. How is she rigged?'

Stephen paused. 'I am ashamed to say I did not ask,' he said. 'But from the satisfaction with which her name was pronounced, I take her to be some prepotent great argosy.'

'Well, we must try to keep out of her way: and since she knows what we look like, we must try to change our appearance. It is wonderful what a coat of paint and a waist-cloth will do, or even an oddly patched jib or a fished topmast – by the way, I suppose they told you in the boat why we were compelled to maroon you?'

'They told me about the frigates and your boarding the American.'

'Yes: and precious stuff it was, too. There were no such people aboard – Dillon searched her for close on an hour. I was just as glad, for I remembered you had told me the United Irishmen were good creatures, on the whole – far better than those other fellows, whose name I forget. Steel boys, white boys, orange boys?'

'United Irishmen? I had understood them to be French. They told me the American ship had been searched for some Frenchmen.'

'They were only pretending to be Frenchmen. That is to say, if they had been there at all, they might have pretended to be French. That is why I sent Dillon, who speaks it so well. But they were not, you see; and in my opinion the whole thing was so much cock. I was just as glad, as I say; but it seemed to upset Dillon most strangely. I suppose he was very eager to take them: or he was very much put out at our cruise being cut short. Ever since then – however, I must not bore you with all that. You heard about the prisoners?'

'That the frigates had been so good as to give you fifty of theirs?'

'Merely for their own convenience! It was not for the good of the service at all. A most shabby, unscrupulous thing!' cried Jack, his eyes starting from his head at the recollection. 'But I dished 'em, though. As soon as we were done with the American we bore away for the *Amelia*, told her we had drawn a blank and made our signal for parting company; and a couple of hours later, the wind serving, we landed every man jack on Dragon Island.'

'Off Majorca?'

'Just so.'

'But is not that wrong? Will you not be reproved – court-martialled?'

Jack winced, and clapping his hand to wood he said, 'Pray never say that ill-conditioned word. The mere sound of it is enough to spoil the day.'

'But will you not get into trouble?'

'Not if I put into Mahon with a thundering great prize at my tail,' said Jack, laughing. 'For now we may just have time to go and lie off Barcelona, do you see, if the wind is kind – I had quite set my heart upon it. We shall just have time for a quick stroke or two and then we must bear away for Mahon with anything we may have caught, for we certainly cannot spare another prize-crew, with our numbers so reduced. And we certainly cannot stay out much longer, without we eat our boots.'

'Still and all . . .'

'Never look so concerned, dear Doctor. There was no specific order as to where to land them, no order at all; and, of course, I'll square the head-money. Besides, I am covered: all my officers formally agreed that our shortage of water and provisions compelled us to do so – Marshall and Ricketts and even Dillon, although he was so chuff and pope-holy about it all.'

The *Sophie* reeked of grilled sardines and fresh paint. She lay fifteen miles off Cape Tortosa in a dead calm, wallowing on the oily swell; and the blue smoke of the sardines she had bought out of a night-fishing barca-longa (she had bought the whole catch) still hung sickeningly about her 'tweendecks, her sails and rigging, half an hour after dinner.

The bosun had a large working-party slung over her side, spreading yellow paint over the neat dockyard black and white; the sailmaker and a dozen palm-and-pricket men were busy at a long narrow strip of canvas designed to conceal her warlike character; and her lieutenant was pulling round her in the jolly-boat to judge of the effect. He was alone, except for her surgeon, and he was saying '. . . everything. I did everything in my power to avoid it. *Everything*, breaking all measures. I altered course, I shortened sail – unthinkable in the service – blackmailing the master to do so; and yet in the morning there she lay, two miles away under our lee, where she had no conceivable right to be. Ahoy, Mr Watt! Six inches lower all round.'

'It was just as well. If any other man had gone aboard they might have been taken.'

A pause, and James said, 'He leant over the table, so close I had his stinking breath in my face, and with a hateful yellow look he poured out this ugly stuff. I had already made up my mind, as I said; yet it looked exactly as though I were yielding to a vulgar threat. And two minutes later I was sure I had.'

'But you had not: it is a sick fancy. Indeed, it is not far from morose delectation: take great care of that sin, James, I beg. As for the rest, it is a pity you mind it so. What does it amount to, in the long run?'

'A man would have to be three parts dead not to mind it so; and quite dead to a sense of duty, to say nothing of . . . Mr Watt, that will do very well.'

Stephen sat there, weighing the advantage of saying 'Do not hate Jack Aubrey for it: do not drink so much: do not destroy yourself for what will not last' against the disadvantage of setting off an explosion; for in spite of his apparent calm, James Dillon was on a hair-trigger, in a state of pitiful exacerbation. Stephen could not decide, shrugged, lifting his right hand, palm upwards, in a gesture that meant 'Bah, let it go,' and to himself he observed, 'However, I shall oblige him to take a black draught this evening – that at least I *can* do – and some comfortable mandragora; and in my diary I shall write "JD, required to play Iscariot either with his right hand or with his left, and hating the necessity (the absolute necessity), concentrates all this hatred upon poor JA, which is a remarkable instance of the human process; for, in fact, JD does not dislike JA at all – far from it."'

'At least,' said James, pulling back to the *Sophie*, 'I do hope that after all this discreditable shuffling we may be taken into action. It has a wonderful way of reconciling a man with himself: and with everybody else, sometimes.'

'What is that fellow in the buff waistcoat doing on the quarterdeck?'

'That is Pram. Captain Aubrey is dressing him as a Danish officer; it is part of our plan of disguise. Do not you remember the yellow waistcoat the master of the *Clomer* wore? It is customary with them.'

'I do not. Tell me, do such things often happen, at sea?'

'Oh, yes. It is a perfectly legitimate *ruse de guerre*. Often we amuse the enemy with false signals too – anything but those of distress. Take great care of the paint, now.'

At this point Stephen fell straight into the sea – into the hollow of the sea between the boat and the side of the sloop as they drew away from one another. He sank at once, rose just as they came together, struck his head between the two and sank again, bubbling. Most of the *Sophie*'s people who could swim leapt into the water, Jack among them; and others ran with boat-hooks, a dolphin-striker, two small grapnels, an ugly barbed hook on a chain; but it was the brothers Sponge that found him, five fathoms down (heavy bones for his size, no fat, lead-soled half-boots) and brought him up, his clothes blacker than usual, his face more white, and he streaming with water, furiously indignant.

It was no epoch-making event, but it was a useful one, since it provided the gun-room with a topic of conversation at a moment when very hard work was needed to maintain the appearance of a civilized community. A good deal of the time James was heavy, inattentive and silent; his eyes were bloodshot from the grog he swallowed, but it seemed neither to cheer nor yet to fuddle him. The master was almost equally withdrawn, and he sat there stealing covert glances at Dillon from time to time. So when they were all at table they went into the subject of swimming quite exhaustively – its rarity among seamen, its advantages (the preservation of life: the pleasure to be derived from it, in suitable climates: the carrying of a line ashore in an emergency), its disadvantages (the prolongation of death-agonies in shipwreck, in falling overboard unseen: flying in the face of nature – had

God meant men to swim, etc.), the curious inability of young seals to swim, the use of bladders, the best ways of learning and practising the art of swimming.

'The only right way to swim,' said the purser for the seventh time, 'is to join your hands like you were saying your prayers' – he narrowed his eyes, joined his hands very exactly – 'and shoot them out so –' This time he did strike the bottle, which plunged violently into the solomongundy and thence, deep in thick gravy, into Marshall's lap.

'I knew you would do it,' cried the master, springing about and mopping himself. 'I told you so. I said "Soonar or latar you'll knock down that damned decantar", and you can't swim a stroke – prating like a whoreson ottar. You have wrecked my best nankeen trousars.'

'I didn't go for to do it,' said the purser sullenly; and the evening relapsed into a barbarous gloom.

Indeed, as the *Sophie* beat up, tack upon tack, to the northward, she could not have been described as a very cheerful sloop. In his beautiful little cabin Jack sat reading Steel's Navy List and feeling low, not so much because he had over-eaten again, and not so much because of the great number of men senior to him on the list, as because he was so aware of this feeling aboard. He could not know the precise nature of the complicated miseries inhabiting Dillon and Marshall. He could not tell that three yards from him James Dillon was trying to fend off despair with a series of invocations and a haggard attempt at resignation, while the whole of his mind that was not taken up with increasingly mechanical prayer converted its unhappy turmoil into hatred for the established order, for authority and so for captains, and for all those who, never having had a moment's conflict of duty or honour in their lives, could condemn him out of hand. And although Jack could hear the master's shoes crunching on the deck some inches above his head, he could not possibly divine the particular emotional disturbance and the sickening dread of exposure that filled the poor man's loving heart. But he knew very well that his tight, self-contained world was hopelessly out of tune and he was haunted by the depressing sentiment of failure – of not having succeeded in what he had set out to do. He would very much have liked to ask Stephen Maturin the reasons for this failure; he would very much have liked to talk to him on indifferent subjects and to have played a little music; but he knew that an invitation to the captain's cabin was very like an order, if only because the refusing of it was so extraordinary – that had been borne in upon him very strongly the other morning, when he had been so amazed by Dillon's refusal. Where there was no equality there was no companionship: when a man was obliged to say 'Yes, sir,' his agreement was of no worth even if it happened to be true. He had known these things all his service life; they were perfectly evident; but he had never thought they would apply so fully, and to *him*.

Farther down in the sloop, in the almost deserted midshipmen's berth, the melancholy was even more profound: the youngsters were, in fact, weeping as they sat. Ever since Mowett and Pullings had gone off in prizes these two had been at watch and watch, which meant that neither ever had more than four hours' sleep – hard at that dormouse, lovebed age that so clings to its warm hammock; then again in writing their dutiful letters they had contrived to cover themselves with ink, and had been sharply rebuked for their appearance; what is more, Babbington, unable to think of *anything to put*, had filled his pages with asking after everybody at home and in the village, human beings, dogs, horses, cats, birds, and even the great hall clock, to such an extent that he was now filled with an overwhelming nostalgia. He was also afraid that his hair and teeth were going to fall out and his bones soften, while sores and blotches covered his face and body – the inevitable result of conversing with harlots, as the wise old-experienced clerk Richards had assured him. Young Ricketts' woe had quite another source: his father had been talking of a transfer into a store-ship or a transport, as being safer and far more homelike, and young Ricketts had accepted the prospect of separation with wonderful for-titude; but now it appeared that there was to be no separation – that he, young Ricketts, was to go too, torn from the *Sophie* and the life he loved so passionately. Marshall, seeing him staggering with weariness, had sent him below, and there he sat on his sea-chest, resting his face in his hands at half-past three in the morning, too tired even to creep into his hammock; and the tears oozed between his fingers.

Before the mast there was much less sadness, although there were several men – far more than usual – who looked forward with no pleasure to Thursday morning, when they were to be flogged. Most of the others had nothing positive to be glum about, apart from the hard work and the short commons; yet nevertheless the *Sophie* was already so very much of a community that every man aboard was conscious of something out of joint, something more than their officers' snappishness – what, they could not tell; but it took away from their ordinary genial flow. The gloom on the quarter-deck seeped forward, reaching as far as the goat-house, the manger, and even the hawse-holes themselves.

The *Sophie*, then, considered as an entity, was not at the top of her form as she worked through the night on the dying tramontana; nor yet in the morning, when the north-erly weather was followed (as it so often happens in those waters) by wreathing mists from the south-west, very lovely for those who do not have to navigate a vessel through them, close in shore, and the forerunners of a blazing day. But this state was nothing in comparison with the tense alarm, not to say the dejection and even dread, that Stephen discovered when he stepped on to the quarter-deck just at sunrise.

He had been woken by the drum beating to quarters. He had gone directly to the cockpit, and there with Cheslin's help he had arranged his instruments. A bright eager face from the upper regions had announced 'a thundering great xebec round the cape, right in with the land'. He acknowl-edged this with mild approval, and after a while he fell to sharpening his catlin; then he sharpened his lancets and then his fleam-toothed saw with a little hone that he had bought for the purpose in Tortosa. Time passed, and the face was replaced by another, a very much altered pallid face that delivered the captain's compliments and desired him to come on deck.

'Good morning, Doctor,' said Jack, and Stephen noticed that his smile was strained, his eyes hard and wary. 'It looks as though we had caught a Tartar.' He nodded over the water towards a long, sharp, strikingly beautiful vessel, bright light red against the sullen cliffs behind. She lay low in the water for her size (four times the *Sophie*'s bulk), but a high kind of flying platform carried out her stern, so that it jutted far over her counter, while a singular beak-like projection advanced her prow a good twenty feet beyond her stem. Her main and mizzen masts bore immense curved double tapering lateen yards, whose sails were spilling the south-east air to allow the *Sophie* to come up with her; and even at this distance Stephen noticed that the yards, too, were red. Her starboard broadside, facing the *Sophie*, had no less than sixteen gunports in it; and her decks were extraordinarily crowded with men.

'A thirty-two-gun xebec-frigate,' said Jack, 'and she cannot be anything but Spanish. Her hanging-ports deceived us entirely – thought she was a merchantman until the last moment – and nearly all her hands were down below. Mr Dillon, get a few more people out of sight without its showing. Mr Marshall, three or four men, no more, to shake out the reef in the fore topsail – they are to do it slowly, like lubbers. Anderssen, call out something in Danish again and let that bucket dangle over the side.' In a lower voice to Stephen, 'You see her, the fox? Those ports opened two minutes ago, quite hidden by all that bloody paintwork. And although she was thinking of swaying up her square yards – look at her foremast – she can have that lateen back in a moment, and snap us up directly. We must stand on – no choice – and see whether we can't amuse her. Mr Ricketts, you have the flags ready to hand? Slip off your jacket at once and toss it into the locker. Yes, there she goes.' A gun spoke from the frigate's quarter-deck: the ball skipped across the *Sophie*'s bows, and the Spanish colours appeared, clear of the warning smoke. 'Carry on, Mr Ricketts,' said Jack. The Dannebrog broke out at the *Sophie*'s gaff-end, followed by the yellow quarantine flag at the fore. 'Pram, come up here and wave your arms about. Give orders in Danish. Mr Marshall, heave to awkwardly in half a cable's length. No nearer.'

Closer and closer. Dead silence aboard the *Sophie*: gabble drifting across from the xebec. Standing just behind Pram, in his shirt sleeves and breeches – no uniform coat – Jack took the wheel. 'Look at all those people,' he said, half to himself and half to Stephen. 'There must be three hundred and more. They will hail us in a couple of minutes. Now, sir, Pram is going to tell them we are a Dane, a few days out of Algiers: I beg you will support him in Spanish, or any other language you see fit, as the opportunity offers.'

The hail came clear over the morning sea. 'What brig?'

'Good and loud, Pram,' said Jack.

'*Clomer*!' called the quartermaster in the buff waistcoat, and very faintly off the cliffs there came back the cry '*Clomer*!' with the same hint of defiance, though so diminished.

'Back the foretopsail slowly, Mr Marshall,' murmured Jack, 'and keep the hands to the braces.' He murmured, for he knew very well that the frigate's officers had their glasses trained on the quarter-deck, and a persuasive fallacy assured him that the glasses would magnify his voice as well.

The way began to come off the brig, and at the same time the close groups aboard the xebec, her gun-crews, began to disperse. For a moment Jack thought it was all over and his heart, hitherto tranquil, began to bound and thump. But no. A boat was putting off.

'Perhaps we shall not be able to avoid this action,' he said. 'Mr Dillon, the guns are double-shotted, I believe?'

'Treble, sir,' said James, and looking at him Stephen saw that look of mad happiness he had known often enough, in former years – the contained look of a fox about to do something utterly insane.

The breeze and the current kept heaving the *Sophie* in towards the frigate, whose crew were going back to their task of changing from a lateen to a square rig: they swarmed thick into the shrouds, looking curiously at the docile brig, which was just about to be boarded by their launch.

'Hail the officer, Pram,' said Jack, and Pram went to the rail. He uttered a loud, seamanlike, emphatic statement in Danish; but very ludicrously in pidgin-Danish. And no recognizable form of Algiers appeared – only the Danish for *Barbary coast*, vainly repeated.

The Spanish bowman was about to hook on when Stephen, speaking a Scandinavian but instantly comprehensible Spanish, called out, 'Have you a surgeon that understands the plague aboard your ship?'

The bowman lowered his hook. The officer said, 'Why?'

'Some of our men were taken poorly at Algiers, and we are afraid. We cannot tell what it is.'

'Back water,' said the Spanish officer to his men. 'Where did you say you had touched?'

'Algiers, Alger, Argel: it was there the men went ashore. Pray what is the plague like? Swellings? Buboes? Will you come and look at them? Pray, sir, take this rope.'

'Back water,' said the officer again. 'And they went ashore at Algiers?'

'Yes. Will you send your surgeon?'

'No. Poor people, God and His Mother preserve you.'

'May we come for medicines? Pray let me come into your boat.'

'No,' said the officer, crossing himself. 'No, no. Keep off, or we shall fire into you. Keep out to sea – the sea will cure them. God be with you, poor people. And a happy voyage to you.' He could be seen ordering the bowman to throw the boathook into the sea, and the launch pulled back fast to the bright-red xebec.

They were within very easy hailing distance now, and a

voice from the frigate called out some words in Danish;
Pram replied; and then a tall thin figure on the quarter-deck,
obviously the captain, asked, had they seen an English sloop-
of-war, a brig?

'No,' they said; and as the vessels began to draw away
from one another Jack whispered, 'Ask her name.'

'*Cacafuego*,' came the answer over the widening lane of
sea. 'A happy voyage.'

'A happy voyage to you.'

'So that is a frigate,' said Stephen, looking attentively at
the *Cacafuego*.

'A *xebec*-frigate,' said Jack. 'Handsomely with those
braces, Mr Marshall: no appearance of hurry. A xebec-
frigate. A wonderfully curious rig, ain't it? There's nothing
faster, I suppose – broad in the beam to carry a vast great
press of sail, but with a very narrow floor – but they need
a prodigious crew; for, do you see, when she is sailing on a
wind, she is a lateen, but when the wind comes fair, right
aft or thereabouts, she strikes 'em down on deck and sways
up square yards instead, a great deal of labour. She must
have three hundred men, at the least. She is changing to her
square rig now, which means she is going up the coast. So
we must stand to the south – we have had quite enough of
her company. Mr Dillon, let us take a look at the chart.'

'Dear Lord,' he said in the cabin, striking his hands
together and chuckling, 'I thought we were dished that time
– burnt, sunk and destroyed; hanged, drawn and quartered.
What a jewel that Doctor is! When he waved the guess-rope
and begged them so earnestly to come aboard! I understood
him, though he spoke so quick. Ha, ha, ha! Eh? Did not you
think it the drollest thing in life?'

'Very droll indeed, sir.'

'*Que vengan*, says he, most piteously, waving the line, and
they start back as grave and solemn as a parcel of owls. *Que
vengan*! Ha, ha, ha ... Oh dear. But you don't seem very
amused.'

'To tell you the truth, sir, I was so astonished at our sheering off that I have scarcely had time to relish the joke.'

'Why,' said Jack, smiling, 'what would you have had us do? Ram her?'

'I was persuaded that we were about to attack,' said James passionately. 'I was persuaded that was your intention. I was delighted.'

'A fourteen-gun brig against a thirty-two-gun frigate? You are not speaking in earnest?'

'Certainly. When they were hoisting in their launch and half their people were busy in the rigging our broadside and small-arms would have cut them to pieces, and with this breeze we should have been aboard before they had recovered.'

'Oh, come now! And it would scarcely have been a very honourable stroke, either.'

'Perhaps I am no great judge of what is honourable, sir,' said Dillon. 'I speak as a mere fighting man.'

Mahon, and the *Sophie* surrounded by her own smoke, firing both broadsides all round and one over in salute to the admiral's flag aboard the *Foudroyant*, whose imposing mass lay just between Pigtail Stairs and the ordnance wharf.

Mahon, and the *Sophie*'s liberty-men stuffing themselves with fresh roast pork and soft-tack, to a state of roaring high spirits, roaring merriment: wine-barrels with flowing taps, a hecatomb of pigs, young ladies flocking from far and near.

Jack sat stiffly in his chair, his hands sweating, his throat parched and rigid. Lord Keith's eyebrows were black with strong silver bristles interspersed, and from beneath them he directed a cold, grey, penetrating gaze across the table. 'So you were driven to it by necessity?' he said.

He was speaking of the prisoners landed on Dragon Island: indeed, the subject had occupied him almost since the beginning of the interview.

'Yes, my lord.'

The admiral did not reply for some time. 'Had you been

driven to it by a want of discipline,' he said slowly, 'by a dislike for subordinating your judgment to that of your seniors, I should have been compelled to take a very serious view of the matter. Lady Keith has a great kindness for you, Captain Aubrey, as you know; and myself I should be grieved to see you harm your own prospects; so you will allow me to speak to you very frankly . . .'

Jack had known that it was going to be unpleasant as soon as he had seen the secretary's grave face, but this was far rougher than his worst expectations. The admiral was shockingly well informed; he had all the details – official reprimand for petulance, neglect of orders on stated occasions, reputation for undue independence, for temerity, and even for insubordination, rumours of ill behaviour on shore, drunkenness; and so it ran. The admiral could not see the smallest likelihood of promotion to post rank: though Captain Aubrey should not take that too much to heart – plenty of men never rose even to commander; and the commanders were a very respectable body of men. But could a man be entrusted with a line of battle ship if he were liable to take it into his head to fight a fleet engagement according to his own notions of strategy? No, there was not the least likelihood, unless something very extraordinary took place. Captain Aubrey's record was by no means all that could be wished. Lord Keith spoke steadily, with great justice, great accuracy in his facts and his diction; at first Jack had merely suffered, ashamed and uneasy; but as it went on he felt a glow somewhere about his heart or a little lower, the beginning of that rising jet of furious anger that might take control of him. He bowed his head, for he was certain it would show in his eye.

'Yet on the other hand,' said Lord Keith, 'you do possess one prime quality in a commander. You are lucky. None of my other cruisers has played such havoc with the enemy's trade; none has taken half as many prizes. So when you come back from Alexandria I shall give you another cruise.'

'Thank you, my lord.'

'It will arouse a certain amount of jealousy, a certain amount of criticism; but luck is something that rarely lasts – at least that is my experience – and we should back it while it is with us.'

Jack made his acknowledgements, thanked the admiral not ungracefully for his kindness in giving him advice, sent his duty – his affectionate duty, if he might say so – to Lady Keith, and withdrew. But the fire in his heart was burning so high in spite of the promised cruise that it was all he could do to get his words out smoothly, and there was such a look on his face as he came out that the sentry at the door instantly changed his expression of knowing irony to one of deaf, dumb, unmoving wood.

'If that scrub Harte presumes to use the same tone to me,' said Jack to himself, walking out into the street and crushing a citizen hard against the wall, 'or anything like it, I shall wring his nose off his head, and damn the service.'

'Mercy, my dear,' he roared, stepping into the Crown on his way, 'bring me a glass of vino, there's a good girl, and a copito of aguardiente. God damn all admirals,' he said, letting the young green flowery wine run cool and healing down his throat.

'But he is a topping old admiral, dear Capitano,' said Mercedes, brushing dust off his blue lapels. 'He will give you a cruise when you are coming back from Alexandria.'

Jack cocked a shrewd eye at her, observed 'Mercy querido, if you knew half as much about Spanish sailings as you do about ours, how happy, felix, you would make me,' tossed down the burning drop of brandy and called for another glass of wine, that appeasing, honest brew. 'I have an auntie,' said Mercedes, 'that know a great deal.' 'Have you, my dear? Have you indeed?' said Jack. 'You shall tell me about her this evening.' He kissed her absently, tapped his lace hat more firmly on to his new wig and said, 'Now for that scrub.'

But as it happened, Captain Harte received him with more than ordinary civility, congratulated him upon the Almoraira affair – 'that battery was a damned nuisance; hulled the

Pallas three times and knocked away one of the *Emerald*'s topmasts; should have been dealt with long ago' – and asked him to dinner. 'And bring your surgeon along, will you? My wife particularly desires me to invite him.'

'I am sure he will be very happy, if he is not already bespoke. Mrs Harte is well, I trust? I must pay my respects.'

'Oh, she's very well, I thank you. But it's no use calling on her this morning – she's out riding with Colonel Pitt. How she does it in this heat, I don't know. By the by, you can do me a service, if you will.' Jack looked at him attentively, but did not commit himself. 'My money-man wants to send his son to sea – you have a vacancy for a youngster: it is as simple as that. He is a perfectly respectable fellow, and his wife was at school with Molly. You will see them both at dinner.'

On his knees, and with his chin level with the top of the table, Stephen watched the male mantis step cautiously towards the female mantis. She was a fine strapping green specimen, and she stood upright on her four back legs, her front pair dangling devoutly; from time to time a tremor caused her heavy body to oscillate over the thin suspending limbs, and each time the brown male shot back. He advanced lengthways, with his body parallel to the table-top, his long, toothed, predatory front legs stretching out tentatively and his antennae trained forwards: even in this strong light Stephen could see the curious inner glow of his big oval eyes.

The female deliberately turned her head through forty-five degrees, as though looking at him. 'Is this recognition?' asked Stephen, raising his magnifying glass to detect some possible movement in her feelers. 'Consent?'

The brown male certainly thought it was, and in three strides he was upon her; his legs gripped her wing-covers; his antennae found hers and began to stroke them. Apart from a vibratory, well-sprung quiver at the additional weight, she made no apparent response, no resistance; and in a little while the strong orthopterous copulation began. Stephen set his watch and noted down the time in a book, open upon the floor.

Minutes passed. The male shifted his hold a little. The female moved her triangular head, pivoting it slightly from left to right. Through his glass Stephen could see her sideways jaws open and close; then there was a blur of movements so rapid that for all his care and extreme attention he could not follow them, and the male's head was off, clamped there, a detached lemon, under the crook of her green praying arms. She bit into it, and the eye's glow went out; on her back the headless male continued to copulate rather more strongly than before, all his inhibitions having been removed. 'Ah,' said Stephen with intense satisfaction, and noted down the time again.

Ten minutes later the female took off three pieces of her mate's long thorax, above the upper coxal joint, and ate them with every appearance of appetite, dropping crumbs of chitinous shell in front of her. The male copulated on, still firmly anchored by his back legs.

'There you are,' cried Jack. 'I have been waiting for you this quarter of an hour.'

'Oh,' said Stephen, starting up. 'I beg your pardon. I beg your pardon. I know what importance you attach to punctuality – most concerned. I had put my watch back to the beginning of the copulation,' he said, very gently covering the mantis and her dinner with a hollow ventilated box. 'I am with you now.'

'No you aren't,' said Jack. 'Not in those infamous half-boots. Why do you have them soled with lead, anyhow?'

At any other time he would have received a very sharp reply to this, but it was clear to Stephen that he had not spent a pleasant forenoon with the admiral; and all he said, as he changed into his shoes, was, 'You do not need a head, nor even a heart, to be all a female can require.'

'That reminds me,' said Jack, 'have you anything that will keep my wig on? A most ridiculous thing happened as I was crossing the square: there was Dillon on the far side, with a woman on his arm – Governor Wall's sister, I believe – so I returned his salute with particular attention, do you see. I lifted my hat right off my head and the damned wig came with it. You may laugh, and it is damned amusing, of course; but I would have given a fifty-pound note not to have looked ridiculous with him there.'

'Here is a piece of court plaster,' said Stephen. 'Let me double it over and stick it to your head. I am heartily sorry there should be this – constraint, between Dillon and you.'

'So am I,' said Jack, bending for the plaster: then with a sudden burst of confidence – the place being so different, and they on land, with no sort of sea-going relationship – he said, 'I never have been so puzzled what to do in all my life. He practically accused me – I hardly like to name it – of want of conduct, after that *Cacafuego* business. My first impulse was to ask him for an explanation, and for satisfaction, naturally. But then the position is so very particular – it is heads I win tails you lose in such a case; for if I were to sink him, why, there he would be, of course; and if he were to do the same by me, he would be out of the Navy before you could say knife, which would amount to much the same thing, for him.'

'He is passionately attached to the service, sure.'

'And in either case, there is the *Sophie* left in a pitiable state . . . damn the man for a fool. And then again he is the best first lieutenant a man could wish for – taut, but not a slave-driver; a fine seaman; and you never have to give a thought to the daily running of the sloop. I like to think that that was not his meaning.'

'He would certainly never have meant to impugn your courage,' said Stephen.

'Would he not?' asked Jack, gazing into Stephen's face and balancing his wig in his hand. 'Should you like to dine at the Hartes'?' he asked, after a pause. 'I must go, and I should be glad of your company, if you are not engaged.'

'Dinner?' cried Stephen, as though the meal had just been invented. 'Dinner? Oh, yes: charmed – delighted.'

'You don't happen to have a looking-glass, I suppose?' said Jack.

'No. No. But there is one in Mr Florey's room. We can step in on our way downstairs.'

In spite of a candid delight in being fine, in putting on his best uniform and his golden epaulette, Jack had never had the least opinion of his looks, and until this moment he had scarcely thought of them for two minutes together. But now, having gazed long and thoughtfully, he said, 'I suppose I am rather on the hideous side?'

'Yes,' said Stephen. 'Oh yes. Very much so.'

Jack had cut off the rest of his hair when they came into port and had bought this wig to cover his cropped poll; but there was nothing to hide his burnt face which, moreover, had caught the sun in spite of Stephen Maturin's medicated grease, or the tumefaction of his battered brow and eye, which had now reached the yellow stage, with a blue outer ring; so that his left-hand aspect was not unlike that of the great West African mandrill.

When they had finished their business at the prize-agent's house (a gratifying reception – such bows and smiles) they walked up to their dinner. Leaving Stephen contemplating a tree-frog by the patio fountain, Jack saw Molly Harte alone for a moment in the cool anteroom.

'Lord, Jack!' she cried, staring. 'A wig?'

''Tis only for the moment,' said Jack, pacing swiftly towards her.

'Take care,' she whispered, getting behind a jasper, onyx and cornelian table, three feet broad, seven and a half feet long, nineteen hundredweight. 'The servants.'

'The summerhouse tonight?' whispered he.

She shook her head and mutely, with great facial expression, said, 'Indisposée.' And then in a low but audible tone, a sensible tone, 'Let me tell you about these people who are coming to dinner, the Ellises. She was of some sort of family, I believe – anyhow, she was at Mrs Capell's school with me. Very much older, of course: quite one of the great girls. And then she married this Mr Ellis, of the City. He is a respectable, well-behaved man, extremely rich and he looks after our money very cleverly. Captain Harte is uncommonly obliged to him, I know; and I have known Laetitia this age; so there is the double whatever you call it – bond? They want their boy to go to sea, so it would give me great pleasure if . . .'

'I would do anything in my power to give you pleasure,' said Jack heavily. The words *our money* had stabbed very deep.

'Dr Maturin, I am so glad you were able to come,' cried Mrs Harte, turning towards the door. 'I have a very learned lady to introduce you to.'

'Indeed, ma'am? I rejoice to hear it. Pray what is she learned in?'

'Oh, in everything,' said Mrs Harte cheerfully; and this, indeed, seemed to be Laetitia's opinion too, for she at once gave Stephen her views on the treatment of cancer and on the conduct of the Allies – prayer, love and Evangelism was the answer, in both cases. She was an odd, doll-like little creature with a wooden face, both shy and extremely self-satisfied, rather alarmingly young; she spoke slowly, with an odd writhing motion of her upper body, staring at her interlocutor's stomach or elbow, so her exposition took some time. Her husband was a tall, moist-eyed, damp-handed man, with a meek, Evangelical expression, and knock-knees: had it not been for those knees he would have looked exactly like a butler. 'If that man lives,' reflected Stephen, as Laetitia prattled on about Plato, 'he will become a miser: but it is more likely that he will hang himself. Costive; piles; flat feet.'

They sat down ten to dinner, and Stephen found that Mrs Ellis was his left-hand neighbour. On his right there was a Miss Wade, a plain, good-natured girl with a splendid appetite, unhampered by a humid ninety degrees or the calls of fashion; then came Jack, then Mrs Harte, and on her right Colonel Pitt. Stephen was engaged in a close discussion of the comparative merits of the crayfish and the true lobster with Miss Wade when the insistent voice on his left broke in so strongly that soon it was impossible to ignore it. 'But I don't understand – you are a real physician, he tells me, so how come you to be in the Navy? How come you to be in the Navy if you are a real doctor?'

'Indigence, ma'am, indigence. For all that clysters is not gold, on shore. And then, of course, a fervid desire to bleed for my country.'

'The gentleman is joking, my love,' said her husband across the table. 'With all these prizes he is *a very warm man*, as we say in the City' – nodding and smiling archly.

'Oh,' cried Laetitia, startled. 'He is a wit. I must take care of him, I declare. But still, you have to look after the common sailors too, Dr Maturin, not only the midshipmen and officers: that must be very horrid.'

'Why, ma'am,' said Stephen, looking at her curiously: for so small and Evangelical a woman she had drunk a remarkable quantity of wine and her face was coming out in blotches. 'Why, ma'am, I cut 'em off pretty short, I assure you. Oil of cat is my usual dose.'

'Quite right,' said Colonel Pitt, speaking for the first time. 'I allow no complaints in my regiment.'

'Dr Maturin is admirably strict,' said Jack. 'He often desires me to have the men flogged, to overcome their torpor and to open their veins both at the same time. A hundred lashes at the gangway is worth a stone of brimstone and treacle, we always say.'

'*There's* discipline,' said Mr Ellis, nodding his head.

Stephen felt the odd bareness on his knee that meant his napkin had glided to the floor; he dived after it, and in the hooded tent below he beheld four and twenty legs, six belonging to the table and eighteen to his temporary messmates. Miss Wade had kicked off her shoes: the woman opposite him had dropped a little screwed-up handkerchief:

Colonel Pitt's gleaming military boot lay pressed upon Mrs Harte's right foot, and upon her left – quite a distance from the right – reposed Jack's scarcely less massive buckled shoe.

Course followed course, indifferent Minorcan food cooked in English water, indifferent wine doctored with Minorcan verjuice; and at one point Stephen heard his neighbour say, 'I hear you have a very high moral tone in your ship.' But in time Mrs Harte rose and walked, limping slightly, into the drawing-room: the men gathered at the top end of the table, and the muddy port went round and round and round.

The wine brought Mr Ellis into full bloom at last; the diffidence and the timidity melted away from the mound of wealth, and he told the company about discipline – order and discipline were of primordial importance; the family, the *disciplined* family, was the cornerstone of Christian civilization; commanding officers were (as he might put it) the fathers of their numerous families, and their love was shown by their firmness. Firmness. His friend Bentham, the gentleman that wrote the *Defence of Usury* (it deserved to be printed in gold), had invented a whipping machine. Firmness and dread: for the two great motives in the world were greed and fear, gentlemen. Let them look at the French revolution, the disgraceful rebellion in Ireland, to say nothing – looking archly at their stony faces – of the unpleasantness at Spithead and the Nore – all greed, and to be put down by fear.

Mr Ellis was clearly very much at home in Captain Harte's house, for without having to ask the way he walked to the sideboard, opened the lead-lined door and took out the chamber-pot, and looking over his shoulder he went on without a pause to state that fortunately the lower classes naturally looked up to gentlemen and loved them, in their humble way; only gentlemen were fit to be officers. God had ordered it so, he said, buttoning the flap of his breeches; and as he sat down again at the table he observed that he knew one house where the article was silver – solid silver. The family was a good thing: he would drink a toast to discipline. The rod was a good thing: he would drink a toast to the rod, in *all* its forms. Spare the rod and spoil the child – loveth, chastitheth.

'You must come to us one Thursday morning and see how the bosun's mate loveth our defaulters,' said Jack.

Colonel Pitt, who had been staring heavily at the banker with an undisguised, boorish contempt, broke out into a guffaw and then left, excusing himself on the grounds of regimental business. Jack was about to follow him when Mr Ellis desired him to stay – he begged the favour of a few words.

'I do a certain amount of business for Mrs Jordan, and I have the honour, the great honour, of being presented to the Duke of Clarence,' he began, impressively. 'Have you ever seen him?'

'I am acquainted with His Highness,' said Jack, who had been shipmates with that singularly unattractive hot-headed cold-hearted bullying Hanoverian.

'I ventured to mention *our* Henry and said we hoped to make an officer of him, and he condescended to advise the sending of him to sea. Now, my wife and I have considered it carefully, and we prefer a little boat to a ship of the line, because they are sometimes rather *mixed*, if you understand me, and my wife is very particular – she is a Plantagenet; besides, some of these captains want their young gentlemen to have an allowance of fifty pounds per annum.'

'I always insist that their friends should guarantee my midshipmen at least fifty,' said Jack.

'Oh,' said Mr Ellis, a little dashed. 'Oh. But I dare say a good many of the things can be picked up second-hand. Not that I care about that – at the beginning of the war all of us in the alley sent His Majesty an address saying we should support him with our lives and fortunes. I don't mind fifty quid, or *even more*, so long as the ship is genteel. My wife's old friend Mrs H was telling us about you, sir; and what is more, you are a thorough-going Tory, just like me. And yesterday we caught sight of Lieutenant Dillon, who is Lord

Kenmare's nephew, I understand, and has a pretty little estate of his own – seems quite the gentleman. So to put it in a nutshell, sir, if you will take my boy I shall be very much obliged to you. And allow me to add,' he said, with an awkward jocularity, clearly against his own better judgment, 'what with my inside knowledge and experience of the market, you won't regret it. You'll find your advantage, I warrant you, hee, hee!'

'Let us join the ladies,' said Captain Harte, actually blushing for his guest.

'The best thing is to take him to sea for a month or so,' said Jack, standing up. 'Then he can see how he likes the service and whether he is suited for it; and we can speak of it again.'

'I am sorry to have let you in for that,' he said, taking Stephen's arm and guiding him down Pigtail Stairs, where the green lizards darted along the torrid wall. 'I had no notion Molly Harte was capable of giving such a wretched dinner – cannot think what has come over her. Did you remark that soldier?'

'The one in scarlet and gold, with boots?'

'Yes. Now he was a perfect example of what I was saying, that the army is divided into two sorts – the one as kind and gentle as ever you could wish, just like my dear old uncle, and the other heavy, lumpish brutes like that fellow. Quite unlike the Navy. I have seen it again and again, and I still cannot understand it. How do the two sorts live together? I wish he may not be a nuisance to Mrs Harte – she is sometimes very free and unguarded, quite unsuspecting – can be imposed upon.'

'The man whose name I forget, the money-man, was an eminently curious study,' said Stephen.

'Oh, him,' said Jack, with an utter want of interest. 'What do you expect, when a fellow sits thinking about money all day long? And they can never hold their wine, those sorts of people. Harte must be very much in his debt to have him in the house.'

'Oh, he was a dull ignorant superficial darting foolish prating creature in himself, to be sure, but I found him truly fascinating. The pure bourgeois in a state of social ferment. There was that typical costive, haemorrhoidal facies, the knock-knees, the drooping shoulders, the flat feet splayed out, the ill breath, the large staring eyes, the meek complacency; and, of course, you noticed that womanly insistence upon authority and beating once he was thoroughly drunk? I would wager that he is *very nearly* impotent: that would account for the woman's restless garrulity, her desire for predominance, absurdly combined with those girlish ways, and her thinning hair – she will be bald in a year or so.'

'It might be just as well if everybody were impotent,' said Jack sombrely. 'It would save a world of trouble.'

'And having seen the parents I am impatient to see this youth, the fruit of their strangely unattractive loins: will he be a wretched mammothrept? A little corporal? Or will the resiliency of childhood . . . ?'

'He will be the usual damned little nuisance, I dare say; but at least we shall know whether there is anything to be made of him by the time we are back from Alexandria. We are not saddled with him for the rest of the commission.'

'Did you say Alexandria?'

'Yes.'

'In Lower Egypt?'

'Yes. Did I not tell you? We are to run an errand to Sir Sydney Smith's squadron before our next cruise. He is watching the French, you know.'

'Alexandria,' said Stephen, stopping in the middle of the quay. 'O joy. I wonder you did not cry out with delight the moment you saw me. What an indulgent admiral – *pater classis* – O how I value that worthy man!'

'Why, 'tis no more than a straight run up and down the Mediterranean, about six hundred leagues each way, with precious little chance of seeing a prize either coming or going.'

'I did not think you could have been such an earthling,' cried Stephen. 'For shame. Alexandria is classic ground.'

'So it is,' said Jack, his good nature and pleasure in life flooding back at the sight of Stephen's delight. 'And with any luck I dare say we shall have a sight of the mountains of Candia, too. But come, we must get aboard: if we go on standing here we shall be run down.'

Chapter Nine

'It is ungrateful in me to repine,' he wrote, 'but when I think that I might have paced the burning sands of Libya, filled (as Goldsmith tells us) with serpents of various malignity; that I might have trodden the Canopic shore, have beheld the ibis, the Mareotic grallatores in their myriads, even perhaps the crocodile himself; that I was whirled past the northern coast of Candia, with Mount Ida in sight all day long; that at a given moment Cythera was no more than half an hour away, and yet for all my pleas no halt to be made, no "heaving to"; and when I reflect upon the wonders that lay at so short a distance from our course – the Cyclades, the Peloponnese, great Athens, and yet no deviation allowed, no not for half a day – why, then I am obliged to restrain myself from wishing Jack Aubrey's soul to the devil. Yet on the other hand, when I look over these notes not as a series of unfulfilled potentialities but as the record of positive accomplishment, how many causes have not I for rational exultation! The Homeric sea (if not the Homeric land); the pelican; the great white shark the seamen so obligingly fished up; the holothurians; euspongia mollissima (the same that Achilles stuffed his helmet with, saith Poggius); the nondescript gull; the turtles! Again, these weeks have been among the most peaceful I have known: they might have been among the happiest, if I had not been so aware that JA and JD might kill one another, in the civillest way in the world, at the next point of land: for it seems these things cannot take place at sea. JA is still deeply wounded about some remarks concerning the *Cacafuego* – feels there is a reflexion upon his courage – cannot bear it – it preys upon him. And JD, though quieter now, is wholly unpredictable: he is full of contained rage and unhappiness that will break out in some way; but I cannot tell what. It is not unlike sitting on a barrel of gunpowder in a busy forge, with sparks flying about (the sparks of my figure being the occasions of offence).'

Indeed, but for this tension, this travelling cloud, it would have been difficult to imagine a pleasanter way of spending the late summer than sailing across the whole width of the Mediterranean as fast as the sloop could fly. She flew a good deal faster now that Jack had hit upon her happiest trim, restowing her hold to bring her by the stern and restoring her masts to the rake her Spanish builders had intended. What is more, the brothers Sponge, with a dozen of the *Sophie*'s swimmers under their instruction, had spent every moment of the long calms in Greek waters (their native element) scraping her bottom; and Stephen could remember an evening when he had sat there in the warm, deepening twilight, watching the sea; it had barely a ruffle on its surface, and yet the *Sophie* picked up enough moving air with her topgallants to draw a long straight whispering furrow across the water, a line brilliant with unearthly phosphorescence, visible for quarter of a mile behind her. Days and nights of unbelievable purity. Nights when the steady Ionian breeze rounded the square mainsail – not a brace to be touched, watch relieving watch – and he and Jack on deck, sawing away, sawing away, lost in their music, until the falling dew untuned their strings. And days when the perfection of dawn was so great, the emptiness so entire, that men were almost afraid to speak.

A voyage whose two ends were out of sight – a voyage sufficient in itself. And on the plain physical side, she was a well-manned sloop, now that her prize-crews were all aboard again: not a great deal of work; a fair sense of urgency; a steady routine day after day; and day after day the exercise with the great guns that knocked the seconds off one by one until the day in 16°31'E., when the larboard watch succeeded in firing three broadsides in exactly five minutes. And, above all, the extraordinarily fine weather and (apart from a languid week or so of calm far to the east, a little after they had left Sir Sidney's squadron) fair winds: so much so that when a moderate Levanter sprang up as soon as their chronic short-age of water made it really necessary to put into Malta, Jack said uneasily, 'It is too good to last. I am afraid we must pay for this, presently.'

He had a very particular wish to make a rapid passage, a strikingly rapid passage that would persuade Lord Keith of his undeviating attention to duty, his reliability; nothing he had ever heard in his adult life had so chilled him (upon reflexion) as the admiral's remarks about post rank. They had been kindly meant; they were totally convincing; they haunted his mind.

'I wonder you should be so concerned over a mere title – a tolerably Byzantine title,' observed Stephen. 'After all, you are called Captain Aubrey now, and you would still only be called Captain Aubrey after that eventual elevation; for no man, as I understand it, ever says "Post-captain So-and-so". Surely it cannot be a peevish desire for symmetry – a longing to wear two epaulettes?'

'That does occupy a great share of my heart, of course, along with eagerness for an extra eighteenpence a day. But you will allow me to point out, sir, that you are mistaken in everything you advance. At present I am called captain only by courtesy – I am dependent upon the courtesy of a parcel of damned scrubs, much as surgeons are by courtesy called Doctor. How should you like it if any cross-grained brute could call you *Mr* M the moment he chose to be uncivil? Whereas, was I to be made post some day, I should be captain by right; but even so I should only shift my swab from one shoulder to the other. I should not have the right to wear both until I had three years' seniority. No. The reason why every sea-officer in his right wits longs so ardently to be made post is this – once you are over that fence, why, there you are! My dear sir, you are there! What

I mean is, that from then onwards all you have to do is to remain alive to be an admiral in time.'

'And that is the summit of human felicity?'

'Of course it is,' cried Jack, staring. 'Does it not seem plain to you?'

'Oh, certainly.'

'Well then,' said Jack, smiling at the prospect, 'well then, up the list you go, once you are there, whether you have a ship or no, all according to seniority, in perfect order – rear-admiral of the blue, rear-admiral of the white, rear-admiral of the red, vice-admiral of the blue, and so on, right up – no damned merit about it, no selection. That's what I like. Up until that point it is interest, or luck, or the approbation of your superiors – a pack of old women, for the most part. You must truckle to them – yes, sir; no, sir; by your leave, sir; your most humble servant . . . Do you smell that mutton? You will dine with me, will you not? I have asked the officer and midshipman of the watch.'

The officer in question happened to be Dillon, and the acting midshipman young Ellis. Jack had very early determined that there should be no evident breach, no barbarous sullen inveteracy, and once a week he invited the officer (and sometimes the midshipman) of the forenoon watch to dinner, whoever he was; and once a week he in turn was invited to dine in the gun-room. Dillon had tacitly acquiesced in this arrangement, and on the surface there was a perfect civility between them – a state of affairs much helped in their daily life by the invariable presence of others.

On this occasion Henry Ellis formed part of their protection. He had proved an ordinary boy, rather pleasant than otherwise: exceedingly timid and modest at first and outrageously made game of by Babbington and Ricketts, but now, having found his place, somewhat given to prating. Not at his captain's table, however: he sat rigid, mute, the tips of his fingers and the rims of his ears bleeding with cleanliness, his elbows pressed to his sides, eating wolf-like gulps of mutton, which he swallowed whole. Jack had always liked the young, and in any case he felt that a guest was entitled to consideration at his table, so having invited Ellis to drink a glass of wine with him, he smiled affably and said, 'You people were reciting some verses in the foretop this morning. Very capital verses, I dare say – Mr Mowett's verses? Mr Mowett turns a pretty line.' So he did. His piece on the bending of the new mainsail was admired throughout the sloop: but most unhappily he had also been inspired to write, as part of a general description:

White as the clouds beneath the blaze of noon
Her bottom through translucent waters shone.

For the time being this couplet had quite destroyed his authority with the youngsters; and it was this couplet they had been reciting in the foretop, hoping thereby to provoke him still further.

'Pray, will you not recite them to us? I am sure the Doctor would like to hear.'

'Oh, yes, pray do,' said Stephen.

The unhappy boy thrust a great lump of mutton into his cheek, turned a nasty yellow and gathered to his heart all the fortitude he could call upon. He said, 'Yes, sir,' fixed his eyes upon the stern-window and began,

'*White as the clouds beneath the blaze of noon* Oh God don't let me die

'*White as the clouds beneath the blaze of noon*

Her b –' His voice quavered, died, revived as a thin desperate ghost and squeaked out '*Her bottom*'; but could do no more.

'A damned fine verse,' cried Jack, after a very slight pause. 'Edifying too. Dr Maturin, a glass of wine with you?'

Mowett appeared, like a spirit a little late for its cue, and said, 'I beg your pardon, sir, for interrupting you, but there's a ship topsails up three points on the starboard bow.'

In all this golden voyage they had seen almost nothing on the open sea, apart from a few caiques in Greek waters and a transport on her passage from Sicily to Malta, so when at length the newcomer had come close enough for her topsails and a hint of her courses to be seen from the deck, she was stared at with an even greater intensity than usual. The *Sophie* had cleared the Sicilian Channel that morning and she was steering west-north-west, with Cape Teulada in Sardinia bearing north by east twenty-three leagues, a moderate breeze at north-east, and only some two hundred and fifty miles of sea between her and Port Mahon. The stranger appeared to be steering west-south-west or something south, as though for Gibraltar or perhaps Oran, and she bore north-west by north from the sloop. These courses, if persisted in, would intersect; but at present there was no telling which would cross the other's wake.

A detached observer would have seen the *Sophie* heel slightly as all her people gathered along her starboard side, would have noticed the excited talk die away on the fo'c'sle and would have smiled to see two-thirds of the crew and all the officers simultaneously purse their lips as the distant ship set her topgallants. That meant she was almost certainly a man-of-war; almost certainly a frigate, if not a ship of the line. And those topgallants had not been sheeted home in a very seamanlike way – scarcely as the Royal Navy would have liked it.

'Make the private signal, Mr Pullings. Mr Marshall, begin to edge away. Mr Day, stand by for the gun.'

The red flag soared up the foremast in a neat ball and broke out smartly, streaming forwards, while the white flag and pendant flacked overhead at the main and the single gun fired to windward.

'Blue ensign, sir,' reported Pullings, glued to his telescope. 'Red pendant at the main. Blue Peter at the fore.'

'Hands to the braces,' called Jack. 'South-west by south a half south,' he said to the man at the wheel, for that signal was the answer of six months ago. 'Royals, lower and tops'l stuns'ls. Mr Dillon, pray let me know what you make of her.'

James hoisted himself into the crosstrees and trained his glass on the distant ship: as soon as the *Sophie* had steadied on her new course, bowing the long southern swell, he compensated for her movement with an even pendulum motion of his far hand and fixed the stranger in the shining round. The flash of her brass bow-chaser winked at him across the sea in the afternoon sun. She was a frigate sure enough: he could not count her gun-ports yet but she was a heavy frigate: of that there was no doubt. An elegant ship. She, too, was setting her lower studdingsails; and they were having difficulty in rigging out a boom.

'Sir,' said the midshipman of the maintop as he made his way down, 'Andrews here thinks she's the *Dédaigneuse*.'

'Look again with my glass,' said Dillon, passing his telescope, the best in the sloop.

'Yes. She's the *Dédaigneuse*,' said the sailor, a middle-aged man with a greasy red waistcoat over his bare copper-brown upper half. 'You can see that new-fangled round bow. I was prisoner aboard of her a matter of three weeks and more: took out of a collier.'

'What does she carry?'

'Twenty-six eighteen-pounders on the main deck, sir, eighteen long eights on the quarter-deck and fo'c'sle, and a brass long twelve for a bow-chaser. They used to make me polish 'un.'

'She is a frigate, sir, of course,' reported James. 'And Andrews of the maintop, a sensible man, says she is the *Dédaigneuse*. He was a prisoner in her.'

'Well,' said Jack, smiling, 'how fortunate that the evenings are drawing in.' The sun would, in fact, set in about four hours' time; the twilight did not last long in these latitudes; and this was the dark of the moon. The *Dédaigneuse* would have to sail nearly two knots faster than the *Sophie* to catch her, and he did not think there was any likelihood of her doing so – she was heavily armed, but she was no famous sailer like the *Astrée* or the *Pomone*. Nevertheless, he turned the whole of his mind to urging his dear sloop to her very utmost speed. It was possible that he might not manage to slip away in the night – he had taken part in a thirty-two-hour chase over more than two hundred miles of sea on the West Indies station himself – and every yard might count. She had the breeze almost on her larboard quarter at present, not far from her best point of sailing, and she was running a good seven knots; indeed, so briskly had her numerous and well-trained crew set the royals and studdingsails that for the first quarter of an hour she appeared to be gaining on the frigate.

'I wish it may last,' thought Jack, glancing up at the sun through the poor flimsy canvas of the topsail. The prodigious spring rains of the western Mediterranean, the Greek sun and piercing winds had removed every particle of the contractor's dressing as well as most of the body of the stuff, and the bunt and reefs showed poor and baggy: well enough before the wind, but if they were to try a tacking-match with the frigate it could only end in tears – they would never lie so close.

It did not last. Once the frigate's hull felt the full effect of the sails she spread in her leisurely fashion, she made up her loss and began to overhaul the *Sophie*. It was difficult to be sure of this at first – a far-off triple flash on the horizon with a hint of darkness beneath at the top of the rise – but in three-quarters of an hour her hull was visible from the *Sophie*'s quarter-deck most of the time, and Jack set their old-fashioned spritsail topsail, edging away another half point.

At the taffrail Mowett was explaining the nature of this sail to Stephen, for the *Sophie* set it flying, with a jack-stay clinched round the end of the jib-boom, having an iron traveller on it, a curious state of affairs in a man-of-war, of course; and Jack was standing by the aftermost starboard four-pounder with his eyes recording every movement aboard the frigate and his mind taken up with the calculation of the risks involved in setting the topgallant studdingsails in this freshening breeze, when there was a confused bellowing forward and the cry of *man overboard*. Almost at the same moment, Henry Ellis swept by in the smooth curving stream beneath him, his face straining up out of the water, amazed. Mowett threw him the fall of the empty davit. Both arms reached up from the sea to catch the flying line: head went under – hands missed their hold. Then he was away behind, bobbing on the wake.

Every face turned to Jack. His expression was terribly hard. His eyes darted from the boy to the frigate coming up at eight knots. Ten minutes would lose a mile and more: the havoc of studdingsails taken aback: the time to get way on her again. Ninety men endangered. These considerations and many others, including a knowledge of the extreme intensity of the eyes directed at him, a recollection of the odious nature of the parents, the status of the boy as a sort of guest, Molly Harte's protégé, flew through his racing mind before his stopped breath had begun to flow again.

'Jolly-boat away,' he said harshly. 'Stand by, fore and aft. Stand by. Mr Marshall, bring her to.'

The *Sophie* flew up into the wind: the jolly-boat splashed into the water. Very few orders were called for. The yards came round, her great spread of canvas shrank in, halliards, bunt-lines, clew-lines, brails racing through their blocks with scarcely a word; and even in his cold black fury Jack admired the smooth competence of the operation.

Painfully the jolly-boat crept out over the sea to cut the curve of the *Sophie*'s wake again: slowly, slowly. They were peering over the side of the boat, poking about with a boat-hook. Interminably. Now at last they had turned; they were a quarter of the way back; and in his glass Jack saw all the rowers fall violently into the bottom of the boat. Stroke had been pulling so hard that his oar had broken, flinging him backwards.

'Jesus, Mary . . .' muttered Dillon, at his side.

The *Sophie* was on the hover, with some way on her already, as the jolly-boat came alongside and the drowned boy was passed up. 'Dead,' they said. 'Make sail,' said Jack. Again the almost silent manoeuvres followed one another with admirable rapidity. Too much rapidity. She was not yet on her course, she had not reached half her former speed, before there was an ugly rending crack and the foretopgallantyard parted in the slings.

Now the orders flew: looking up from Ellis' wet body, Stephen saw Jack utter three bouts of technicalities to Dillon, who relayed them, elaborated, through his speaking-trumpet to the bosun and the foretopmen as they flew aloft; saw him give a separate set of orders to the carpenter and his crew; calculate the altered forces acting on the sloop and give the helmsman a course accordingly; glance over his shoulder at the frigate and then look down with a sharp attentive glance. 'Is there anything you can do for him? Do you need a hand?'

'His heart has stopped,' said Stephen. 'But I should like to try . . . could he be slung up by the heels on deck? There is no room below.'

'Shannahan. Thomas. Bear a hand. Clap on to the burton-tackle and that spun-yarn. Carry on as the Doctor directs you. Mr Lamb, this fish . . .'

Stephen sent Cheslin for lancets, cigars, the galley bellows; and as the lifeless Henry Ellis rose free of the deck so he swung him forwards two or three times, face down and tongue lolling, and emptied some water out of him. 'Hold him just so,' he said, and bled him behind the ears. 'Mr Ricketts, pray be so good as to light me this cigar.' And what part of the *Sophie*'s crew that was not wholly occupied with the fishing of the sprung yard, the bending of the sail afresh and swaying all up, with the continual trimming of the sails and with furtively peering at the frigate, had the inexpressible gratification of seeing Dr Maturin draw tobacco smoke into the bellows, thrust the nozzle into his patient's nose, and while his assistant held Ellis' mouth and other nostril closed, blow the acrid smoke into his lungs, at the same time swinging his suspended body so that now his bowels pressed upon his diaphragm and now they did not. Gasps, choking, a vigorous plying of the bellows, more smoke, more and steadier gasps, coughing. 'You may cut him down now,' said Stephen to the fascinated seamen. 'It is clear that he was born to be hanged.'

The frigate had covered a great deal of sea in this time, and now her gun-ports could be counted without a glass. She was a heavy frigate – her broadside would throw three hundred pounds of metal as against the *Sophie*'s twenty-eight – but she was deep-laden and even in this moderate wind she was making heavy weather of it. The swell broke regularly under her bows, sending up white water, and she had a labouring air. She was still gaining perceptibly on the *Sophie*. 'But,' said Jack to himself, 'I swear with that crew he will have the royals off her before it is quite dark.' His intent scrutiny of the *Dédaigneuse*'s sailing had convinced him that she had a great many raw hands aboard, if not a new crew altogether – no uncommon thing in French ships. 'He may try a ranging shot before that, however.'

He looked up at the sun. It was still a long way from the horizon. And when he had taken a hundred counted turns from the taffrail to the gun, from the gun to the taffrail, it was still a long way from the horizon, in exactly the same place, shining with idiot good humour between the arched foot of the topsail and the yard, whereas the frigate had moved distinctly closer.

Meanwhile, the daily life of the sloop went on, almost automatically. The hands were piped to supper at the beginning of the first dog-watch; and at two bells, as Mowett was heaving the log James Dillon said, 'Will I beat to quarters, sir?' He spoke a little hesitantly, for he was not sure of Jack's mind: and his eyes were fixed beyond Jack's face at the *Dédaigneuse*, coming on with a most impressive show of canvas, brilliant in the sun, and her white moustache giving an impression of even greater speed.

'Oh, yes, by all means. Let us hear Mr Mowett's reading; and then by all means beat to quarters.'

'Seven knots four fathoms, sir, if you please,' said Mowett to the lieutenant, who turned, touched his hat and repeated this to the captain.

The drum-roll, the muffled thunder of bare feet on the hollow, echoing deck, and quarters; then the long process of lacing bonnets to the topsails and topgallants; the sending-up of extra preventer-backstays to the topgallant mastheads (for Jack was determined to set more sail by night); a hundred minute variations in the spread, tension and angle of the sails – all this took time; but still the sun took longer, and still the *Dédaigneuse* came closer, closer, closer. She was carrying far too much sail aloft, and far too much aft: but everything aboard her seemed to be made of steel – she neither carried anything away nor yet (his highest hope of all) broached to, in spite of a couple of wild yawing motions in the last dog-watch that must have made her captain's heart stand still. 'Why does he not haul up the weather skirt of his mainsail and ease her a trifle?' asked Jack. 'The pragmatical dog.'

Everything that could be done aboard the *Sophie* had been done. The two vessels raced silently across the warm kind sea in the evening sun; and steadily the frigate gained.

'Mr Mowett,' called Jack, pausing at the end of his beat. Mowett came away from the group of officers on the larboard side of the quarter-deck, all gazing very thoughtfully at the *Dédaigneuse*. 'Mr Mowett . . .' he paused. From below, half-heard through the song of the quartering wind and the creak of the rigging, came snatches of a 'cello suite. The young master's mate looked attentive, ready and dutiful, inclining his tube-like form towards his captain in a deferential attitude continually and unconsciously adapted to the long urgent corkscrewing motion of the sloop. 'Mr Mowett, perhaps you would be so kind as to tell me over your piece about the new mainsail. I am very fond of poetry,' he added with a smile, seeing Mowett's look of wary dismay, his tendency to deny everything.

'Well, sir,' said Mowett hesitantly, in a low, human voice; he coughed and then, in quite another, rather severe, tone, said, '*The New Mainsail*', and went on –

> *'The mainsail, by the squall so lately rent,*
> *In streaming pendants flying, is unbent:*
> *With brails refixed, another soon prepared,*
> *Ascending, spreads along beneath the yard.*
> *To each yardarm the head-rope they extend,*
> *And soon their earings and their robans bend.*
> *That task performed, they first the braces slack,*
> *Then to the chesstree drag th'unwilling tack:*
> *And, while the lee clew-garnet's lowered away,*
> *Taut aft the sheet they tally and belay.'*

'Excellent – capital,' cried Jack, clapping him on the shoulder. 'Good enough for the Gentleman's Magazine, upon my honour. Tell me some more.'

Mowett looked modestly down, drew breath and began again, *'Occasional Piece'*:

> *'Oh were it mine with sacred Maro's art,*
> *To wake to sympathy the feeling heart,*
> *Then might I, with unrivalled strains, deplore,*
> *Th'impervious horrors of a leeward shore.'*

'Ay, a leeward shore,' murmured Jack, shaking his head; and at this moment he heard the frigate's first ranging shot. The thump of the *Dédaigneuse*'s bow-chaser punctuated Mowett's verse for a hundred and twenty lines, but no fall of shot did they see until the moment the sun's lower limb touched the horizon, when a twelve-pound ball went skipping by twenty yards away along the starboard side of the sloop, just as Mowett reached the unfortunate couplet,

> *'Transfixed with terror at th'approaching doom*
> *Self-pity in their breasts alone has room.'*

and he felt obliged to break off and explain 'that of course, sir, they were only people in the merchant service.'

'Why, that is a consideration, to be sure,' said Jack. 'But now I am afraid I must interrupt you. Pray tell the purser we need three of his largest butts, and rouse them up on to the fo'c'sle. Mr Dillon, Mr Dillon, we will make a raft to carry a stern lantern and three or four smaller ones; and let it be done behind the cover of the forecourse.'

A little before the usual time Jack had the *Sophie*'s great stern-lantern lit, and himself he went into the cabin to see that the stern-windows were as conspicuous as he could wish: and as the twilight deepened they saw lights appear on the frigate too. What is more, they saw her main and mizen royals disappear. Now, with her royals handed, the *Dédaigneuse* was a black silhouette, sharp against the violet sky; and her bow-chaser spat orange-red every three minutes or so, the stab showing well before the sound reached them.

By the time Venus set over their starboard bow (and the starlight diminished sensibly with her going) the frigate had not fired for half an hour: her position could only be told by her lights, and they were no longer gaining – almost certainly not gaining any more.

'Veer the raft astern,' said Jack, and the awkward contraption came bobbing down the side, fouling the studdingsail booms and everything else it could reach: it carried a spare stern-lantern on a pole the height of the *Sophie*'s taffrail and four smaller lanterns in a line below. 'Where is a handy nimble fellow?' asked Jack. 'Lucock.'

'Sir?'

'I want you to go on to the raft and light each lantern the very moment the same one on board is put out.'

'Aye aye, sir. Light as put out.'

'Take this darky and clap a line round your middle.'

It was a tricky operation, with the sea running and the sloop throwing the water about; and there was always the possibility of some busy fellow with a glass aboard the *Dédaigneuse* picking out a figure acting strangely abaft the *Sophie*'s stern; but presently it was done, and Lucock came over the taffrail on to the darkened quarter-deck.

'Well done,' said Jack softly. 'Cast her off.'

The raft went far astern and he felt the *Sophie* give a skip as she was relieved of its drag. It was a creditable imitation of her lights, although it did bob about too much; and the bosun had rigged a criss-cross of old rope to simulate the casement.

Jack gazed at it for a moment and then said, 'Topgallant stuns'ls.' The topmen vanished upwards, and everyone on deck listened with grave attention, unmoving, glancing at one another. The wind had lessened a trifle, but there was that wounded yard; and in any case such a very great press of canvas . . .

The fresh sails were sheeted home; the extra preventer-back-stays tightened; the rigging's general voice rose a quarter-tone; the *Sophie* moved faster through the sea. The topmen reappeared and stood with their listening shipmates, glancing aft from time to time to watch the dwindling lights. Nothing carried away; the strain eased a little; and suddenly their attention was wholly shifted, for the *Dédaigneuse* had begun to fire again. Again and again and again; and then her lit side appeared as she yawed to give the raft her whole broadside – a very noble sight, a long line of brilliant flashes and a great sullen roar. It did the raft no harm, however, and a low contented chuckle rose from the *Sophie*'s deck. Broadside after broadside – she seemed in quite a passion – and at last the raft's lights went out, all of them at once.

'Does he think we have sunk?' wondered Jack, gazing back at the frigate's distant side. 'Or has he discovered the cheat? Is he at a stand? At all events, I swear he will not expect me to carry straight on.'

It was one thing to swear it, however, and quite another to believe it with the whole of his heart and head, and the rising of the Pleiades found Jack at the masthead with his night-glass swinging steadily from north-north-west to east-north-east; first light still found him there, and even sunrise, although by then it was clear that they had either completely outsailed the frigate or that she had set a new course, easterly or westerly, in pursuit.

'West-north-west is the most likely,' observed Jack, stabbing his bosom with the telescope to close it and narrowing his eyes against the intolerable brilliance of the rising sun.

'That is what I should have done.' He lowered himself heavily, stiffly down through the rigging, stumped into his cabin, sent for the master to work out their present position and closed his eyes for a moment until he should come.

They were within five leagues of Cape Bougaroun in North Africa, it appeared, for they had run over a hundred miles during the chase, many of them in the wrong direction. 'We shall have to haul our wind – what wind there is –' (for it had been backing and dying all through the middle watch) 'and lie as close as ever we can. But even so, kiss my hand to a quick passage.' He leant back and closed his eyes again, thought of saying what a good thing it was that Africa had not moved northwards half a degree during the night, and smiling at the notion went fast asleep.

Mr Marshall offered a few observations that brought no response, then contemplated him for a while and then, with infinite tenderness, eased his feet up on to the locker, cradled him back with a cushion behind his head, rolled up the charts and tiptoed away.

Farewell to a quick passage, indeed. The *Sophie* wished to sail to the north-west. The wind, when it blew, blew from the north-west. But for days on end it did nothing whatever, and at last they had to sweep for twelve hours on end to reach Minorca, where they crept up the long harbour with their tongues hanging out, water having been down to quarter-allowance for the past four days.

What is more, they crept down it too, with the launch and cutter towing ahead and the men heaving crossly on the heavy sweeps, while the reek of the tanneries pursued them, spreading by mere penetration in the still and fetid air.

'What a disappointing place that is,' said Jack, looking back from Quarantine Island.

'Do you think so?' said Stephen, who had come aboard with a leg wrapped in sailcloth, quite a fresh leg, a present from Mr Florey. 'It seems to me to have its charms.'

'But then you are much attached to toads,' said Jack. 'Mr

Watt, those men are supposed to be heaving at the sweeps, I believe.'

The most recent disappointment or rather vexation – a trifle, but vexing – had been singularly gratuitous. He had given Evans, of the *Aetna* bomb, a lift in his boat, although it was out of his way to thread through all the victuallers and transports of the Malta convoy; and Evans, peering at his epaulette in that underbred way of his, had said, 'Where did you get your swab?'

'At Paunch's.'

'I thought as much. They are nine parts brass at Paunch's, you know: hardly any real bullion at all. It soon shows through.'

Envy and ill-nature. He had heard several remarks of that kind, all prompted by the same pitiful damned motives: for his part he had never felt unkindly towards any man for being given a cruise, nor for being lucky in the way of prizes. Not that he had been so very lucky in the way of prizes either – had made nothing like so much as people thought. Mr Williams had met him with a long face: part of the *San Carlo*'s cargo had not been condemned, having been consigned by a Ragusan Greek under British protection; the admiralty court's expenses had been very high; and really it was scarcely worthwhile sending in some of the smaller vessels, as things were at present. Then the dockyard had made a childish scene about the topgallant yard – a mere stick, most legitimately expended. And the backstays. But above all, Molly Harte had not been there for more than a single afternoon. She had gone to stay with Lady Warren at Ciudadela: a long-standing engagement, she said. He had had no idea of how much it would matter to him, how deeply it would affect his happiness.

A series of disappointments. Mercy and what she had to tell him had been pleasant enough: but that was all. Lord Keith had sailed two days before, saying he wondered Captain Aubrey did not make his number, as Captain Harte was quick to let him know. But Ellis' horrible parents had not

285

yet left the island, and he and Stephen had been obliged to undergo their hospitality – the only occasion in his life he had ever seen a half bottle of small white wine divided between four. Disappointments. The Sophies themselves, indulged with a further advance of prize-money, had behaved badly; quite badly, even by the standards of port behaviour. Four were in prison for rape; four had not been recovered from the stews when the *Sophie* sailed; one had broken his collarbone and a wrist. 'Drunken brutes,' he said, looking at them coldly; and, indeed, many of the waisters at the sweeps were deeply unappetizing at this moment – dirty, mazed still, unshaven; some still in their best shore-going rigs all foul and beslobbered. A smell of stale smoke, chewed tobacco, sweat and whore-house scent. 'They take no notice of punishment. I shall rate that dumb Negro bosun's mate. King is his name. And rig a proper grating: that will make them mind what they are about.' Disappointments. The bolts of honest number three and four sailcloth he had ordered and paid for himself had not been delivered. The shops had run out of fiddle strings. His father's letter had spoken in eager, almost enthusiastic, tones of the advantages of remarriage, the great conveniency of a woman to supervise the housekeeping, the desirability of the marriage state, from *all* points of view, particularly from that of society – society had a call upon a man. Rank was a matter of no importance whatever, said General Aubrey: a woman took rank from her husband; *goodness of heart* was what signified; and good hearts, Jack, and damned fine women, were to be found even in cottage kitchens; the difference between not quite sixty-four and twenty-odd was of *very little importance*. The words 'an old stallion to a young –' had been crossed out, and an arrow pointing to 'supervising the housekeeping' said 'Very like your first lieutenant, I dare say.'

He glanced across the quarter-deck at his lieutenant, who was showing young Lucock how to hold a sextant and bring the sun down to the horizon. Lucock's entire being showed a restrained but intense delight in understanding this mystery, carefully explained, and (more generally) in his elevation; the sight of him gave the first thrust to shift Jack's black humour, and at the same moment he made up his mind to go south about the island and to call in at Ciudadela – he would see Molly – there was perhaps some little foolish misunderstanding that he would clear away directly – they would pass an exquisite hour together in the high walled garden overlooking the bay.

Out beyond St Philip's a dark line ruled straight across the sea showed a wafting air, the hope of a westerly breeze: after two sweaty hours in the increasing heat they reached it, hoisted in the launch and cutter and prepared to make sail.

'You can run inside Ayre Island,' said Jack.

'South about, sir?' asked the master with surprise, for north round Minorca was the directest course for Barcelona, and the wind would serve.

'Yes, sir,' said Jack sharply.

'South by west,' said the master to the helmsman.

'South by west it is, sir,' he replied, and the headsails filled with a gentle urgency.

The moving air came off the open sea, clean, salt and sharp, pushing all the squalor before it. The *Sophie* heeled just a trifle, with life flowing back into her, and Jack, seeing Stephen coming aft from his elm-tree pump, said, 'My God, it is prime to be at sea again. Don't you feel like a badger in a barrel, on shore?'

'A badger in a barrel?' said Stephen, thinking of badgers he had known. 'I do not.'

They talked, in a quiet, desultory fashion, of badgers, otters, foxes – the pursuit of foxes – instances of amazing cunning, perfidy, endurance, lasting memory in foxes. The pursuit of stags. Of boars. And as they talked so the sloop ranged close along the Minorcan shore.

'I remember eating boar,' said Jack, his good humour quite restored, 'I remember eating a dish of stewed boar, the first time I had the pleasure of dining with you; and you told me what it was. Ha, ha: do you remember that boar?'

'Yes: and I remember we spoke of the Catalan language at the same time, which brings to mind something I had meant to tell you yesterday evening. James Dillon and I walked out beyond Ulla to view the ancient stone monuments – druidical, no doubt – and two peasants called out to one another from a distance, alluding to us. I will relate the conversation. First peasant: Do you see those heretics walking along so pleased with themselves? The red-haired one is descended from Judas Iscariot, no doubt. Second peasant: Wherever the English walk the ewes miscarry and abort; they are all the same; I wish their bowels may gush out. Where are they going? Where do they come from? First peasant: They are going to see the navetta and the taula d'en Xatart: they come from the disguised two-masted vessel opposite Bep Ventura's warehouse. They are sailing at dawn on Tuesday to cruise on the coast from Castellon up to Cape Creus, for six weeks. They have been paying four dollars a score for hogs. I, too, wish their bowels may gush out.'

'He had no great fund of originality, your second peasant,' said Jack, adding in a pensive, wondering tone, 'They do not seem to love the English. And yet, you know, we have protected them most of this past hundred years.'

'It is astonishing, is it not?' said Stephen Maturin. 'But my point was rather to hint that our appearance on the main may not be quite so unexpected as you suppose, perhaps. There is a continual commerce of fishermen and smugglers between this and Majorca. The Spanish governor's table is furnished with our Fornells crayfish, our Xambo butter and Mahon cheese.'

'Yes, I had taken your point, and am much obliged to you for your attention in –'

A dark form drifted from the sombre cliff-face on the starboard beam – an enormous pointed wingspan: as ominous as fate. Stephen gave a swinish grunt, snatched the telescope from under Jack's arm, elbowed him out of the way and squatted at the rail, resting the glass on it and focusing with great intensity.

'A bearded vulture! It is a bearded vulture!' he cried. 'A *young* bearded vulture.'

'Well,' said Jack instantly – not a second's hesitation – 'I dare say he forgot to shave this morning.' His red face crinkled up, his eyes diminished to a bright blue slit and he slapped his thigh, bending in such a paroxysm of silent mirth, enjoyment and relish that for all the *Sophie*'s strict discipline the man at the wheel could not withstand the infection and burst out in a strangled 'Hoo, hoo, hoo,' instantly suppressed by the quartermaster at the con.

'There are times,' said James quietly, 'when I understand your partiality for your friend. He derives a greater pleasure from a smaller stream of wit than any man I have ever known.'

It was the master's watch; the purser was away forward discussing accounts with the bosun; Jack was in his cabin, his spirits still high, one part of his mind designing a new disguise for the *Sophie* and the other revelling (by anticipation) in the happy outcome of his evening's interview with Molly Harte. She would be so surprised to see him at Ciudadela, so pleased: how happy they would be! Stephen and James were playing chess in the gun-room: James' furious attack, based upon the sacrifice of a knight, a bishop and two pawns, had very nearly reached its culminating point of error, and for a long placid stretch of time Stephen had been wondering how he could avoid mating him in three or four moves by any means less obvious than throwing down the board. He decided (James minded these things terribly) to sit it out until the drum beat to quarters, and meanwhile he waved his queen thoughtfully in the air, humming the Black Joke.

'It seems,' said James, dropping the words into the silence, 'that there may be some danger of peace.' Stephen pursed his lips and closed one eye. He, too, had heard these rumours in Port Mahon. 'So I hope to God we may see a touch of real action before it is too late. I am very curious to know what you will think of it: most men find it entirely unlike what they had expected – like love in that. Very disappointing, and yet you cannot wait to be starting again. It is your move, you know.'

'I am perfectly aware of it,' said Stephen sharply. He glanced at James, and he was surprised at the look of naked, unguarded distress on his face. Time was not doing what Stephen had expected of it: not by any means. The American ship was still there on the horizon. 'And would you not say we had seen any action, then?' he went on.

'These scuffles? I was thinking of something on a rather larger scale.'

'No, Mr Watt,' said the purser, ticking the last item in the private arrangement by which he and the bosun made thirteen and a half per cent on a whole range of stores on the borderland of their respective kingdoms, 'you may say what you please, but this young chap will end up by losing the *Sophie*; and what is more, he will either get us all knocked on the head or taken prisoner. And I've no wish to drag out my days in a French or Spanish prison, let alone be chained to an oar in an Algerine galley, rained upon, sunned upon and sitting there over my own stink. And I don't want my Charlie knocked on the head, either. That's why I'm transferring. It's a profession that has its risks, I grant you, and I'm willing for him to run them. But understand me, Mr Watt: willing for him to run the ordinary risks of the profession, not these. Not capers like that huge bloody great battery; nor lying right inshore by night as though we owned the place; nor watering here there and everywhere, just to stay out a little longer; nor setting about anything you see, regardless of size or number. The main chance is all very well; but we must not only be thinking of the main chance, Mr Watt.'

'Very true, Mr Ricketts,' said the bosun. 'And I can't say

I have ever really liked those cross-catharpings. But you're wide of the mark when you say it's all the main chance. Look at this hawser-laid stuff, now: better rope you'll never see. And there's no rogue's yarn in it,' he said, teasing out an end with his marlin-spike. 'Look for yourself. And why is there no rogue's yarn in it, Mr Ricketts? Because it never come off of the King's yard, that's why: Mr Screw-penny Bleeding Commissioner Brown never set eyes on it. Which Goldilocks bought it out of his own pocket, as likewise the paint you're a-sitting on. So there, you mean-souled dough-faced son of a cow-poxed bitch,' he would have added, if he had not been a peaceable, quiet sort of a man, and if the drum had not begun to beat to quarters.

'Pass the word for my cox'n,' said Jack after the drum had beat the retreat. The word passed – cap'n's cox'n, cap'n's cox'n, come on George, show a leg George, at the double George, you're in trouble George, George is going to be crucified, ha, ha, ha – and Barret Bonden appeared. 'Bonden, I want the boat's crew to look their best: washed, shaved, trimmed, straw hats, Guernsey frocks, ribbons.'

'Aye aye, sir,' said Bonden with an impassive face and his heart brimming with inquiry. Shaved? Trimmed? Of a Tuesday? They mustered clean to divisions on Thursdays and Sundays: but to be shaved on Tuesday – on a Tuesday at sea! He hurried off to the ship's barber, and by the time half the cutter's crew were as rosy and smooth as art could make them the answer to his questions appeared. They rounded Cape Dartuch, and Ciudadela came into view on the starboard bow; but instead of sailing steadily north-west the *Sophie* bore up for the town, heaving to in fifteen fathom water with her foretopsail aback a quarter of a mile from the mole.

'Where's Simmons?' asked James, quickly passing the cutter's crew in review.

'Reported sick, sir,' said Bonden, and in a lower voice, 'His birthday, sir.'

James nodded. Yet the substitution of Davies was not very clever, for although he was much of a size, and filled the straw hat with *Sophie* embroidered on its ribbon, he was an intense blue-black and could not but be noticed. However, there was no time to do anything about it now, for here was the captain, very fine in his best uniform, best sword and gold-laced hat.

'I do not expect to be more than an hour or so, Mr Dillon,' said Jack, with an odd mixture of conscious stiffness and hidden excitement; and as the bosun sprung his call he stepped down into the scrubbed and gleaming cutter. Bonden had judged better than James Dillon: the cutter's crew might have been all the colours of the rainbow, or even pied, for all Captain Aubrey cared at this moment.

The sun set in a somewhat troubled sky; the bells of Ciudadela rang for the Angelus and the *Sophie*'s for the last dog watch; the moon rose, very near the full, swimming up gloriously behind Black Point. Hammocks were piped down. The watch changed. Seized by Lucock's passion for navigation, all the midshipmen took observations of the moon as it mounted, and of the fixed stars, one by one. Eight bells, and the middle watch. The lights of Ciudadela all going out.

'Cutter's away, sir,' reported the sentry at last, and ten minutes later Jack came up the side. He was very pale, and in the strong moonlight he looked deathly – black hole for a mouth, hollows for his eyes. 'Are you still on deck, Mr Dillon?' he said, with an attempt at a smile. 'Make sail, if you please: the tail of the sea-breeze will carry us out,' he said, and walked uncertainly into his cabin.

Chapter Ten

'Maimonides has an account of a lute-player who, required to perform upon some stated occasion, found that he had entirely forgot not only the piece but the whole art of playing, fingering, everything,' wrote Stephen. 'I have sometimes had a dread of the same thing happening to me; a not irrational dread, since I once experienced a deprivation of a similar nature: coming back to Aghamore when I was a boy, coming back after an eight years' absence, I went to see Bridie Coolan, and she spoke to me in Irish. Her voice was intimately familiar (none more, my own wet-nurse); so were the intonations and even the very words; yet nothing could I understand – her words conveyed no meaning whatever. I was dumbfounded at my loss. What puts me in mind of this is my discovery that I no longer know what my friends feel, intend, or even mean. It is clear that JA met with a severe disappointment in Ciudadela, one that he feels more deeply than I should have supposed possible, in him; and it is clear that JD is still in a state of great unhappiness: but beyond that I know almost nothing – they do not speak and I can no longer look into them. My own testiness does not help, to be sure. I must guard against a strong and increasing tendency to indulge in dogged, sullen conduct – the conduct of vexation (much promoted by want of exercise); but I confess that much as I love them, I could wish them both to the Devil, with their high-flown, egocentrical points of honour and their purblind spurring one another on to remarkable exploits that may very well end in unnecessary death. In *their* death, which is their concern: but also in *mine*, to say nothing of the rest of the ship's company. A slaughtered crew, a sunken ship, and my collections destroyed – these do not weigh at all against their punctilios. There is a systematic flocci-naucinihili-pilification of all other aspects of existence that angers me. I spend half my time purging them, bleeding them, prescribing low diet and soporifics. They both eat far too much, and drink far too much, especially JD. Sometimes I am afraid they have closed themselves to me because they have agreed upon a meeting next time we come ashore, and they know very well I should stop it. How they vex my very spirit! If *they* had the scrubbing of the decks, the hoisting of the sails, the cleaning of the heads, we should hear little enough of these fine vapourings. I have no patience with them. They are strangely immature for men of their age and their position: though, indeed, it is to be supposed that if they were not, they would not be here – the mature, the ponderate mind does not embark itself upon a man-of-war – is not to be found wandering about the face of the ocean in quest of violence. For all his sensibility (and he played his transcription of *Deh vieni* with a truly exquisite delicacy, just before we reached Ciudadela), JA is in many ways more suited to be a pirate chief in the Caribbean a hundred years ago: and for all his acumen JD is in danger of becoming an enthusiast – a latter-day Loyola, if he is not knocked on the head first, or run through the body. I am much exercised in my mind by that unfortunate conversation . . .

The *Sophie*, to the astonishment of her people, had not headed for Barcelona after leaving Ciudadela, but west-north-west; and at daybreak, rounding Cape Salou within hail of the shore, she had picked up a richly-laden Spanish coaster of some two hundred tons, mounting (but not firing) six six-pounders – had picked her up from the landward side as neatly as though the rendezvous had been fixed weeks ahead and the Spanish captain had kept his hour to the minute. 'A very profitable commercial venture,' said James, watching the prize disappear in the east, bound with a favourable wind for Port Mahon, while they beat up, tack upon tack, to their northern cruising-ground, one of the busiest sea-lanes in the world. But that (though unhappy in itself) was not the conversation Stephen had in mind.

No. That came later, after dinner, when he was on the quarterdeck with James. They were talking, in an easy, off-hand manner, about differences in national habit – the Spaniards' late hours; the French way of all leaving the table together, men and women, and going directly into the drawing-room; the Irish habit of staying with the wine until one of the guests suggested moving; the English way of leaving this to the host; the remarkable difference in duelling habits.

'Rencounters are most uncommon in England,' observed James.

'Indeed they are,' said Stephen. 'I was astonished, when first I went to London, to find that a man might not go out from one year's end to the other.'

'Yes,' said James. 'Ideas upon matters of honour are altogether different in the two kingdoms. Before now I have given Englishmen provocation that would necessarily have called for a meeting in Ireland, with no result. *We* should call that remarkably timid; or is shy the word?' He shrugged, and he was about to continue when the cabin skylight in the surface of the quarter-deck opened and Jack's head and massive shoulders appeared. 'I should never have thought so ingenuous a face could look so black and wicked,' thought Stephen.

'Did JD say that on purpose?' he wrote. 'I do not know for sure, though I suspect he did – it would be all of a piece with the remarks he has been making recently, remarks that may be unintentional, merely tactless, but that all tend to present reasonable caution in an odious and, indeed, a contemptible light. I do not know. I should have known once. But all I know now is that when JA is in a rage with his superiors, irked by the subordination of the service, spurred on by his restless, uneasy temperament, or (as at present) lacerated by his mistress' infidelity, he flies to violence as a relief – to action. JD, urged on by entirely different furies, does the same. The difference is that whereas I believe JA merely longs for the shattering noise, immense activity of mind and body, and the all-embracing sense of the present moment, I am very much afraid that JD wants more.' He closed the book and stared at its cover for a long while, far, far away, until a knock recalled him to the *Sophie*.

'Mr Ricketts,' he said, 'what may I do for you?'

'Sir,' said the midshipman, 'the captain says, will you please to come on deck and view the coast?'

'To the left of the smoke, southwards, that is the hill of Montjuich, with the great castle; and the projection to the right is Barceloneta,' said Stephen. 'And rising there behind the city you can make out Tibidabo: I saw my first red-footed falcon there, when I was a boy. Then continuing the line from Tibidabo through the cathedral to the sea, there is the Moll de Santa Creu, with the great mercantile port: and to the left of it the basin where the King's ships and the gunboats lie.'

'Many gunboats?' asked Jack.

'I dare say: but I never made it my study.'

Jack nodded, looked keenly round the bay to fix its details in his mind once more and, leaning down, he called, 'Deck? Lower away: handsomely now. Babbington, look alive with that line.'

Stephen rose six inches from his perch at the masthead, and with his hands folded to prevent their involuntary clutching at passing ropes, yards, blocks, and with the ape-nimble Babbington keeping pace, heaving him in towards the weather backstay, he descended through the dizzy void to the deck, where they let him out of the cocoon in which they had hoisted him aloft; for no one on board had the least opinion of his abilities as a seaman.

He thanked them absently and went below, where the sailmaker's mates were sewing Tom Simmons into his hammock.

'We are just waiting for the shot, sir,' they said; and as they spoke Mr Day appeared, carrying a net of the *Sophie*'s cannonballs.

'I thought I would pay him the attention myself,' said the gunner, arranging them at the young man's feet with a practised hand. 'He was shipmates with me in the *Phoebe*: though always unhealthy, even then,' he added, as a quick afterthought.

'Oh, yes: Tom was never strong,' said one of the sailmaker's mates, cutting the thread on his broken eye-tooth.

These words, and a certain unusual delicacy of regard, were intended to comfort Stephen, who had lost his patient: in spite of all his efforts the four-day coma had deepened to its ultimate point.

'Tell me, Mr Day,' he said, when the sailmakers had gone, 'just how much did he drink? I have asked his friends, but they give evasive answers – indeed, they lie.'

'Of course they do, sir: for it is against the law. How much did he drink? Why, now, Tom was a popular young chap, so I dare say he had the whole allowance, bating maybe a sip or two just to moisten their victuals. That would make it close on a quart.'

'A quart. Well, it is a great deal: but I am surprised it should kill a man. At an admixture of three to one, that amounts to six ounces or so – inebriating, but scarcely lethal.'

'Lord, Doctor,' said the gunner, looking at him with affectionate pity, 'that ain't the mixture. That's the rum.'

'A quart of rum? Of neat rum?' cried Stephen.

'That's right, sir. Each man has his half-pint a day, at twice, so that makes a quart for each mess for dinner and for supper: and that is what the water is added to. Oh dear me,' he said, laughing gently and patting the poor corpse on the deck between them, 'if they was only to get half a pint of three-water grog we should soon have a bloody mutiny on our hands. And quite right, too.'

'Half a pint of spirits a day for every man?' said Stephen,

flushing with anger. 'A great tumbler? I shall tell the captain – shall insist upon its being poured over the side.'

'And so we commit his body to the deep,' said Jack, closing the book. Tom Simmons' messmates tilted the grating: there was the sound of sliding canvas, a gentle splash and a long train of bubbles rising up through the clear water.

'Now, Mr Dillon,' he said, with something of the formal tone of his reading still in his voice, 'I think we may carry on with the weapons and the painting.'

The sloop was lying to, well over the horizon from Barcelona; and a little while after Tom Simmons had reached the bottom in four hundred fathoms she was far on her way to becoming a white-painted snow with black top-sides, with a horse – a length of cable bowsed rigidly vertical – to stand for the trysail mast of that vessel; while at the same time the grindstone mounted on the fo'c'sle turned steadily, putting a keener edge, a sharper point, on cutlasses, pikes, boarding-axes, marines' bayonets, midshipmen's dirks, officers' swords.

The *Sophie* was as busy as she could well be, but there was a curious gravity with it all: it was natural that a man's messmates should be low after burying him, and even his whole watch (for Tom Simmons had been well liked – would never have had so deadly a birthday present otherwise); but this solemnity affected the whole ship's company and there was none of those odd bursts of song on the fo'c'sle, none of those ritual jokes called out. There was a quiet, brooding atmosphere, not at all angry or sullen, but – Stephen, lying in his cot (he had been up all night with poor Simmons) tried to hit upon the definition – oppressive? – fearful? – vaticinatory? But in spite of all the deeply shocking noise of Mr Day and his party overhauling the shot-lockers, scaling all the balls with any rust or irregularity upon them, and trundling them back down an echoing plane, hundreds and hundreds of four-pound cannon-balls clashing and growling and being beaten, he went to sleep before he could accomplish it.

He woke to the sound of his own name. 'Dr Maturin? No, certainly you may not see Dr Maturin,' said the master's voice in the gun-room. 'You may leave a message with me, and I will tell him at dinner-time, if he wakes up by then.'

'I was to ask him what physic would answer for a slack-going horse,' quavered Ellis, now filled with doubt.

'And who told you to ask him that? That villain Babbington, I swear. For shame, to be such a flat, after all these weeks at sea.'

This particular atmosphere had not reached the midshipmen's berth, then; or if so it had already dissipated. What private lives the young led, he reflected, how very much apart: their happiness how widely independent of circumstance. He was thinking of his own childhood – the then intensity of the present – happiness not then a matter of retrospection nor of undue moment – when the howling of the bosun's pipe for dinner caused his stomach to give a sharp sudden grinding wring and he swung his legs over the side. 'I am grown a naval animal,' he observed.

These were the fat days of the beginning of a cruise; there was still soft tack on the table, and Dillon, standing bowed under the beams to carve a noble saddle of mutton, said, 'You will find the most prodigious transformation when you go on deck. We are no longer a brig, but a snow.'

'With an extra mast,' explained the master, holding up three fingers.

'Indeed?' said Stephen, eagerly passing up his plate. 'Pray, why is this? For speed, for expediency, for comeliness?'

'To amuse the enemy.'

The meal continued with considerations on the art of war, the relative merits of Mahon cheese and Cheshire, and the surprising depth of the Mediterranean only a short way off the land; and once again Stephen noticed the curious skill (the outcome, no doubt, of many years at sea and the tradition of generations of tight-packed mariners) with which even so gross a man as the purser helped to keep the conversation going, smoothing over the dislikes and tensions – with platitudes, quite often, but with flow enough to make the dinner not only easy, but even mildly enjoyable.

'Take care, Doctor,' said the master, steadying him from behind on the companion ladder. 'She's beginning to roll.'

She was indeed, and although the *Sophie*'s deck was only so trifling a height from what might be called her subaqueous gun-room, the motion up there was remarkably greater: Stephen staggered, took hold of a stanchion and gazed about him expectantly.

'Where is your prodigious great transformation?' he cried. 'Where is this third mast, that is to amuse the enemy? Where is the merriment in practising upon a landman, where the wit? Upon my honour, Mr Farcical Comic, any poteen-swilling shoneen off the bog would be more delicate. Are you not sensible it is very wrong?'

'Oh, sir,' cried Mr Marshall, shocked by the sudden extreme ferocity of Stephen's glare, 'upon my word – Mr Dillon, I appeal to you . . .'

'Dear shipmate, joy,' said James, leading Stephen to the horse, that stout rope running parallel to the mainmast and some six inches behind it, 'allow me to assure you that to a seaman's eye this is a mast, a third mast: and presently you will see something very like the old fore-and-aft mainsail set upon it as a trysail, *at the same time as a cro'jack on the yard above our heads.* No seaman afloat would ever take us for a brig.'

'Well,' said Stephen, 'I must believe you. Mr Marshall, I ask your pardon for speaking hastily.'

'Why, sir, you would have to speak more hasty by half to put me out,' said the master, who was aware of Stephen's liking for him and who valued it highly. 'It looks as though they had had a blow away to the south,' he remarked, nodding over the side.

The long swell was setting from the far-off African coast, and although the small surface-waves disguised it, the rise and fall of the horizon showed its long even intervals. Stephen could very well imagine it breaking high against the rocks of the Catalan shore, rushing up the shingle beaches and drawing back with a monstrous grating indraught. 'I hope it does not rain,' he said, for again and again, at the beginning of the fall, he had known this sea swelling up out of calmness to be followed by a south-eastern wind and a low yellow sky, pouring down warm beating rain on the grapes just as they were ready to be picked.

'Sail ho!' called the look-out.

She was a medium-sized tartan, deep in the water, beating up into the fresh easterly breeze, obviously from Barcelona; and she lay two points on their port bow.

'How lucky this did not happen an hour ago,' said James. 'Mr Pullings, my duty to the captain, and there is a strange sail two points on the larboard bow.' Before he had finished speaking Jack was on deck, his pen still in his hand, and a look of hard excitement kindling in his eye.

'Be so kind . . .' he said, handing Stephen the pen, and he ran up to the masthead like a boy. The deck was teeming with sailors clearing away the morning's work, trimming the sails as they surreptitiously changed course to cut the tartan off from the land, and running about with very heavy loads; and after Stephen had been bumped into once or twice and had 'By your leave, sir,' and 'Way there – oh parding, sir' roared into his ear often enough, he walked composedly into the cabin, sat on Jack's locker and reflected upon the nature of a community – its reality – its difference from every one of the individuals composing it – communication within it, how effected.

'Why, there you are,' said Jack returning. 'She is only a tub of a merchantman, I fear. I had hoped for something better.'

'Shall you catch her, do you suppose?'

'Oh, yes, I dare say we shall, even if she goes about this minute. But I had so hoped for a dust-up, as we say. I can't tell you how it stretches your mind – your black draughts and blood-letting are nothing to it. Rhubarb and senna. Tell me, if we are not prevented, shall we have some music this evening?'

'It would give me great pleasure,' said Stephen. Looking at Jack now he could see what his appearance might be when the fire of his youth had gone out: heavy, grey, authoritarian, if not savage and morose.

'Yes,' said Jack, and hesitated as though he were going to say much more. But he did not, and after a moment he went on deck.

The *Sophie* was slipping rapidly through the water, having set no more sail and showing no sort of inclination to close with the tartan – the steady, sober, mercantile course of a snow bound for Barcelona. In half an hour's time they could see that she carried four guns, that she was short-handed (the cook joined in the manoeuvres) and that she had a disagreeably careless, neutral air. However, when the tartan prepared to tack at the southern end of her board, the *Sophie* heaved out her staysails in a flash, set her topgallants and bore up with surprising speed – so surprising to the tartan, indeed, that she missed stays and fell off again on the larboard tack.

At half a mile Mr Day (he dearly loved to point a gun) put a shot across her forefoot, and she lay to with her yard lowered until the *Sophie* ranged alongside and Jack hailed her master to come aboard.

'He was sorry, gentleman, but he could not: if he could, he should with joy, gentleman, but he had burst the bottom of his launch,' he said, through the medium of a quite lovely young woman, presumably Mrs Tartan or the equivalent. 'And in any case he was only a neutral Ragusan, a neutral bound for Ragusa in ballast.' The little dark man beat on his boat to mark the point: and holed it was.

'What tartan?' called Jack again.

'*Pola*,' said the young woman.

He stood, considering: he was in an ugly mood. The two vessels rose and fell. Behind the tartan the land appeared with every upward heave, and to add to his irritation he saw a fishing-boat in the south, running before the wind, with another beyond it – sharp-eyed barca-longas. The Sophies stood silently gazing at the woman: they licked their lips and swallowed.

That tartan was not in ballast – a stupid lie. And he doubted it was Ragusan-built, too. But *Pola* – was that the right name? 'Bring the cutter alongside,' he said. 'Mr Dillon, who have we aboard that speaks Italian? John Baptist is an Italian.'

'And Abram Codpiece, sir – a purser's name.'

'Mr Marshall, take Baptist and Codpiece and satisfy yourself as to that tartan – look at her papers – look into her hold – rummage her cabin if needs be.'

The cutter came alongside, the boat-keeper booming her off from the fresh paint with the utmost care, and the heavily-armed men dropped into her by a line from the main yardarm, far more willing to break their necks or drown than spoil their fine black paint, so fresh and trim.

They pulled across, boarded the tartan: Marshall, Codpiece and John Baptist disappeared into the cabin: there was the sound of a female voice raised high in anger, then a piercing scream. The men on the fo'c'sle began to skip, and turned shining faces to one another.

Marshall reappeared. 'What did you do to that woman?' called Jack.

'Knocked her down, sir,' replied Marshall phlegmatically. 'Tartan's no more a Ragusan than I am. Captain only talks the lingua franca, says Codpiece, no right Italian at all; Missis has a Spanish set of papers in her pinny; hold's full of bales consigned to Genoa.'

'The infamous brute to strike a woman,' said James aloud. 'To think we have to mess with such a fellow.'

'You wait till you're married, Mr Dillon,' said the purser, with a chuckle.

'Very well done, Mr Marshall,' said Jack. 'Very good indeed. How many hands? What are they like?'

'Eight, sir, counting passengers: ugly, froward-looking buggars.'

'Send 'em over, then. Mr Dillon, steady men for the prize-crew, if you please.' As he spoke rain began to fall, and with the first drops came a sound that made every head aboard turn, so that in a moment each man's nose was pointing north-east. It was not thunder. It was gunfire.

'Light along those prisoners,' cried Jack. 'Mr Marshall, keep in company. It will not worry you, looking after the woman?'

'I do not mind it, sir,' said Marshall.

Five minutes later they were under way, running diagonally across the swell through the sweeping rain with a lithe corkscrewing motion. They had the wind on their beam now, and although they had handed the topgallants almost at once, they left the tartan behind in less than half an hour.

Stephen was gazing over the taffrail at the long wake, his mind a thousand miles away, when he became aware of a hand gently plucking at his coat. He turned and saw Mowett smiling at him, and some way beyond Mowett, Ellis on his hands and knees being carefully, desperately sick through a small square hole in the bulwark, a scuttle. 'Sir, sir,' said Mowett, 'you are getting wet.'

'Yes,' said Stephen; and after a pause he added, 'It is the rain.'

'That's right, sir,' said Mowett. 'Should not you like to step below, to get out of it? Or may I bring you a tarpaulin jacket?'

'No. No. No. You are very good. No . . .' said Stephen, his attention wandering, and Mowett, having failed in the first part of his mission, went cheerfully on to the second: this was to stop Stephen's whistling, which made the after-guard and quarter-deckmen – the crew in general – so very nervous and uneasy. 'May I tell you something nautical, sir – do you hear the guns again?'

'If you please,' said Stephen, unpursing his lips.

'Well then, sir,' said Mowett, pointing over the grey hissing sea to his right in the general direction of Barcelona, 'that is what we call a lee shore.'

'Ah?' said Stephen, with a certain interest lighting his eye. 'The phenomenon you dislike so much? It is not a mere prejudice – a weak superstitious traditional belief?'

'Oh, no, sir,' cried Mowett, and explained the nature of leeway, the loss of windward distance in wearing, the impossibility of tacking in a very great wind, the inevitability of leeward drift in the case of being embayed with a full gale blowing dead on short, and the impervious horror of this situation. His explanation was punctuated by the deep boom of gunfire, sometimes a continuous low roaring for half a minute together, sometimes a single sharp report. 'Oh, how I wonder what it is!' he cried, breaking off and craning up on tiptoe.

'You need not be afraid,' said Stephen. 'Soon the wind will blow in the direction of the waves – this often happens towards Michaelmas. If only one could protect the vines with a vast umbrella.'

Mowett was not alone in wondering what it was: the *Sophie*'s captain and lieutenant, each burning for the uproar and the more than human liberation of a battle, stood side by side on the quarterdeck, infinitely remote from one another, all their senses straining towards the north-east. Almost all the other members of the crew were equally intent; and so were those of the *Felipe V*, a seven-gun Spanish privateer.

She came racing up out of the blinding rain, a dark squall a little way abaft the beam on the landward side, making for the sound of battle with all the canvas she could bear. They saw one another at the same moment: the *Felipe* fired, showed her colours, received the *Sophie*'s broadside in reply, grasped her mistake, put up her helm and headed straight back to Barcelona with the strong wind on her larboard quarter and her big lateens bellying out and swaying wildly on the roll.

The *Sophie*'s helm was over within a second of the privateer's: the tompions of the starboard guns were out: cupping hands sheltered the sputtering slow-match and the priming.

'All at her stern,' cried Jack, and the crows and handspikes heaved the guns through five degrees. 'On the roll. Fire as they bear.' He brought the wheel up two spokes and the guns went off three and four. Instantly the privateer yawed as though she meant to board; but then her flapping mizen came down on deck, she filled again and went off before the wind. A shot had struck the head of her rudder, and without it she could bear no sail aft. They were putting out a sweep to steer with and working furiously at the mizen-yard. Her two larboard guns fired, one hitting the *Sophie* with the strangest sound. But the sloop's next broadside, a careful, collected fire within pistol-range, together with a volley of musketry, put a stop to all resistance. Just twelve minutes after the first gun fired her colours came down and a fierce, delighted cheer broke out – men clapping one another on the back, shaking hands, laughing.

The rain had stopped and it was drifting westwards in a dense grey swathe, blotting out the port, very much nearer now. 'Take possession of her, Mr Dillon, if you please,' said Jack, looking up at the dog-vane. The wind was veering, as it so often did in these waters after rain, and presently it would be coming from well south of east.

'Any damage, Mr Lamb?' he asked, as the carpenter came up to report.

'Wish you joy of the capture, sir,' said the carpenter. 'No damage, rightly speaking; no structural damage; but that one ball made a sad mess in the galley – upset all the coppers and unshipped the smoke-funnel.'

'We will take a look at it presently,' said Jack. 'Mr Pullings, those for'ard guns are not properly secured. What the devil?' he cried. The gun-crews were strangely, even shockingly pied, and horrible imaginations flashed through his mind until he realized that they were covered with wet black paint and with the galley's soot: and now, in the exuberance of their hearts, those farthest forward were daubing their fellows. 'Avast that God-damned – foolery, God rot your – eyes,' he called out in an enormous line-of-battle voice. He rarely swore, apart from an habitual damn or an unmeaning blasphemy, and the men, who in any case had expected him to be far more pleased with the taking of a neat privateer, fell perfectly mute, with nothing more than the rolling of an eye or a wink to convey secret understanding and delight.

'Deck,' hailed Lucock from the top. 'There are gunboats coming out from Barcelona. Six. Eight – nine – eleven behind 'em. Maybe more.'

'Out launch and jolly-boat,' cried Jack. 'Mr Lamb, go across, if you please, and see what can be done to her steering.'

Getting the boats to the yardarms and launching them in this swell was no child's play, but the men were in tearing spirits and they heaved like maniacs – it was as though they had been filled with rum and yet had lost none of their ability. Muffled laughter kept bursting out: it was damped by the cry of a sail to windward – a sail that might place them between two fires – then revived by the news that it was only their own prize, the tartan.

The boats plied to and fro; the glum or surly prisoners made their way down into the fore-hold, their bosoms swollen with personal possessions; the carpenter and his crew could be heard working away with their adzes to make a new tiller; Stephen caught Ellis as he darted by. 'Just when did you stop being sick, sir?' 'Almost the moment the guns began to go, sir,' said Ellis. Stephen nodded. 'I thought as much,' said he. 'I was watching you.'

The first shot sent up a white plume of water topmast high, right between the two vessels. Infernally good practice for a ranging shot, thought Jack, and a damned great heavy ball.

The gunboats were still over a mile away, but they were coming up surprisingly fast, straight into the eye of the wind. Each of the three foremost carried a long thirty-six-pounder and rowed thirty oars. Even at a mile a chance hit from one of these would pierce the *Sophie* through and through. He had to restrain a violent urge to tell the carpenter to hurry. 'If a thirty-six-pound ball does not hasten him, nothing I can say will do so,' he observed, pacing up and down, cocking an eye at the dog-vane and at the gunboats at each turn. All seven of the foremost had tried the range, and now there was a spasmodic firing, most falling short, but some howling right overhead.

'Mr Dillon,' he called over the water, after half a dozen turns, and the splash from a ball plunging into the swell just astern wetted the back of his neck. 'Mr Dillon, we will transfer the rest of the prisoners later, and make sail as soon as you can conveniently do so. Or should you like us to pass you a tow?'

'No, thank you, sir. The tiller will be shipped in two minutes.'

'In the meantime we might as well pepper them, for what it is worth,' reflected Jack, for the now silent Sophies were looking somewhat tense. 'At least the smoke will hide us a little. Mr Pullings, the larboard guns may fire at discretion.'

This was much more agreeable, with the banging, the rumble, the smoke, the immense intent activity; and he smiled to see the earnestness of every man at the brass gun nearest him as they glared out for the fall of their shot. The *Sophie*'s fire stung the gunboats to a great burst of activity, and the dull grey western sea sparkled with their flashes over a front of a quarter of a mile.

Babbington was in front of him, pointing: wheeling about, Jack saw Dillon hailing through the din – the new tiller had been fitted.

'Make sail,' he said: the *Sophie*'s backed foretopsail came round and filled. Speed was called for, and setting all her headsails he took her down with the wind well abaft her beam before hauling up into the north-north-west. This took the sloop nearer to the gunboats and across their front: the larboard guns were firing continuously, the enemies' shots were kicking up the water or passing overhead, and for a moment his spirits rose to a wild pitch of delight at the idea of dashing down among them – they were unwieldy brutes at close quarters. But then he reflected that he had the prizes with him and that Dillon still had a dangerous number of prisoners aboard; and he gave the order to brace the yards up sharp.

The prizes hauled their wind at the same time, and at a smooth five or six knots they ran out to sea. The gunboats followed for half an hour, but as the light faded and the range lengthened to impossibility, one by one they turned and went back to Barcelona.

'I played that very badly,' said Jack, putting down his bow.

'Your heart was not in it,' said Stephen. 'It has been an active day – a fatiguing day. A satisfactory day, however.'

'Why, yes,' said Jack, his face brightening somewhat. 'Yes, certainly. I am most uncommonly delighted.' A pause. 'Do you remember a fellow named Pitt we dined with one day at Mahon?'

'The soldier?'

'Yes. Now, would you call him good-looking – handsome?'

'No. Oh, no.'

'I am happy to hear you say so. I have a great regard for your opinion. Tell me,' he added, after a long pause, 'have you noticed how things return to your mind when you are hipped? It is like old wounds breaking out when you come down with scurvy. Not, indeed, that I have ever for a moment forgotten what Dillon said to me that day: but it has been rankling in my heart, and I have been turning it over this last day or so. I find that I must ask him for an explanation – I should certainly have done so before. I shall do so as soon as we go into port: unless, indeed, the next few days make it unnecessary.'

'Pom, pom, pom, pom,' went Stephen in unison with his 'cello, glancing at Jack: there was an exceedingly serious look on that darkened, heavy face, a kind of red light in his clouded eyes. 'I am coming to believe that laws are the prime cause of unhappiness. It is not merely a case of born under one law, required another to obey – you know the lines: I have no memory for verse. No, sir: it is born under half a dozen, required another fifty to obey. There are parallel sets of laws in different keys that have nothing to do with one another and that are even downright contradictory. You, now – you wish to do something that the Articles of War and (as you explained to me) the rules of generosity forbid, but that your present notion of the moral law and your present notion of the point of honour require. This is but one instance of what is as common as breathing. Buridan's ass died of misery between equidistant mangers, drawn first by one then by the other. Then again, with a slight difference, there are these double loyalties – another great source of torment.'

'Upon my word, I cannot see what you mean by double loyalty. You can only have one King. And a man's heart can only be in one place at a time, unless he is a scrub.'

'What nonsense you do talk, to be sure,' said Stephen. 'What "balls", as you sea-officers say: it is a matter of common observation that a man may be sincerely attached to two women at once – to three, to four, to a very surprising number of women. However,' he said, 'no doubt you know more of these things than I. No: what I had in mind were those wider loyalties, those more general conflicts – the candid American, for example, before the issue became envenomed; the unimpassioned Jacobite in '45; Catholic priests in France today – Frenchmen of many complexions, in and out of France. So much pain; and the more honest the man the worse the pain. But there at least the conflict is direct: it seems to me that the greater mass of confusion and distress must arise from these less evident divergencies – the moral law, the civil, military, common laws, the code of honour, custom, the rules of practical life, of civility, of amorous conversation, gallantry, to say nothing of Christianity for those that practise it. All sometimes, indeed generally, at variance; none ever in an entirely harmonious relation to the rest; and a man is perpetually required to choose one rather than another, perhaps (in his particular case) its contrary. It is as though our strings were each tuned according to a completely separate system – it is as though the poor ass were surrounded by four and twenty mangers.'

'You are an antinomian,' said Jack.

'I am a pragmatist,' said Stephen. 'Come, let us drink up our wine, and I will compound you a dose – requies Nicholai. Perhaps tomorrow you should be let blood: it is three weeks since you was let blood.'

'Well, I will swallow your dose,' said Jack. 'But I tell you what – tomorrow night I shall be in among those gunboats and I shall do the blood-letting. And don't they wish they may relish it.'

The *Sophie*'s allowance of fresh water for washing was very small, and she made no allowance of soap at all. Those men who had blackened themselves and one another with paint remained darker than was pleasant; and those who had worked in the wrecked galley, covering themselves with grease and soot from the coppers and the stove, looked, if anything, worse – they had a curiously bestial and savage appearance, worst of all in those that had fair hair.

'The only respectable-looking fellows are the black men,' said Jack. 'They are all still aboard, I believe?'

'Davies went with Mr Mowett in the privateer, sir,' said James, 'but the rest are still with us.'

'Counting the men left in Mahon and the prize-crews, how many are we short at the moment?'

'Thirty-six, sir. We are fifty-four all told.'

'Very good. That gives us elbow-room. Let them have as much sleep as possible, Mr Dillon: we shall stand in at midnight.'

Summer had come back after the rain – a gentle, steady tramontana, warm, clear air, and phosphorescence on the sea. The lights of Barcelona twinkled with uncommon brilliance, and over the middle part of the city floated a luminous cloud: the gunboats guarding the approaches to the port could be made out quite clearly against this background before ever they saw the darkened *Sophie*: they were farther out than usual, and they were obviously on the alert.

'As soon as they start to come for us,' reflected Jack, 'we will set topgallants, steer for the orange light, then haul our wind at the last moment and run between the two on the northern end of the line.' His heart was going with a steady, even beat, a little faster than usual. Stephen had drawn off ten ounces of blood, and he thought he felt much the better for it. At all events his mind was as clear and sharp as he could wish.

The moon's tip appeared above the sea. A gunboat fired: deep, booming note – the voice of an old solitary hound.

'The light, Mr Ellis,' said Jack, and a blue flare soared up, designed to confuse the enemy. It was answered with Spanish signals, hoists of coloured lights, and then another gun, far over to the right. 'Topgallants,' he said. 'Jeffreys, steer for that orange mark.'

This was splendid: the *Sophie* was running in fast, prepared, confident and happy. But the gunboats were not coming on as he had hoped. Now one would spin about and fire, and now another; but on the whole they were falling back. To stir them up the sloop yawed and sent her broadside skipping among them – with some effect, to judge by a distant howl. Yet still the gunboats moved away. 'Damn this,' said Jack. 'They are trying to lead us on. Mr Dillon, trysail and staysails. We'll make a dash for that fellow farthest out.'

The *Sophie* came round fast and brought the wind on to her beam: heeling over so that the silk black water lapped at her port-sills, she raced towards the nearest gunboat. But now the others showed what they could do if they chose: they all faced about in a moment and kept up a continuous raking fire, while the chosen gunboat fled quartering away, keeping the *Sophie*'s unprotected stern towards them. A glancing blow from a thirty-six-pounder made her whole hull ring again; another passed just above head-height the whole length of the deck; two neatly severed backstays fell across Babbington, Pullings and the man at the wheel, knocking them down; a heavy block clattered on to the wheel itself as James leapt for its spokes.

'We'll tack, Mr Dillon,' said Jack; and a few moments later the *Sophie* flew up into the wind.

The men working the sloop moved with the unthinking smoothness of long practice; but seen suddenly picked out by the flashes of the gunboats' fire they seemed to be jerking like so many puppets. Just after the order 'let go and haul' there were six shots in quick succession, and he saw the marines at the mainsheet in a rapid series of galvanic motions – a few inches between each illumination – but throughout they wore exactly the same concentrated diligent expressions of men tallying with all their might.

'Close hauled, sir?' asked James.

'One point free,' said Jack. 'But gently, gently: let us see if we can draw *them* out. Drop the maintopsailyard a couple of feet and slacken away the starboard lift – let us look as though we were winged. Mr Watt, the topgallant backstays are our first care.'

And so they all moved back again across the same miles of sea, the *Sophie* knotting and splicing, the gunboats following and firing steadily, the old left-handed moon climbing with her usual indifference.

There was not much conviction in the pursuit: but even so, a little while after James Dillon had reported the completion of the essential repairs, Jack said, 'If we go about and set all sail like lightning, I believe we can cut those heavy chaps off from the land.'

'All hands about ship,' said James. The bosun started his call, and racing to his post by the maintopsail bowline Isaac Isaacs said to John Lakey, 'We are going to cut those two heavy buggers off from the land,' with intense satisfaction.

So they might have, if an unlucky shot had not struck the *Sophie*'s foretopgallant yard. They saved the sail, but her speed dropped at once and the gunboats pulled away ahead, away and away until they were safe behind their mole.

'Now, Mr Ellis,' said James, as the light of dawn showed just how much the sloop's rigging had suffered in the night, 'here is a most capital opportunity for learning your profession; why, I dare say there is enough to keep you busy until sunset, or even longer, with every variety of splice, knot, service and parcelling you could desire.' He was singularly gay, and from time to time, as he hurried about the deck, he hummed or chanted a sort of song.

There was the swaying up of the new yard, too, some shotholes to be repaired and the bowsprit to be new gammoned, for the strangest grazing ricochet had cut half the turns without ever touching the wood – something the oldest seamen aboard had never yet beheld, a wonder to be recorded in the log. The *Sophie* lay there unmolested, putting herself to rights all through that sunny gentle day, as busy as a hive, watchful, prepared, bristling with pugnacity. It was a curious atmosphere aboard her: the men knew very well they were going in again very soon, perhaps for some raid on the coast, perhaps for some cutting-out expedition; their mood was affected by many things – by their captures of yesterday and last Tuesday (the consensus was that each man was worth fourteen guineas more than when he sailed); by their captain's continuing gravity; by the strong conviction aboard that he had private intelligence of Spanish sailings; and by the sudden strange merriment or even levity of their lieutenant. He had found Michael and Joseph Kelly, Matthew Johnson and John Melsom busily pilfering aboard the *Felipe V*, between decks, a very serious court-martial offence (although custom winked at the taking of anything above hatches) and one that he particularly abhorred as being 'a damned privateer's trick'; yet he had not reported them. They kept peering at him from behind masts, spars, boats; and so did their guilty messmates, for the Sophies were much given to rapine. The outcome of all these factors was an odd busy restrained quietly cheerful attentiveness, with a note of anxiety in it.

With all hands so busy, Stephen scrupled to go forward to his elm-tree pump, through whose unshipped head he daily observed the wonders of the deep and where his presence was now so usual that he might have been the pump itself for all the restraint he placed upon the men's conversation; but he caught this note and he shared the uneasiness that produced it.

James was in tearing spirits at dinner; he had invited Pullings and Babbington informally, and their presence, together with Marshall's absence, gave the meal something of the air of a festivity, in spite of the purser's brooding silence. Stephen watched him as he joined in the chorus of Babbington's song, thundering out

> *And this is law, I will maintain*
> *Until my dying day, sir,*
> *That whatsoever king shall reign,*
> *I will be Vicar of Bray, sir*

in a steady roar.

'Well done,' he cried, thumping the table. 'Now a glass of wine all round to whet our whistles, and then we must be on deck again, though that is a cursed thing for a host to say. What a relief it is, to be fighting with king's ships again, rather than these damned privateers,' he observed, à propos of nothing, when the young men and the purser had withdrawn.

'What a romantic creature you are, to be sure,' said Stephen. 'A ball fired from a privateer's cannon makes the same hole as a king's.'

'Me, romantic?' cried James with real indignation, an angry light coming into his green eyes.

'Yes, my dear,' said Stephen, taking snuff. 'You will be telling me next about their divine right.'

'Well, at least even you, with your wild enthusiastic levelling notions, will not deny that the King is the sole fount of honour?'

'Not I,' said Stephen. 'Not for a moment.'

'When I was last at home,' said James, filling Stephen's glass, 'we waked old Terence Healy. He had been my grandfather's tenant. And there was a song they sang there has been in the middle part of my mind all day – I cannot quite bring it to the front, to sing it.'

'Was it an Irish song or an English?'

'There were English words as well. One line went
Oh the wild geese a-flying a-flying a-flying,
The wild geese a-swimming upon the grey sea.'

Stephen whistled a bar and then, in his disagreeable crake, he sang
'They will never return, for the white horse has scunnered
Has scunnered has scunnered
The white horse has scunnered upon the green lea.'

'That's it – that's it. Bless you,' cried James, and walked off, humming the air, to see that the *Sophie* was gathering the utmost of her strength.

She made her way out to sea at sunset, with a great show of farewell for ever and set her course soberly for Minorca; and some time before dawn she ran inshore again, still with the same good breeze a little east of north. But now there was a true autumnal nip in it, and a dampness that brought fungi in beech woods to Stephen's mind; and over the water lay impalpable wafting hazes, some of them a most uncommon brown.

The *Sophie* was standing in with her starboard tacks aboard, steering west-north-west; hammocks had been piped up and stowed in the nettings; the smell of coffee and frying bacon mingled together in the eddies that swirled on the weatherside of her taut trysail. Wide on the port bow the brown mist still hid the Llobregat valley and the mouth of the river, but farther up the coast towards the dim city looming there on the horizon, the rising sun had burnt off all but a few patches of haze – those that remained might have been headlands, islands, sandbanks.

'I know, I *know*, those gunboats were trying to lead us into some trap,' said Jack, 'and am with child to know what it was.' Jack was no great hand at dissembling, and Stephen was instantly persuaded that he knew the nature of the trap perfectly well, or at least had a very good notion of what it was likely to be.

The sun worked upon the surface of the water, doing wonderful things to its colour, raising new mists, dissolving others, sending exquisite patterns of shadow among the taut lines of the rigging and the pure curves of the sails and down on to the white deck, now being scrubbed whiter, to the steady grinding noise of holystones: with a swift yet imperceptible movement it breathed away a blue-grey cape and revealed a large ship three points on the starboard bow, running southwards under the land. The look-out called that she was there, but in a matter-of-fact voice, formally, for as the cloud-bank dissolved she was hull-up from the deck.

'Very well,' said Jack, clasping his glass to after a long stare. 'What do you make of her, Mr Dillon?'

'I rather think she is our old friend, sir,' said James.

'So do I. Set the mainstaysail and haul up to close her. Swabs aft, dry the deck. And let the hands go to breakfast at once, Mr Dillon. Should you care to take a cup of coffee with the Doctor and me? It would be a sad shame to waste it.'

'Very happy, sir.'

There was almost no conversation during their breakfast. Jack said, 'I suppose you would like us to put on silk stockings, Doctor?'

'Why silk stockings, for all love?'

'Oh, everyone says it is easier for the surgeon, if he has to cut one up.'

'Yes. Yes, certainly. Pray do by all means put on silk stockings.'

No conversation, but there was a remarkable feeling of easy companionship, and Jack, standing up to put on his uniform coat, said to James, 'You are certainly right, you know,' as though they had been talking about the identity of the stranger throughout the meal.

On deck again he saw that it was so, of course: the vessel over there was the *Cacafuego*; she had altered course to meet the *Sophie*, and she was in the act of setting her studdingsails. In his telescope he could see the vermilion gleam of her side in the sun.

'All hands aft,' he said, and as they waited for the crew to assemble Stephen could see that a smile kept spreading on his face – that he had to make a conscious effort to repress it and look grave.

'Men,' he said, looking over them with pleasure. 'That's the *Cacafuego* to windward, you know. Now some of you were not quite pleased when we let her go without a compliment last time; but now, with our gunnery the best in the fleet, why, it is another thing. So, Mr Dillon, we will clear for action, if you please.'

When he began to speak perhaps half the Sophies were gazing at him with uncomplicated pleasurable excitement; perhaps a quarter looked a little troubled; and the rest had downcast and anxious faces. But the self-possessed happiness radiating from their captain and his lieutenant, and the spontaneous delighted cheer from the first half of the crew, changed this wonderfully; and as they set about clearing the sloop there were not above four or five who looked glum – the others might have been going to the fair.

The *Cacafuego*, square-rigged at present, was running down, turning in a steady westward sweep to get to windward and seaward of the *Sophie*; and the *Sophie* was pointing up close into the wind; so that by the time they were a long half-mile apart she was directly open to a raking broadside from the frigate, the thirty-two-gun frigate.

'The pleasant thing about fighting with the Spaniards, Mr Ellis,' said Jack, smiling at his great round eyes and solemn face, 'is not that they are shy, for they are not, but that they are never, never ready.'

The *Cacafuego* had now almost reached the station that her captain had set his mind upon: she fired a gun and broke out the Spanish colours.

'The American flag, Mr Babbington,' said Jack. 'That will give them something to think about. Note down the time, Mr Richards.'

The distance was lessening very fast now. Second after second; not minute after minute. The *Sophie* was pointing astern of the *Cacafuego*, as though she meant to cut her wake; and not a gun could the sloop bring to bear. There was a total silence aboard as every man stood ready for the order to tack – an order that might not come before the broadside.

'Stand by with the ensign,' said Jack in a low voice: and louder, 'Right, Mr Dillon.'

'Helm's a-lee,' and the bosun's call sounded almost at the same moment; the *Sophie* spun on her heel, ran up the English colours, steadied and filled on her new course and ran close-hauled straight for the Spaniard's side. The *Cacafuego* fired at once, a crashing broadside that shot over and among the *Sophie*'s topgallants, making four holes, no more. The Sophies cheered to a man and stood tense and eager by their treble-shotted guns.

'Full elevation. Not a shot till we touch,' cried Jack in a tremendous voice, watching the hen-coops, boxes and lumber tossing overboard from the frigate. Through the smoke he could see ducks swimming away from one coop, and a panic-stricken cat on a box. The smell of powder-smoke reached them, and the dispersing mist. Closer, closer: they would be becalmed under the Spaniard's lee at the last moment, but they would have way enough . . . He could see the round blackness of her guns' mouths now, and as he watched so they erupted, the flashes brilliant in the smoke and a great white bank of it hiding the frigate's side. Too high again, he observed, but there was no room for any particular emotion as he searched through the faults in the smoke to put the sloop right up against the frigate's main-chains.

'Hard over,' he shouted; and as the grinding crash came, 'Fire!'

The xebec-frigate was low in the water, but the *Sophie* was lower still. With her yards locked in the *Cacafuego*'s rigging she lay there, and her guns were below the level of the frigate's ports. She fired straight up through the *Cacafuego*'s deck, and her first broadside, at a six-inch range, did shocking devastation. There was a momentary silence after the Sophie's cheer, and in that half-second's pause Jack could hear a confused screaming on the Spaniard's quarter-deck. Then the Spanish guns spoke again, irregular now, but immensely loud, firing three feet above his head.

The *Sophie*'s broadside was firing in a splendid roll, one-two-three-four-five-six-seven, with a half-beat at the end and a rumbling of the trucks; and in the fourth or fifth pause James seized his arm and shouted, 'They gave the order to board.'

'Mr Watt, boom her off,' cried Jack, directing his speaking trumpet forward. 'Sergeant, stand by.' One of the *Cacafuego*'s backstays had fallen aboard, fouling the carriage of a gun; he passed it round a stanchion and as he looked up a swarm of Spaniards appeared on the *Cacafuego*'s side. The marines and small-arms men gave them a staggering volley, and they hesitated. The gap was widening as the bosun at the head and Dillon's party aft thrust on their spars. Amidst a crackling of pistols some Spaniards tried to jump, some tried to throw grapnels; some fell in and some fell back. The *Sophie*'s guns, now ten feet from the frigate's side, struck right into the midst of the waverers, tore seven most dreadful holes.

The *Cacafuego*'s head had fallen off: she was pointing nearly south, and the *Sophie* had all the wind she needed to range alongside again. Again the thundering din roared and echoed round the sky, with the Spaniards trying to depress their guns, trying to fire down with muskets and blindly-held chance pistols over the side, to kill the gun-crews. Their efforts were brave enough – one man balanced there to fire until he had been hit three times – but they seemed totally disorganized. Twice again they tried to board, and each time the sloop sheered off, cutting them up with terrible slaughter, lying off five or ten minutes, battering her upper-works, before coming in again to tear out her bowels. By now the guns were so hot that they could scarcely be touched; they were kicking furiously with every round. The sponges hissed and charred as they went in, and the guns were growing almost as dangerous to their crews as to their enemies.

And all this time the Spaniards fired on and on, irregularly, spasmodically, but never stopping. The *Sophie*'s maintop had been hit again and again, and now it was coming to pieces – great lumps of timber falling down on deck, stanchions, hammocks. Her foresail yard was held only by its chains. Rigging hung in every direction and the sails had innumerable holes: burning wad was flying aboard all the time and the unengaged starboard crews were running to and fro with their fire-buckets. Yet within its confusion the *Sophie*'s deck showed a beautiful pattern of movement – the powder passing up from the magazine and the shot, the gun-crews with their steady heave-crash-heave, a wounded man, a dead man carrying below, his place instantly taken without a word, every man intent, threading the dense smoke – no collisions, no jostling, almost no orders at all.

'We shall be a mere hull presently, however,' reflected Jack: it was unbelievable that no mast or yard had gone yet; but it could not last. Leaning down to Ellis he said in his ear, 'Cut along to the galley. Tell the cook to put all his dirty pans and coppers upside-down. Pullings, Babbington, stop the firing. Boom off, boom off. Back topsails. Mr Dillon, let the starboard watch black their faces in the galley as soon as I have spoken to them. Men, men,' he shouted as the *Cacafuego* slowly forged ahead, 'we must board and carry her. Now's the time – now or never – now or no quarter

– now while she's staggering. Five minutes' hearty and she's ours. Axes and broadswords and away – starbowlines black their faces in the galley and forward with Mr Dillon – the rest aft along of me.'

He darted below. Stephen had four quiet wounded men, two corpses. 'We're boarding her,' said Jack. 'I must have your man – every man-jack aboard. Will you come?'

'I will not,' said Stephen. 'I will steer, if you choose.'

'Do – yes, do. Come on,' cried Jack.

On the littered deck and in the smoke Stephen saw the towering xebec's poop some twenty yards ahead on the port bow; the *Sophie*'s crew in two parties, the one blackfaced and armed racing from the galley and gathering at the head, the other already aft, lining the rail – the purser pale and glaring, wild; the gunner blinking from the darkness below; the cook with his cleaver; Jack-in-the-dust; the ship's barber and his own loblolly boy were there. Stephen noticed his hare-lip grinning and he cherishing the curved spike of a boarding-axe, saying over and over again, 'I'll hit the buggers, I'll hit the buggers, I'll hit the buggers.' Some of the Spanish guns were still firing out into the vacancy.

'Braces,' called Jack, and the yards began to come round to fill the topsails. 'Dear Doctor, you know what to do?' Stephen nodded, taking over the spokes and feeling the life of the wheel. The quartermaster stepped away, picked up a cutlass with a grim look of delight. 'Doctor, what's the Spanish for fifty more men?'

'Otros cincuenta.'

'Otros cincuenta,' said Jack, looking into his face with a most affectionate smile. 'Now lay us alongside, I beg.' He nodded to him again, walked to the bulwark with his coxswain close behind and hoisted himself up, massive but lithe, and stood there holding the foremost shroud and swinging his sword, a long heavy cavalry sabre.

Holes and all, the topsails filled: the *Sophie* ranged up: Stephen put the wheel hard over: the grinding crunch, the twang of some rope parting, a jerk, and they were fast

322

together. With an enormous shrieking cheer fore and aft the Sophies leapt up the frigate's side.

Jack was over the shattered bulwark straight down on to a hot gun run in and smoking, and its swabber thrust at him with the pole. He cut sideways at the swabber's head; the swabber ducked fast and Jack leapt over his bowed shoulder on to the *Cacafuego*'s deck. 'Come on, come on,' he roared, and rushed forwards striking furiously at the fleeing gun-crew and then at the pikes and swords opposing him – there were hundreds, *hundreds* of men crowding the deck, he noticed; and all the time he kept roaring 'Come on!'

For some moments the Spaniards gave way, as though amazed, and every one of the *Sophie*'s men and boys came aboard, amidships and over the bow: the Spaniards gave way from abaft the mainmast, backing into the waist; but there they rallied. And now there was hard fighting, now there were cruel blows given and received – a dense mass of struggling men, tripping among the spars, scarcely room to fall, beating, hacking, pistolling one another; and detached fights of two or three men together round the edges, yelling like beasts. In the looser part of the main battle Jack had forced his way some three yards in: he had a soldier in front of him, and as their swords clashed high so a pikeman drove under his right arm, ripping the flesh outside his ribs and pulling out to stab again. Immediately behind him Bonden fired his pistol, blowing off the lower part of Jack's ear and killing the pikeman where he stood. Jack feinted at the soldier, a quick double slash, and brought his sword down on his shoulder with terrible force. The fight surged back: the soldier fell. Jack heaved out his sword, tight in bone, and glanced quickly fore and aft. 'This won't do,' he said.

Forward, under the fo'c'sle, the sheer weight and number of the three hundred Spaniards, now half recovered from their surprise, was pushing the Sophies back, driving a solid wedge between his band and Dillon's in the bows. Dillon must have been held up. The tide might turn at any second now. He leapt on to a gun and with a hail that ripped his throat he roared, 'Dillon, Dillon, the starboard gangway! Thrust for the starboard gangway!' For a fleeting moment, at the edge of his field of vision, he was aware of Stephen far below, on the deck of the *Sophie*, holding her wheel and gazing collectedly upwards. 'Otros cincuenta!' he shouted, for good measure: and as Stephen nodded, calling out something in Spanish, he raced back into the fight, his sword high and his pistol searching.

At this moment there was a frightful shrieking on the fo'c'sle, a most bitter, furious drive for the head of the gangway, a desperate struggle; something gave, and the dense mass of Spaniards in the waist turned to see these black faces rushing at them from behind. A confused milling round the frigate's bell, cries of every kind, the blackened Sophies cheering like madmen as they joined their friends, shots, the clash of arms, a trampling huddled retreat, all the Spaniards in the waist hampered, crowded in upon, unable to strike. The few on the quarter-deck ran forward along the larboard side to try to rally the people, to bring them into some order, at least to disengage the useless marines.

Jack's opponent, a little seaman, writhed away behind the capstan, and Jack heaved back out of the press. He looked up and down the clear run of deck. 'Bonden,' he shouted, plucking his arm, 'Go and strike those colours.'

Bonden ran aft, leaping over the dead Spanish captain. Jack hallooed and pointed. Hundreds of eyes, glancing or staring or suddenly looking back, half-comprehending, saw the *Cacafuego*'s ensign race down – her colours struck.

It was over. ''Vast fighting,' cried Jack, and the order ran round the deck. The Sophies backed away from the packed mob in the waist and the men there threw down their weapons, suddenly dispirited, frightened, cold and betrayed. The senior surviving Spanish officer struggled out of the crowd in which he had been penned and offered Jack his sword.

'Do you speak English, sir?' asked Jack.

'I understand it, sir,' said the officer.

'The men must go down into the hold, sir, at once,' said Jack. 'The officers on deck. The men down into the hold. Down into the hold.'

The Spaniard gave the order: the frigate's crew began to file down the hatchways. As they went so the dead and wounded were discovered – a tangled mass amidships, many more forward, single bodies everywhere – and so, too, the true number of the attackers grew clear.

'Quickly, quickly,' cried Jack, and his men urged the prisoners below, herded them fast, for they understood the danger as well as their captain. 'Mr Day, Mr Watt, get a couple of their guns – those carronades – pointing down the hatchways. Load with canister – there's plenty in the garlands aft. Where's Mr Dillon? Pass the word for Mr Dillon.'

The word passed, and no answer came. He was lying there near the starboard gangway, where the most desperate fighting had been, a couple of steps from little Ellis. When Jack picked him up he thought he was only hurt; but turning him he saw the great wound in his heart.

Chapter Eleven

H. M. Sloop *Sophie*
off Barcelona

Sir,
I have the honour to acquaint you, that the sloop I
have the honour to command, after a mutual chase
and a warm action, has captured a Spanish xebec
frigate of 32 guns, 22 long twelve-pounders, 8 nines,
and 2 heavy carronades, viz. the *Cacafuego*, commanded by Don Martin de Langara, manned by 319
officers, seamen and marines. The disparity of force
rendered it necessary to adopt some measure that
might prove decisive. I resolved to board, which
being accomplished almost without loss, after a violent close engagement the Spanish colours were
obliged to be struck. I have, however, to lament the
loss of Lieutenant Dillon, who fell at the height of
the action, leading his boarding-party, and of Mr
Ellis, a supernumerary; while Mr Watt the boatswain
and five seamen were severely wounded. To render
just praise to the gallant conduct and impetuous
attack of Mr Dillon, I am perfectly unequal to.

'I saw him for a while,' Stephen had said, 'I saw him through
that gap where two ports were beaten into one: they were
fighting by the gun, and then when you called out at the
head of those stairs into the waist; and he was in front –
black faces behind him. I saw him pistol a man with a pike,
pass his sword through a fellow who had beaten down the

bosun and come to a redcoat, an officer. After a couple of quick passes he caught this man's sword on his pistol and lunged straight into him. But his sword struck on the breast-bone or a metal plate, and doubled and broke with the thrust: and with the six inches left he stabbed him faster than you could see – inconceivable force and rapidity. You would never believe the happiness on his face. The light on his face!'

I must be permitted to say, that there could not have been greater regularity, nor more cool determined conduct shown by men, than by the crew of the *Sophie*. The great exertions and good conduct of Mr Pullings, a passed midshipman and acting lieutenant whom I beg to recommend to their Lordships' attention, and of the boatswain, carpenter, gunner and petty officers, I am particularly indebted for.

I have the honour to be, etc.

Sophie's force at commencement of action: 54 officers, men, and boys. 14 4-pounders. 3 killed and 8 wounded.

Cacafuego's force at commencement of action: 274 officers, seamen and supernumeraries. 45 marines. Guns 32.
The captain, boatswain, and 13 men killed; 41 wounded.

He read it through, changed 'I have the honour' on the first page to 'I have the pleasure', signed it Jno. Aubrey and addressed it to M. Harte, Esqr. – not to Lord Keith alas, for the admiral was at the other end of the Mediterranean, and everything passed through the hands of the commandant.

It was a passable letter; not very good, for all his efforts and revisions. He was no hand with a pen. Still, it gave the facts – some of them – and apart from being dated 'off

Barcelona' in the customary way, whereas it was really being written in Port Mahon the day after his arrival, it contained no falsehood: and he thought he had done everyone justice – had done all the justice he could, at least, for Stephen Maturin had insisted upon being left out. But even if it had been a model of naval eloquence it would still have been utterly inadequate, as every sea-officer reading it would know. For example, it spoke of the engagement as something isolated in time, coolly observed, reasonably fought and clearly remembered, whereas almost everything of real importance was before or after the blaze of fighting; and even in that he could scarcely tell what came first. As to the period after the victory, he was unable to recapture the sequence at all, without the log: it was all a dull blur of incessant labour and extreme anxiety and weariness. Three hundred angry men to be held down by two dozen, who also had to bring the six-hundred-ton prize to Minorca through an ugly sea and some cursed winds; almost all the sloop's standing and running rigging to be set up anew, masts to be fished, yards shifted, fresh sails bent, and the bosun among the badly wounded; that hobbling voyage along the edge of disaster, with precious little help from the sea or the sky. A blur, and a sense of oppression; a feeling more of the *Cacafuego*'s defeat than the *Sophie*'s victory; and exhausted perpetual hurrying, as though that were what life really consisted of. A fog punctuated by a few brilliantly clear scenes.

Pullings, there on the bloody deck of the *Cacafuego*, shouting in his deafened ear that gunboats were coming down from Barcelona; his determination to fire the frigate's undamaged broadside at them; his incredulous relief when he saw them turn at last and dwindle against the threatening horizon – why?

The sound that woke him in the middle watch: a low cry mounting by quarter tones or less and increasing in volume to a howling shriek, then a quick series of spoken or chanted words, the mounting cry again and the shriek – the Irish men of the crew waking James Dillon, stretched there with a cross in his hands and lanterns at his head and his feet.

The burials. That child Ellis in his hammock with the flag sewed over him looked like a little pudding, and now at the recollection his eye clouded again. He had wept, wept, his face streaming with tears as the bodies went over the side and the marines fired their volley.

'Dear Lord,' he thought. 'Dear Lord.' For the re-writing of the letter and this casting back of his mind brought all the sadness flooding up again. It was a sadness that had lasted from the end of the action until the breeze had died on them some miles off Cape Mola and they had fired urgent guns for a pilot and assistance: a sadness that fought a losing battle against invading joy, however. Trying to fix the moment when the joy broke through he looked up, stroking his wounded ear with the feather of his pen; and through the cabin window he saw the tall proof of his victory at her moorings by the yard; her undamaged larboard side was towards the *Sophie*, and the pale water of the autumn day reflected the red and shining gold of her paintwork, as proud and trim as the first day he had seen her.

Perhaps it was when he received the first unbelieving amazed congratulations from Sennet of the *Bellerophon*, whose gig was the first boat to reach him: then there was Butler of the *Naiad* and young Harvey, Tom Widdrington and some midshipmen, together with Marshall and Mowett, almost out of their minds with grief at not having taken part in the action, yet already shining with reflected glory. Their boats took the *Sophie* and her prize in tow; their men relieved the exhausted marines and idlers guarding the prisoners; he felt the accumulated weight of those days and nights come down on him in a soft compelling cloud, and he went to sleep in the midst of their questions. That marvellous sleep, and his waking in the still harbour to be given a quick unsigned note in a double cover from Molly Harte.

Perhaps it was then. The joy, the great swelling delight was certainly in him when he woke. He grieved, of course he grieved, he grieved bitterly for the loss of his shipmates – would have given his right hand to save them – and mixed in his sorrow for Dillon there was a guilt whose cause and nature eluded him; but a serving officer in an active war has an intense rather than a lasting grief. Sober objective reason told him that there had not been many successful single-ship actions between quite such unequal opponents and that unless he did something spectacularly foolish, unless he blew himself as high as the *Boyne*, the next thing that would reach him from the Admiralty would be the news of his being gazetted – of his being made a post-captain.

With any kind of luck he would be given a frigate: and his mind ran over those glorious high-bred ships – *Emerald*, *Seahorse*, *Terpsichore*, *Phaëton*, *Sibylle*, *Sirius*, the lucky *Ethalion*, *Naiad*, *Alcmène* and *Triton*, the flying *Thetis*. *Endymion*, *San Fiorenzo*, *Amelia*. . . dozens of them: more than a hundred in commission. Had he any right to a frigate? Not much: a twenty-gun post-ship was more his mark, something just in the sixth rate. Not much right to a frigate. Not much right to set about the *Cacafuego*, either; nor to make love to Molly Harte. Yet he had done so. In the post-chaise, in a bower, in another bower, all night long. Perhaps that was why he was so sleepy now, so apt to doze, blinking comfortably into the future as though it were a sea-coal fire. And perhaps that was why his wounds hurt so. The slash on his left shoulder had opened at the far end. How he had come by it he could not tell; but there it was after the action, and Stephen had sewn it up at the same time he dressed the pike-wound across the front of his chest (one bandage for the two) and clapped a sort of dressing on what was left of his ear.

But dozing would not do. This was the time for riding in with the tide of flood, for making a dash for a frigate, for seizing fortune while she was in reach, running her aboard. He would write to Queeney at once, and half a dozen letters more that afternoon, before the party – perhaps to his father too, or would the old boy make a cock of it again? He was the worst hand imaginable at plot, intrigue or the management of what tiny amount of interest they had with the grander members of the family – should never have reached the rank of general, by rights. However, the public letter was the first of these things, and Jack got up carefully, smiling still.

This was the first time he had been openly ashore, and early though it was he could not but be conscious of the looks, the murmurs and the pointing that accompanied his passage. He carried his letter into the commandant's office, and the compunction, the stirrings if not of conscience or principle then at least of decency, that had disturbed him on his way up through the town and even more in the anteroom, disappeared with Captain Harte's first words. 'Well, Aubrey,' he said, without getting up, 'we are to congratulate you upon your prodigious good luck again, I collect.'

'You are too kind, sir,' said Jack. 'I have brought you my official letter.'

'Oh, yes,' said Captain Harte, holding it some way off and looking at it with an affectation of carelessness. 'I will forward it, presently. Mr Brown tells me it is perfectly impossible for the yard here to supply half your wants – he seems quite astonished that you should want so much. How the devil did you contrive to get so many spars knocked away? And such a preposterous amount of rigging? Your sweeps destroyed? There are no sweeps here. Are you sure your bosun is not coming it a trifle high? Mr Brown says there is not a frigate on the station, nor even a ship of the line, that has called for half so much cordage.'

'If Mr Brown can tell me how to take a thirty-two gun frigate without having a few spars knocked away I shall be obliged to him.'

'Oh, in these sudden surprise attacks, you know . . . however, all I can say is you will have to go to Malta for most of your requirements. *Northumberland* and *Superb* have made a clean sweep here.' It was so evidently his intention to be ill-natured that his words had little effect; but his next stroke slipped under Jack's guard and stabbed right home. 'Have you written to Ellis' people yet? This sort of thing' – tapping the public letter – 'is easy enough: anyone can do this. But I do not envy you the other. What I shall say myself I don't know . . .' Biting the joint of his thumb he darted a furious look from under his eyebrows, and Jack had a moral certainty that the financial setback, misfortune, disaster, or whatever it was, affected him far more than the debauching of his wife.

Jack had, in fact, written that letter, as well as the others – Dillon's uncle, the seamen's families – and he was thinking of them as he walked across the patio with a sombre look on his face. A figure under the dark gateway stopped, obviously peering at him. All Jack could see in the tunnel through to the street was an outline and the two epaulettes of a senior post-captain or a flag-officer, so although he was ready with his salute his mind was still blank when the other stepped through into the sunlight, hurrying forward with his hand outstretched. 'Captain Aubrey, I do believe? Keats, of the *Superb*. My dear sir, you must allow me to congratulate you with all my heart – a most splendid victory indeed. I have just pulled round your capture in my barge, and I am amazed, sir, *amazed*. Was you very much clawed? May I be of any service – my bosun, carpenter, sailmakers? Would you do me the pleasure of dining aboard, or are you bespoke? I dare say you are – every woman in Mahon will wish to exhibit you. Such a victory!'

'Why, sir, I thank you most heartily,' cried Jack, flushing with undisguised open ingenuous pleasure and returning the pressure of Captain Keats' hand with such vehemence as to cause a dull crepitation, followed by a shattering dart of agony. 'I am infinitely obliged to you, for your kind opinion. There is none I value more, sir. To tell you the truth, I am engaged to dine with the Governor and to stay for the concert; but if I might beg the loan of your bosun and a small party – my people are all most uncommon weary, quite fagged out – why, I should look upon it as a most welcome, indeed, a Heaven-sent relief.'

'It shall be done. Most happy,' said Captain Keats. 'Which way do you go, sir? Up or down?'

'Down, sir. I have appointed to meet a – a person at the Crown.'

'Then our ways lie together,' said Captain Keats, taking Jack's arm; and as they crossed the street to walk in the shade he called out to a friend, 'Tom, come and see who I have in tow. This is Captain Aubrey of the *Sophie*! You know Captain Grenville, I am sure?'

'This gives me very great pleasure,' cried the grim, battle-scarred Grenville, breaking out into a one-eyed smile: he shook Jack by the hand and instantly asked him to dinner.

Jack had refused five more invitations by the time he and Keats parted at the Crown: from mouths he respected he had heard the words 'as neat an action as ever I knew', 'Nelson will rejoice in this', and 'if there is justice on earth, the frigate will be bought by Government and Captain Aubrey given command of her'. He had seen looks of unfeigned respect, good will and admiration upon the faces of seamen and junior officers passing in the crowded street; and two commanders senior to him, unlucky in prizes and known to be jealous, had hurried across to make their compliments, handsomely and with good grace.

He walked in, up the stairs to his room, threw off his coat and sat down. 'This must be what they call the vapours,' he said, trying to define something happy, tremulous, poignant, churchlike and not far from tears in his heart and bosom. He sat there: the feeling lasted, indeed grew stronger; and when Mercedes darted in he gazed at her with a mild benevolence, a kind and brotherly look. She darted in, squeezed him passionately and uttered a flood of Catalan into his ear, ending 'Brave, brave Captain – good, *pretty* and brave.'

'Thank you, thank you, Mercy dear; I am infinitely obliged to you. Tell me,' he said, after a decent pause, trying to shift to an easier position (a plump girl: a good ten stone), 'diga me, would you be a good creature, bona creatura, and fetch me some iced negus? Sangria colda? Thirst, soif, very thirst, I do assure you, my dear.'

'Your auntie was quite right,' he said, putting down the beaded jug and wiping his mouth. 'The Vinaroz ship was there to the minute, and we found the false Ragusan. So here, acqui, aqui is auntie's reward, the recompenso de tua tia, my dear' – pulling a leather purse out of his breeches pocket – 'y aqui' – bringing out a neat sealing-waxed packet – 'is a little regalo para vous, sweetheart.'

'Present?' cried Mercedes, taking it with a sparkling eye, nimbly undoing the silk, tissue-paper, jeweller's cotton, and finding a pretty little diamond cross with a chain. She shrieked, kissed him, darted to the looking-glass, shrieked some more – eek, eek! – and came back with the stone flashing low on her neck. She pulled herself in below and puffed herself out above, like a pouter-pigeon, and lowered her bosom, the diamonds winking in the hollow, down towards him, saying, 'You like him? You like him? You like him?'

Jack's eyes grew less brotherly, oh far less brotherly, his glottis stiffened and his heart began to thump. 'Oh, yes, I like him,' he said, hoarsely.

'Timely, sir, bosun of the *Superb*,' said a tremendous voice at the opening door. 'Oh, beg pardon, sir . . .'

'Not at all, Mr Timely,' said Jack. 'I am very happy to see you.'

'And indeed perhaps it was just as well,' he reflected, landing again at the Rope-Walk stairs, leaving behind him a numerous body of skilful, busy Superbs rattling down the newly set-up shrouds, 'there being so much to do. But what a sweet girl it is . . .' He was now on his way to the Governor's dinner. That, at least, was his intention; but a bemused state of mind, swimming back into the past and onwards into the future, together with a reluctance to seem to parade himself in what the sailors called the High Street, brought him by obscure back ways filled with the smell of new fermenting wine and purple-guttered with the lees, to the Franciscan church at the top of the hill. Here, summoning his wits into the present, he took new bearings; and looking with some anxiety at his watch he paced rapidly along by the armoury, passed the green door of Mr Florey's house with a quick upward glance and headed north-west by north for the Residence.

Behind the green door and some floors up Stephen and Mr Florey were already sat down to a haphazard meal, spread wherever there was room on odd tables and chairs. Ever since coming back from the hospital they had been dissecting a well-preserved dolphin, which lay on a high bench by the window, next to something covered by a sheet.

'Some captains think it the best policy to include every case of bloodshed or temporary incapacity,' said Mr Florey, 'because a long butcher's bill looks well in the Gazette. Others will admit no man that is not virtually dead, because a small number of casualties means a careful commander. I think your list is near the happy mean, though perhaps a trifle cautious – you are looking at it from the point of view of your friend's advancement of course?'

'Just so.'

'Yes . . . Allow me to give you a slice of this cold beef. Pray reach me a sharp knife – beef, above all, *must be cut thin*, if it is to savour well.'

'There is no edge on this one,' said Stephen. 'Try the catling.' He turned to the dolphin. 'No,' he said, peering under a flipper. 'Where can we have left it? Ah' – lifting the sheet – 'here is another. Such a blade: Swedish steel, no doubt. You began your incision at the Hippocratic point, I see,' he said, raising the sheet a little more, and gazing at the young lady beneath it.

'Perhaps we ought to wash it,' said Mr Florey.

'Oh, a wipe will do,' said Stephen, using a corner of the sheet. 'By the way, what was the cause of death?' he asked, letting the cloth fall back.

'That is a nice point,' said Mr Florey, carving a first slice and carrying it to the griffon vulture tied by the leg in a

335

corner of the room. 'That is a nice point, but I rather incline to believe that the battering did her business before the water. These amiable weaknesses, follies . . . Yes. Your friend's advancement.' Mr Florey paused, gazing at the long straight double-edged catling and waving it solemnly over the joint. 'If you provide a man with horns, he may gore you,' he observed with a detached air, covertly watching to see what effect his remark might have.

'Very true,' said Stephen, tossing the vulture a piece of gristle. 'In general *fenum habent in cornu*. But surely,' he said, smiling at Mr Florey, 'you are not throwing out a generality about cuckolds? Do not you choose to be more specific? Or do you perhaps refer to the young person under the sheet? I know you speak from your excellent heart, and I assure you no degree of frankness can possibly offend.'

'Well,' said Mr Florey, 'the point is, that your young friend – our young friend, I may say, for I have a real regard for him, and look upon this action as reflecting great credit upon the service, upon us all – our young friend has been very indiscreet: so has the lady. You follow me, I believe?'

'Oh, certainly.'

'The husband resents it, and he is in such a position that he may be able to indulge his resentment, unless our friend is very careful – most uncommon cautious. The husband will not ask for a meeting, for that is not his style at all – a pitiful fellow. But he may try to entrap him into some act of disobedience and so bring him to a court-martial. Our friend is famous for his dash, his enterprise and his good luck rather than for his strict sense of subordination: and some few of the senior captains here feel a good deal of jealousy and uneasiness at his success. What is more, he is a Tory, or his family is; and the husband and the present First Lord are rabid Whigs, vile ranting dogs of Whigs. Do you follow me, Dr Maturin?'

'I do indeed, sir, and am much obliged to you for your candour in telling me this: it confirms what was in my mind, and I shall do all I can to make him conscious of the delicacy of his position. Though upon my word,' he added with a sigh, 'there are times when it seems to me that nothing short of a radical ablation of the membrum virile would answer, in this case.'

'That is very generally the peccant part,' said Mr Florey.

Clerk David Richards was also having his dinner; but he was eating it in the bosom of his family. 'As everyone knows,' he told the respectful throng, 'the captain's clerk's position is the most dangerous there is in a man-of-war: he is up there all the time on the quarter-deck with his slate and his watch, to take remarks, next to the captain, and all the small-arms and a good many of the great guns concentrate their fire upon him. Still, there he must stay, supporting the captain with his countenance and his advice.'

'Oh, Davy,' cried his aunt, 'and did he ask your advice?'

'Did he ask my advice, ma'am? Ha, ha, upon my sacred word.'

'Don't swear, Davy dear,' said his aunt automatically. 'It ain't genteel.'

'"La, Mr Richards bach," says he, when the maintop begins to tumble about our ears, tearing down through the quarter-deck splinter-netting like so much Berlin wool, "I don't know what to do. I am quite at a loss, I protest." "There's only one thing for it, sir," says I. "Board 'em. Board 'em fore and aft, and I give you my sacred word the frigate's ours in five minutes." Well, ma'am and cousins, I do not like to boast, and I confess it took us ten minutes; but it was worth it, for it won us as pretty a copper-fastened, new-sheathed xebec frigate as any I have seen. And when I came aft, having dirked the Spanish captain's clerk, Captain Aubrey shook me by the hand, and with tears in his eyes, "Richards," says he, "we ought all to be very grateful to you," says he. "Sir, you are very good," says I, "but I have done nothing but what any taut captain's clerk would do." "Well," says he, "'tis very well."' He took a draught of porter and went on, 'I very nearly said to him, "I tell you

what, Goldilocks" – for we call him Goldilocks in the service, you know, in much the same way as they call me Hell-
fire Davy, or Thundering Richards – "just you rate me
midshipman aboard the *Cacafuego* when she's bought by
Government, and we'll cry quits." Perhaps I may,
tomorrow; for I feel I have the genius of command. She
ought to fetch twelve pound ten, thirteen pound a ton, don't
you think, sir?' he said to his uncle. 'We did not cut up her
hull a great deal.'

'Yes,' said Mr Williams slowly. 'If she was bought in by
Government she would fetch that and her stores as much
again: Captain A would clear a neat five thou' apart from
the head-money; and your share would be, let's see, two
hundred and sixty-three, fourteen, two. *If* she was bought
by Government.'

'What do you mean, Nunckie, with your *if*?'

'Why, I mean that a *certain person* does the Admiralty
buying; and a *certain person* has a lady that is not over-shy;
and a *certain person* may cut up horrid rough. O Goldilocks,
Goldilocks, wherefore are thou Goldilocks?' asked Mr Williams, to the unspeakable amazement of his nieces. 'If he
had attended to business instead of playing Yardo, the parish
bull, he . . .'

'It was she as set her bonnet at him!' cried Mrs Williams,
who had never yet let her husband finish a sentence since
his 'I will' at Trinity Church, Plymouth Dock, in 1782.

'O the minx!' cried her unmarried sister; and the nieces'
eyes swung towards her, wider still.

'The hussy,' cried Mrs Thomas. 'My Paquita's cousin
was the driver of the shay she came down to the quay in;
and you would never credit . . .'

'She should be flogged through the town at the cart's tail,
and don't I wish I had the whip.'

'Come, my dear . . .'

'I know what you are thinking, Mr W.,' cried his wife, 'and
you are to stop it this minute. The nasty cat; the wretch.'

* * *

The wretch's reputation had indeed suffered, had been much blown upon in recent months, and the Governor's wife received her as coldly as she dared; but Molly Harte's looks had improved almost out of recognition – she had been a fine woman before, and now she was positively beautiful. She and Lady Warren arrived together for the concert, and a small troop of soldiers and sailors had waited outside to meet their carriage: now they were crowding about her, snorting and bristling with aggressive competition, while their wives, sisters and, even, sweethearts sat in dowdy greyish heaps at a distance, mute, and looking with pursed lips at the scarlet dress almost hidden amidst the flocking uniforms.

The men fell back when Jack appeared, and some of them returned to their womenfolk, who asked them whether they did not find Mrs Harte much aged, ill dressed, a perfect frump? Such a pity at her age, poor thing. She must be at least thirty, forty, forty-five. Lace mittens! They had no idea of wearing lace mittens. This strong light was unkind to her; and surely it was very outré to wear all those enormous great pearls?

She *was* something of a whore, thought Jack, looking at her with great approval as she stood there with her head high, perfectly aware of what the women were saying, and defying them: she was something of a whore, but the knowledge spurred his appetite. She was only for the successful; but with the *Cacafuego* moored by the *Sophie* in Mahon harbour, Jack found that perfectly acceptable.

After a few moments of inane conversation – a piece of dissembling which Jack thought he accomplished with particular brilliance, alas – they all surged in a shuffling mob into the music-room, Molly Harte to sit looking beautiful by her harp and the rest to arrange themselves on the little gilt chairs.

'What are we to have?' asked a voice behind him, and turning Jack saw Stephen, powdered, respectable apart from having forgotten his shirt, and eager for the treat.

'Some Boccherini – a 'cello piece – and the Haydn trio

that we arranged. And Mrs Harte is going to play the harp. Come and sit by me.'

'Well, I suppose I shall have to,' said Stephen, 'the room being so crowded. Yet I had hoped to enjoy this concert: it is the last we shall hear for some time.'

'Nonsense,' said Jack, taking no notice. 'There is Mrs Brown's party.'

'We shall be on our way to Malta by then. The orders are writing at this moment.'

'The sloop is not nearly ready for sea,' said Jack. 'You must be mistaken.'

Stephen shrugged. 'I have it from the secretary himself.'

'The damned rogue . . .' cried Jack.

'Hush,' said all the people round them; the first violin gave a nod, brought down his bow, and in a moment they were all dashing away, filling the room with a delightful complexity of sound, preparing for the 'cello's meditative song.

'Upon the whole,' said Stephen, 'Malta is a disappointing place. But at least I did find a very considerable quantity of squills by the sea-shore: these I have conserved in a woven basket.'

'It is,' said Jack. 'Though God knows, apart from poor Pullings, I should not complain. They have fitted us out nobly, apart from the sweeps – nobody could have been more attentive than the Master Attendant – and they entertained us like emperors. Do you suppose one of your squills would be a good thing, in a general way, to set a man up? I feel as low as a gib cat – quite out of order.'

Stephen looked at him attentively, took his pulse, gazed at his tongue, asked squalid questions, examined him. 'Is it a wound going bad?' asked Jack, alarmed by his gravity.

'It is a wound, if you wish,' said Stephen. 'But not from our battle with the *Cacafuego*. Some lady of your acquaintance has been too liberal with her favours, too universally kind.'

'Oh, Lord,' cried Jack, to whom this had never happened before.

'Never mind,' said Stephen, touched by Jack's horror. 'We shall soon have you on your feet again: taken early, there is no great problem. It will do you no harm to keep close, drink nothing but demulcent barley-water and eat gruel, thin gruel – no beef or mutton, no wine or spirits. If what Marshall tells me about the westward passage at this time of the year is true, together with our stop at Palermo, you will certainly be in a state to ruin your health, prospects, reason, features and happiness again by the time we raise Cape Mola.'

He left the cabin with what seemed to Jack an inhuman want of concern and went directly below, where he mixed a draught and a powder from the large stock that he (like all other naval surgeons) kept perpetually at hand. Under the thrust of the gregale, coming in gusts off Delamara Point, the *Sophie*'s lee-lurch slopped out too much by half.

'It is too much by half,' he observed, balancing like a seasoned mariner and pouring the surplus into a twenty-drachm phial. 'But never mind. It will just do for young Babbington.' He corked it, set it on a rail-locked rack, counted its fellows with their labelled necks and returned to the cabin. He knew very well that Jack would act on the ancient seafaring belief that *more is better* and dose himself into Kingdom Come if not closely watched, and he stood there reflecting upon the passage of authority from one to the other in relationships of this kind (or rather of potential authority, for they had never entered into any actual collision) as Jack gasped and retched over his nauseous dose. Ever since Stephen Maturin had grown rich with their first prize he had constantly laid in great quantities of asafetida, castoreum and other substances, to make his medicines more revolting in taste, smell and texture than any others in the fleet; and he found it answered – his hardy patients *knew* with their entire beings that they were being physicked.

'The Captain's wounds are troubling him,' he said at

dinner-time, 'and he will not be able to accept the gun-room's invitation tomorrow. I have confined him to his cabin and to slops.'

'Was he very much cut up?' asked Mr Dalziel respectfully. Mr Dalziel was one of the disappointments of Malta: every-body aboard had hoped that Thomas Pullings would be confirmed lieutenant, but the admiral had sent down his own nominee, a cousin, Mr Dalziel of Auchterbothie and Sodds. He had softened it with a private note promising to 'keep Mr Pullings in mind and to make particular mention of him to the Admiralty', but there it was – Pullings remained a master's mate. He was not 'made' – the first spot on their victory. Mr Dalziel felt it, and he was particularly concili-atory; though, indeed, he had very little need to be, for Pullings was the most unassuming creature on earth, pain-fully diffident anywhere except on the enemy's deck.

'Yes,' said Stephen, 'he was. Sword, pistol and pike wounds; and probing the deepest I have found a piece of metal, a slug, that he had received at the Battle of the Nile.'

'Enough to trouble any man,' said Mr Dalziel, who through no fault of his own had seen no bloodshed whatever and who suffered from the fact.

'I speak under correction, Doctor,' said the master, 'but surely fretting will open wounds? And he must be fretting something cruel not to be on our cruising-ground, the season growing so late.'

'Ay, to be sure,' said Stephen. And certainly Jack had reason to fret, like everybody else aboard: to be sent to Malta while they had a right to cruise in fine rich waters was very hard, in any case, and it was made all the worse by the persistent rumour of a galleon earmarked by fate and by Jack's private intelligence for the *Sophie* – a galleon, or even galleons, a parcel of galleons, that might at this very moment be creeping along the Spanish coast, and they five hundred miles away.

They were extremely impatient to be back to their cruise, to the thirty-seven days that were owing to them, thirty-seven days of making hay; for although there were many aboard who possessed more guineas than they had ever owned shillings ashore, there was not one who did not ardently long for more. The general reckoning was that the ordinary seaman's share would be close on fifty pounds, and even those who had been blooded, thumped, scorched and battered in the action thought it good pay for a morning's work – more interesting by far than the uncertain shilling a day they might earn at the plough or the loom, by land, or even than the eight pounds a month that hard-pressed merchant captains were said to be offering.

Successful action together, strong driving discipline and a high degree of competence (apart from Mad Willy, *Sophie*'s lunatic, and a few other hopeless cases, every man and boy aboard could now hand, reef and steer) had welded them into a remarkably united body, perfectly acquainted with their vessel and her ways. It was just as well, for their new lieutenant was no great seaman, and they got him out of many a sad blunder as the sloop made her way westwards as fast as ever she could, through two shocking gales, through high battering seas and maddening calms, with the *Sophie* wallowing in the great swell, her head all round the compass and the ship's cat as sick as a dog. As fast as ever she could, for not only had all her people a month's mind to be on the enemy's coast again, but all the officers were intensely eager to hear the news from London, the Gazette and the official reaction to their exploit – a post-captain's commission for Jack and perhaps advancement for all the rest.

It was a passage that spoke well for the yard at Malta, as well as for the excellence of her crew, for it was in these same waters that the sixteen-gun sloop *Utile* foundered during their second gale – she broached to going before the wind not twenty miles to the south of them, and all hands perished. But the weather relented on the last day, sending them a fine steady close-reef topsail tramontana: they raised the high land of Minorca in the forenoon, made their number a little after dinner and rounded Cape Mola before the sun was half-way down the sky.

All alive once more, though a little less tanned from his confinement, Jack looked eagerly at the wind-clouds over Mount Toro, with their promise of continuing northerly weather, and he said, 'As soon as we are through the narrows, Mr Dalziel, let us hoist out the boats and begin to get the butts on deck. We shall be able to start watering tonight and be on our way as soon as possible in the morning. There is not a moment to lose. But I see you have hooks to the yards and stays already – very good,' he added with a chuckle, going into his cabin.

This was the first poor Mr Dalziel had heard of it: silent hands that knew Jack's ways far better than he did had foreseen the order, and the poor man shook his head with what philosophy he could muster. He was in a difficult position, for although he was a respectable, conscientious officer he could not possibly stand any sort of comparison with James Dillon: their former lieutenant was wonderfully present in the mind of the crew that he had helped to form – his dynamic authority, his immense technical ability and his seamanship grew in their memories.

Jack was thinking of him as the *Sophie* glided up the long harbour, past the familiar creeks and the islands one after another: they were just abreast of the hospital island and he was thinking how much less noise James Dillon used to make when he heard the hail of 'Boat ahoy' on deck and far away the answering cry that meant the approach of a captain. He did not catch the name, but a moment later Babbbington, looking alarmed, knocked on his door to announce 'Commandant's barge pulling alongside, sir.'

There was a good deal of plunging about on deck as Dalziel set about trying to do three things at once and as those who should dress the sloop's side tried to make themselves look respectable in a violent hurry. Few captains would have darted from behind an island in this way; few would have worried a vessel about to moor; and most, even in an emergency, would have given them a chance, would have allowed them a few minutes' grace; but not Captain Harte, who came up the side as quickly as he could. The calls twittered and howled; the few properly dressed officers stood rigid, bare-headed; the marines presented arms and one dropped his musket.

'Welcome aboard, sir,' cried Jack, who was in such charity with the present shining world that he could feel pleased to see even this ill-conditioned face, it being familiar. 'I believe this is the first time we have had the honour.'

Captain Harte saluted the quarter-deck with a sketchy motion towards his hat and stared with elaborate disgust at the grubby sideboys, the marines with their crossbelts awry, the heap of water-butts and Mr Dalziel's little fat meek cream-coloured bitch, that had come forward into the only open space, and that there, apologizing to one and all, her ears and whole person drooping, was in the act of making an immeasurable pool.

'Do you usually keep your decks in this state, Captain Aubrey?' he asked. 'By my living bowels, it's more like a Wapping pawnshop than the deck of a King's sloop.'

'Why, no, sir,' said Jack, still in the best humour in the world, for the waxed-canvas Admiralty wrapper under Harte's arm could only be a post-captain's commission addressed to J. A. Aubrey, Esqr., and brought with delightful speed. 'You have caught the *Sophie* in her shift, I am afraid. Will you step into the cabin, sir?'

The crew were tolerably busy as she made her way through the shipping and prepared to moor, but they were used to their sloop and they were used to their anchorage, which was just as well, for a disproportionate amount of their attention was taken up with listening to the voices that came out of the cabin.

'He's coming it the Old Jarvie,' whispered Thomas Jones to William Witsover, with a grin. Indeed, this grin was fairly general abaft the mainmast, where those in earshot quickly gathered that their captain was being blown up. They loved him much, would follow him anywhere; but they were pleasantly amused at the thought of his copping it, his being dressed down, hauled over the coals, taken to task a little.

'"When I give an order I expects it to be punctually obeyed,"' mouthed Robert Jessup in silent pomp to William Agg, quartermaster's mate.

'Silence there,' cried the master, who could not hear.

But presently the grin faded, first on the faces of the brighter men nearest the skylight, then on those within reach of their communicative eyes, meaning gestures and significant grimaces, and so forward. And as the best bower splashed into the sea the whisper ran 'No cruise.'

Captain Harte reappeared on deck. He was seen into his barge with rigid ceremony, in an atmosphere of silent suspicion, much strengthened by the look of stony reserve on Captain Aubrey's face.

The cutter and the launch began watering at once; the jolly-boat carried the purser ashore for stores and the post; bumboats came off with their usual delights; and Mr Watt, together with most of the other Sophies who had survived their wounds, hurried out in the hospital wherry to see what those sods in Malta had done to his rigging.

To these their shipmates cried, 'Do you know what?'

'What, mate?'

'So you don't know what?'

'Tell us, mate.'

'We ain't going to have no more cruise, that's what. – We've had it, says old Whoreson Prick, we've had our time. – We'm used it up, going to Malta. – Our thirty-seven days! – We convoy that damned lubberly packet down to Gib, that's what we do; and thank you kindly for your efforts in the cruising line. – *Cacafuego* was not bought in – sold to them bloody Moors for eighteen-pence and a pound of shit, the swiftest bleeding xebec that ever swam. – We come back too slow: "Don't you tell me, sir," says he, "for I knows better." – Nothing in the Gazette about us, and Old Fart never brought Goldilocks his step. – They say she weren't regular and her captain had no commission – all bloody lies. – Oh, if I had his cullions in my hand, wouldn't I serve him out, just? I'd . . .' At this point they were cut short by a peremptory message from the quarter-deck, delivered by a bosun's mate with a rope's end; but their passionate indignation flowed on in what they meant to be whispers, and if Captain Harte had reappeared at that moment they might have broken out in mutinous riot and flung him in the harbour. They were furious for their victory, furious for themselves and furious for Jack; and they knew perfectly well that their officers' reproaches were totally devoid of conviction; the rope's end might have been a wafting handkerchief; and even the newcomer Dalziel was shocked by their treatment, at least as it was delivered by rumour, eavesdropping, inference, bumboat talk and the absence of the lovely *Cacafuego*.

In fact, their treatment was even shabbier than rumour had it. The *Sophie*'s commander and her surgeon sat in the cabin amidst a heap of papers, for Stephen Maturin had been helping with some of the paper work as well as writing returns and letters of his own, and now it was three in the morning: the *Sophie* rocked gently at her moorings, and her tight-packed crew were snorting the long night through (the rare joys of harbour-watch). Jack had not gone ashore at all – had no intention of going ashore; and now the silence, the lack of real motion, the long sitting with pen and ink seemed to insulate them from the world in their illuminated cell; and this made their conversation, which would have been indecent at almost any other time, seem quite ordinary and natural. 'Do you know that fellow Martinez?' asked Jack quietly. 'The man whose house the Hartes have part of?'

'I know of him,' said Stephen. 'He is a speculator, a sort of would-be rich man, the left-handed half.'

'Well, he has got the contract for carrying the mails – a damned job, I'm sure – and has bought that pitiful tub the *Ventura* to be the packet. She has never sailed six miles in an hour since she was launched and we are to convoy her to the Rock. Fair enough, you say. Yes, but *we* are to take the sack, put it aboard her when we are just outside the mole and then return back here directly, without landing or communicating with Gibraltar. And I will tell you another thing: he did not forward my official letter by *Superb*, that was going down the Mediterranean two days after we left, nor by *Phoebe*, that was going straight home; and I will lay you any odds you choose to mention that it is here, in this greasy sack. What is more, I know as certainly as if I had read it that his covering letter will be full of this fancied irregularity about the *Cacafuego*'s command, this quibble over the officer's status. Ugly hints and delay. That is why there was nothing in the Gazette. No promotion, either: that Admiralty wrapper only held his own orders, in case I should insist upon having them in writing.'

'Sure, his motive is obvious to a child. He hopes to provoke you into an outburst. He hopes you will disobey and ruin your career. I do beg you will not be blinded with anger.'

'Oh, I shan't play the fool,' said Jack, with a somewhat dogged smile. 'But as for provoking me, I confess he has succeeded to admiration. I doubt I could so much as finger a scale, my hand trembles so when I think of it,' he said, picking up his fiddle. And while the fiddle was passing through the two feet of air from the locker to the height of his shoulder, purely self-concerned and personal thoughts presented themselves to his mind, scarcely in succession but as a cluster: these weeks and months of precious seniority slipping away – already Douglas of the *Phoebe*, Evans on the West Indies station, and a man he did not know called Raitt had been made; they were in the last Gazette and now they were ahead of him on the immutable list of post-captains; he would be junior to them for ever. Time lost; and these disturbing rumours of peace. And a deep, barely acknowledged suspicion, a dread that the whole thing might have gone wrong: no promotion: Lord Keith's warning truly prophetic. He tucked the fiddle under his chin, tightening his mouth and raising his head as he did so: and the tightening of his mouth was enough to release a flood of emotion. His face reddened, his breath heaved deep, his eyes grew larger and, because of the extreme contraction of their pupils, bluer: his mouth tightened still further, and with it his right hand. *Pupils contract symmetrically to a diameter of about a tenth part of an inch*, noted Stephen on a corner of a page. There was a loud, decided crack, a melancholy confused twanging, and with a ludicrous expression of doubt and wonder and distress, Jack held out his violin, all dislocated and unnatural with its broken neck. 'It snapped,' he cried. 'It snapped.' He fitted the broken ends together with infinite care and held them in place. 'I would not have had it happen for the world,' he said in a low voice. 'I have known this fiddle, man and boy, since I was breeched.'

Indignation at the *Sophie*'s treatment was not confined to the sloop, but naturally it was strongest there, and as the crew heaved the capstan round to unmoor they sang a new song, a song that owed nothing whatever to Mr Mowett's chaste muse.

> *– old Harte, – old Harte,*
> *That red-faced son of a dry French fart.*
> *Hey ho, stamp and go,*
> *Stamp and go, stamp and go,*
> *Hey ho, stamp and go.*

The cross-legged fifer on the capstan-head lowered his pipe and sang the quiet solo part:

> *Says old Harte to his missis*
> *O what do I see?*
> *Bold Sophie's commander*
> *With his fiddle-dee-dee.*

Then the deep cross rhythmical bellow again

> *– old Harte, – old Harte,*
> *That one-eyed son of a blue French fart.*

James Dillon would never have allowed it, but Mr Dalziel had no notion of any of the allusions and the song went on and on until the cable was all below in tiers, smelling disagreeably of Mahon ooze, and the *Sophie* was hoisting her jibs and bracing her foretopsailyard round. She dropped down abreast of the *Amelia*, whom she had not seen since the action with the *Cacafuego*, and all at once Mr Dalziel observed that the frigate's rigging was full of men, all carrying their hats and facing the *Sophie*.

'Mr Babbington,' he said in a low voice, in case he should be mistaken, for he had only seen this happen once before, 'tell the captain, with my duty, that I believe *Amelia* is going to cheer us.'

Jack came blinking on deck as the first cheer roared out, a shattering wave of sound at twenty-five yards' range. Then came the *Amelia*'s bosun's pipe and the next cheer, as precisely timed as her own broadside: and the third. He and his officers stood rigidly with their hats off, and as soon as the last roar had died away over the harbour, echoing back and forth, he called out, 'Three cheers for the *Amelia*!' and the Sophies, though deep in the working of the sloop, responded like heroes, scarlet with pleasure and the energy needed for huzzaying proper – huge energy, for they knew what was manners. Then the *Amelia*, now far astern, called 'One cheer more,' and so piped down.

It was a handsome compliment, a noble send-off, and it gave great pleasure: but still it did not prevent the Sophies from feeling a strong sense of grievance – it did not prevent them from calling out 'Give us back our thirty-seven days' as a sort of slogan or watchword between decks, and even above hatches when they dared – it did not wholly recall them to their duty, and in the following days and weeks they were more than ordinarily tedious.

The brief interlude in Port Mahon harbour had been exceptionally bad for discipline. One of the results of their fierce contraction into a single defiant ill-used body was that the hierarchy (in its finer shades) had for a time virtually disappeared; and among other things the ship's corporal had let the wounded men returning to their duty bring in bladders and skins full of Spanish brandy, anisette and a colourless liquid said to be gin. A discreditable number of men had succumbed to its influence, among them the captain of the foretop (paralytic) and both bosun's mates. Jack disrated Morgan, promoting the dumb negro Alfred King, according to his former threat – a *dumb* bosun's mate would surely be more terrible, more deterrent; particularly one with such a very powerful arm.

'And, Mr Dalziel,' he said, 'we will rig a proper grating at the gangway at last. They do not give a damn for a flogging at the capstan, and I am going to stop this infernal drunkenness, come what may.'

'Yes, sir,' said the lieutenant: and after a slight pause, 'Wilson and Plimpton have represented to me that it would grieve them very much to be flogged by King.'

'Of course it will grieve them very much. I sincerely hope it *will* grieve them very much. That is why they are to be flogged. They were drunk, were they not?'

'Blind drunk, sir. They said it was their Thanksgiving.'

'What in God's name have they got to be thankful about? And the *Cacafuego* sold to the Algerines.'

'They are from the colonies, sir, and it seems that it is a feast in those parts. However, it is not the flogging they object to, but the colour of the flogger.'

'Bah,' said Jack. 'I'll tell you another man who will be flogged if this goes on,' he said, bending and peering sideways through the cabin window, 'and that is the master of that damned packet. Just give him a gun, Mr Dalziel, will you? Shotted, not too far from his stern, and desire him to keep to his station.'

The wretched packet had had a miserable time of it since leaving Port Mahon. She had expected the *Sophie* to sail straight to Gibraltar, keeping well out in the offing, out of sight of privateers, and certainly out of range of shore batteries. But although the *Sophie* was still no Flying Childers, in spite of all her improvements, she could nevertheless sail two miles for the packet's one, either close-hauled or going large, and she made the most of her superiority to work right down along the coast, peering into every bay and inlet, obliging the packet to keep to the seaward of her, at no great distance and in a very high state of dread.

Hitherto, this eager, terrier-like searching had led to nothing but a few brisk exchanges of fire with guns on shore, for Jack's harsh restrictive orders allowed no chasing and made it almost certain that he should take no prize. But that was an entirely secondary consideration: action was what he was looking for; and at this juncture, he reflected, he would give almost anything for a direct uncomplicated head-on clash with some vessel about his own size.

So thinking he stepped on deck. The breeze off the sea had been fading all the afternoon, and now it was dying in irregular gasps; although the *Sophie* still had it the packet was almost entirely becalmed. To starboard the high brown rocky coast trended away north and south with something of a protrusion, a small cape, a headland with a ruined Moorish castle, on the beam, perhaps a mile away.

'You see that cape?' said Stephen, who was gazing at it with an open book dangling from his hand, his thumb marking the place. 'It is Cabo Roig, the seaward limit of Catalan speech: Orihuela is a little way inland, and after Orihuela you hear no more Catalan – 'tis Murcia, and the barbarous jargon of the Andalou. Even in the village round the point they speak like Morescoes – algarabia, gabble-gabble, munch, munch.' Though perfectly liberal in all other senses, Stephen Maturin could not abide a Moor.

'There is a village, is there?' asked Jack, his eyes brightening.

'Well, a hamlet: you will see it presently.' A pause, while the sloop whispered through the still water and the landscape imperceptibly revolved. 'Strabo tells us that the ancient Irish regarded it as an honour to be eaten by their relatives – a form of burial that kept the soul in the family,' he said, waving the book.

'Mr Mowett, pray be so good as to fetch me my glass. I beg your pardon, dear Doctor: you were telling me about Strabo.'

'You may say he is no more than Eratosthenes redivivus, or shall I say new-rigged?'

'Oh, do, by all means. There is a fellow riding hell for leather along the top of the cliff, under that castle.'

'He is riding to the village.'

'So he is. I see it now, opening behind the rock. I see something else, too,' he added, almost to himself. The sloop glided steadily on, and steadily the shallow bay turned, showing a white cluster of houses at the water's edge. There were three vessels lying at anchor some way out, a quarter of a mile to the south of the village: two houarios and a pink, merchantmen of no great size, but deeply laden.

Even before the sloop stood in towards them there was great activity ashore, and every eye aboard that could command a glass could see people running about, boats launching and pulling industriously for the anchored vessels. Presently men could be seen hurrying to and fro on the merchantmen, and the sound of their vehement discussion came clearly over the evening sea. Then came the rhythmic shouting as they worked at their windlasses, weighing their anchors: they loosed their sails and ran themselves straight on shore.

Jack stared at the land for some time with a hard calculating look in his eye: if no sea were to get up it would be easy to warp the vessels off – easy both for the Spaniards and for him. To be sure, his orders left no room for a cutting-out expedition. Yet the enemy lived on his coastwise trade – roads execrable – mule-trains absurd for anything in bulk – no waggons worth speaking of – Lord Keith had been most emphatic on that point. And it was his duty to take, burn, sink or destroy. The Sophies stared at Jack: they knew very well what was in his mind, but they also had a pretty clear notion of what was in his orders too – this was not a cruise but a piece of strict convoy-work. They stared so hard that the sands of time ran out. Joseph Button, the marine sentry whose function it was to turn the half-hour glass the moment it emptied and to strike the bell, was roused from his contemplation of Captain Aubrey's face by nudges, pinches, muffled cries of 'Joe, Joe, wake up Joe, you fat son of a bitch,' and lastly by Mr Pullings' voice in his ear, 'Button, turn that glass.'

The last tang of the bell died away and Jack said, 'Put her about, Mr Pullings, if you please.'

With a smooth perfection of curve and the familiar, almost unnoticed piping and cries of 'Ready about – helm's a-lee – rise tacks and sheets – mainsail haul,' the *Sophie* came round, filled and headed back towards the distant packet, still becalmed in a smooth field of violet sea.

She lost the breeze herself when she had run a few miles off the little cape, and she lay there in the twilight and the falling dew, with her sails limp and shapeless.

'Mr Day,' said Jack, 'be so good as to prepare some fire barrels – say half a dozen. Mr Dalziel, unless it comes on to blow I think we may take the boats in at about midnight. Dr Maturin, let us rejoice and be gay.'

Their gaiety consisted of ruling staves and copying a borrowed duet filled with hemidemisemiquavers. 'By God,' said Jack, looking up with red-rimmed streaming eyes after an hour or so, 'I am getting too old for this.' He pressed his hands over his eyes and kept them there for a while: in quite another voice he said, 'I have been thinking about Dillon all day. All day long I have been thinking about him, off and on. You would scarcely credit how much I miss him. When you told me about that classical chap, it brought him so to mind . . . because it was about Irishmen, no doubt; and Dillon was Irish. Though you would never have thought so – never to be seen drunk, almost never called anyone out, spoke like a Christian, the most gentleman-like creature in the world, nothing of the hector at all – oh Christ. My dear fellow, my dear Maturin, I do beg your pardon. I say these damned things . . . I regret it extremely.'

'Ta, ta, ta,' said Stephen, taking snuff and waving his hand from side to side.

Jack pulled the bell, and through the various ship-noises, all muted in this calm, he heard the quick pittering of his steward. 'Killick,' he said, 'bring me a couple of bottles of that Madeira with the yellow seal, and some of Lewis' biscuits. I can't get him to make a decent seed-cake,' he explained to Stephen, 'but these petty fours go down tolerably well and give the wine a relievo. Now this wine,' he said, looking attentively through his glass, 'was given me in Mahon by our agent, and it was bottled the year Eclipse was foaled. I produce it as a sin-offering, conscious of my offence. Your very good health, sir.'

'Yours, my dear. It is a most remarkable ancient wine. Dry, yet unctuous. Prime.'

'I say these damned things,' Jack went on, musing as they drank their bottle, 'and don't quite understand at the time, though I see people looking black as hell, and frowning, and my friends going "Pst, pst", and then I say to myself, "You're brought by the lee again, Jack." Usually I make out what's amiss, given time, but by then it's too late. I am afraid I vexed Dillon often enough, that way' – looking down sadly – 'but, you know, I am not the only one. Do not think I mean to run him down in any way – I only mention it as an instance, that even a very well-bred man can make these blunders sometimes, for I am sure he never meant it – but Dillon once hurt me very much, too. He used the word *commercial*, when we were speaking rather warmly about taking prizes. I am sure he did not mean it, any more than I meant any uncivil reflexion, just now; but it has always stuck hard in my gullet. That is one of the reasons why I am so happy . . .'

Knock-knock on the door. 'Beg pardon, your honour. Loblolly boy's all in a mother, sir. Young Mr Ricketts has swallowed a musket-ball and they can't get it out. Choking to death, sir, if you please.'

'Forgive me,' said Stephen, carefully putting down his glass and covering it with a red spotted handkerchief, a bandanna.

'Is all well – did you manage . . . ?' asked Jack five minutes later.

'We may not be able to do all we could wish in physic,' said Stephen with quiet satisfaction, 'but at least we can give an emetic that answers, I believe. You were saying, sir?'

'*Commercial* was the word,' said Jack. 'Commercial. And that is why I am so happy to have this little boat expedition tonight. For although my orders will not allow me to bring 'em off, yet I have to wait for the packet to come up, and there is nothing to prevent me from burning 'em. I lose no time; and the most scrupulous mind could not but say that this is the most uncommercial enterprise imaginable. It is too late, of course – these things always are too late – but it is a great satisfaction to me. And how James Dillon would have delighted in it! The very thing for him! You remember him with the boats at Palamos? And at Palafrugell?'

The moon set. The star-filled sky wheeled about its axis, sweeping the Pleiades right up overhead. It was a midwinter sky (though warm and still) before the launch, the cutter and the jolly-boat came alongside and the landing-party dropped down into them, the men in their blue jackets and wearing white armbands. They were five miles from their prey, but already no voice rose much above a whisper – a few smothered laughs and the clink of weapons handing down – and when they paddled off with muffled oars they melted so silently into the darkness that in ten minutes Stephen's straining eyes lost them altogether.

'Do you see them still?' he asked the bosun, lame from his wound and now in charge of the sloop.

'I can just make out the darkie the captain's looking at the compass with,' said Mr Watt. 'A little abaft the cathead.'

'Try my night-glass, sir,' said Lucock, the only midshipman left aboard.

'I wish it were over,' said Stephen.

'So do I, Doctor,' said the bosun. 'And I wish I were with them. 'Tis much worse for us left aboard. Those chaps are all together, jolly like, and time goes by like Horndean fair. But here we are, left all thin and few, nothing to do but wait, and the sand chokes in the watch-glass. It will seem years and years before we hear anything of them, sir, as you will surely see.'

Hours, days, weeks, years, centuries. Once there was an ominous clangour high overhead – flamingoes on their way to the Mar Menor, or maybe as far as the marshes of the Guadalquivir: but for the most part it was featureless darkness, almost a denial of time.

The flashes of musketry and the subsequent crackle of firing did not come from the small arc on which his stare had been concentrated, but from well to the right of it. Had the boats gone astray? Run into opposition? Had he been looking in the wrong direction? 'Mr Watt,' he said, 'are they in the right place?'

'Why, no, sir,' said the bosun comfortably. 'And if I know anything of it, the captain is a-leading of 'em astray.'

The crackling went on and on, and in the intervals a faint shouting could be heard. Then to the left there appeared a deep red glow; then a second, and a third; and all at once the third grew enormously, a tongue of flame that leapt up and up and higher still, a most prodigious fountain of light – a whole ship-load of olive-oil ablaze.

'Christ almighty,' murmured the bosun, deep struck with awe. 'Amen,' said one among the silent, staring crew.

The blaze increased: in its light they could see the other fires and their smoke, quite pale; the whole of the bay, the village; the cutter and the launch pulling away from the shore and the jolly-boat crossing to meet them; and all round behind, the brown hills, sharp in light and shade.

At first the column had been perfectly straight, like a

cypress; but after the first quarter of an hour its tip began to lean southwards and inland, towards the hills, and the smoke-cloud above to stream away in a long pall, lit from below. The brilliance was if anything greater, and Stephen saw gulls drifting across between the sloop and the land, all heading for the fire. 'It will be attracting every living thing,' he reflected, with anxiety. 'What will be the conduct of the bats?'

Presently the top two-thirds was leaning over strongly, and the *Sophie* began to roll, with the waves slapping up against her larboard side.

Mr Watt broke from his long state of wonder to give the necessary orders, and coming back to the rail he said, 'They will have a hard pull, if this goes on.'

'Could we not bear down and pick them up?' asked Stephen.

'Not with this wind come round three points, and those old shoals off of the headland. No, sir.'

Another group of gulls passed low over the water. 'The flame is attracting every living thing for miles,' said Stephen.

'Never mind, sir,' said the bosun. 'It will be daylight in an hour or two, and they will pay no heed then, no heed at all.'

'It lights up the whole sky,' said Stephen.

It also lit up the deck of the *Formidable*, Captain Lalonde, a beautifully built French eighty-gun ship of the line wearing the flag of Rear-Admiral Linois at the mizen: she was seven or eight miles off shore, on her way from Toulon to Cadiz, and with her in line ahead sailed the rest of the squadron, the *Indomptable*, 80, Captain Moncousu, the *Desaix*, 74, Captain Christy-Pallière (a splendid sailer), and the *Muiron*, a thirty-eight-gun frigate that had until recently belonged to the Venetian Republic.

'Let us put in and see what is afoot,' said the admiral, a small, dark, round-headed, lively gentleman in red breeches, very much the seaman; and a few moments later the hoists of coloured lanterns ran up. The ships tacked in succession with a quiet efficiency that would have done credit to any navy afloat, for they were largely manned from the Rochefort squadron, and as well as being commanded by efficient professional officers they were filled with prime sailormen.

They ran inshore on the starboard tack with the wind one point free, bringing up the daylight, and when they were first seen from the *Sophie*'s deck they were greeted with joy. The boats had just reached the sloop after a long wearisome pull, and the French men-of-war were not sighted as early as they might have been: but sighted they were, in time, and at once every man forgot his hunger, fatigue, aching arms, and the cold and the wet, for the rumour instantly filled the sloop – 'Our galleons are coming up, hand over fist!' The wealth of the Indies, New Spain and Peru: gold ingots by way of their ballast. Ever since the crew had come to know of Jack's private intelligence about Spanish shipping there had been this persistent rumour of a galleon, and now it was fulfilled.

The splendid flame was still leaping up against the hills, though more palely as dawn broke all along the eastern sky; but in the cheerful animation of putting all to rights, of making everything ready for the chase, no one took notice of it any more – whenever a man could look up from his business his eyes darted eager, delighted glances over the three or four miles of sea at the *Desaix*, and at the *Formidable*, now some considerable way astern of her.

It was difficult to say just when all the delight vanished: certainly the captain's steward was still reckoning up the cost of opening a pub on the Hunstanton road when he brought Jack a cup of coffee on the quarter-deck, heard him say 'A horrid bad position, Mr Dalziel,' and noticed that the *Sophie* was no longer standing towards the supposed galleons but sailing from them as fast as she could possibly go, close-hauled, with everything she could set, including bonnets and even drabblers.

By this time the *Desaix* was hull-up – had been for some time – and so was the *Formidable*: behind the flagship there showed the topgallants and topsails of the *Indomptable*, and out to sea, a couple of miles to windward of her, the frigate's sails nicked the line of the sky. It was a horrid bad position; but the *Sophie* had the weather-gage, the breeze was uncertain and she might be taken for a merchant brig of no importance – something a busy squadron would not trouble with for more than an hour or so: they were not in very grave earnest, concluded Jack, lowering his glass. The behaviour of the press of men on the *Desaix*'s fo'c'sle, the by no means extraordinary spread of canvas, and countless indefinable trifles, persuaded him that she had not the air of a ship chasing in deadly earnest. But even so, how she slipped along! Her light, high, roomy, elegant round French bows and her beautifully cut, taut, flat sails brought her smoothly over the water, sailing as sweetly as the *Victory*. And she was well handled: she might have been running along a path ruled out upon the sea. He hoped to cross her bows before she had satisfied her curiosity about the fire on shore and so lead her such a dance of it that she would give it up – that the admiral would eventually make her signal of recall.

'Upon deck,' called Mowett from the masthead. 'The frigate has taken the packet.'

Jack nodded, sweeping his glass out to the miserable *Ventura* and back beyond the seventy-four to the flagship. He waited: perhaps five minutes. This was the crucial stage. And now signals did indeed break out aboard the *Formidable*, signals with a gun to emphasize them. But they were not signals of recall, alas. The *Desaix* instantly hauled her wind, no longer interested in the shore: her royals appeared, sheeted home and hoisted with a brisk celerity that made Jack round his mouth in a silent whistle. More canvas was appearing aboard the *Formidable* too; and now the *Indomptable* was coming up fast, all sails abroad, sweeping along with a freshening of the breeze.

It was clear that the packet had told what the *Sophie* was. But it was clear, too, that the rising sun was going to make the breeze still more uncertain, and perhaps swallow it up altogether. Jack glanced up at the *Sophie*'s spread: everything was there, of course; and at present everything was drawing in spite of the chancy wind. The master was at the con, Pram, the quartermaster, was at the wheel, getting everything out of her that she was capable of giving, poor fat old sloop. And every man was at his post, ready, silent and attentive: there was nothing for him to say or do; but his eye took in the threadbare, sagging Admiralty canvas, and his heart smote him cruelly for having wasted time – for not having bent his own new topsails, made of decent sailcloth, though unauthorized.

'Mr Watt,' he said, a quarter of an hour later, looking at the glassy patches of calm in the offing, 'stand by to out sweeps.'

A few minutes after this the *Desaix* hoisted her colours and opened with her bow-chasers; and as though the rumbling double crash had stunned the air, so the opulent curves of her sails collapsed, fluttered, swelled momentarily and slackened again. The *Sophie* kept the breeze another ten minutes, but then it died for her too. Before the way was off her – long before – all the sweeps that Malta had allowed her (four short, alas) were out and she was creeping steadily along, five men to each loom, and the long oars bending perilously under the urgent, concentrated heave and thrust, right into what would have been the wind's eye if there had still been any blowing. It was heavy, heavy work: and suddenly Stephen noticed that there was an officer to almost every sweep. He stepped forward to one of the few vacant places, and in forty minutes all the skin was gone from his palms.

'Mr Dalziel, let the starboard watch go to breakfast. Ah, there you are, Mr Ricketts: I believe we may serve out a double allowance of cheese – there will be nothing hot for a while.'

'If I may say so, sir,' said the purser with a pale leer, 'I fancy there will be something uncommon hot, presently.'

The starboard watch, summarily fed, took over the

labouring sweeps while their shipmates set to their biscuit, cheese and grog, with a couple of hams from the gun-room – a brief, uneasy meal, for out there the wind was ruffling the sea, and it had chopped round two points. The French ships picked it up first, and it was striking to see how their tall, high-reaching sails sent them running on little more than an air. The *Sophie*'s hard-won advance was wiped out in twenty minutes; and before her sails were drawing the *Desaix* already had a bow-wave, whiskers that could be seen from the quarter-deck. *Sophie*'s sails were drawing now, but this creeping pace would never do.

'In sweeps,' said Jack. 'Mr Day, throw the guns overboard.'

'Aye aye, sir,' said the gunner briskly, but his movements were strangely slow, unnatural and constrained as he sprung the capsquares, like those of a man walking along the edge of a cliff, by will-power alone.

Stephen came on deck again, his hands neatly mittened. He saw the team of the starboard brass quarter-deck four-pounder with crows and handspike in their hands and a common look of anxious, almost frightened concern, waiting for the roll: it came, and they gently urged their gleaming, highly-polished gun overboard – their pretty number four-teen over the side. Its splash coincided exactly with the fountain thrown up not ten yards away by a ball from the *Desaix*'s bow-chaser, and the next gun went overboard with less ceremony. Fourteen splashes at half a ton apiece; then the heavy carriages over the rail after them, leaving the slashed breeching and the unhooked tackles on either side of the gaping ports – a desolation to be seen.

He glanced forward, then astern, and understood the position: he pursed his lips and retired to the taffrail. The light-ened *Sophie* gathered speed minute by minute, and as all this weight had gone from well above the water-line she swam more upright – stiffer to the wind.

The first of the *Desaix*'s shot whipped through the top-gallantsail, but the next two pitched short. There was still time for manoeuvre – for plenty of manoeuvre. For one thing, reflected Jack, he would be very much surprised if the *Sophie* could not come about twice as quickly as the seventy-four. 'Mr Dalziel,' he said, 'we will go about and back again. Mr Marshall, let her have plenty of way on her.' It would be quite disastrous if the *Sophie* were to miss stays on her second turn: and these light airs were not what she liked – she never gave of her best until there was something of a sea running and at least one reef in her topsails.

'Ready about . . .' The pipe twittered, the sloop luffed up, came into the wind, stayed beautifully and filled on the larboard tack: her bowlines were as taut as harpstrings before the big seventy-four had even begun her turn.

The swing began, however; the *Desaix* was in stays; her yards were coming round; her checkered side began to show; and Jack, seeing the first hint of her broadside in his glass, called out, 'You had better go below, Doctor.' Stephen went, but no farther than the cabin; and there, craning from the stern-window, he saw the *Desaix*'s hull vanish in smoke from stem to stern, perhaps a quarter of a minute after the *Sophie* had begun her reverse turn. The massive broadside, nine hundred and twenty-eight pounds of iron, plunged into a wide area of sea away on the starboard beam and rather short, all except for the two thirty-six pound balls, which hummed ominously through the rigging, leaving a trail of limp, dangling cordage. For a moment it seemed that the *Sophie* might not stay – that she would fall impotently off, lose all her advantage and expose herself to another such salute, more exactly aimed. But a sweet puff of air in her backed headsails pushed her round and there she was on her former tack, gathering way before the *Desaix*'s heavy yards were firmly braced – before her first manoeuvre was complete at all.

The sloop had gained perhaps a quarter of a mile. 'But he will not let me do that again,' reflected Jack.

The *Desaix* was round on the starboard tack again, making good her loss; and all the while she fired steadily with her bowchasers, throwing her shot with remarkable accuracy as the range narrowed, just missing, or else clipping the sails, compelling the sloop to jig every few minutes, slightly losing speed each time. The *Formidable* was lying on the other tack to prevent the *Sophie* slipping through, and the *Indomptable* was running westwards, to haul her wind in half a mile or so for the same purpose. The *Sophie*'s pursuers were roughly in line abreast behind her and coming up fast as she ran sloping across their front. Already the eighty-gun flagship had yawed to fire one broadside at no unlikely distance; and the grim *Desaix*, making short boards, had done so on each turn. The bosun and his party were busy knotting, and there were some sad holes in the sails; but so far nothing essential had been struck, nor any man wounded.

'Mr Dalziel,' said Jack, 'start the stores over the side, if you please.'

The hatch-covers came off, the holds emptied into the sea – barrels of salt beef, barrels of pork, biscuit by the ton, peas, oatmeal, butter, cheese, vinegar. Powder, shot. They started their water and pumped it overboard. A twenty-four pounder hulled the *Sophie* low under the counter, and at once the pumps began gushing sea as well as fresh water.

'See how the carpenter is doing, Mr Ricketts,' said Jack.

'Stores overboard, sir,' reported the lieutenant.

'Very good, Mr Dalziel. Anchors away now, and spars. Keep only the kedge.'

'Mr Lamb says two foot and a half in the well,' said the midshipman, panting. 'But he has a comfortable plug in the shot-hole.'

Jack nodded, glancing back at the French squadron. There was no longer any hope of getting away from them close-hauled. But if he were to bear up, turning quickly and unexpectedly, he might be able to double back through their line; and then, with this breeze one or two points on her quarter, and with the help of the slight following sea, her lightness and her liveliness, why, she might live to see Gibraltar yet. She was so light now – a cockleshell – she might outrun them before the wind; and with any luck, turning briskly, she would gain a mile before the line-of-battle ships could gather way on the new tack. To be sure, she would have to survive a couple of broadsides as she passed through . . . But it was the only hope; and surprise was everything.

'Mr Dalziel,' he said, 'we will bear up in two minutes' time, set stuns'ls and run between the flagship and the seventy-four. We must do it smartly, before they are aware.' He addressed these words to the lieutenant, but they were instantly understood by all hands, and the topmen hurried to their places, ready to race up and rig out the studdingsail booms. The whole crowded deck was intensely alive, poised. 'Wait . . . wait,' murmured Jack, watching the *Desaix* coming up wide on the starboard beam. She was the one to beware of: she was terribly alert, and he longed to see her beginning to engage in some manoeuvre before he gave the word. To port lay the *Formidable*, overcrowded, no doubt, as flagships always were, and therefore less efficient in an emergency. 'Wait . . . wait,' he said again, his eyes fixed on the *Desaix*. But her steady approach never varied and when he had counted twenty he cried 'Right!'

The wheel span, the buoyant *Sophie* turned like a weathercock, swinging towards the *Formidable*. The flagship instantly let fly, but her gunnery was not up to the *Desaix*'s, and the hurried broadside lashed the sea where the sloop had been rather than where she was: the *Desaix*'s more deliberate offering was hampered by the fear of ricochets skipping as far as the admiral, and only half a dozen of her balls did any harm – the rest fell short.

The *Sophie* was through the line, not too badly mauled – certainly not disabled; her studdingsails were set and she was running fast, with the wind where she liked it best. The surprise had been complete, and now the two sides were drawing away from one another fast – a mile in the first five minutes. The *Desaix*'s second broadside, delivered at well over a thousand yards, showed the effects of irritation and precipitancy; a splintering crash forward marked the utter destruction of the elm-tree pump, but that was all. The flagship had obviously countermanded her second discharge, and for a while she kept to her course, close-hauled, as though the *Sophie* did not exist.

'We may have done it,' said Jack inwardly, leaning his hands on the taffrail and staring back along the *Sophie*'s lengthening wake. His heart was still beating with the tension of waiting for those broadsides, with the dread of what they might do to his *Sophie*; but now its beat had a different urgency. 'We may have done it,' he said again. Yet the words were scarcely formed in his mind before he saw a signal break out aboard the admiral, and the *Desaix* began to turn into the wind.

The seventy-four came about as nimbly as a frigate: her yards traversed as though by clockwork, and it was clear that everything was tallied and belayed with the perfect regularity of a numerous and thoroughly well trained crew. The *Sophie* had an excellent ship's company too, as attentive to their duty and as highly-skilled as Jack could wish; but nothing that they could do would make her move through the water at more than seven knots with this breeze, whereas in another quarter of an hour the *Desaix* was running at well over *eight without her studdingsails*. She was not going to trouble herself with setting them: when they saw that – when the minutes went by and it was clear that she had not the least intention of setting them – then the Sophies' hearts died within them.

Jack looked up at the sky. It looked down on him, a broad and meaningless expanse, with stray clouds passing over it – the wind would not die away that afternoon: night was still hours and hours away.

How many? He glanced at his watch. Fourteen minutes past ten. 'Mr Dalziel,' he said, 'I am going into my cabin. Call me if anything whatever occurs. Mr Richards, be so good as to tell Dr Maturin I should like to speak to him. And Mr Watt, let me have a couple of fathoms of logline and three or four belaying-pins.'

In his cabin he made a parcel of his lead-covered signal-book and some other secret papers, put the copper belaying-pins into the bag of mail, lashed its neck tight, called for his best coat and put his commission into its inner pocket. The words 'hereof nor you nor any of you may fail as you will answer the contrary at your peril' floated before his mind's eye, wonderfully clear; and Stephen came in. 'There you are, my dear fellow,' said Jack. 'Now, I am afraid that unless something very surprising happens we are going to be taken or sunk in the next half hour.' Stephen said, 'Just so,' and Jack continued, 'So if you have anything you particularly value perhaps it would be wise to entrust it to me.'

'They rob their prisoners, then?' asked Stephen.

'Yes: sometimes. I was stripped to the bone when the *Leander* was taken, and they stole our surgeon's instruments before he could operate on our wounded.'

'I will bring my instruments at once.'

'And your purse.'

'Oh, yes, and my purse.'

Hurrying back on deck, Jack looked astern. He would never have believed the seventy-four could have come up so far. 'Masthead!' he cried. 'What do you see?'

Seven ships of the line just ahead? Half the Mediterranean fleet? 'Nothing, sir,' answered the look-out slowly, after a most conscientious pause.

'Mr Dalziel, should I be knocked on the head, by any chance, these go over the side at the last moment, of course,' he said, tapping the parcel and the bag.

Already the strict pattern of the sloop's behaviour was growing more fluid. The men were quiet and attentive; the watch-glass turned to the minute; four bells in the afternoon watch rang with singular precision but there was a certain amount of movement, unreproved movement up and down the fore-hatch – men putting on their best clothes (two or three waistcoats together, and a shoregoing jacket on top), asking their particular officers to look after money or curious treasures, in the faint hope they might be preserved – Babbington had a carved whale's tooth in his hand, Lucock a Sicilian bull's pizzle. Two men had already managed to get drunk: some wonderfully hidden savings, no doubt.

'Why does he not fire?' thought Jack. The *Desaix*'s bow-chasers had been silent these twenty minutes, though for the last mile or so of their course the *Sophie* had been well within range. Indeed, by now she was in musket-shot, and the people in her bows could easily be told from one another: seamen, marines, officers – one man had a wooden leg. What splendidly cut sails, he reflected, and at the same time the answer to his question came: 'By God, he's going to riddle us with grape.' That was why he had silently closed the range. Jack moved to the side; leaning over the hammock-netting he dropped his packets into the sea and saw them sink.

In the bows of the *Desaix* there was a sudden movement, a response to an order. Jack stepped to the wheel, taking the spokes from the quartermaster's hands and looking back over his left shoulder. He felt the life of the sloop under his fingers: and he saw the *Desaix* begin to yaw. She answered her helm as quickly as a cutter, and in three heartbeats there were her thirty-seven guns coming round to bear. Jack heaved strongly at the wheel. The broadside's roar and the fall of the *Sophie*'s maintopgallantmast and foretopsail yard came almost together – in the thunder a hail of blocks, odd lengths of rope, splinters, the tremendous clang of a grape-shot striking the *Sophie*'s bell; and then a silence. The greater part of the seventy-four's roundshot had passed a few yards ahead of her stem: the scattering grape-shot had utterly wrecked her sails and rigging – had cut them to pieces. The next broadside must destroy her entirely.

'Clew up,' called Jack, continuing the turn that brought the *Sophie* into the wind. 'Bonden, strike the colours.'

Chapter Twelve

The cabin of a ship of the line and the cabin of a sloop of war differ in size, but they have the same delightful curves in common, the same inward-sloping windows; and in the case of the *Desaix* and the *Sophie* a good deal of the same quietly agreeable atmosphere. Jack sat gazing out of the seventy-four's stern-windows, out beyond the handsome gallery to Green Island and Cabrita Point, while Captain Christy-Pallière searched through his portfolio for a drawing he had made when he was last in Bath, a prisoner on parole.

Admiral Linois' orders had required him to join the Franco-Spanish fleet in Cadiz; and he would have carried them out directly if, on reaching the straits, he had not learnt that instead of one or two ships of the line and a frigate Sir James Saumarez had no less than six seventy-fours and an eighty-gun ship watching the combined squadron. This state of affairs called for some reflexion, so here he lay with his ships in Algeciras Bay, under the guns of the great Spanish batteries, over against the Rock of Gibraltar.

Jack was aware of all this – it was obvious, in any case – and as Captain Pallière muttered through his prints and drawings, 'Landsdowne Terrace, another view – Clifton – the Pump Room –' his mind's eye pictured messengers riding at a great pace between Algeciras and Cadiz; for the Spaniards had no semaphore. His bodily eye, however, looked steadily through the window panes at Cabrita Point, the extremity of the bay; and presently it saw the topgallant masts and pendant of a ship moving across, behind the neck of land. He watched it placidly for some two or three seconds before his heart gave a great leap, having recognized the pendant as British before his head had even begun to weigh the matter.

He darted a furtive look at Captain Pallière, who cried, 'Here we are! Laura Place. Number sixteen, Laura Place. This is where my Christy cousins always stay, when they come to Bath. And here, behind this tree – you could see it better, was it not for the tree – is my bedroom window!'

A steward came in and began to lay the table, for Captain Pallière not only possessed English cousins and the English language in something like perfection, but he had solid notions of what made a proper breakfast for a seafaring man: a pair of ducks, a dish of kidneys and a grilled turbot the size of a moderate cartwheel were preparing, as well as the usual ham, eggs, toast, marmalade and coffee. Jack looked at the water-colour as attentively as he could, and said, 'Your bedroom window, sir? You astonish me.'

Breakfast with Dr Ramis was a very different matter – austere, if not penitential: a bowl of milkless cocoa, a piece of bread with *a very little* oil. '*A very little* oil cannot do us much harm,' said Dr Ramis, who was a martyr to his liver. He was a severe and meagre, dusty man, with a harsh grey-ish-yellow face and deep violet rings under his eyes; he did not look capable of any pleasant emotion, yet he had both blushed and simpered when Stephen, upon being confided to his care as a prisoner-guest, had cried, 'Not the illustrious Dr Juan Ramis, the author of the *Specimen Animalium*?' Now they had just come back from visiting the *Desaix*'s sick-bay, a sparsely inhabited place, because of Dr Ramis' passion for curing other people's livers too by a low diet and no wine: it had a dozen of the usual diseases, a fair amount of pox, the *Sophie*'s four invalids and the French wounded from the recent action – three men bitten by Mr Dalziel's little bitch, whom they had presumed to caress: they were now confined upon suspicion of hydrophobia. In Stephen's view there was an error in his colleague's reasoning – a Scotch dog that bit a French seaman was not therefore and necessarily mad; though it might, in this particular case, be strangely wanting in discrimination. He kept this reflexion to himself, however, and said, 'I have been contemplating on emotion.'

'Emotion,' said Dr Ramis.

'Yes,' said Stephen. 'Emotion, and the *expression* of emotion. Now, in your fifth book, and in part of the sixth, you treat of emotion as it is shown by the cat, for example, the bull, the spider – I, too, have remarked the singular intermittent brilliance in the eyes of lycosida: have you ever detected a glow in those of the mantis?'

'Never, my dear colleague: though Busbequius speaks of it,' replied Dr Ramis with great complacency.

'But it seems to me that emotion and its expression are almost the same thing. Let us take your cat: now suppose we shave her tail, so that it cannot shall I say *perscopate* or bristle; suppose we attach a board to her back, so that it cannot arch; suppose we then exhibit a displeasing sight – a sportive dog, for instance. Now, she cannot express her emotions fully: Quaere: will she feel them fully? She will *feel* them, to be sure, since we have suppressed only the grossest manifestations; but will she feel them *fully*? Is not the arch, the bottle-brush, an integral part and not merely a potent reinforcement – though it is that too?'

Dr Ramis inclined his head to one side, narrowed his eyes and lips, and said, 'How can it be measured? It cannot be measured. It is a notion; a most valuable notion, I am sure; but, my dear sir, where is your measurement? It cannot be measured. Science is measurement – no knowledge without measurement.'

'Indeed it can,' cried Stephen eagerly. 'Come, let us take our pulses.' Dr Ramis pulled out his watch, a beautiful Bréguet with a centre seconds hand, and they both sat gravely counting. 'Now, dear colleague, pray be so good as to imagine – to imagine vehemently – that I have taken up your watch and wantonly flung it down; and I for my part will imagine that you are a very wicked fellow. Come, let us simulate the gestures, the expressions of extreme and violent rage.'

Dr Ramis' face took on a tetanic look; his eyes almost vanished; his head reached forward, quivering. Stephen's lips writhed back; he shook his fist and gibbered a little. A servant came in with a jug of hot water (no second bowls of cocoa were allowed).

'Now,' said Stephen Maturin, 'let us take our pulses again.'

'That pilgrim from the English sloop is mad,' the surgeon's servant told the second cook. 'Mad, twisted, tormented. And ours is not much better.'

'I will not say it is conclusive,' said Dr Ramis. 'But it is wonderfully interesting. We must try the addition of harsh reproachful words, cruel flings and bitter taunts, but without any physical motion, which could account for part of the increase. You intend it as a proof per contra of what you advance, I take it? Reversed, inverted, or *arsy-versy*, as you say in English. Most interesting.'

'Is it not?' said Stephen. 'My mind was led into this train of thought by the spectacle of our surrender, and of some others that I have seen. With your far greater experience of naval life, sir, no doubt you have been present at many more of these interesting occasions than I.'

'I imagine so,' said Dr Ramis. 'For example, I myself have had the honour of being your prisoner no less than four times. That,' he said with a smile, 'is one of the reasons why we are so very happy to have you with us. It does not happen quite as often as we could wish. Allow me to help you to another piece of bread – *half* a piece, with a very little garlic? Just a scrape of this wholesome, antiphlogistical garlic?'

'You are too good, dear colleague. And you have no doubt taken notice of the impassive faces of the captured men? It is always so, I believe?'

'Invariably. Zeno, followed by all his school.'

'And does it not seem to you that this suppression, this denial of the outward signs, and as I believe reinforcers if not actually ingredients of the distress – does it not seem to you that this stoical appearance of indifference in fact diminishes the pain?'

'It may well be so: yes.'

'I believe it is so. There were men aboard whom I knew intimately well, and I am morally certain that without this what one might call *ceremony of diminution*, it would have broken their . . .'

'Monsieur, monsieur, monsieur,' cried Dr Ramis' servant. 'The English are filling the bay!'

'On the poop they found Captain Pallière and his officers watching the manoeuvres of the *Pompée*, the *Venerable*, the *Audacious* and, farther off, the *Caesar*, the *Hannibal* and the *Spencer* as they worked in on the light, uncertain westerly airs, through the strong, shifting currents running between the Atlantic and the Mediterranean: they were all of them seventy-fours except for Sir James' flagship, the *Caesar*, and she carried eighty guns. Jack stood at some distance, with a detached look on his face; and at the farther rail there were the other quarter-deck Sophies, all making a similar attempt at decency.

'Do you think they will attack?' asked Captain Pallière, turning to Jack. 'Or do you think they will anchor off Gibraltar?'

'To tell you the truth, sir,' said Jack, looking over the sea at the towering Rock, 'I am quite sure they will attack. And you will forgive me for saying, that when you reckon up the forces in presence, it seems clear that we shall all be in Gibraltar tonight. I confess I am heartily glad of it, for it will allow me to repay a little of the great kindness I have met with here.'

There had been kindness, great kindness, from the moment they exchanged formal salutes on the quarter-deck of the *Desaix* and Jack stepped forward to give up his sword: Captain Pallière had refused to take it, and with the most obliging expressions about the *Sophie*'s resistance, had insisted upon his wearing it still.

'Well,' said Captain Pallière, 'let it not spoil our breakfast, at all events.'

'Signal from the Admiral, sir,' said a lieutenant. '*Warp in as close as possible to the batteries.*'

'Acknowledge and make it so, Dumanoir,' said the captain. 'Come, sir: gather we rose-pods while we may.'

It was a gallant effort, and they both of them talked away with a fine perseverance, their voices rising as the batteries on Green Island and the mainland began to roar and the thundering broadsides filled the bay; but Jack found that presently he was spreading marmalade upon his turbot and answering somewhat at random. With a high-pitched shattering crash the stern-windows of the *Desaix* fell in ruin; the padded locker beneath, Captain Pallière's best wine-bin, shot half across the cabin, projecting a flood of champagne, Madeira and broken glass before it; and in the midst of the wreckage trundled a spent ball from HMS *Pompée*.

'Perhaps we had better go on deck,' said Captain Pallière. It was a curious position. The wind had almost entirely dropped. The *Pompée* had glided on past the *Desaix* to anchor very close to the *Formidable*'s starboard bow, and she was pounding her furiously as the French flagship warped farther in through the treacherous shoals by means of cables on shore. The *Venerable*, for want of wind, had anchored about half a mile from the *Formidable* and the *Desaix* and was plying them briskly with her larboard broadside, while the *Audacious*, as far as he could see through clouds of smoke, was abreast of the *Indomptable*, some three or four hundred yards out. The *Caesar* and the *Hannibal* and the *Spencer* were doing their utmost to come up through the calms and the patchy gusts of west-north-west breeze: the French ships were firing steadily; and all the time the Spanish batteries, from the Torre del Almirante in the north right down to Green Island in the south, thundered in the background, while the big Spanish gunboats, invaluable in this calm, with their mobility and their expert knowledge of the reefs and the strong turning currents, swept out to rake the anchored enemy.

The rolling smoke drifted off the land, wafting now this way and now that, often hiding the Rock at the far end of the bay and the three ships out to sea; but at last a steadier breeze sprang up and the *Caesar*'s royals and topgallants appeared above the obscurity. She was wearing Admiral Saumarez' flag and she was flying the signal *anchor for mutual support*. Jack saw her pass the *Audacious* and swing broadside on to the *Desaix* within hailing distance: the cloud around her closed, hiding everything: there was a great stab as of lightning within the murk, a ball at head-height reaped a file of marines on the *Desaix*'s poop and the whole frame of the powerful ship shuddered with the force of the impact – at least half the broadside striking home.

'This is no place for a prisoner,' reflected Jack, and with a parting look of particular consideration at Captain Pallière, he hurried down on to the quarter-deck. He saw Babbington and young Ricketts standing doubtfully at the hances and called out, 'Get below, you two. This is no time to come it the old Roman – proper flats you would look, cut in half with our own chain-shot' – for chain was coming in now, shrieking and howling over the sea. He shepherded them down into the cable-tier and then made his way to the ward-room quarter-gallery – the officers' privy: it was not the safest place in the world, but there was little room for a spectator between the decks of a man-of-war in action, and he desperately wanted to see the course of the battle.

The *Hannibal* had anchored a little ahead of the *Caesar*, having run up the line of the French ships as they lay pointing north, and she was playing on the *Formidable* and the Santiago battery: the *Formidable* had almost ceased firing, which was as well, since for some reason the *Pompée* had swung round in the current – her spring shot away, perhaps – and she was head-on to the *Formidable*'s broadside, so that she could now only engage the shore-batteries and the gunboats with her starboard guns. The *Spencer* was still far out in the bay: but even so there were five ships of the line attacking three – everything was going very well, in spite of the Spanish artillery. And now through a gap in the smoke torn by the west-north-west breeze, Jack saw the *Hannibal* cut her cable, make sail towards Gibraltar and tack as soon as she had way enough, coming down close inshore to run between the French admiral and the land, and to cross his hawse and rake him. 'Just like the Nile,' thought Jack, and at that moment the *Hannibal* ran aground, very hard aground, and brought up all standing right opposite the heavy guns of the Torre del Almirante. The cloud closed again; and when at last it lifted boats were plying to and fro from the other English ships, and an anchor was carrying out; the *Hannibal* was roaring furiously at three shore-batteries, at the gunboats and, with her forward larboard guns and bowchasers, at the *Formidable*. Jack found that he was clasping his hands so hard that it needed strong determination to unknot them. The situation was not desperate – was not bad at all. The westerly air had fallen quite away, and now a right breeze was parting the heavy powder-fog, coming from the north-east. The *Caesar* cut her cable, and coming down round the *Venerable* and the *Audacious* she battered the *Indomptable*, astern of the Desaix, with the heaviest fire that had yet been heard. Jack could not make out what signal it was she had abroad, but he was certain it was *cut and wear*, together with *engage the enemy more closely*: there was a signal aboard the French admiral too – *cut and run aground* – for now, with a wind that would allow the English to come right in, it was better to risk wrecking than total disaster: furthermore, his was a signal easier to carry out than Sir James', for not only did the breeze stay with the French after it had left the English becalmed, but the French already had their warps out and boats by the dozen from the shore.

Jack heard the orders overhead, the pounding of feet, and the bay with its smoke and floating wreckage turned slowly before his eyes as the *Desaix* wore and ran straight for the land. She grounded with a thumping lurch that threw him off his balance, on a reef just in front of the town: the *Indomptable*, with her foretopmast gone, was already ashore on Green Island, or precious near. He could not see the French flagship at all from where he was, but she would certainly have grounded herself too.

And yet suddenly the battle went sour. The English ships did not come in, sweep the stranded Frenchmen clean and burn or destroy them far less tow them out; for not only did the breeze drop completely, leaving the *Caesar*, *Audacious* and *Venerable* with no steerage-way, but almost all the surviving boats of the squadron were busy towing the shattered *Pompée* towards Gibraltar. The Spanish batteries had been throwing red-hot shot for some time, and now the grounded French ships were sending their excellent gun-crews ashore by the hundred. Within a few minutes the fire of the shore guns increased enormously in volume and in accuracy. Even the poor *Spencer*, that had never managed to get up, suffered cruelly as she lay out there in the bay; the *Venerable* had lost her mizen topmast; and it looked as though the *Caesar* were on fire amidships. Jack could bear it no longer: he hurried up on deck in time to see a breeze spring up off the land and the squadron make sail on the starboard tack, standing eastwards for Gibraltar and leaving the dismasted, helpless *Hannibal* to her fate under the guns of the Torre del Almirante. She was firing still, but it could not last; her remaining mast fell, and presently her ensign came wavering down.

'A busy morning, Captain Aubrey,' said Captain Pallière, catching sight of him.

'Yes, sir,' said Jack. 'I hope we have not lost too many of our friends.' The *Desaix*'s quarter-deck was very ugly in patches, and there was a deep gutter of blood running along to the scupper under the wreckage of the poop-ladder. The hammock-netting had been torn to pieces; there were four dismounted guns abaft the mainmast, and the splinter-netting over the quarter-deck bowed and sagged under the weight of fallen rigging. She was canted three or four strakes on her rock, and the least hint of a sea would pound her to pieces.

'Many, many more than I could have wished,' said Captain Pallière. 'But the *Formidable* and the *Indomptable* have suffered worse – both their captains killed, too. What are they doing aboard the captured ship?'

The *Hannibal*'s colours were rising again. It was her own ensign, not the French flag: but it was the ensign reversed, flying with the union downwards. 'I suppose they forgot to take a tricolour when they went to board her and take possession,' observed Captain Pallière, turning to give orders for the heaving of his ship off the reef. Some time later he came back to the shattered rail, and staring out at the little fleet of boats that were pulling with all their might from Gibraltar and from the sloop *Calpe* towards the *Hannibal*, he said to Jack, 'You do not suppose they mean to retake the ship, do you? What *are* they about?'

Jack knew very well what they were about. In the Royal Navy the reversed ensign was an emphatic signal of distress: the *Calpe* and the people in Gibraltar, seeing it, had supposed the *Hannibal* meant she was afloat again and was begging to be towed off. They had filled every available boat with every available man – with unattached seamen and, above all, with the highly-skilled shipwrights and artificers of the dockyard. 'Yes,' he said, with all the open sincerity of one bluff seaman talking to another. 'I do. That is what they are about, for sure. But certainly if you put a shot across the bow of the leading cutter they will turn round – they imagine everything is over.'

'Ah, that's it,' said Captain Pallière. An eighteen-pounder creaked round and settled squarely on the nearest boat. 'But come,' said Captain Pallière, putting his hand on the lock and smiling at Jack, 'perhaps it would be better not to fire.' He countermanded the gun, and one by one the boats reached the *Hannibal*, where the waiting Frenchmen quietly led their crews below. 'Never mind,' said Captain Pallière, patting him on the shoulder. 'The Admiral is signalling: come ashore with me, and we will try to find decent quarters for you and your people, until we can heave off and refit.'

The quarters allotted to the *Sophie*'s officers, a house up at the back of Algeciras, had an immense terrace overlooking the bay, with Gibraltar to the left, Cabrita Point to the right and the dim land of Africa looming ahead. The first person Jack saw upon it, standing there with his hands behind his back and looking down on his own dismasted ship, was Captain Ferris of the *Hannibal*. Jack had been shipmates with him during two commissions and had dined with him only last year, but the post-captain was hardly recognizable as the same man – had aged terribly, and shrunk; and although they now fought the battle over again, pointing out the various manoeuvres, misfortunes and baffled intentions, he spoke slowly, with an odd uncertain hesitation, as though what had happened were not quite real, or had not happened to him.

'So you were aboard the *Desaix*, Aubrey,' he said, after a while. 'Was she much cut up?'

'Not so badly as to be disabled, sir, as far as I could collect. She was not much holed below the waterline, and none of her lower masts was badly wounded: if she don't bilge they will put her to rights presently – she has an uncommon seamanlike set of officers and men.'

'How many did she lose, do you suppose?'

'A good many, I am sure – but here is my surgeon, who certainly knows more about it than I do. May I name Dr Maturin? Captain Ferris. My God, Stephen!' he cried, starting back. He was tolerably used to carnage, but he had never seen anything quite like this. Stephen might have come straight out of a busy slaughterhouse. His sleeves, the whole of the front of his coat up to his stock and the stock itself were deeply soaked, soaked through and through and stiff with drying blood. So were his breeches: and wherever his linen showed it, too, was dark red-brown.

'I beg pardon,' he said, 'I should have shifted my clothes, but it seems that my chest was shattered – destroyed entirely.'

'I can let you have a shirt and some breeches,' said Captain Ferris. 'We are much of a size.' Stephen bowed.

'You have been lending the French surgeons a hand?' said Jack.

'Just so.'

'Was there a great deal to do?' asked Captain Ferris.

'About a hundred killed and a hundred wounded,' said Stephen.

'We had seventy-five and fifty-two,' said Captain Ferris.

'You belong to the *Hannibal*, sir?' asked Stephen.

'I did, sir,' said Captain Ferris. 'I struck my colours,' he said in a wondering tone and at once began to sob, staring open-eyed at them – at one and then at the other.

'Captain Ferris,' said Stephen, 'pray tell me, how many mates has your surgeon? And have they all their instruments? I am going down to the convent to see your wounded as soon as I have had a bite, and I dispose of two or three sets.'

'Two mates, sir,' said Captain Ferris. 'As for their instruments I fear I cannot say. It is good in you, sir – most Christian – let me fetch you this shirt and breeches – you must be damned uncomfortable.' He came back with a bundle of clean clothes wrapped in a dressing-gown, suggested that Dr Maturin might operate in the gown, as he had seen done after the First of June, when there was a similar shortage of clean linen. And during their odd, scrappy meal, brought to them by staring, pitiful maidservants, with red and yellow sentries guarding the door, he said, 'After you have looked to my poor fellows, Dr Maturin – if you have any benevolence left after you have looked to them, I say, it would be a charitable act to prescribe me something in the poppy or mandragora line. I was strangely upset today, I must confess, and I need what is it? The knitting up of ravelled care? And what is more, since we are likely to be exchanged in a few days, I shall have a court-martial on top of it all.'

'Oh, as for that, sir,' cried Jack, throwing himself back in his chair, 'you cannot possibly have any misgivings – never was a clearer case of –'

'Don't you be so sure, young man,' said Captain Ferris. 'Any court-martial is a perilous thing, whether you are in the right or the wrong – justice has nothing much to do with it. Remember poor Vincent of the *Weymouth*: remember Byng – shot for an error of judgment and for being unpopular with the mob. And think of the state of feeling in Gibraltar and at home just now – six ships of the line beaten off by three French, and one taken – a defeat, and the *Hannibal* taken.'

This degree of apprehension in Captain Ferris seemed to Jack a kind of wound, the result of lying hard aground under the fire of three shore-batteries, a ship of the line and a dozen heavy gun-boats, and of being terribly hammered for hours, dismasted and helpless. The same thought, in a slightly different shape, occurred to Stephen. 'What is this trial of which he speaks?' he asked later. 'Is it factual, or imaginary?'

'Oh, it is factual enough,' said Jack.

'But he has done nothing amiss, surely? No one can pretend he ran away or did not fight as hard as ever he could.'

'But he lost his ship. Every captain of a King's ship that is lost must stand his trial at court-martial.'

'I see. A mere formality in his case, no doubt.'

'In *his* case, yes,' said Jack. '*His* anxiety is unfounded – a sort of waking nightmare, I take it.'

But the next day, when he went down with Mr Dalziel to see the *Sophie*'s crew in their disaffected church and to tell them of the flag of truce from the Rock, it seemed to him a little more reasonable – less of a sick fantasy. He told the Sophies that both they and the Hannibals were to be exchanged – that they should be in Gibraltar for dinner – dried peas and salt horse for dinner, no more of these foreign messes – and although he smiled and waved his hat at the roaring cheers that greeted his news, there was a black shadow in the back of his mind.

The shadow deepened as he crossed the bay in the *Caesar*'s barge; it deepened as he waited in the antechamber to report himself to the Admiral. Sometimes he sat and sometimes he walked up and down the room, talking to other officers as people with urgent business were admitted by the secretary. He was surprised to receive so many congratulations on the *Cacafuego* action – it seemed so long ago now as almost to belong to another life. But the congratulations (though both generous and kind) were a little on the cursory side, for the atmosphere in Gibraltar was one of severe and general condemnation, dark depression, strict attention to arduous work, and a sterile wrangling about what ought to have been done.

When at last he was received he found Sir James almost as old and changed as Captain Ferris; the Admiral's strange, heavy-lidded eyes looked at him virtually without expression as he made his report; there was not a word of interruption, not a hint of praise or blame, and this made Jack so uneasy that if it had not been for a list of heads he had written on a card that he kept in the palm of his hand, like a schoolboy, he would have deviated into rambling explanations and excuses. The Admiral was obviously very tired, but his quick mind extracted the necessary facts and he noted them down on a slip of paper. 'What do you make of the state of the French ships, Captain Aubrey?' he asked.

'The *Desaix* is now afloat, sir, and pretty sound; so is the *Indomptable*. I do not know about the *Formidable* and *Hannibal*, but there is no question of their being bilged; and in Algeciras the rumour is that Admiral Linois sent three officers to Cadiz yesterday and another early this morning to beg the Spaniards and Frenchmen there to come round and fetch him out.'

Admiral Saumarez put his hand to his forehead. He had honestly believed they would never float again, and he had said as much in his report. 'Well, thank you, Captain Aubrey,' he said, after a moment, and Jack stood up. 'I see you are wearing your sword,' observed the Admiral.

'Yes, sir. The French captain was good enough to give it back to me.'

'Very handsome in him, though I am sure the compliment was quite deserved; and I have little doubt the court-martial will do the same. But, you know, it is not quite etiquette to ship it until then: we will arrange your business as soon as possible – poor Ferris will have to go home, of course, but we can see to you here. You are only on parole, I believe?'

'Yes, sir: waiting for an exchange.'

'What a sad bore. I could have done with your help – the squadron is in such a state . . . Well, good day to you, Captain Aubrey,' he said, with a hint of a smile, or at least a lightening in his expression. 'As you know, of course, you are under nominal arrest, so pray be discreet.'

He had known it perfectly well, of course, in theory; but the actual words were a blow to his heart, and he walked through the crowded, busy streets of Gibraltar in a state of quite remarkable unhappiness. When he reached the house where he was staying, he unbuckled his sword, made an ungainly parcel of it and sent it down to the Admiral's secretary with a note. Then he went for a walk, feeling strangely naked and unwilling to be seen.

The officers of the *Hannibal* and the *Sophie* were on parole: that is to say, until they were exchanged for French prisoners of equal rank they were bound in honour to do nothing against France or Spain – they were merely prisoners in more agreeable surroundings.

The days that followed were singularly miserable and lonely – lonely, although he sometimes walked with Captain Ferris, sometimes with his own midshipmen and sometimes with Mr Dalziel and his dog. It was strange and unnatural to be cut off from the life of the port and the squadron at such a moment as this, when every able-bodied man and a good many who should never have got out of their beds at all, were working furiously to repair their ships – an active hive, an ant-hill down below, and up here on these heights, on the thin grass and the bare rock between the Moorish wall and the tower above Monkey's Cove, solitary self-communing, doubt, reproach and anxiety. He had looked through all the Gazettes, of course, and there was nothing about either the *Sophie*'s triumph or her disaster: one or two garbled accounts in the newspapers and a paragraph in the Gentleman's Magazine that made it seem like a surprise attack, that was all. As many as a dozen promotions in the Gazettes, but none for him or Pullings and it was a fair bet that the news of the *Sophie*'s capture had reached London at about the same time as that of the *Cacafuego*. If not before: for the good news (supposing it to have been lost – supposing it to have been in the bag he himself sank in ninety fathoms off Cape Roig) could only have come in a dispatch from Lord Keith, far up the Mediterranean, among the Turks. So there could not be any promotion now until after the court-martial – no such thing as the promotion of prisoners, ever. And what if the trial went wrong? His conscience was very far from being perfectly easy. If Harte had meant this, he had been devilish successful; and he, Jack, had been a famous greenhorn, an egregious flat. Was such malignity possible? Such cleverness in a mere horned scrub? He would have liked to put this to Stephen, for Stephen had a head-piece; and Jack, almost for the first time in his life, was by no means sure of his perfect comprehension, natural intelligence and penetration. The Admiral had not congratulated him: could that conceivably mean that the official view was . . . ? But Stephen had no notion of any parole that would keep him out of the naval hospital: the squadron had had more than two hundred men wounded, and he spent almost all his time there. 'You go a-walking,' he said. 'Do for all love go walking up very steep heights – traverse the Rock from end to end – traverse it again and again on an empty stomach. You are an obese subject; your hams quiver as you go. You must weigh sixteen or even seventeen stone.'

'And to be sure I do sweat like a mare in foal,' he reflected, sitting under the shade of a boulder, loosening his waistband and mopping himself. In an attempt at diverting his mind he privately sang a ballad about the Battle of the Nile:

> *We anchored alongside of them like lions bold and free.*
> *When their masts and shrouds came tumbling down, what*
> *   a glorious sight to see!*
> *Then came the bold* Leander, *that noble fifty-four,*
> *And on the bows of the* Franklin *she caused her guns to*
> *   roar;*
> *Gave her a dreadful drubbing, boys, and did severely*
> *   maul;*
> *Which caused them loud for quarter cry and down French*
> *   colours haul.*

The tune was charming, but the inaccuracy vexed him: the poor old *Leander* had fifty-two guns, as he knew very well, having directed the fire of eight of them. He turned to another favourite naval song:

> *There happened of late a terrible fray,*
> *Begun upon our St James's day,*
> *With a thump, thump, thump, thump, thump,*
> *Thump, thump a thump, thump.*

An ape on a rock no great way off threw a turd at him, quite unprovoked; and when he half rose in protest it shook its wizened fist and gibbered so furiously that he sank down again, so low were his spirits.

'Sir, sir!' cried Babbington, tearing up the slope, scarlet with hailing and climbing. 'Look at the brig! Sir, look over the point!'

The brig was the *Pasley*: they knew her at once. The hired brig *Pasley*, a fine sailer, and she was crowding sail on the brisk north-west breeze fit to carry everything away.

'Have a look, sir,' said Babbington, collapsing on the grass

in a singularly undisciplined manner and handing up a little
brass spyglass. The tube only magnified weakly, but at once
the signal flying from the *Pasley*'s masthead leapt out clear
and plain – *enemy in sight*.

'And there they are, sir,' said Babbington, pointing to a
glimmer of topsails over the dark curve of the land beyond
the end of the Gut.

'Come on,' cried Jack, and began labouring up the hill,
gasping and moaning, running as fast as he could for the
tower, the highest point on the Rock. There were some
masons up there, working on the building, an officer of the
garrison artillery with a splendid great telescope, and some
other soldiers. The gunner very civilly offered Jack his glass:
Jack leant it on Babbington's shoulder, focused carefully,
gazed, and said, 'There's the *Superb*. And the *Thames*. Then
two Spanish three-deckers – one's the *Real Carlos*, I am
almost sure: vice-admiral's flagship, in any event. Two seventy-fours. No, a seventy-four and probably an eighty-gun
ship.'

'*Argonauta*,' said one of the masons.

'Another three-decker. And three frigates, two French.'

They sat there silently watching the steady, calm procession, the *Superb* and the *Thames* keeping their stations
just a mile ahead of the combined squadron as they came
up the Gut, and the huge, beautiful Spanish first-rates
moving along with the inevitability of the sun. The masons
went off to their dinner: the wind backed westerly. The
shadow of the tower swept through twenty-five degrees.

When they had rounded Cabrita Point the *Superb* and the
frigate carried straight on for Gibraltar, while the Spaniards
hauled their wind for Algeciras; and now Jack could see that
their flagship was indeed the *Real Carlos*, of a hundred and
twelve guns, one of the most powerful ships afloat; that one
of the other three-deckers was of the same force; and the
third of ninety-six. It was a most formidable squadron –
four hundred and seventy-four great guns, without counting
the hundred odd of the frigates – and the ships were surpris-

ingly well handled. They anchored over there under the guns of the Spanish batteries as trimly as though they were to be reviewed by the King.

'Hallo, sir,' said Mowett. 'I thought you would be up here. I have brought you a cake.'

'Why, thankee, thankee,' cried Jack. 'I am devilish hungry, I find.' He at once cut a slice and ate it up. How extraordinarily the Navy had changed, he thought, cutting another: when he was a midshipman it would never in a thousand years have occurred to him to speak to his captain, far less bring him cakes; and if it had occurred to him he would never have done so, for fear of his life.

'May I share your rock, sir?' asked Mowett, sitting down. 'They have come to fetch the Frenchmen out, I do suppose. Do you think we shall go for 'em, sir?'

'*Pompée* will never be fit for sea these three weeks,' said Jack dubiously. '*Caesar* is cruelly knocked about and must get all her new masts in: but even if they can get her ready before the enemy sail, that only gives us five of the line against ten, or nine if you leave the *Hannibal* out – three hundred and seventy-six guns to their seven hundred odd, both their squadrons combined. We are short-handed, too.'

'*You* would go for them, would not you, sir?' said Babbington; and both the midshipmen laughed very cheerfully.

Jack gave a meditative jerk of his head, and Mowett said, '*As when enclosing harpooners assail, In hyperborean seas the slumbering whale.* What huge things these Spaniards are. The Caesars have petitioned to be allowed to work all day and night, sir. Captain Brenton says they may work all day, but only watch and watch at night. They are piling up juniper-wood fires on the mole to have light.'

It was by the light of these juniper fires that Jack ran into Captain Keats of the *Superb*, with two of his lieutenants and a civilian. After the first surprise, greetings, introductions, Captain Keats asked him to take supper aboard – they were going back now – only a scrap-meal, of course, but some genuine Hampshire cabbage brought straight from Captain Keats' own garden by the *Astraea*.

'It is very kind of you indeed, sir; most grateful, but I believe I must beg to be excused. I had the misfortune to lose the *Sophie*, and I dare say you will be sitting on me presently, together with most of the other post-captains.'

'Oh,' said Captain Keats, suddenly embarrassed.

'Captain Aubrey is quite right,' said the civilian in a sententious voice; and at that moment an urgent messenger called Captain Keats to the Admiral.

'Who was that ill-looking son of a bitch in the black coat?' asked Jack, as another friend, Heneage Dundas of the *Calpe*, came down the steps.

'Coke? Why, he's the new judge-advocate,' said Dundas, with a queer look. Or was it a queer look? The trick of the flames could give anyone a queer look. The words of the tenth Article of War came quite unbidden into his mind: *If any person in the fleet shall cowardly yield or cry for quarter, being convicted thereof by the sentence of a court-martial, shall suffer death.*

'Come and split a bottle of port with me at the Blue Posts, Heneage,' said Jack, drawing his hand across his face.

'Jack,' said Dundas, 'there is nothing I should like better, upon my oath; but I have promised Brenton to give him a hand. I am on my way this minute – there is the rest of my party staying for me.' He hurried off into the brighter light along the mole, and Jack drifted away: dark steep alleys, low brothels, smells, squalid drinking-shops.

The next day, under the lee of the Charles V wall, with his telescope resting on a stone, and with a certain sense of spying or eavesdropping, he watched the *Caesar* (no longer the flagship) being eased alongside the sheer-hulk to receive her new lower mainmast, a hundred feet long and more than a yard across. She got it in so quickly that the top was over before noon, and neither it nor the deck could be seen for the number of men working on the rigging.

The day after that, still from his melancholy height, full

of guilt at his idleness and the intense, ordered busyness below, particularly about the *Caesar*, he saw the *San Antonio*, a French seventy-four that had been delayed, come in from Cadiz and anchor among her friends at Algeciras.

The next day there was great activity on the far side of the bay – boats plying to and fro among the twelve ships of the combined fleet, new sails bending, supplies coming aboard, hoist after hoist of signals aboard the flagships; and all this activity was reproduced in Gibraltar, with even greater zeal. There was no hope for the *Pompée*, but the *Audacious* was almost entirely ready, while the *Venerable*, the *Spencer* and, of course, the *Superb*, were in fighting trim, and the *Caesar* was so near the final stages of her refitting that it was just possible she might be fit for sea in twenty-four hours.

During the night a hint of a Levanter began to breathe from the east: this was the wind the Spaniards were praying for, the wind that would carry them straight out of the Gut, once they had weathered Cabrita Point, and waft them up to Cadiz. At noon the first of their three-deckers loosed her foretopsail and began to move out of the crowded road; then the others followed her. They were weighing and coming out at intervals of ten minutes or a quarter of an hour to their rendezvous off Cabrita Point. The *Caesar* was still tied up alongside the mole, taking in her powder and shot, with officers, men, civilians and garrison soldiers working with silent concentrated earnestness.

At length the whole of the combined fleet was under way: even their jury-rigged capture, the *Hannibal*, towed by the French frigate *Indienne*, was creeping out to the point. And now the shrill squealing fife and fiddle broke out aboard the *Caesar* as her people manned the capstan bars and began to warp her out of the mole, taut, trim and ready for war. A thundering cheer ran all along the crowded shore, from the batteries, walls and hillside black with spectators; and when it died away there was the garrison band playing *Come cheer up my lads, 'tis to glory we steer* as loud as ever they could go, while the *Caesar*'s marines answered with *Britons strike home*. Through the cacophony the fife could still be heard: it was most poignantly moving.

As the *Caesar* passed under the stern of the *Audacious* she hoisted Sir James's flag once more and immediately afterwards heaved out the signal *weigh and prepare for battle*. The execution of this was perhaps the most beautiful naval manoeuvre Jack had ever seen: they had all been waiting for the signal, they were all waiting and ready with their cables up and down; and in an unbelievably short space of time the anchors were catted and the masts and yards broke out in tall white pyramids of sail as the squadron, five ships of the line, two frigates, a sloop and a brig, moved out of the lee of the Rock and formed in line ahead on the larboard tack.

Jack pushed his way out of the tight-packed crowd on the mile-head, and he was half-way to the hospital, meaning to persuade Stephen to mount the Rock with him, when he saw his friend running swiftly through the deserted streets.

'Has she got out of the mole?' cried Stephen, at a considerable distance. 'Has the battle begun?' Reassured, he said, 'I would not have missed it for a hundred pounds: that damned fellow in Ward B and his untimely fancies – a fine time to cut one's throat, good lack a-day.'

'There's no hurry – no one will touch a gun for hours,' said Jack. 'But I am sorry you did not see the *Caesar* warping out: it was a glorious sight. Come up the hill with me, and you will have a perfect view of both squadrons. Do come. I will call in at the house and pick up a couple of telescopes; and a cloak – it grows cold at night.'

'Very well,' said Stephen, after a moment's thought. 'I can leave a note. And we will fill our pockets with ham: then we shall have none of your wry looks and short answers.'

'There they lay,' said Jack, pausing for breath again. 'Still on the larboard tack.'

'I see them perfectly well,' said Stephen, a hundred yards

ahead and climbing fast. 'Pray do not stop so often. Come on.'

'Oh Lord, oh Lord,' said Jack at last, sinking under his familiar rock. 'How quick you go. Well, there they are.'

'Aye, aye, there they are: a noble spectacle, indeed. But why are they standing over towards Africa? And why only courses and topsails, with this light breeze? That one is even backing her maintopsail.'

'She's the *Superb*; she does so to keep her station and not over-run the Admiral, for she is a *superb* sailer, you know, the best in the fleet. Did you hear that?'

'Yes.'

'It was rather clever, I thought – witty.'

'Why do they not make sail and bear up?'

'Oh, there is no question of a head-on encounter – probably no action at all by daylight. It would be downright madness to attack their line of battle at this time. The Admiral wants the enemy to get out of the bay and into the Gut, so there will be no doubling back and so that he will have sea-room to make a dash at them: once they get well into the offing I dare say he will try to cut off their rear if this wind holds; and it looks like a true three-day Levanter. Look, there the *Hannibal* cannot weather the point. Do you see? She will be on shore directly. The frigate is making sad work of it. They are towing her head round. Handsomely does it – there we are – she fills – set the jib, man – just so. She is going back.'

They sat watching in silence, and all around them they could hear other groups, scattered all over the surface of the Rock – remarks about the strengthening of the wind, the probable strategy to be observed, the exact broadside weight of metal on either side, the high standard of French gunnery, the currents to be met with off Cape Trafalgar.

With a good deal of backing and filling, the combined fleet, now nine ships of the line and three frigates, had formed their line of battle, with the two great Spanish first-rates in the rear, and now they bore away due westwards before the freshening breeze.

A little before this the British squadron had worn together by signal, and now they were on the starboard tack, under easy sail. Jack's telescope was firmly on the flagship, and as soon as he saw the hoist running up he murmured, 'Here we go.'

The signal appeared: at once the press of canvas almost doubled, and within a few minutes the squadron was racing away after the French and the Spaniards, dwindling in his view – growing smaller every moment as he watched.

'Oh God, how I wish I were with them,' said Jack, with a groan of something like despair. And some ten minutes later, 'Look, there's *Superb* going ahead – the Admiral must have hailed her.' The *Superb*'s topgallant studdingsails appeared as though by magic, port and starboard. 'How she flies,' said Jack, lowering his glass and wiping it: but the dimness was neither his tears nor any dirt on the glass – it was the fading of the day. Down below it had already gone; a tawny late evening filled the town, and lights were breaking out all over it. Presently lanterns could be seen creeping up the Rock to the high points from which perhaps the battle might be seen; and over the water Algeciras began to twinkle, a low-lying curve of lights.

'What do you say to some of that ham?' said Jack.

Stephen said he thought ham might prove a valuable preservative against the falling damps; and when they had been eating for some time in the darkness, with their pocket-handkerchiefs spread upon their knees, he suddenly observed, 'They tell me I am to be tried for the loss of the *Sophie*.'

Jack had not thought of the court-martial since early that morning, when it became certain that the combined fleet was coming out: now it came back to him with an extraordinarily unpleasant shock, quite closing his stomach. However, he only replied, 'Who told you that? The physical gentlemen at the hospital, I suppose?'

'Yes.'

'Theoretically they are right, of course. The thing is officially called the trial of the captain, officers and ship's company; and they formally ask the officers if they have any complaints to make against the captain, and the captain whether he has any to make against the officers; but obviously in this it is only my conduct that is in question. You have nothing to worry about, I do assure you, upon my word and honour. Nothing at all.'

'Oh, I shall plead guilty at once,' said Stephen. 'And I shall add that I was sitting in the powder-magazine with a naked light at the time, imagining the death of the King, wasting my medical stores, smoking tobacco and making a fraudulent return of the portable soup. What solemn nonsense it is' – laughing heartily – 'I am surprised so sensible a man as you should attribute any importance to the matter.'

'Oh, I do not mind it,' cried Jack. 'How you lie,' said Stephen affectionately, but within his own bosom. After a longish pause Jack said, 'You do not rate post-captains and admirals very high among intelligent beings, I believe? I have heard you say some tolerably severe things about admirals, and great men in general.'

'Why, to be sure, something sad seems to happen to your great men and your admirals, with age, pretty often: even to your post-captains. A kind of atrophy, a withering-away of the head and the heart. I conceive it may arise from . . .'

'Well,' said Jack, laying his hand upon his friend's dimly-seen shoulder in the starlight, 'how would you like to place your life, your profession and your good name between the hands of a parcel of senior officers?'

'Oh,' cried Stephen. But what he had to say was never heard, for away on the horizon towards Tangiers there was a flash flash-flash, not unlike the repeated dart of lightning. They leapt to their feet and cupped their ears to the wind to catch the distant roar; but the wind was too strong and presently they sat down again, fixing the western sea with their telescopes. They could distinctly make out two sources, between twenty and twenty-five miles away, scarcely any distance apart – not above a degree: then three: then a fourth and fifth, and then a growing redness that did not move.

'There is a ship on fire,' said Jack in horror, his heart pumping so hard that he could scarcely keep the steady deep-red glow in his object-glass. 'I hope to God it is not one of ours. I hope to God they drown the magazines.'

An enormous flash lit the sky, dazzled them, put out the stars; and nearly two minutes later the vast solemn long rumbling boom of explosion reached them, prolonged by its own echo off the African shore.

'What was it?' asked Stephen at last.

'The ship blew up,' said Jack: his mind was filled with the Battle of the Nile and the long moment when *L'Orient* exploded, all brought back to him with extraordinary vividness – a hundred details he thought forgotten, some very hideous. And he was still among those memories when a second explosion shattered the darkness, perhaps even greater than the first.

After this, nothing. Not the remotest light, not a gunflash. The wind increased steadily, and the rising moon put out the smaller stars. After a while some of the lanterns began to go down; others remained, and some even climbed higher still; Jack and Stephen stayed where they were. Dawn found them under their rock, with Jack steadily sweeping the Gut – calm now, and deserted – and Stephen Maturin fast asleep, smiling.

Not a word, not a sign: a silent sea, a silent sky and the wind grown treacherous again – all round the compass. At half-past seven Jack saw Stephen back to the hospital, revived himself with coffee and climbed again.

In his journeys up and down he came to know every wind in the path, and the rock against which he leaned was as familiar as an old coat. It was when he was going up after tea on Thursday, with his supper in a sailcloth bag, that he saw Dalziel, Boughton of the *Hannibal* and Marshall bounding down the steep slope so fast that they could not stop: they called out '*Calpe*'s coming in, sir,' and blundered on, with the little dog running round and round them, very nearly bringing them down, and barking with delight.

Heneage Dundas of the fast-sailing sloop *Calpe* was an amiable young man, much caressed by those who knew him for his shining parts and particularly for his skill in the mathematics; but never before had he been the best-loved man in Gibraltar. Jack broke through the crowd surrounding him with brutal force and an unscrupulous use of his weight and his elbows: five minutes later he broke out again and ran like a boy through the streets of the town.

'Stephen,' he cried, bursting open the door, his shining face far larger and higher than usual. 'Victory! Come out at once and drink to a victory! Give you joy of a famous victory, old cock,' he cried, shaking him terribly by the hand. 'Such a magnificent fight.'

'Why, what happened?' asked Stephen, slowly wiping his scalpel and covering up his Moorish hyena.

'Come on, and I will tell you as we drink,' said Jack, leading him into the street full of people, all talking eagerly, laughing, shaking hands and beating one another on the back: down by the New Mole there was the sound of cheering. 'Come on. I have a thirst like Achilles, no, Andromache. It is Keats has the glory of the day – Keats has borne the bell away. Ha, ha, ha! That was a famous line, was it not? In here. Pedro! Bear a hand there! Pedro, champagne. Here's to the victory! Here's to Keats and the *Superb*! Here's to Admiral Saumarez! Pedro, another bottle. Here's to the victory again! Three times three! Huzza!'

'You would oblige me extremely by just giving the news,' said Stephen. 'With all the details.'

'I don't know all the details,' said Jack, 'but this is the gist of it. That noble fellow Keats – you remember how we saw him shoot ahead? – came up with their rear, the two Spanish first-rates, just before midnight. He chose his moment, clapped his helm a lee and dashed between 'em firing both broadsides – a seventy-four taking on two first-rates! He shot straight on, leaving his smoke-cloud between 'em as thick as peasoup; and each, firing into it, hit the other; and so the *Real Carlos* and the *Hermenegildo* went for each other like fury in the dark. Someone, the *Superb* or the *Hermenegildo*, had knocked away the *Real Carlos'* fore-topmast, and it was her topsail that fell over the guns and took fire. And after a while the *Real Carlos* fell on board the *Hermenegildo* and fired her too. Those were the two explosions we saw, of course. But while they were burning Keats had pushed on to engage the *San Antonio*, who hauled her wind and fought back like a rare plucked 'un; but she had to strike in half an hour for, do you see, *Superb* was firing three broadsides to her two, and pointing 'em straight. So Keats took possession of her; and the rest of the squadron chased as hard as ever they could to the north-north-west in a gale of wind. They very nearly took the *Formidable*, but she just got into Cadiz; and we very nearly lost the *Venerable*, dismasted and aground; but they got her off and she is on her way back now, jury-rigged, with a stuns'l boom for a mizenmast, ha, ha, ha! – There's Dalziel and Marshall going by. Ahoy! Dalziel ahoy! Marshall! Ahoy there! Come and drink a glass to the victory!'

The flag broke out aboard the *Pompée*; the gun boomed; the captains assembled for the court-martial.

It was a very grave occasion, and in spite of the brilliance of the day, the abounding cheerfulness on shore and the deep chuckling contentment aboard, each post-captain put away his gaiety and came up the side as solemn as a judge, to be greeted with all due ceremony and led into the great cabin by the first lieutenant.

Jack was already aboard, of course; but his was not the first case to be dealt with. Waiting there in the screened-off larboard part of the dining-cabin there was a chaplain, a hunted-looking man who paced up and down, sometimes making private ejaculations and dashing his hands together. It was pitiful to see how carefully he was dressed, and how he had shaved until the blood came; for if half the general report of his conduct was true there was no hope for him at all.

The moment the next gun sounded the master-at-arms took the chaplain away, and there was a pause, one of those great lapses of time that presently come to have no flow at all, but grow stagnant or even circular in motion. The other officers talked in low voices – they, too, were dressed with particular attention, in the exact uniform regularity that plenty of prize-money and the best Gibraltar outfitters could provide. Was it respect for the court? For the occasion? A residual sense of guilt, a placating of fate? They spoke quietly, equably, glancing at Jack from time to time.

They had each received an official notification the day before, and for some reason each had brought it with him, folded or rolled. After a while Babbington and Ricketts took to changing all the words they could into obscenities, secretly in a corner, while Mowett wrote and scratched out on the back of his, counting syllables on his fingers and silently mouthing. Lucock stared straight ahead of him into vacancy. Stephen intently watched the busy unsatisfied questing of a shining dark-red rat-flea on the chequered sailcloth floor.

The door opened. Jack returned abruptly to this world, picked up his laced hat and walked into the great cabin, ducking his head as he came in, with his officers filing in behind him. He came to a halt in the middle of the room, tucked his hat under his arm and made his bow to the court, first to the president, then to the captains to the right of him, then to the captains to the left of him. The president gave a slight inclination of his head and desired Captain Aubrey and his officers to sit down. A marine placed a chair for Jack a few paces in front of the rest, and there he sat, his hand going to hitch forward his non-existent sword, while the judge advocate read the document authorizing the court to assemble.

This took a considerable time, and Stephen looked steadily about him, examining the cabin from side to side:

it was like a larger version of the *Desaix*'s stateroom (how glad he was the *Desaix* was safe) and it, too, was singularly beautiful and full of light – the same range of curved stern-windows, the same inward-leaning side-walls (the ship's tumblehome, in fact) and the same close, massive white-painted beams overhead in extraordinarily long pure curves right across from one side to another: a room in which common domestic geometry had no say. At the far end from the door, parallel with the windows, ran a long table; and between the table and the light sat the members of the court, the president in the middle, the black-coated judge-advocate at a desk in front and three post-captains on either side. There was a clerk at a small table on the left, and to the left again a roped-off space for bystanders.

The atmosphere was austere: all the heads above the blue and gold uniforms on the far side of the shining table were grave. The last trial and the sentence had been quite shockingly painful.

It was these heads, these faces, that had all Jack's attention. With the light behind them it was difficult to make them out exactly; but they were mostly overcast, and all were withdrawn. Keàts, Hood, Brenton, Grenville he knew: was Grenville winking at him with his one eye, or was it an involuntary blink? Of course it was a blink: any signal would be grossly indecent. The president looked twenty years younger since the victory, but still his face was impassive and there was no distinguishing the expression of his eyes, behind those drooping lids. The other captains he knew only by name. One, a left-handed man, was drawing – scribbling. Jack's eyes grew dark with anger.

The judge-advocate's voice droned on. 'His Majesty's late Sloop *Sophie* having been ordered to proceed . . . and whereas it is represented that in or about 40'W 37° 40' N, Cape Roig bearing . . .' he said, amidst universal indifference.

'That man loves his trade,' thought Stephen. 'But what a wretched voice. It is almost impossible to be understood.

Gabble, a professional deformation in lawyers.' And he was reflecting on industrial disease, on the corrosive effects of righteousness in judges, when he noticed that Jack had relaxed from his first rigid posture: and as the formalities went on and on this relaxation became more evident. He was looking sullen, oddly still and dangerous; the slight lowering of his head and the dogged way in which he stuck out his feet made a singular contrast with the perfection of his uniform, and Stephen had a strong premonition that disaster might be very close at hand.

The judge advocate had now reached '. . . to enquire into the conduct of John Aubrey, commander of His Majesty's late sloop the *Sophie* and her officers and company for the loss of the said sloop by being captured on the third instant by a French squadron under the command of Admiral Linois', and Jack's head was lower still. 'How far is one entitled to manipulate one's friends?' asked Stephen, writing *Nothing would give H greater pleasure than an outburst of indignation on your part at this moment* on a corner of his paper: he passed it to the master, pointing to Jack. Marshall passed it on, by way of Dalziel. Jack read it, turned a lowering, grim face without much apparent understanding in it towards Stephen and gave a jerk of his head.

Almost immediately afterwards Charles Stirling, the senior captain and president of the court-martial, cleared his throat and said, 'Captain Aubrey, pray relate the circumstances of the loss of His Majesty's late sloop the *Sophie*.'

Jack rose to his feet, looked sharply along the line of his judges, drew his breath, and speaking in a much stronger voice than usual, the words coming fast, with odd intervals and an unnatural intonation – a harsh, God-damn-you voice, as though he were addressing a most inimical body of men – he said, 'About six o'clock in the morning of the third, to the eastward and in sight of Cape Roig, we saw three large ships apparently French, and a frigate, who soon after gave chase to the *Sophie*: the *Sophie* was between the shore and the ships that chased her, and to windward of the French vessels: we endeavoured by making all sail and were pulling with sweeps – as the wind was very light – to keep to windward of the enemy; but having found notwithstanding all our endeavours to keep to the wind, that the French ships gained very fast, and having separated on different tacks one or the other gained upon each shift of wind, and finding it impracticable to escape by the wind, about nine o'clock the guns and other things on deck were thrown overboard; and having watched an opportunity, when the nearest French ship was on our quarter, we bore up and set the studdingsails; but again found the French ships outsailed us though their studdingsails were not set: when the nearest ship had approached within musket-shot, I ordered the colours to be hauled down about eleven o'clock a.m., the wind being to the eastward and having received several broadsides from the enemy which carried away the maintopgallantmast and foretopsail yard and cut several of the ropes.'

Then, though he was conscious of the singular ineptitude of this speech, he shut his mouth tight and stood looking straight ahead of him, while the clerk's pen squeaked nimbly after his words, writing *and cut several of the ropes*. Here there was a slight pause, in which the president glanced left and right and coughed again before speaking. The clerk drew a quick flourish after *ropes* and hurried on:

> *Question by the court   Captain Aubrey, have you any reason to find fault with any of your officers or ship's company?*
> *Answer   No. The utmost endeavour was used by every person on board.*
> *Question by the court   Officers and ship's company of the Sophie, have any of you reason to find fault with the conduct of your captain?*
> *Answer   No.*

'Let all the evidence withdraw except Lieutenant Alexander Dalziel,' said the judge-advocate, and presently the midshipmen, the master and Stephen found themselves in the dining-cabin again, sitting perfectly mute in odd corners, while from the one side the distant shrieking of the parson echoed up from the cockpit (he had made a determined attempt at suicide) and from the other the drone of the trial went on. They were all deeply affected by Jack's concern, anxiety and rage: they had seen him unmoved so often and in such circumstances that his present emotion shook them profoundly, and disturbed their judgment. They could hear his voice now, formal, savage and much louder than the rest of the voices in the court, saying, 'Did the enemy fire several broadsides at us and at what distance were we when they fired the last?' Mr Dalziel's reply was a murmur, indistinguishable through the bulkhead.

'This is an entirely irrational fear,' said Stephen Maturin, looking at his wet and clammy palm. 'It is but one more instance of the . . . for surely to God, surely for all love, if they had wished to sink him they would have asked "How came you to be there?"? But then I know very little of nautical affairs.' He looked for comfort at the master's face, but he found none there.

'Dr Maturin,' said the marine, opening the door.

Stephen walked in slowly and took the oath with particular deliberation, trying to sense the atmosphere of the court: he thus gave the clerk time to catch up with Dalziel's evidence, and the shrill pen wrote:

> *Question   Did she gain on the Sophie without her stud-*
> *   dingsails set?*
> *Answer   Yes.*
> *Question by the court   Did they seem to sail much faster*
> *   than you?*
> *Answer   Yes, both by and large.*
> *Dr Maturin, surgeon of the Sophie, called and sworn.*
> *Question by the court   Is the statement you heard made*
> *   by your captain respecting the loss of the Sophie, correct*
> *   as far as your observation went?*

Answer   I think it is.

Question by the court   Are you a sufficient judge of nautical affairs to know whether every effort was used to escape from the force that was pursuing the Sophie?

Answer   I know very little of nautical affairs, but it appeared to me that every exertion was used by every person on board: I saw the captain at the helm, and the officers and ship's company at the sweeps.

Question by the court   Was you on deck at the time the colours were struck and what distance were the enemy from you at the time of her surrender?

Answer   I was on deck, and the Desaix was within musket-shot of the Sophie and was firing at us at the time.

Ten minutes later the court was cleared. The dining-cabin again, and no hesitation about precedence in the doorway this time, for Jack and Mr Dalziel were there: they were all there, and not one of them spoke a word. Could that be laughter in the next room, or did the sound come from the wardroom of the *Caesar*?

A long pause. A long, long pause: and the marine at the door.

'If you please, gentlemen.'

They filed in, and in spite of all his years at sea Jack forgot to duck: he struck the lintel of the door with a force that left a patch of yellow hair and scalp on the wood and he walked on, almost blinded, to stand rigidly by his chair.

The clerk looked up from writing the word *Sentence*, startled by the crash, and then looked down again, to commit the judge-advocate's words to writing. 'At a court-martial assembled and held on board His Majesty's Ship *Pompée* in Rosia Bay . . . the court (being first duly sworn) proceeded in pursuance of an order from Sir James Saumarez Bart. Rear-Admiral of the Blue and . . . and having examined witnesses on the occasion, and maturely and deliberately considered every circumstance . . .'

The droning, expressionless voice went on, and its tone

was so closely allied to the ringing in Jack's head that he heard virtually none of it, any more than he could see the man's face through the watering of his eyes.

'. . . the court is of the opinion that Captain Aubrey, his officers and ship's company used every possible exertion to prevent the King's sloop from falling into the hands of the enemy: and do therefore honourably acquit them. And they are hereby acquitted accordingly,' said the judge-advocate, and Jack heard none of it.

The inaudible voice stopped and Jack's blurred vision saw the black form sit down. He shook his singing head, tightened his jaw and compelled his faculties to return; for here was the president of the court getting to his feet. Jack's clearing eyes caught Keats' smile, saw Captain Stirling pick up that familiar, rather shabby sword, holding it with its hilt towards him, while with his left hand he smoothed a piece of paper by the inkwell. The president cleared his throat again in the dead silence, and speaking in a clear, seamanlike voice that combined gravity, formality and cheerfulness, he said, 'Captain Aubrey: it is no small pleasure to me to receive the commands of the court I have the honour to preside at, that in delivering to you your sword, I should congratulate you upon its being restored by both friend and foe alike; hoping ere long you will be called upon to draw it once more in the honourable defence of your country.'

The Winning Post
at Last

ALAN JUDD

SOMETIMES THINGS come together as they should. They recently have for the novelist and biographer, Patrick O'Brian; within a week of the announcement in the Birthday Honours of his CBE for services to literature, he became the first ever winner of the £10,000 Heywood Hill Literary Prize.

World-wide publishing success already threatens to lionise this energetic and very private octogenarian, but it was clear at the prize-giving that the pleasures of literary recognition do something to render tolerable the passing inconveniences of fame. They do something, too, to make up for decades of unremitting endeavour, for early years of poverty and for numbers of good books written blind – that is, without the comforting assurance of a reading public. It has been a long haul for O'Brian.

Ill-health and parental death resulted in a peripatetic Anglo—Irish childhood, while an education that unusually combined rigour and breadth fed the autodidact in him. Fluency in French, Spanish and Catalan found him useful employment in Intelligence during the Second World War, on which subject he remains firmly discreet, and also led to his marriage to Mary, mother of Count Nikolai Tolstoy. After the war they settled in Wales, then partly for health reasons moved to the coastal village near the Franco-Spanish border where they have lived ever since.

It was easier to be poor in a warm climate.

There was never any question for O'Brian that he should – must – write, and never any wavering or compromise in Mary's essential support. Short stories, reviews, translations and early novels appeared, outstanding amongst which was

Testimonies, an intense and obsessional love story set in rural Wales and now published by HarperCollins. For years, however, it was the translations from French into English – *Papillon*, for instance, and all of de Beauvoir – that kept the wolf from the door. Luck helped; Picasso was a neighbour and became a friend, which subsequently led O'Brian to write a vivid and perceptive biography of him, still acknowledged in Spain (and by the late Lord Clark) as the best.

In 1969 O'Brian published *Master and Commander*, the first of a series of novels – 'tales', he modestly calls them – set in the Royal Navy during the Napoleonic Wars. Although he thought there might be others he no more anticipated that the series would extend to seventeen (so far – the eighteenth is on the way) than that it would ensure his place in the literary pantheon. Indeed, despite early support from such as Mary Renault, T. J. Binyon and John Bayley, the books were not an immediate sensation and actually went out of print in America.

Gradually, however, word-of-mouth, astute publishing, literary merit and – dare one say it? – sheer readability have combined to produce during the last five years a rare tidal wave of literary recognition and commercial success. Sales are now over the million, translations are into nineteen languages, the British Library has published its first bibliography of a living author (with an introduction by William Waldegrave), the University of Indiana is buying the manuscripts and forming an O'Brian study centre, a ship is being built in Chile to the specification of that most often sailed by O'Brian's heroes, his American publishers (Norton) issue a regular newsletter and in the Cayman Isles there is a dining club called the Patrick O'Brian Widows, formed by ladies whose husbands are addicted. Better known admirers include people as diverse as Iris Murdoch and Max Hastings, Antonia Byatt and Charlton Heston.

Master and Commander begins in Port Mahon where the impoverished Lieutenant Jack Aubrey and the impoverished physician, Stephen Maturin, meet and fall out at a concert. Next morning, in the euphora of a longed-for but unexpected promotion to command, Jack offers Stephen a place as ship's surgeon, so beginning a friendship that will surely prove one of the most enduring and endearing in our literature. They are quite different: Jack is English, beefy, cheerful and generous, a fool ashore but a genius afloat; Stephen is Irish–Catalan, moody, subtle, brilliant, a passionate naturalist (O'Brian is also the biographer of Sir Joseph Banks) and a determined spy against Napoleon. They are united by sympathy, respect, acknowledgement of difference, a sense of fairness and justice and affection. All this is suggested more in the spaces between words than expressed directly, except when they make music together. In the portrayal of this friendship we learn something of all friendship, just as in the series as a whole we learn of loyalty and betrayal, love and mutability, interest and humour.

These novels are neither Forester nor Marryat, though O'Brian pays the respect due to both. There is adventure and there are battles. The historic furniture and vernacular you can trust absolutely because O'Brian is so steeped in his period but there is also something of his heroine, Jane Austen. He writes with her irony, humour and moral toughness, almost as she might have written of the adventures of her naval brothers. Above all, they are accessible novels, so well written that you settle into each as into a warm bath, knowing you are in good, considerate hands. In evoking so vividly what it was like to be alive then, O'Brian shows by reflection elements of what it is to be alive now, and of how we should live. He achieves that simultaneous dislocation and bridging that is the essence of all imaginative art and is what distinguishes it from everything else.

The Heywood Hill Literary Prize was the suggestion of the Duke of Devonshire, a director of the bookshop. The judges were John Saumarez Smith, Mark Amory and Roy Jenkins. It is awarded not for somebody's latest work, but for a 'lifetime's contribution to the enjoyment of books' and could easily have gone to a publisher such as Rupert Hart-Davis or the late Jock Murray. For an author to win it his or her books must have held up well over a period of years among the customers of Heywood Hill; in the words of John Saumarez Smith, *we wanted to strike a blow for reading*.

There is a feeling that one or two well-known prize-giving bodies have lost sight of what they think of as the reading aspect of books.

O'Brian was handed his award by another admirer, Tom Stoppard, amidst the bucolic elegance of a large mixed crowd on the lawn at Chatsworth. The sun shone, the bands played cheerfully, the literati were littered about and the gliterati glittered – though not as brightly as the chains adorning the assembled mayors of Derbyshire. The RAF laid on a timely unintended fly-past, the Chatsworth dogs proved that if you're handsome enough you can scrounge any number of free lunches and at the end a lady danced extempore upon a table.

It was, O'Brian told us, his first literary award; in fact, his first prize of any sort since he was given a pen-knife by the headmaster of his prep school in Paignton for keeping on running when everyone else was way ahead and out of sight. Well, they're out of sight now, but no longer ahead, and Patrick O'Brian is running still.

This article first appeared in the *Spectator* of 1st July 1995, and is reprinted here by kind permission of its literary editor, Mark Amery.

For those readers wishing to journey a little further with Jack and Stephen, the following pages contain the first chapter of Post Captain, *the next book in the Aubrey/Maturin series.*

Post Captain is the second novel in Patrick O'Brian's remarkable Aubrey/Maturin series and led Mary Renault to write: '*Master and Commander* raised dangerously high expectations; *Post Captain* triumphantly surpasses them.'

The tale begins with Jack Aubrey arriving home from his exploits in the Mediterranean to find England at peace following the Treaty of Amiens. He and his friend Stephen Maturin, surgeon and secret agent, begin to live the lives of country gentlemen, hunting, entertaining and enjoying more amorous adventures. Their comfortable existence, however, is cut short when Jack is overnight reduced to a pauper with enough debts to keep him in prison for life. He flees to the continent to seek refuge: instead he finds himself a hunted fugitive as Napoleon has ordered the internment of all Englishmen in France. Aubrey's adventures in escaping from France and the debtors' prison will grip the reader as fast as his unequalled actions at sea.

'Mr O'Brian is a master of his period, in which his characters are firmly placed, while remaining three-dimensional, intensely human beings. This book sets him at the very top of his genre ... It is brilliant.'   MARY RENAULT

ISBN: 978 0 00 649916 9

Chapter One

At first dawn the swathes of rain drifting eastwards across the Channel parted long enough to show that the chase had altered course. The *Charwell* had been in her wake most of the night, running seven knots in spite of her foul bottom, and now they were not much above a mile and a half apart. The ship ahead was turning, turning, coming up into the wind; and the silence along the frigate's decks took on a new quality as every man aboard saw her two rows of gun-ports come into view. This was the first clear sight they had had of her since the look-out hailed the deck in the growing darkness to report a ship hull-down on the horizon, one point on the larboard bow. She was then steering north-north-east, and it was the general opinion aboard the *Charwell* that she was either one of a scattered French convoy or an American blockade-runner hoping to reach Brest under cover of the moonless night.

Two minutes after that first hail the *Charwell* set her fore and main topgallants – no great spread of canvas, but then the frigate had had a long, wearing voyage from the West Indies: nine weeks out of sight of land, the equinoctial gales to strain her tired rigging to the breaking-point, three days of lying-to in the Bay of Biscay at its worst, and it was understandable that Captain Griffiths should wish to husband her a little. No cloud of sail, but even so she fetched the stranger's wake within a couple of hours, and at four bells in the morning watch the *Charwell* cleared for action. The drum beat to quarters, the hammocks came racing up, piling into the nettings to form bulwarks, the guns were run out; and the warm, pink, sleepy watch below had been standing to them in the cold rain ever since – an hour and more to chill them to the bone.

Now in the silence of this discovery one of the crew of a gun in the waist could be heard explaining to a weak-eyed staring little man beside him, 'She's a French two-decker, mate. A seventy-four or an eighty: we've caught a tartar, mate.'

'Silence there, God damn you,' cried Captain Griffiths. 'Mr Quarles, take that man's name.'

Then the grey rain closed in. But at present everyone on the crowded quarterdeck knew what lay behind that drifting, formless veil: a French ship of the line, with both her rows of gun-ports open. And there was not one who had missed the slight movement of the yard that meant she was about to lay her foresail to the mast, heave to and wait for them.

The *Charwell* was a 32-gun 12-pounder frigate, and if she got close enough to use the squat carronades on her quarterdeck and forecastle as well as her long guns she could throw a broadside weight of metal of 238 pounds. A French line-of-battle ship could not throw less than 960. No question of a match, therefore, and no discredit in bearing up and running for it, but for the fact that somewhere in the dim sea behind them there was their consort, the powerful 38-gun 18-pounder *Dee*. She had lost a topmast in the last blow, which slowed her down, but she had been well in sight at nightfall, and she had responded to Captain Griffiths's signal to chase: for Captain Griffiths was the senior captain. The two frigates would still be heavily outgunned by the ship of the line, but there was no doubt that they could take her on: she would certainly try to keep her broadside to one of the frigates and maul her terribly, but the other could lie on her bow or her stern and rake her – a murderous fire right along the length of her decks to which she could make almost no reply. It could be done: it had been done. In '97, for example, the *Indefatigable* and the *Amazon* had destroyed a French seventy-four. But then the *Indefatigable* and the *Amazon* carried eighty long guns between them, and the *Droits de l'Homme* had not been able to open her lower-deck ports – the sea was running too high. There was no more than a moderate swell now; and to engage the stranger the *Charwell* would have to cut her off from Brest and fight her for – for how long?

'Mr – Mr Howell,' said the captain. 'Take a glass to the masthead and see what you can make of the *Dee*.'

The long-legged midshipman was half-way to the mizentop before the captain had finished speaking, and his 'Aye-aye, sir' came down through the sloping rain. A black squall swept across the ship, pelting down so thick that for a while the men on the quarterdeck could scarcely see the forecastle, and the water ran spouting from the lee-scuppers. Then it was gone, and in the pale gleam of day that followed there came the hail. 'On deck, sir. She's hull-up on the leeward beam. She's fished her ...'

'Report,' said the captain, in a loud, toneless voice. 'Pass the word for Mr Barr.'

The third lieutenant came hurrying aft from his station. The wind took his rain-soaked cloak as he stepped on to the quarterdeck, and he made a convulsive gesture, one hand going towards the flapping cloth and the other towards his hat.

'Take it off, sir,' cried Captain Griffiths, flushing dark red. 'Take it right off your head. You know Lord St Vincent's order – you have all of you read it – you know how to salute ...' He snapped his mouth shut; and after a moment he said, 'When does the tide turn?'

'I beg your pardon, sir,' said Barr. 'At ten minutes after eight o'clock, sir. It is almost the end of slack-water now, sir, if you please.'

The captain grunted, and said, 'Mr Howell?'

'She has fished her main topmast, sir,' said the midshipman, standing bareheaded, tall above his captain. 'And has just hauled to the wind.'

The captain levelled his glass at the *Dee*, whose top-gallant-sails were now clear above the jagged edge of the sea: her top-sails too, when the swell raised both the frigates high. He wiped the streaming objective-glass, stared again, swung round to look at the Frenchman, snapped the telescope shut and gazed back at the distant frigate. He was alone there, leaning on the rail, alone there on the holy starboard side of the quarterdeck; and from time to time, when they were not looking at the Frenchman or the *Dee*, the officers glanced thoughtfully at his back.

The situation was still fluid; it was more a potentiality than a situation. But any decision now would crystallize it, and the moment it began to take shape all the succeeding events would follow of themselves, moving at first with slow inevitability and then faster and faster, never to be undone. And a decision must be made, made quickly – at the *Charwell*'s present rate of sailing they would be within range of the two-decker in less than ten minutes. Yet there were so many factors ... The *Dee* was no great sailer close-hauled on a wind; and the turning tide would hold her back – it was right across her course; she might have to make another tack. In half an hour the French 36-pounders could rip the guts out of the *Charwell*, dismast her and carry her into Brest – the wind stood fair for Brest. Why had they seen not a single ship of the blockading squadron? They could not have been blown off, not with this wind. It was damned odd. Everything was damned odd, from this Frenchman's conduct onwards. The sound of gunfire would bring the squadron up ... Delaying tactics ...

The feeling of those eyes on his back filled Captain Griffiths with rage. An unusual number of eyes, for the *Charwell* had several officers and a couple of civilians as passengers, one set from Gibraltar and another from Port of Spain. The fire-eating General Paget was one of them, an influential man; and another was Captain Aubrey, Lucky Jack Aubrey, who had set about a Spanish 36-gun xebec-frigate not long ago with the *Sophie*, a 14-gun brig, and had taken her. The *Cacafuego*. It had been the talk of the fleet some months back; and it made the decision no less difficult.

Captain Aubrey was standing by the aftermost larboard carronade, with a completely abstracted, non-committal look upon his face. From that place, being tall, he could see the whole situation, the rapidly, smoothly changing triangle of three ships; and close beside him stood two shorter figures, the one Dr Maturin, formerly his surgeon in the *Sophie*, and the other a man in black – black clothes, black hat and a streaming black cloak – who might have had *intelligence agent* written on his narrow forehead. Or just the word *spy*, there being so little room. They were talking in a language thought by some to be Latin. They were talking eagerly, and Jack Aubrey, intercepting a furious glance across the deck, leant down to whisper in his friend's ear, 'Stephen, will you not go below? They will be wanting you in the cockpit any moment now.'

Captain Griffiths turned from the rail, and with laboured calmness he said, 'Mr Berry, make this signal. *I am about to …*'

At this moment the ship of the line fired a gun, followed by three blue lights that soared and burst with a ghostly effulgence in the dawn: before the last dropping trail of sparks had drifted away downwind she sent up a succession of rockets, a pale, isolated Guy Fawkes' night far out in the sea.

'What the devil can she mean by that?' thought Jack Aubrey, narrowing his eyes, and the wondering murmur along the frigate's decks echoed his amazement.

'On deck,' roared the look-out in the foretop, 'there's a cutter pulling from under her lee.'

Captain Griffiths's telescope swivelled round. 'Duck up,' he called, and as the clewlines plucked at the main and foresails to give him a clear view he saw the cutter, an English cutter, sway up its yard, fill, gather speed, and come racing over the grey sea, towards the frigate.

'Close the cutter,' he said. 'Mr Bowes, give her a gun.'

At last, after all these hours of frozen waiting, there came the quick orders, the careful laying of the gun, the crash of the twelve-pounder, the swirl of acrid smoke eddying briefly on the wind, and the cheer of the crew as the ball skipped across the cutter's bows. An answering cheer from the cutter, a waving of hats, and the two vessels neared one another at a combined speed of fifteen miles an hour.

The cutter, fast and beautifully handled – certainly a smuggling craft – came to under the *Charwell*'s lee, lost her way, and lay there as trim as a gull, rising and falling on the swell. A row of brown, knowing faces grinned up at the frigate's guns.

'I'd press half a dozen prime seamen out of her in the next two minutes,' reflected Jack, while Captain Griffiths hailed her master over the lane of sea.

'Come aboard,' said Captain Griffiths suspiciously, and after a few moments of backing and filling, of fending-off and cries of 'Handsomely now, God damn your soul,' the master came up the stern ladder with a bundle under his arm. He swung easily over the taffrail, held out his hand and said, 'Wish you joy of the peace, Captain.'

'Peace?' cried Captain Griffiths.

'Yes, sir. I thought I should surprise you. They signed not three days since. There's not a foreign-going ship has heard yet. I've got the cutter filled with the newspapers, London, Paris and country towns – all the articles, gentlemen, all the latest details,' he said, looking round the quarterdeck. 'Half a crown a go.'

There was no disbelieving him. The quarterdeck looked utterly blank. But the whispered word had flown along the deck from the radiant carronade-crews, and now cheering broke out on the forecastle. In spite of the captain's automatic 'Take that man's name, Mr Quarles,' it flowed back to the mainmast and spread throughout the ship, a full-throated howl of joy – liberty, wives and sweethearts, safety, the delights of land.

And in any case there was little real ferocity in Captain Griffiths's voice: anyone looking into his close-set eyes would have seen ecstasy in their depths. His occupation was gone, vanished in a puff of smoke; but now no one on God's earth could ever know what signal he had been about to make, and in spite of the severe control that he imposed upon his face there was an unusual urbanity in his tone as he invited his passengers, his first lieutenant, the officer and the midshipman of the watch to dine with him that afternoon.

'It is charming to see how sensible the men are – how sensible of the blessings of peace,' said Stephen Maturin to the Reverend Mr Hake, by way of civility.

'Aye. The blessings of peace. Oh, certainly,' said the chaplain, who had no living to retire to, no private means, and who knew that the *Charwell* would be paid off as soon as she reached Portsmouth. He walked deliberately out of the wardroom, to pace the quarterdeck in a thoughtful silence, leaving Captain Aubrey and Dr Maturin alone.

'I thought he would have shown more pleasure,' observed Stephen Maturin.

'It's an odd thing about you, Stephen,' said Jack Aubrey, looking at him with affection. 'You have been at sea quite some time now, and no one could call you a fool, but you have no more notion of a sailor's life than a babe unborn. Surely you must have noticed how glum Quarles and Rodgers and all the rest were at dinner? And how blue everyone has always looked this war, when there was any danger of peace?'

'I put it down to the anxieties of the night – the long strain, the watchfulness, the lack of sleep: I must not say the apprehension of danger. Captain Griffiths was in a fine flow of spirits, however.'

'Oh,' said Jack, closing one eye. 'That was reyther different; and in any case he is a post-captain, of course. He has his ten shillings a day, and whatever happens he goes up the captains' list as the old ones die off or get their flag. He's quite old – forty, I dare say, or even more – but with any luck he'll die an admiral. No. It's the others I'm sorry for, the lieutenants with their half-pay and very little chance of a ship – none at all of promotion; the poor wretched midshipmen who have not been made and who never will be made now – no hope of a commission. And of course, no half-pay at all. It's the merchant service for them, or blacking shoes outside St James's Park. Haven't you heard the old song? I'll tip you a stave.' He hummed the tune, and in a discreet rumble he sang.

'Says Jack, "There is very good news, there is peace both
    by land and by sea;
Great guns no more shall be used, for we all disbanded
    be."
Says the Admiral, "That's very bad news;" says the
    captain, "My heart will break;"
The lieutenant cries, "What shall I do? For I know not
    what course for to take."
Says the doctor, "I'm a gentleman too, I'm a gentleman of
    the first rank;
I will go to some country fair, and there I'll set up
    mountebank."*

Ha, ha, that's for you, Stephen – ha, ha, ha –

Says the midshipman, "I have no trade; I have
    got my trade for to choose,
I will go to St James's Park gate, and there I'll set black
    of shoes;
And there I will set all day, at everybody's call,
And everyone that comes by, 'Do you want my nice
    shining balls?'"*

Mr Quarles looked in at the door, recognized the tune and drew in a sharp breath; but Jack was a guest, a superior officer – a master and commander, no less, with an epaulette on his shoulder – and he was broad as well as tall. Mr Quarles let his breath out in a sigh and closed the door.

'I should have sung softer,' said Jack, and drawing his chair closer to the table he went on in a low voice, 'No, those are the chaps I am sorry for. I'm sorry for myself too, naturally – no great likelihood of a ship, and of course no enemy to cruise against if I do get one. But it's nothing in comparison of them. We've had luck with prize-money, and if only it were not for this infernal delay over making me post I should be perfectly happy to have a six months' run ashore. Hunting. Hearing some decent music. The opera – we might even go to Vienna! Eh? What do you say, Stephen? Though I must confess this slowness irks my heart and soul. However, it's nothing in comparison of them, and I make no doubt it will be settled directly.' He picked up *The Times* and ran through the *London Gazette*, in case he should have missed his own name in the first three readings. 'Toss me the one on the locker, will you?' he said, throwing it down. 'The *Sussex Courier*.'

'This is more like it, Stephen,' he said, five minutes later. '*Mr Savile's hounds will meet at ten o'clock on Wednesday, the sixth of November 1802, at Champflower Cross.* I had such a run with them when I was a boy: my father's regiment was in camp at Rainsford. A seven-mile point – prodigious fine country if you have a horse that can really go. Or listen to this: *a neat gentleman's residence, standing upon gravel, is to be let by the year, at moderate terms.* Stabling for ten, it says.'

'Are there any rooms?'

'Why, of course there are. It couldn't be called a *neat* gentleman's residence, without there were rooms. What a fellow you are, Stephen. Ten bedrooms. By God, there's a lot to be said for a house, not too far from the sea, in that sort of country.'

'Had you not thought of going to Woolhampton – of going to your father's house?'

'Yes … yes. I mean to give him a visit, of course. But there's my new mother-in-law, you know. And to tell you the truth, I don't think it would exactly answer.' He paused, trying to remember the name of the person, the classical person, who had had such a trying time with his father's second wife; for General Aubrey had recently married his dairy-maid, a fine black-eyed young woman with a moist palm whom Jack knew very well. Actaeon, Ajax, Aristides? He felt that their cases were much alike and that by naming him he would give a subtle hint of the position: but the name would not come, and after a while he reverted to the advertisements. 'There's a great deal to be said for somewhere in the neighbourhood of Rainsford – three or four packs within reach, London only a day's ride away, and neat gentlemen's residences by the dozen, all standing upon gravel. You'll go snacks with me, Stephen? We'll take Bonden, Killick, Lewis and perhaps one or two other old Sophies, and ask some of the youngsters to come and stay. We'll lay in beer and skittles – it will be Fiddler's Green!'

'I should like it of all things,' said Stephen. 'Whatever the advertisements may say, it is a chalk soil, and there are some very curious plants and beetles on the downs. I am with child to see a dew-pond.'

Polcary Down and the cold sky over it; a searching air from the north breathing over the water-meadows, up across the plough, up and up to this great sweep of open turf, the down, with the covert called Rumbold's Gorse sprawling on the lower edge of it. A score of red-coated figures dotted round the Gorse, and far away below them on the middle slope a ploughman standing at the end of his furrow, motionless behind his team of Sussex oxen, gazing up as Mr Savile's hounds worked their way through the furze and the brown remnants of the bracken.

Slow work; uncertain, patchy scent; and the foxhunters had plenty of time to drink from their flasks, blow on their hands, and look out over the landscape below them – the river winding through its patchwork of fields, the towers or steeples of Hither, Middle, Nether and Savile Champflower, the six or seven big houses scattered along the valley, the whale-backed downs one behind the other, and far away the lead-coloured sea.

It was a small field, and almost everyone there knew everyone else: half a dozen farmers, some private gentlemen from
the Champflowers and the outlying parishes, two militia
officers from the dwindling camp at Rainsford, Mr Burton,
who had come out in spite of his streaming cold in the hope
of catching a glimpse of Mrs St John, and Dr Vining, with
his hat pinned to his wig and both tied under his chin
with a handkerchief. He had been led astray early in his
rounds – he could not resist the sound of the horn – and his
conscience had been troubling him ever since the scent had
faded and died. From time to time he looked over the miles
of frigid air between the covert and Mapes Court, where
Mrs Williams was waiting for him. 'There is nothing wrong
with her,' he observed. 'My physic will do no good; but in
Christian decency I should call. And indeed I shall, unless
they find again before I can tell a hundred.' He put his finger
upon his pulse and began to count. At ninety he paused,
looking about for some reprieve, and on the far side of the
covert he saw a figure he did not know. 'That is the medical
man they have been telling me about, no doubt,' he said.
'It would be the civil thing to go over and say a word to
him. A rum-looking cove. Dear me, a very rum-looking
cove.'

The rum-looking cove was sprawling upon a mule, an
unusual sight in an English hunting-field; and quite apart
from the mule there was a strange air about him – his slate-
coloured small-clothes, his pale face, his pale eyes and even
paler close-cropped skull (*his* hat and wig were tied to his
saddle), and the way he bit into a hunk of bread rubbed with
garlic. He was calling out in a loud tone to his companion, in
whom Dr Vining recognized the new tenant of Melbury
Lodge. 'I tell you what it is, Jack,' he was saying, 'I tell you
what it is …'

'You sir – you on the mule,' cried old Mr Savile's furious
voice. 'Will you let the God-damned dogs get on with their
work? Hey? Hey? Is this a God-damned coffee-house? I
appeal to you, is this an infernal debating society?'

Captain Aubrey pursed his lips demurely and pushed his horse over the twenty yards that separated them. 'Tell me later, Stephen,' he said in a low voice, leading his friend round the covert out of the master's sight. 'Tell me later, when they have found their fox.'

The demure look did not sit naturally upon Jack Aubrey's face, which in this weather was as red as his coat, and as soon as they were round the corner, under the lee of a wind-blown thorn, his usual expectant cheerfulness returned, and he looked eagerly up into the furze, where an occasional heave and rustle showed the pack in motion.

'Looking for a *fox*, are they?' said Stephen Maturin, as though hippogriffs were the more usual quarry in England, and he relapsed into a brown study, munching slowly upon his bread.

The wind breathed up the long hillside; remote clouds passed evenly across the sky. Now and then Jack's big hunter brought his ears to bear; this was a recent purchase, a strongly-built bay, quite up to Jack's sixteen stone. But it did not much care for hunting, and then like so many geldings it spent much of its time mourning for its lost stones: a discontented horse. If the moods that succeeded one another in its head had taken the form of words they would have run, 'Too heavy – sits too far forward when we go over a fence – have carried him far enough for one day – shall have him off presently, see if I don't. I smell a mare! A mare! Oh!' Its flaring nostrils quivered, and it stamped.

Looking round Jack saw that there were newcomers in the field. A young woman and a groom came hurrying up the side of the plough, the groom mounted on a cob and the young woman on a pretty little high-bred chestnut mare. When they reached the post and rail dividing the field from the down the groom cantered on to open a gate, but the girl set her horse at the rail and skipped neatly over it, just as a whimpering and then a bellowing roar inside the covert gave promise of great things.

The noise died away: a young hound came out and stared

into the open. Stephen Maturin moved from behind the close-woven thorn to follow the flight of a falcon overhead, and at the sight of the mule the chestnut mare began to caper, flashing her white stockings and tossing her head.

'Get over, you –,' said the girl, in her pure clear young voice. Jack had never heard a girl say – before, and he turned to look at her with a particular interest. She was busy coping with the mare's excitement, but after a moment she caught his eye and frowned. He looked away, smiling, for she was the prettiest thing – indeed, beautiful, with her heightened colour and her fine straight back, sitting her horse with the unconscious grace of a midshipman at the tiller in a lively sea. She had black hair and blue eyes; a certain ram-you-damn-you air that was slightly comic and more than a little touching in so slim a creature. She was wearing a shabby blue habit with white cuffs and lapels, like a naval lieutenant's coat, and on top of it all a dashing tricorne with a tight curl of ostrich-feather. In some ingenious way, probably by the use of combs, she had drawn up her hair under this hat so as to leave one ear exposed; and this perfect ear, as Jack observed when the mare came crabwise towards him, was as pink as …

'There is that fox of theirs,' remarked Stephen, in a conversational tone. 'There is that fox we hear so much about. Though indeed, it is a vixen, sure.'

Slipping quickly along a fold in the ground the leaf-coloured fox went slanting down across them towards the plough. The horses' ears and the mule's followed it, cocked like so many semaphores. When the fox was well clear Jack rose in his stirrups, held up his hat and holla'd it away in a high-seas roar that brought the huntsman tearing round, his horn going twang-twang-twang, and hounds racing from the furze at all points. They hit the scent in the sheltered hollow and they were away with a splendid cry. They poured through the fence; they were half-way across the unploughed stubble, a close-packed body – such music – and the huntsman was right up there with them. The field came thundering round the covert: someone had the gate open and in a moment there was an eager crowd jostling to get through, for it was a devilish unpleasant downhill leap just here. Jack held hard, not choosing to thrust his first time out in a strange country, but his heart was beating to quarters, double-time, and he had already worked out the line he would follow once the press had thinned.

Jack was the keenest of fox-hunters: he loved everything about the chase, from the first sound of the horn to the rancid smell of the torn fox, but in spite of a few unwelcome spells without a ship, he had spent two-thirds of his life at sea – his skill was not all he thought it was.

The gate was still jammed – there would be no chance of getting through it before the pack was in the next field. Jack wheeled his horse, called out, 'Come on, Stephen,' and put it at the rail. Out of the corner of his eye he saw the chestnut flash between his friend and the crowd in the gate. As his horse rose Jack screwed round to see how the girl would get over, and the gelding instantly felt this change of balance. It took the rail flying high and fast, landed with its head low, and with a cunning twist of its shoulder and an upward thrust from behind it unseated its rider.

He did not fall at once. It was a slow, ignominious glide down that slippery near shoulder, with a fistful of mane in his right hand; but the horse was the master of the situation now, and in twenty yards the saddle was empty.

The horse's satisfaction did not last, however. Jack's boot was wedged in his near stirrup; it would not come free, and here was his heavy person jerking and thumping along at the gelding's side, roaring and swearing horribly. The horse began to grow alarmed – to lose its head – to snort – to stare wildly – and to run faster and faster across those dark, flint-strewn, unforgiving furrows.

The ploughman left his oxen and came lumbering up the hill, waving his goad; a tall young man in a green coat, a foot-follower, called out 'Whoa there, whoa there,' and ran towards the horse with his arms spread wide; the mule, the last of the vanishing field, turned and raced back to cut the gelding off, swarming along in its inhuman way, very close to the ground. It outran the men, crossed the gelding's path, stood firm and took the shock: like a hero Stephen flung himself off, seized the reins and clung there until Green Coat and the ploughman came pounding up.

The oxen, left staring half-way along their furrow, were so moved by all this excitement that they came very nearly to the point of cutting a caper on their own. But before they had made up their minds it was over. The ploughman was leading the shamefaced horse to the side of the field, while the other two propped raw bones and bloody head between them, listening gravely to his explanations. The mule walked behind.

Mapes Court was an entirely feminine household – not a man in it, apart from the butler and the groom. Mrs Williams was a woman, in the natural course of things; but she was a woman so emphatically, so totally a woman, that she was almost devoid of any private character. A vulgar woman, too, although her family, which was of some importance in the neighbourhood, had been settled there since Dutch William's time.

It was difficult to see any connection, any family likeness, between her and her daughters and her niece, who made up the rest of the family. Indeed, it was not much of a house for family likeness: the dim portraits might have been bought at various auctions, and although the three daughters had been brought up together, with the same people around them, in the same atmosphere of genteel money-worship, position-worship and suffused indignation – an indignation that did not require any object for its existence, but that could always find one in a short space of time; a housemaid wearing silver buckles on Sunday would bring on a full week's flow – they were as different in their minds as they were in their looks.

Sophia, the eldest, was a tall girl with wide-set grey eyes, a broad, smooth forehead, and a wonderful sweetness of expression – soft fair hair, inclining to gold: an exquisite skin. She was a reserved creature, living much in an inward dream whose nature she did not communicate to anyone. Perhaps it was her mother's unprincipled rectitude that had given her this early disgust for adult life; but whether or no, she seemed very young for her twenty-seven years. There was nothing in the least degree affected or kittenish about this: rather a kind of ethereal quality – the quality of a sacrificial object. Iphigenia before the letter. Her looks were very much admired; she was always elegant, and when she was in looks she was quite lovely. She spoke little, in company or out, but she was capable of a sudden dart of sharpness, of a remark that showed much more intelligence and reflection than would have been expected from her rudimentary education and her very quiet provincial life. These remarks had a much greater force, coming from an amiable, pliant, and as it were sleepy reserve, and before now they had startled men who did not know her well – men who had been prating away happily with the conscious superiority of their sex. They dimly grasped an underlying strength, and they connected it with her occasional expression of secret amusement, the relish of something that she did not choose to share.

Cecilia was more nearly her mother's daughter: a little goose with a round face and china-blue eyes, devoted to ornament and to crimping her yellow hair, shallow and foolish almost to simplicity, but happy, full of cheerful noise, and not yet at all ill-natured. She dearly loved the company of men, men of any size or shape. Her younger sister Frances did not: she was indifferent to their admiration – a long-legged nymph, still given to whistling and shying stones at the squirrels in the walnut-tree. Here was all the pitilessness of youth intact; and she was perfectly entrancing, as a spectacle. She had her cousin Diana's black hair and great dark blue misty pools of eyes, but she was as unlike her sisters as though they belonged to another sex. All they had in common was youthful grace, a good deal of gaiety, splendid health, and ten thousand pounds apiece.

With these attractions it was strange that none of them should have married, particularly as the marriage-bed was never far from Mrs Williams's mind. But the paucity of men, of eligible bachelors, in the neighbourhood, the disrupting effects of ten years of war, and Sophia's reluctance (she had had several offers) explained a great deal; the rest could be accounted for by Mrs Williams's avidity for a good marriage settlement, and by an unwillingness on the part of the local gentlemen to have her as a mother-in-law.

Whether Mrs Williams liked her daughters at all was doubtful: she loved them, of course, and had 'sacrificed everything for them', but there was not much room in her composition for liking – it was too much taken up with being right (*Hast thou considered my servant Mrs Williams, that there is none like her in the earth, a perfect and an upright woman?*), with being tired, and with being ill-used. Dr Vining, who had known her all her life and who had seen her children into the world, said that she did not; but even he, who cordially disliked her, admitted that she truly, whole-heartedly loved their interest. She might damp all their enthusiasms, drizzle grey disapproval from one year's end to another, and spoil even birthdays with bravely-supported headaches, but she would fight parents, trustees and lawyers like a tigress for 'an adequate provision'. Yet still she had three unmarried daughters, and it was something of a comfort to her to be able to attribute this to their being overshadowed by her niece. Indeed, this niece, Diana Villiers, was as good-looking in her way as Sophia. But how unlike these two ways were: Diana with her straight back and high-held head seemed quite tall, but when she stood next to her cousin, she came no higher than her ear; they both had natural grace in an eminent degree, but whereas Sophia's was a willowy, almost languorous flowing perfection of movement, Diana's had a quick, flashing rhythm – on those rare occasions when there was a ball within twenty miles of Mapes she danced superbly; and by candlelight her complexion was almost as good as Sophia's.

Mrs Villiers was a widow: she had been born in the same year as Sophia, but what a different life she had led; at fifteen, after her mother's death, she had gone out to India to keep house for her expensive, raffish father, and she had lived there in splendid style even after her marriage to a penniless young man, her father's aide-de-camp, for he had moved into their rambling great palace, where the addition of a husband and an extra score of servants passed unnoticed. It had been a foolish marriage on the emotional plane – both too passionate, strong, self-willed, and opposed in every way to do anything but tear one another to pieces – but from the worldly point of view there was a great deal to be said for it. It did bring her a handsome husband, and it might have brought her a deer-park and ten thousand a year as well, for not only was Charles Villiers well-connected (one sickly life between him and a great estate) but he was intelligent, cultivated, unscrupulous and active – particularly gifted on the political side: the very man to make a brilliant career in India. A second Clive, maybe, and wealthy by the age of thirty-odd. But they were both killed in the same engagement against Tippoo Sahib, her father owing three lakhs of rupees and her husband nearly half that sum.

The Company allowed Diana her passage home and fifty pounds a year until she should remarry. She came back to England with a wardrobe of tropical clothes, a certain knowledge of the world, and almost nothing else. She came back, in effect, to the schoolroom, or something very like it. For she at once realized that her aunt meant to clamp down on her, to allow her no chance of queering her daughters' pitch; and as she had no money and nowhere else to go she determined to fit into this small slow world of the English countryside, with its fixed notions and its strange morality.

She was willing, she was obliged, to accept a protectorate, and from the beginning she resolved to be meek, cautious and retiring; she knew that other women would regard her as a menace, and she meant to give them no provocation. But her theory and her practice were sometimes at odds, and in any case Mrs Williams's idea of a protectorate was much more like a total annexation. She was afraid of Diana, and dared not push her too far, but she never gave up trying to gain a moral superiority, and it was striking to see how this essentially stupid woman, unhampered by any principle or by any sense of honour, managed to plant her needle where it hurt most.

This had been going on for years, and Diana's clandestine or at least unavowed excursions with Mr Savile's hounds had a purpose beyond satisfying her delight in riding. Returning now she met her cousin Cecilia in the hall, hurrying to look at her new bonnet in the pier-glass between the breakfast-room windows.

'Thou looks't like Antichrist in that lewd hat,' she said in a sombre voice, for the hounds had lost their fox and the only tolerable-looking man had vanished.

'Oh! Oh!' cried Cecilia, 'what a shocking thing to say! It's blasphemy, I'm sure. I declare I've never had such a shocking thing said to me since Jemmy Blagrove called me that rude word. I shall tell Mama.'

'Don't be a fool, Cissy. It's a quotation – literature – the Bible.'

'Oh. Well, I think it's very shocking. You are covered with mud, Di. Oh, you took my tricorne. Oh, what an ill-natured thing you are – I am sure you spoilt the feather. I shall tell Mama.' She snatched the hat, but finding it unhurt she softened and went on, 'Well: and so you had a dirty ride. You went along Gallipot Lane, I suppose. Did you see anything of the hunt? They were over there on Polcary all the morning with their horrid howling and yowling.'

'I saw them in the distance,' said Diana.

'You frightened me so with that dreadful thing you said about Jesus,' said Cecilia, blowing on the ostrich-feather, 'that I almost forgot the news. The Admiral is back!'

'Back already?'

'Yes. And he will be over this very afternoon. He sent Ned with his compliments and might he come with Mama's Berlin wool after dinner. Such fun! He will tell us all about these beautiful young men! Men, Diana!'

The family had scarcely gathered about their tea before Admiral Haddock walked in. He was only a yellow admiral, retired without hoisting his flag, and he had not been afloat since 1794, but he was their one authority on naval matters and he had been sadly missed ever since the unexpected arrival of a Captain Aubrey of the Navy – a captain who had taken Melbury Lodge and who was therefore within their sphere of influence, but about whom they knew nothing and upon whom (he being a bachelor) they, as ladies, could not call.

'Pray, Admiral,' said Mrs Williams, as soon as the Berlin wool had been faintly praised, peered at with narrowed eyes and pursed lips, and privately condemned as useless – nothing like a match, in quality, colour or price. 'Pray, Admiral, tell us about this Captain Aubrey, who they say has taken Melbury Lodge.'

'Aubrey? Oh, yes,' said the Admiral, running his dry tongue over his dry lips, like a parrot, 'I know all about him. I have not met him, but I talked about him to people at the club and in the Admiralty, and when I came home I looked him up in the Navy List. He is a young fellow, only a master and commander, you know –'

'Do you mean he is *pretending* to be a captain?' cried Mrs Williams, perfectly willing to believe it.

'No, no,' said Admiral Haddock impatiently. 'We always call commanders Captain So-and-So in the Navy. Real captains, full captains, we call *post*-captains – we say a man is made post when he is appointed to a sixth-rate or better, an eight-and-twenty, say, or a thirty-two-gun frigate. A *post*-ship, my dear Madam.'

'Oh, indeed,' said Mrs Williams, nodding her head and looking wise.

'Only a commander: but he did most uncommon well in

the Mediterranean. Lord Keith gave him cruise after cruise in that little old quarter-decked brig we took from the Spaniards in ninety-five, and he played Old Harry with the shipping up and down the coast. There were times when he well-nigh filled the Lazaretto Reach in Mahon with his prizes – Lucky Jack Aubrey, they called him. He must have cleared a pretty penny – a most elegant penny indeed. And he it was who took the *Cacafuego*! The very man,' said the Admiral with some triumph, gazing round the circle of blank faces. After a moment's pause of unbroken stupidity on their part he shook his head, saying, 'You never even heard of the engagement, I collect?'

No, they had not. They were sorry to say that they had not heard of the *Cacafuego* – was it the same as the Battle of St Vincent? Perhaps it had happened when they were so busy with the strawberries. They had put up two hundred pots.

'Well, the *Cacafuego* was a Spanish xebec-frigate of two and thirty guns, and he went for her in this little fourteen-gun sloop, fought her to a standstill, and carried her into Minorca. Such an action! The service rang with it. And if it had not been for some legal quirk about her papers, she being lent to the Barcelona merchants and not commanded by her regular captain, which meant that technically she was not for the moment a king's ship but a privateer, he would have been made post and given command of her. Perhaps knighted too. But as it was – there being wheels within wheels, as I will explain at another time, for it is not really suitable for young ladies – she was not bought into the service; and so far he has not been given his step. What is more, I do not think he ever will be. He is a vile ranting dog of a Tory, to be sure – or at least his father is – but even so, it was shameful. He may not be quite the thing, but I intend to take particular notice of him – shall call tomorrow – to mark my sense of the action: and of the injustice.'

'So he is not quite the thing, sir?' asked Cecilia.

'Why no, my dear, he is not. Not at all the thing, they tell me. Dashing he may be! indeed, he is; but disciplined – pah! That is the trouble with so many of your young fellows, and it will never do in the service – will never do for St Vincent. Many complaints about his lack of discipline – independence – disobeying orders. No future in the service for that kind of officer, above all with St Vincent at the Admiralty. And then I fear he may not attend to the fifth commandment quite as he should.' The girls' faces took on an inward look as they privately ran over the Decalogue: in order of intelligence a little frown appeared on each as its owner reached the part about Sunday travelling, and then cleared as they carried on to the commandment the Admiral had certainly intended. 'There was a great deal of talk about Mrs – about a superior officer's wife, and they say that was at the bottom of the matter. A sad rake, I fear; and undisciplined, which is far worse. You may say what you please about old Jarvie, but he will not brook undisciplined conduct. And he does not love a Tory, either.'

'Is Old Jarvie a naval word for the Evil One, sir?' asked Cecilia.

The Admiral rubbed his hands. 'He is Earl St Vincent, my dear, the First Lord of the Admiralty.'

At the mention of authority Mrs Williams looked grave and respectful; and after a reverent pause she said, 'I believe you mentioned Captain Aubrey's father, Admiral?'

'Yes. He is that General Aubrey who made such a din by flogging the Whig candidate at Hinton.'

'How very disgraceful. But surely, to flog a member of parliament he must be a man of considerable estate?'

'Only moderate, ma'am. A moderate little place the other side of Woolhampton; and much encumbered, they tell me. My cousin Hanmer knows him well.'

'And is Captain Aubrey the only son?'

'Yes, ma'am. Though by the bye he has a new mother-in-law: the general married a girl from the village some months ago. She is said to be a fine sprightly young woman.'

'Good heavens, how wicked!' said Mrs Williams. 'But I

presume there is no danger? I presume the general is of a certain age?'

'Not at all, ma'am,' said the Admiral. 'He cannot be much more than sixty-five. Were I in Captain Aubrey's shoes, I should be most uneasy.'

Mrs Williams brightened. 'Poor young man,' she said placidly. 'I quite feel for him, I protest.'

The butler carried away the tea-tray, mended the fire and began to light the candles. 'How the evenings are drawing in,' said Mrs Williams. 'Never mind the sconces by the door. Pull the curtains by the cord, John. Touching the cloth wears it so, and it is bad for the rings. And now, Admiral, what have you to tell us of the other gentleman at Melbury Lodge, Captain Aubrey's particular friend?'

'Oh, him,' said Admiral Haddock. 'I do not know much about him. He was Captain Aubrey's surgeon in this sloop. And I believe I heard he was someone's natural son. His name is Maturin.'

'If you please, sir,' said Frances, 'what is a natural son?'

'Why ...' said the admiral, looking from side to side.

'Are sons more natural than daughters, pray?'

'Hush, my dear,' said Mrs Williams.

'Mr Lever called at Melbury,' said Cecilia. 'Captain Aubrey had gone to London – he is always going to London, it appears – but he saw Dr Maturin, and says that he is quite strange, quite like a foreign gentleman. He was cutting up a horse in the winter drawing-room.'

'How very undesirable,' said Mrs Williams. 'They will have to use cold water for the blood. Cold water is the only thing for the marks of blood. Do not you think, Admiral, that they should be told they must use cold water for the marks of blood?'

'I dare say they are tolerably used to getting rid of stains of that kind, ma'am,' said the admiral. 'But now I come to think of it,' he went on, gazing round the room, 'what a capital thing it is for you girls, to have a couple of sailors with their pockets full of guineas, turned ashore and pitched down on your very doorstep. Anyone in want of a husband has but to whistle, and they will come running, ha, ha, ha!'

The admiral's sally had a wretched reception; not one of the young ladies joined in his mirth. Sophia and Diana looked grave, Cecilia tossed her head, Frances scowled, and Mrs Williams pursed up her mouth, looked down her nose and meditated a sharp retort.

'However,' he continued, wondering at the sudden chill in the room, 'it is no go, no go at all, now that I recollect. He told Trimble, who suggested a match with his sister-in-law, that he had *quite given up women*. It seems that he was so unfortunate in his last attachment, that he has quite given up women. And indeed he is an unlucky wight, whatever they may call him: there is not only this wretched business of his promotion and his father's cursed untimely marriage, but he also has a couple of neutral prizes in the Admiralty court, on appeal. I dare say that is why he is perpetually fagging up and down to London. He is an unlucky man, no doubt; and no doubt he has come to understand it. So he has very rightly given up all thoughts of marriage, in which luck is everything – has quite given up women.'

'It is perfectly true,' cried Cecilia. 'There is not a single woman in the house! Mrs Burdett, who *just happened to be passing by*, and our Molly, whose father's cottage is directly behind and can see everything, say there is not a woman in the house! There they live together, with a parcel of sailors to look after them. La, how strange! And yet Mrs Burdett, who had a good look, you may be sure, says the window-panes were shining like diamonds, and all the frames and doors had been new-painted white.'

'How can they hope to manage?' asked Mrs Williams. 'Surely, it is very wrong-headed and unnatural. Dear me, I should not fancy sitting down in that house. I should wipe my chair with my handkerchief, I can tell you.'

'Why, ma'am,' cried the Admiral, 'we manage tolerably well at sea, you know.'

'Oh, at sea …' said Mrs Williams with a smile.

'What can they do for mending, poor things?' asked Sophia. 'I suppose they buy new.'

'I can just see them with their stockings out at heel,' cried Frances, with a coarse whoop, 'pegging away with their needles – "Doctor, may I trouble you for the blue worsted? After you with the thimble, if you please." Ha, ha, ha, ha!'

'I dare say they can cook,' said Diana. 'Men can broil a steak; and there are always eggs and bread-and-butter.'

'But how wonderfully strange,' cried Cecilia. 'How romantic! As good as a ruin. Oh, how I long to see 'em.'

H.M.S. Surprise

H.M.S. Surprise follows the variable fortunes of Captain Jack Aubrey's career in Nelson's navy as he attempts to hold his ground against admirals, colleagues and the enemy, accepting a commission to convey a British ambassador to the East Indies. The voyage takes him and his friend Stephen Maturin to the strange sights and smells of the Indian sub-continent, and through the archipelago of spice islands where the French have a near-overwhelming local superiority.

Rarely has a novel managed to convey more vividly the fragility of a sailing ship in a wild sea. Rarely has a historical novelist combined action and lyricism of style in the way that O'Brian does. His superb sense of place, brilliant characterisation and a vigour and joy of writing lifts O'Brian above any but the most exalted of comparisons.

'He is perhaps unique ... in that his books can absorb and enthral landlubbers who do not even know the difference between 'a jib-boom and a taffrail.'

VALERIE WEBSTER, *Scotsman*

'*H.M.S. Surprise* is the third in the series, and one can hardly give it higher praise than to say that it maintains the level of the other two. The language is just right, with a full late eighteenth-century weightiness that is still free from any trace of strain or affectation.' JULIAN SYMONS, *Sunday Times*

ISBN: 978 0 00 649917 6